I0678359

HIS WAR

Descent Into Darkness

*His Own**

*Her Lord**

*His Beast**

Vol. 1: He Begins

*His Command**

*His Revenge**

Vol. 2: His War

*His Conquest***

Hidden Reaches

Blood & Rain

*E-Book Only
**Coming Soon

DESCENT INTO DARKNESS
VOLUME 2

HIS WAR

DORIS ROSS

TRINITY GATEWAYS LLC

DESCENT INTO DARKNESS, VOL. 2: HIS WAR

This is a work of fiction. All characters and events portrayed are fictional, and any resemblance to real people or incidents is purely coincidental.

Copyright © 2014 Doris Ross
All rights reserved.

Cover Art by Doris Ross, based on Concept Art by Blue
Cover Design by Doris Ross

A Trinity Gateways LLC Publication
www.TrinityGateways.net

ISBN: 1941426166
ISBN-13:   978-1941426166

DEDICATIONS

For my inner circle,
Jenni & Bill Plumer, Angela & Anderson Schuyler,
Lisa & Scott Gastineau, Tim Ross, and Tricia Sparks.
Thank you for the support., the enthusiasm, & the laughter.
You are among the greatest gifts any writer could wish for.

Descent Into Darkness
Volume 2

THE NORTHERN

PIETE TOWN ▪

ASHBURGH ▪

WINEDE ▪

CARTER'S ROCK ▪

LAST HOSTELRY ●

NORTHERN

IVERNESS ▪

JEVANEL ☆

SRADIEEN

TRADE ROUTE

THE RELDS

CAPIL OCEAN

MENIE ⚓

GOOSE-BREE

‡ GLASTEN PORT

VELTAN ▪

SUNDOWN VILLAGE ▪

THE BROKEN FALLS

THE TRINITY

THE SPIRLAN FOREST (THE SKELETON COAST)

PLAINS

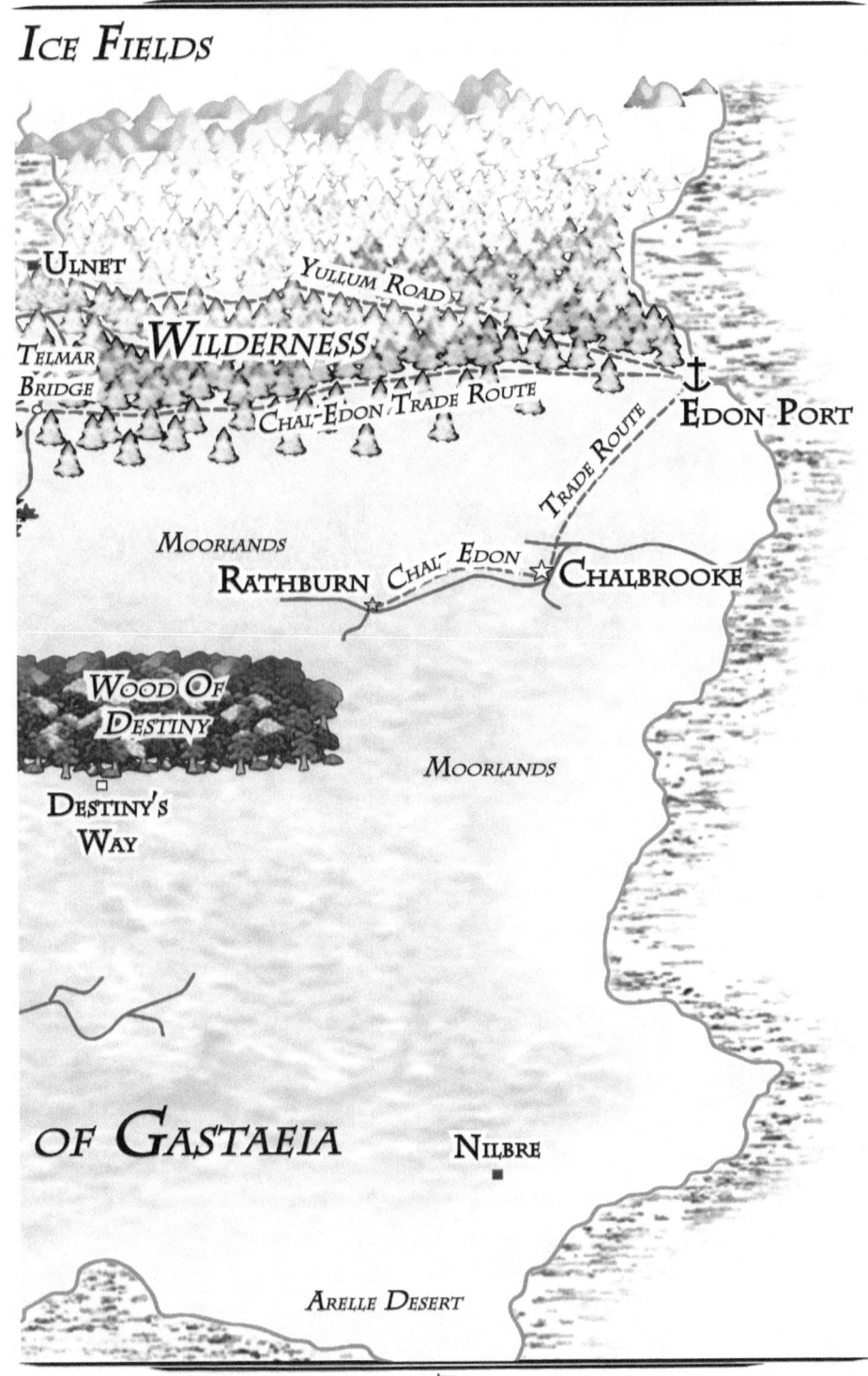

ICE FIELDS

ULNET

YULLUM ROAD

WILDERNESS

TELMAR
BRIDGE

CHAL-EDON TRADE ROUTE

EDON PORT

TRADE ROUTE

MOORLANDS

RATHBURN CHAL-EDON CHALBROOKE

WOOD OF
DESTINY

DESTINY'S
WAY

MOORLANDS

OF GASTAEIA

NILBRE

ARELLE DESERT

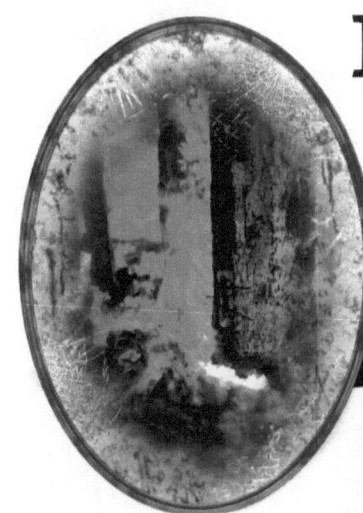

DESCENT
INTO
DARKNESS

PART 4

HIS
COMMAND

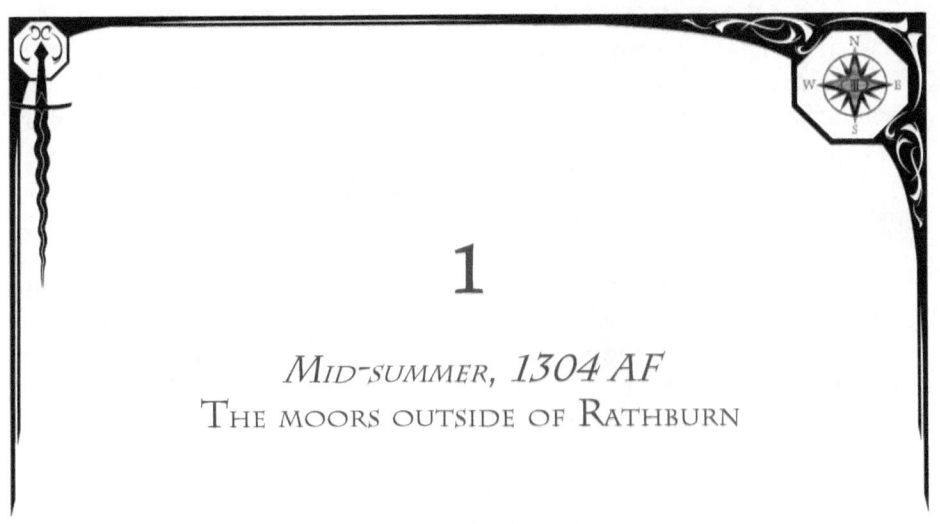

1

THEY"D come to dump the little bitch.

Prialla Filoche crept out into the nightscape, scanning the open moors for signs that other people were around. Behind her lay the woods of the Tretoan Estate. On the far side of the moor was the road leading into city of Rathburn.

The moonlight washed the color out of everything. Prialla's upswept, sunny blonde hair looked white, a stark beacon amid the shade of black and gray that the surrounding wilderness had been demoted to. She hiked up her dress – the only thing out here that was portrayed in its true ebon. Keeping her body bent low as she picked her way through the tall clumps of grass that covered the ground. Once she reached a point halfway between the estate and the road, she paused, scanned again, and saw no one. She stood up, letting the moon illuminate her features fully.

She was a tall, slender woman of eighteen with skin that looked whiter than her hair in the night-time setting. Confident, aware of how much she stood out in the open, she turned her beauteous face back towards the woods. Using just a touch of magic to carry her words across to her companions, she whispered, "There's no one about."

Two men came out to join her. Prialla watched them with faint amusement as they trudged toward her. The hoods of their cloaks were drawn up to hide their identities, as well as the blood spatter. Halvark Tretoan, her legitimate, noble-born half-brother, led the way, with Raptu Carthier carrying the body behind him – the price for his rather messy enthusiasm during their rite. Halvark hadn't been

7

pleased to have his shirt ruined.

She'd smoothed it over before the two started fighting again. Despite that, she could hear her brother grumbling under his breath as they drew near.

"Halvark, please," she began, exasperated, as she went to him to run her hand down his chest to soothe. "You know he gets...excited. Why didn't you wear something else?"

Halvark scowled down at her. Six feet high, he shared her coloring, but where she resembled her pretty mother, he bore the masculine stamp of their mutual sire. Perhaps in another life, she thought, they might have been a matched pair.

We might have been still, if our father had seen fit to die before he found out about us.

"That's assuming that he has something disposable to wear." Flashing a grin, Raptu let the corpse, wrapped in burlap for the journey, slide off his shoulder to hit the ground. "He's worse than you when it comes to his wardrobe."

"Push off, Raptu," Halvark snapped. "Lay it out. Let's be done here."

Prialla let her hands roam his body as she leaned into him, turning her head to watch their friend display their work on the ground. The girl, a maid from the estate, had been Halvark's choice of sacrifice. She'd made for a good victim, with plenty of vitality, durability, and the aesthetic looks that drew all three of them. Seeing the burlap unfurled to reveal what had been made of her, made Prialla's blood heat up again.

She angled her head, pushing up on tip-toe to scrap her teeth along Halvark's jugular.

"Think she'll be found?" Raptu straightened from his task, coming over to run a hand down Prialla's back.

"I'm more concerned that her death will be linked to us." Halvark glowered at the body, for the moment ignoring his sister's attentions. With a sigh, she pulled back from him to lean into Raptu. She felt his readiness pressed against her backside and smiled, though her next words, directed at her brother, held censure.

"If you hadn't taken the old man's current favorite, we wouldn't be in this predicament."

"How was I to know that she was his whore?" he hissed. "The old bastard tells no one of his affairs."

"Let's not forget, Prialla, my sweet," Raptu chimed in, adding to his friend's defense even as his hands slid up her body to cup her breasts. "That you were the one to suggest the little bitch."

"She was an annoying twit." She shrugged, letting the subject drop as she turned her face to brush her lips over Raptu's neck. "We should be going. We can't be caught here."

"I'm afraid that it's too late for that."

The trio stiffened at the unfamiliar voice. Prialla pushed away from Raptu as Halvark stepped forward to confront the speaker, who stood not fifteen feet away, between them and the road. It was a man dressed in tailored dark apparel, the red color of his hair intense enough that the moonlight couldn't leech it out. He wore it pulled back, sported a neatly trimmed beard. His golden eyes held a faint glow in the night.

"You've been attracting attention from the wrong sort of people," he said, one hand clasping the wrist of the other in front of him as he spoke. "The disappearance of Lord Tretoan's whore has gained too much notice and not just from the local law. There's a Mancer in the area, children. Your leavings are under investigation."

"Who are you?" Halvark's demand was stiff.

"You can call me Red." The man inclined his head in formal greeting. "I am a blood mage, one who's had to curtail his activities due to your…indiscretions."

Raptu muttered a vile oath. Prialla quelled him a look before moving to her brother's side before he could deliver a scathing retort. She laid a hand on his arm, touching his mind with hers.

Careful, brother. I sense a great deal of power in this one – power that is as blood stained as our own. He speaks truth about being a blood mage. Allow me to speak here.

Halvark gave her a sidelong glance, then gave a curt nod. She was the better negotiator. Prialla turned to address the newcomer.

"What do you suggest we do? And for what price will you keep our secrets in addition to your own?"

Red studied her, raising a slim eyebrow. "Are you proposing a deal?"

"We are…open to the possibility of one." She let her lips curve just a bit. "We understand that what is dangerous for one is dangerous for all who follow our path. We have done what we can to cover our tracks, though it isn't enough if you could do so easily."

Red returned her smile with a cold one of his own.

"Are you asking for instruction or aid, Prialla of Rathburn?"

That he knew her name startled her. She refused to show it. Halvark stiffened under her hand, as Raptu came up alongside her. She didn't look at either of them, keeping her gaze steady on Red.

"Which would you offer?"

Red let his eyes drop to the mutilated body on the ground. Silence stretched between them.

"A bit of both. Two favors for the price of one." He looked up at the trio. Prialla thought she saw a hint of red in the golden eyes. "I will cover this up and...educate you on how best to avoid detection. In return, I want a favor to be fulfilled at a later time."

"What kind of favor?" Raptu sounded suspicious. "We can't agree to just anything."

"I'll need something done." Red's response was cool. "What it will be, depends on what happens between now and then. It will be nothing that you cannot afford to do, I promise you."

"Will it expose us?" Prialla tightened her grip on her brother's arm as he shifted. "We can't agree to anything that may be a danger to us."

"The contract, should you agree to it, outlines the terms clearly." Red held up a hand. Red mist coalesced out of the air, solidifying into a rolled document tied with twine, sealed with wax. He handed it to Halvark.

He broke the seal, undid the string. Rolling out the parchment, he scanned its contents as Prialla craned her neck to read it. Raptu remained where he was, watching Red in distrust.

"It stipulates conditions that would protect us," Halvark stated, though he sounded doubtful. Prialla pursed her lips as she studied the terms.

"So it seems." She met Red's eyes. "You were very confident to have this drawn up ahead of time."

"I am in the market of information, you could say. I also make a point of knowing the other blood mages in the area." He flicked gaze from one member of the trio to the other. "Even if they remain ignorant of me."

"What would you do if we refused this contract?" Raptu gestured toward the dead girl. "Tell the Mancer, or whoever else, that we dumped her here?"

"No. I would let events play out and keep a low profile for a while." He shrugged. "There are already enough nails in this coffin to shut the lid on the three of you if the Mancer is the one to find the body."

That much is truth, sister.

She nodded in agreement, sensed Halvark have a wordless exchange with his friend. Raptu shrugged, though his suspicion lingered. Prialla would have to...reassure him once this was done.

"Very well, then. We'll sign the contract."

"In blood." Red snapped his fingers. A quill appeared in his hand, the feathery barbs along the shaft trimmed down to a sleek, saturnine shape. He proffered to them. "Your blood, as I shall in mine."

Prialla reached through a slit in her skirts for the dagger she kept strapped to her thigh. She ran the blade over her arm. The cut stung, the blood flowed.

She took the quill and sealed her future.

2

Late winter, 1306 AF
The Northern Wilderness of Orthanor,
East of the Telmar River

THEY hunted.

Shadowed Ones flowed over the ground, through the trees.

Following close behind were three riders, mounted on things that had been deer and horses in a previous life. Now they were both, yet neither, keeping the best traits of both while possessing an endurance that the natural animals lacked.

Ba'tvian Delthanurk rode ahead of his companions. Clad in the dark clothing of trapper, cloaked and hooded, most of his mind concentrated on the hunt. One portion kept track of the time of month; the full moon was in a few days. He had a contract to uphold, a fee to pay. It meant that after this hunt, there must be another. There would be little time between the two.

He was beginning to resent to obligation, yet wasn't brash enough to renege on it. He'd signed the contract in blood. That was more binding than anything signed in ink.

He had to admit, however, that the information Red provided him in exchange for victims was worth the aggravation. It had kept him ahead of the pursuit. Now it allowed him to hunt his hunters.

There was a Mancer in the area. Ba'tvian was determined to find him.

So winter-bound forest provided them with a boon: tracks in the snow. His prey wasn't following a road; those were few and far between in the northern half of the continent. It meant no witnesses. Another asset was the snow itself. Freshly fallen from the night before, it was just a few inches deep – enough to muffle sound while allowing their beasts an easy gallop when needed.

His creatures surged forward, putting on more speed. Their mounts matched the pace. Ba'tvian narrowed his eyes. He arrowed a thought at the leader of the pack.

What have you found?

The responding mental voice slithered into his mind with a hiss.

The Mancer you seek, lord. He is not far.

Good.

He kept a corner of his mind tuned to his minion, glancing over his shoulder at his companions. Nerisse se li Astorae, the Elvanarae girl he'd taken from his former master, rode close behind him. Ibestor the barbarian-mage they had made their own, kept in line with Nerisse, his gaze taking in the scenery. Sensing Ba'tvian's eyes on him, he turned his attention to his lord.

"He's been sighted." Ba'tvian pitched his voice low. He didn't need to raise it much in the quiet of the forest. "You know what to do."

Ibestor nodded once before veering off to the right. Part of the Shadow pack went with him. Nerisse hesitated for the barest instant.

"Be careful, lord. This one is supposed to be more experienced than the last." She flushed, then angled her mount to the left. She was out of sight within seconds, an escort of his creatures trailing after her.

Keep them both in line, he ordered. He felt the assent from the myriad minds of his loyal followers.

He dropped all mental links, redoubled his personal shielding. A whisper of power deadened any sounds his steed made as it cantered through the snow. Then he reached for the small, loaded crossbow hanging by its strap from the saddle horn. It was the almost impossible to re-load while mounted, and took time to do so on foot. The one shot was all he'd have. The others had similar crossbows, each with bolts dipped in a special concoction that Nerisse had come up with.

Surprise was their primary weapon.

Tapping into the nearest Shadow he used as living reservoir, he drew the power he needed. He formed an arcane 'net' – a kind of shield that would capture mage messages and dampen a mage's ability to fight back. It had taken weeks of work to devise the thing. It wasn't perfect, working best when anchored to something physical such as a cross bolt. Still, it sufficed. It would last long enough for Nerisse's drug to take effect.

Within minutes, he spotted his prey. His followers had faded into the merest hints of outlines, just flickers of darkness at the edge of vision. He picked up the psychic threads that linked him with the minds of his comrades, syncing with them on the mental plane. They had reached their positions.

He made his move.

His mount launched a full gallop as he raised the crossbow, aimed, fired. The bolt hit the cloaked man in the shoulder. A second bolt hit his thigh as he stumbled. The leg collapsed under him. The Mancer fell to the ground.

Two good hits; the third – Nerisse's – wasn't needed. Ba'tvian allowed his beast to carry him past the Mancer into the trees beyond, then wheeled the steed around. He kept out of sight of his prey, checking the net he'd created. He could see it in his mind's eye, a dome of woven power lines the color of blood.

Around the wounded man, the Shadows swirled. The Mancer held a hand in front of him, palm out. It glowed, flaring bright yellow as a burst of magic shot out to disperse the half-seen creatures surrounding him. It passed through the net, losing momentum and power as the net flickered around it. For a bare instant, it was visible to the naked eye. So, too, was the emblem that Ba'tvian had devised, a set of arcane runes that identified him as the maker.

He wanted his enemy to know who was killing him.

He tightened the net around the man as he struggled to his feet. The dark things crept in closer. His prey let another volley loose with less effect than the first. He yanked the bolt from his thigh, went for the bow and arrows at his back. Ba'tvian ordered his Shadowed Ones to disperse as the arrows began to fly. The blood mage engaged his mind with Nerisse's.

How long do we have?

There was a pause. He could sense her checking the integrity of the Mancer's shielding.

A minute, perhaps less. His personal shields are beginning to fail. Once they do, the only defense he will have is his physical weaponry.

He re-focused his attention, probing the crumbling shielding. They were fading, one after another, as the drug shut down the arcane centers of the man's mind. He could his panic now, the confusion, as he tried another power blast to no avail.

Ibestor. Ba'tvian felt the dog-like acknowledgement of the barbarian's mind. *Disarm him.*

He sat back to watch as Ibestor galloped into view, throwing himself from his saddle to tackle the Mancer from behind. What the barbarian lacked in intellect, he made up for in brute strength.

Ba'tvian sat back on his mount to watch the show.

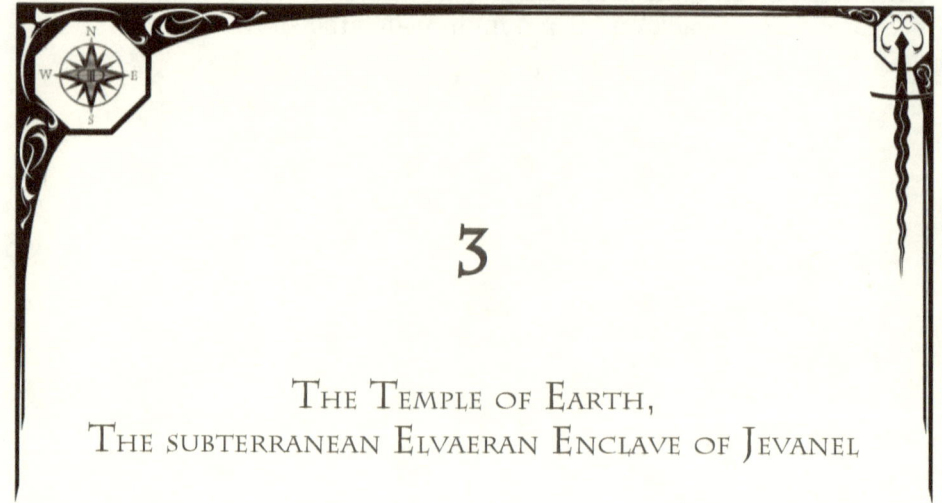

3

The Temple of Earth,
The subterranean Elvaeran Enclave of Jevanel

SAERLAN si le Therian, High Priest of the Elvanarae, laid his hands on the earth's altar. The smooth, granite looked almost white under the slate blue skin of his hands. His silver eyes picked out the flecks of gray, black, and pink in the stone. They roamed the lines of the altar until they focused on the center-piece, a rockery set within a recessed section of the stone. Each piece within it, from the loose sand to the rich soil, from the lack-luster sandstone to the rough crystals, represented the earth in all its forms.

Homely or beautiful, sterile or nourishing, the earth provides and shelters...

Saerlan closed his eyes, murmured another prayer. As he finished, he smoothed a hand over his alabaster hair, its long length pulled back in a queue. His fingers moved to touch the amulet he wore, an engraved silver disk with a rough-hewn topaz mounted in its center. It was the symbol of his office, the etchings on it his oath to nurture and protect his people.

It felt cold now, lying heavy against the fabric of his woolen white robes. The weight of it reminded him of the burden he had to bear.

He was alone in the main temple, striving to make peace with the disturbing news he'd received from the Mancer Absol Omine. In a few minutes, he would meet with the family a would-be priestess, one that he'd known since she was a child, one that he had chosen for the priesthood. He needed to tell them that, after vanishing for two years, she had been found.

He would have to tell them that she was a blood mage.

It made no sense. He was unable to comprehend how Nerisse se li Astorae – an Empath – could have been able to aid a blood mage, let alone participate in the rites. Yet Absol had been adamant that it was true. She had helped to kill a Mancer.

It should not be possible for an Empath. How…why? She was such a sweet girl, a true child of the earth…

Saerlan heard the temple doors open behind him. He would have to give this news without inner peace.

The priest turned from the altar, watching as Nerthet si le and Elisse se li Astorae, Nerisse's parents, approached. They, too, sported the trademark slate blue skin and white hair of their race. Garbed in simple earth-colored tunics, darker trousers for the man, a skirt for the woman, the represented the typical Elvanarae living in the subterranean city of Jevanel. They stopped at the base of the steps leading up to the altar to bow. The respect engendered by the gesture held hints of their anxiety. He returned the formality, then descended to join them.

"High One, have you received word of our daughter?" Nerthet stroked his wife's mane of white hair. It occurred to Saerlan that Elisse most closely resembled her daughter. As with Nerisse, there was a shy, sweet air about her.

Again, he wondered what had happened to her that she'd taken this darker path.

"Yes, I have. Sit." He motioned to the steps, waiting for the couple to be seated before continuing. "What I need to tell you is… difficult."

"She's dead." The flat declaration came from the mother. She raised sorrowful eyes to the priest's. "My child is dead. Killed by that monster."

I wish it were that easy, that her death was what I had to tell them.

"No." He kept his voice soft, gentle. "This, I'm afraid, is much worse than death." He reached within his white robes, pulled out a scroll detailing what the Mancers had discovered concerning Nerisse. He turned it over in his hands. "Ba'tvian Delthanurk, the Monster of Menie, has turned her. She has allied herself with him."

Her parents paled, their minute hope – every parent's hope – crushed by disbelieving shock.

"No, that can't be." Frantic, Elisse looked between the High Priest and her husband. "She's empathic. How can an Empath be a blood mage?"

"The earth has confirmed that she has spilled blood for him.

Willingly." His heart ached for them, for himself. Their loss was also his own. "I am sorry."

Face graying, Nerthet wrapped one arm around his wife as she crumpled onto his shoulder. He stared at the scroll in Saerlan's hands.

"They sent written notice of this?" he demanded. "Of our daughter's betrayal?"

"Yes. Absol Omine, the Mancer who sent the notice, has had little knowledge about us. Without personal knowledge of whom to contact, he could not send us a mage sending. So we learn of her betrayal a month after he discovered it." He looked down at the scroll in his hands, remembering what it said.

Nerisse se li Astorae has been found to be complicit in blood rites performed by the blood mage Ba'tvian Delthanurk...

"They found her arcane signature at a horrific scene outside of Piete Town," he said aloud. "There is no question."

Elisse was weeping now, rocked by her husband. They both were aware what their laws demanded in cases such as this. Nerthet, bleak and grief-stricken, stared at nothing as he asked, "When will the ostracism rites begin?"

"Today. The priesthood will undergo them first, then the general populace. So many people knew her...it will take weeks, if not months, to complete."

"Then we have time to mourn, to...come to terms." He buried his face in his wife's hair. "My daughter, my only child..."

Saerlan placed a hand on his shoulder.

"We mourn with you, my friend." The High Priest sat beside them to share their pain.

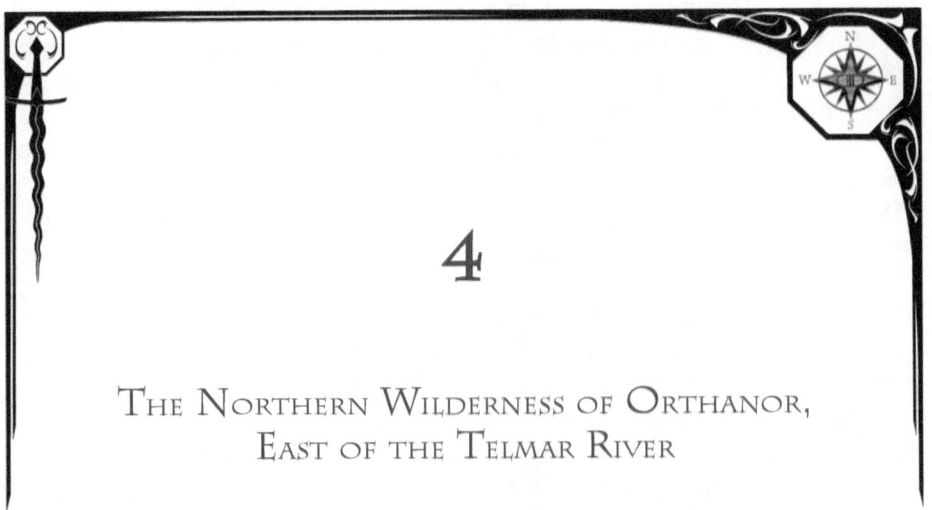

4

The Northern Wilderness of Orthanor, East of the Telmar River

NERISSE wasn't thinking of her people, let alone her parents or her faith. She was too caught up in the ritual playing out before her, in the man who presided over the sacrifice. Any thought of wrongness, disgust, or resistance was diminished. Driven by her devotion, she'd taken the medicinal draught to quell her empathy so that she could join her chosen lord.

Their victim had been stretched over a fallen tree trunk, bound in place with strips of hide collected from other sacrifices, both animal and human. She watched as Ba'tvian plunged the knife into the Mancer's chest. The blade was sharp, cutting through flesh and cartilage with ease. Bone cracked, snapping, as he forced the ribcage to splay open wide, then plunged his hand in for the still-beating heart. He tore it free, held it up above his head as he chanted. Crimson wisps of power rose from the twitching body to gather at the heart. It glowed, pulsing, before bursting into arcane flames. The fire absorbed into his hand, making her lord's aura flare into full visibility for a moment.

Part of her stood back from the scene, horrified. It sensed the sickness, the fear, the utter dismay. Yet it was shrinking, becoming a smaller part of her each time they did this.

She was thankful for that. The rites gave her nightmares sometimes, after the drug she'd used had worn off – dreams of blood, pain, death, hints that the sacrifice Ba'tvian laid on the makeshift altar might one day be her. They were coming on less now, as that part of her that was resistant to the blood magery faded.

She'd confided in her lord after waking up screaming the night after they had killed the Mancer Timbrel Jodrek. Ba'tvian had not responded with irritation or anger, as she'd feared he might. Instead, he had assured her in that cool, logical way of his that he would never sacrifice her.

You are too useful to kill, even if I wanted to. You are someone I need, Nerisse. Because of that I will never let you go.

They were as close to love words as he ever came. After giving them, he'd seduced her – his brand of comfort – and she'd slept soundly through the rest of the night in his bedroll. Remembering that, a glow of warmth, of love, lit up inside her.

He was her lord. She was his lover.

The chanting ceased. Drawn from her reverie, she looked up to see him beckoning her forward, his dark eyes intent. Her heart skipped a beat, her blood quickened. Heedless of any stains her winter dress might garner, she went to him, clasping his blood-slick hand with hers. A jolt of power bled through the contact, from him to her. She experienced another, as he tugged her to him, tilting her face up so he could claim her mouth, smearing blood on her cheek, her chin, her throat.

Her mind buzzing with excitement, she barely registered his mutter to Ibestor to deal with the corpse. She was so focused in him, in how he made her feel, that she didn't hear the earth weeping in the recesses of her awareness.

INTERLUDE 1

THE MOORLANDS OUTSIDE OF RATHBURN

LABIYAL Biyalban watched the rite's conclusion using the small mirror he kept with him. He cupped it in his palm as Ba'tvian took Nerisse, heedless of their companion or the blood they'd shed. Thoughtful, he dismissed the image, tucking the mirror back into his jacket pocket.

He stood on the moors today, a vacant landscape that stretched over the region around the city of Rathburn. In the distance were the woods of the Tretoan Estate. Beyond them, the castle built almost two hundred years ago by the Tretoan family. There lived the ruler of Rathburn, his son, and his bastard daughter. The offspring, Labiyal mused, would long outlive the usefulness of the sire.

He gave his attention to the road, spotting the black speck that was Lord Tretoan's coach, escorted by mounted guards. With careless grace, Labiyal strode to a nearby bush, using a bit of magery to 'extend' the image of the bush over himself. It wouldn't fool anyone who was close, but at a distance, it served him well. He continued to watch the coach as it passed along the road, heading for Chalbrooke, the largest city state in eastern Orthanor, and home to the Mancer Guild House.

A raven flitted overhead, spiraling down to land on his shoulder. It looked at him with eyes as red as hot coals.

"Follow the coach. Track it. Make certain that Tretoan stays in Chalbrooke until this is done." He turned his head to look the bird in the eye. "Do not kill him. He has a role yet to perform."

I do not like your tone, half-breed.

The snarling voice belonged to the daemon trapped within the raven's body. As one of the Chained, it was bound to serve – and Labiyal held its leash.

"My orders are under-written by our king." He kept his tone cool, commanding. "You will obey them."

The raven mantled its wings, issuing a credible hiss.

Why waste time with the humans in this way? It would be much easier to use the old methods.

"They didn't work. If they had, you wouldn't be Chained." He let that sink in. "Go."

The raven took off. Labiyal stepped away from the bush, calling one of his pets to him. This one was a simple dove, one of several dozen he'd stationed in the area to observe the Tretoan family. It flew to his hand, sat there as he produced a message tube and affixed it to the bird's leg. The small bit of paper in that tube would launch the next act of this elaborate play. With careful planning and manipulation, he would succeed in something at which even Daemon Lords had failed.

Ba'tvian Delthanurk had killed Timbrel Jodrek with the help of Nerisse se li Astorae. Then they'd killed another Mancer who'd been patrolling the north. This news had galvanized the Mancers. They were now training local law enforcement in identifying blood mages. Even people with the merest trace of magic at their disposal were being recruited by the city guards to aid in the effort.

Doubtless, the Mancers would increase their activities when they discovered that a third of their number were dead.

For his part, Labiyal was pleased with his chosen's initiative. The only down-side was that the Mancers were beginning to impact his own ability to operate on the sly. Unlike Ba'tvian, Labiyal was had several public personas that interacted with society. So the Mancers now had to be dealt with in a more…direct manner.

With a single favor, and Ba'tvian's current crusade, he would accomplish just that.

His thoughts touched the bird's tiny mind, branding its target recipient in its brain. He sent it winging off in the direction of the castle. As it flew, he took out the mirror again. It was time to report to his king.

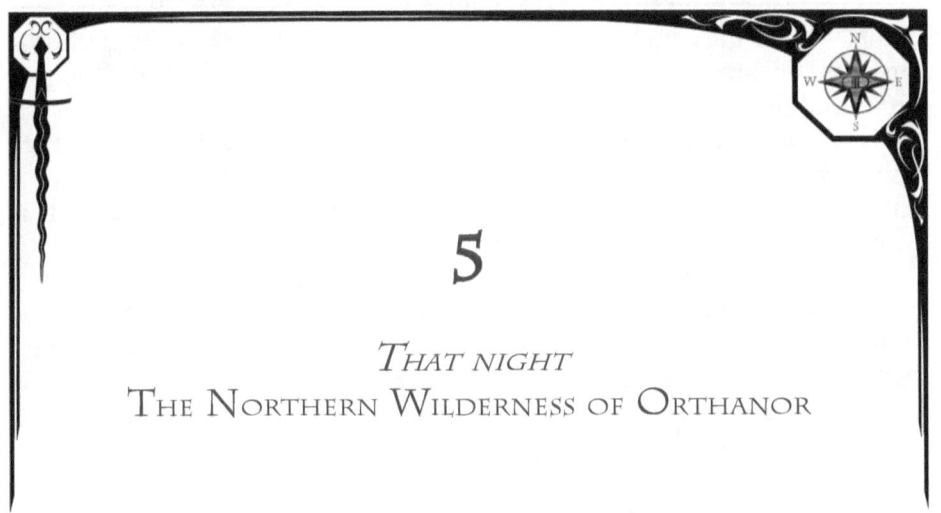

5

THAT NIGHT

THE NORTHERN WILDERNESS OF ORTHANOR

BA'TVIAN left Nerisse to sleep in his bed roll. She had done well that day, in the hunt, in the rite, in pleasing him. The potion she was now taking had a side effect that he liked: she lost most of her natural inhibitions when it came to sex.

If only it could take care of her insecurities as well...

That was wishful thinking, however, and a waste of time. He was resigned to having to deal with them, as irritating as they were. Still, what he gained from doing so – her loyalty, her ability to enslave the minds of others – was worth the aggravation that task presented.

Her weaknesses, her uncertainties, become a way to keep her chained.

He looked back at the elf as she lay curled up in the blankets. Gingerly, he touched her mind with his own. She was deep in sleep, not likely to rouse anytime soon. He would enjoy the reprieve while he could.

There was also another task. It would give him the opportunity to test the usefulness of his other tool.

He scanned their small camp for any sign of Ibestor. The barbarian was nowhere to be seen. Reaching out with his mind, he lets is awareness comb the surrounding area to find him nearby, just out of sight. Ba'tvian stepped through the snow crusted trees to see Ibestor examining their mounts. He looked up as his master approached, grunted a greeting, then went back to what he was doing.

Knowing how fruitless it was to expect an intelligent answer from the man, Ba'tvian linked to him, slipping into his thoughts with ease. He was looking for flaws, signs of deterioration. So far, there were none. Since they had begun incorporating blood rites in the melding process Ibestor used, the makeshift things were lasting longer, functioning better.

Ba'tvian let him complete the examination. When he was done, the barbarian came to stand in front of him with an expectant look on his hairy face. The blood mage touched Ibestor's forehead with a single finger, reinforcing the words he spoke with mental commands.

"Locate a nearby settlement. A lone cabin, a village, a town – any kind of human habitation will do. Bring me a living human. This human must be uninjured – no cuts, no bruises, no rape. It does not matter if this human is male, female, a child, or an infant. Leave no witnesses. Do not get caught. Do not lead anyone else back to me. Understand?"

He nodded.

"Return within a day." That would allow him time to set up a meeting with his contact, Red, and make their monthly transaction. "Go now."

Without a word, Ibestor turned to his steed, saddled it, mounted up, and rode off. Once he was out of hearing range, Ba'tvian turned to the Shadows that lurked in the night's gloom.

"Follow him. Ensure that my orders are obeyed. If there is any pursuit, you will alert me well before it arrives at our camp."

Yes, lord. The sibilant hiss sounded in his consciousness from the unseen creatures. He could sense their presence receding as they moved farther away, then felt the largest of those that remained with him glide to his side.

We have found Absol Omine, lord.

"Where?" Ba'tvian looked down at the creature, noting in the muted light of its white eyes that the head was beginning to show a mottled pattern. The ones that had been with him since he had been stranded on the Spirlan Coast were becoming distinctive. They assumed a physical form more often, were beginning to develop markings that made them easier to identify as individuals. He made a mental to look through texts for an explanation of the phenomenon when he visited his stolen cache of books again.

In the village of Destiny's Way, at the edge of the Wood. It blinked its leprous eyes. Ba'tvian frowned at the location. The Shadows avoided the Wood of Destiny. Its uncanny nature made most, even Ba'tvian, wary of it.

"How long is he likely to stay there?" He wanted that Mancer dead. Omine had been the first to hunt him. It was because of him that Ba'tvian had been harried across the continent for the last several years.

We do not know. He appeared in pain when he arrived.

"Was he." He narrowed his eyes. If Absol was hurt, then he would not be leaving the village any time soon.

Yet Omine was not the whole of his problem. It encompassed the Mancer Order. He needed a way to eliminate the order if he was ever to become a reckoning force in Orthanor. He had to. How else could he ensure that he would never, ever, be rendered as nothing? As the dirt beneath the feet of the world?

"Do the Mancers have a…" What would he call it? "…Central building? A training facility?"

They have a Guild House in Chalbrooke. The mental tone of the response was thoughtful. *It is the only one they have.*

"Are there Shadows in that area? Can we gain any information from them?"

It is an area to which we do not go. The Mancers keep it clear of us.

"That will change." The coldness of his tone was implacable. His followers were his spies, his eyes, his ears, the greatest of his tools; they could be barred from any place in the world. "Keep an eye on Omine. We will continue east and see what opportunities present themselves."

If they didn't, Ba'tvian would manufacture a few.

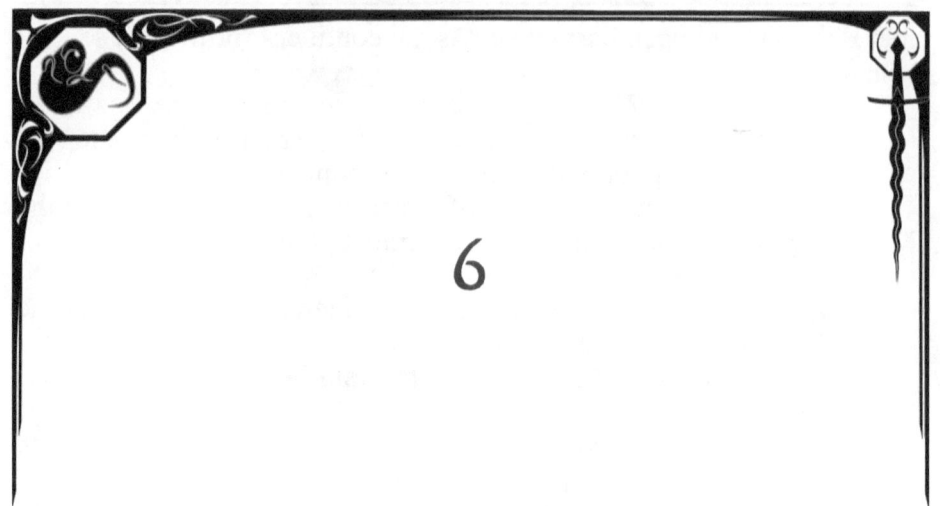

6

N ERISSE dreamed. A kaleidoscope of fractured images cascaded through her mind. She could pick out pieces of them. The docking cavern of the Trinity's Red Tower. The trapper's cabin in the northern wilds. The skeletal remains of the Spirlan Forest. Others were images she didn't recognize. A room of robed judges attending Master Oknare as he gazed at her with accusing eyes. A dilapidated hovel where a bedraggled family slept. A fishing village where each home had become a charnel house. A ship adrift at sea with its crew consumed in darkness.

As she shied away from the unfamiliar, she heard sobbing echoing in the back of her mind. With it came grief, unbearable grief. In a bid for comfort, she instinctively sought out her tie with the earth. Finding it, she clung to it yet the psychic bond was frayed, not as strong as it once was. Frantic, she called out to the earth, her mind seeking out the one thing that had always been there for her. It responded in a bare whisper.

...blood...such blood...such pain...foul death...why?

Choked with fear, sorrow, and desperation, Nerisse answered.

I love. My love is as vital to me as you. Are we not to cherish and protect those we love? Are we not to nurture them?

There was silence then, so deep that it deafened her to all else. As her heart threatened to break, the earth whispered again.

Love is love, not evil, not wrong...yet...blood...

Please do not judge him for what he is driven to do. Nerisse could feel tears gathering, knew that if she woke now there would be tears on her cheeks. *Ba'tvian is a child misjudged, misused. He saved people, and they spurned him. He was the Trinity's salvation during the Great Earthquake yet they persecuted him. My love is a savior. Can that not excuse the method used?*

It seemed like an eternity passed before the earth replied.

Perhaps...

As the word echoed, the sobbing ceased, the flickering images stopped.

Nerisse opened her eyes in the dark, aware of the cold, the blankets wrapped around her. Lifting her head, trying not to move too much lest she woke her lover, she looked over her shoulder at him. He was clothed, which he hadn't been when she'd drifted off earlier that night. That wasn't unusual, though. He often rose at least once in the night to confer with his Shadows.

In sleep, without the intensity that was so much part of who he was, he looked defenseless, exposed somehow. Her lord, her lover, had vulnerabilities that few could comprehend. The world stood against him, the Mancers hunted him – those were the reasons he'd turned to blood, to death. They had not given him a choice.

I will keep you as safe as I can, she promised fiercely. *I will not let them drive you to failure.*

Deep in her heart, she prayed that the earth understood her need of him, and his need of her.

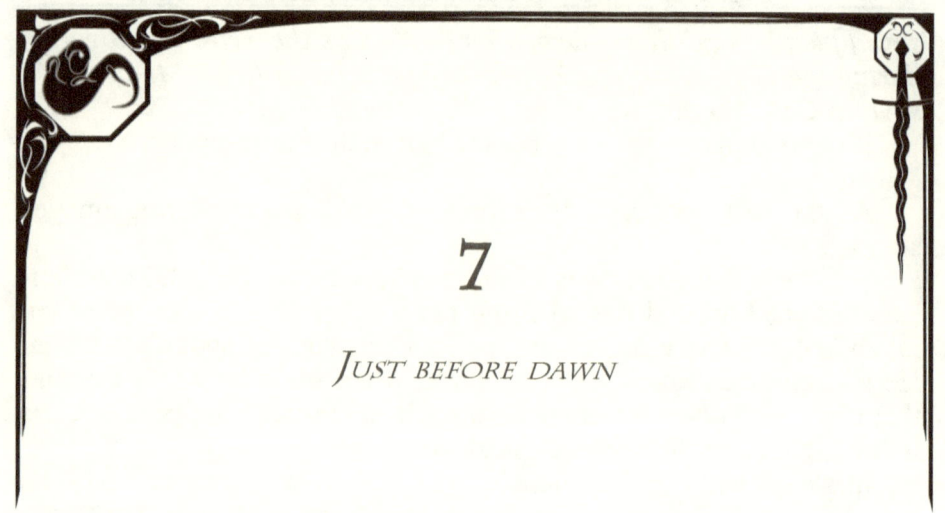

7

Just before dawn

B A'TVIAN was dozing beside Nerisse when Ibestor returned. He preferred to sleep alone, often banishing her to her own bedroll. However, last night had not just been about his pleasure; it had been her reward. She would have seen his dismissal as sign that she had performed well.

He didn't mind letting her know that she failed him. He liked to keep her hungry enough for his approval, for his touch, that she continued to work hard to gain them. Yet he understood that a reward could not be coupled with punishment. Nerisse was sensitive enough to such things that it would...damage his hold on her. Undoing that damage would take more time and effort than preventing it would. So he suppressed his distaste, allowing her to sleep with her body against his. He took consolation in the fact that she was the only one that would require this kind of intimacy. No other female, willing or not, would share his bed.

He'd fallen asleep with that determination in mind and woke with it as his first thought. His second thought was to find the source of noise coming through the frosted brush in the twilight gloom.

He slipped out of the bedroll, donned the over-tunic and cloak he'd discarded before reclining. As he clasped the cloak at his neck, one of his creatures slithered up to him.

The barbarian returns.

"That was quick." He frowned, eyes narrowed. "What does he bring? How did he acquire it?"

He brings a girl-child. It gave a slow blink of its leprous white eyes, satisfaction reflected in its mental tone. *He ambushed a trader* along the Chal-Edon Trade Route. *It is not far from here.*

"Was he followed?"

No, lord. It paused. *The barbarian has not rested. The full moon is nearly upon you.*

"I am aware." He knew his obligations, kept track of them. "Have your brethren scout the countryside. If there is no reason to move the camp, I will leave him to rest while I meet with Red."

What of the elf?

Ba'tvian glanced back at her where she huddled under the blankets. There was nothing to do to reinforce Ibestor's enslavement further. Time would do that for them. Still, there would be other opportunities. If Ba'tvian was to accomplish his latest goal, the one of most immediate importance, then he would need to gather others to his cause. It would be Nerisse's job to make them unequivocally his.

He sent a message to Red requesting a meeting before turning his attention to Nerisse. Kneeling beside the covers, he woke her with a touch on her shoulder. Her silver eyes fluttered open, focused on him. With a frown, she sat up.

"Is something wrong, my lord?" She looked around the small camp, took in the lingering darkness, heard the noise of something unseen approaching. "What is it?"

"Ibestor." He watched her as she relaxed a little at his words. "He brings me a sacrifice for my contact. I will need to deliver it."

"Of course." She had some knowledge of the arrangement, though he'd kept many of the details to himself. He had never taken her that far into his confidence. "What would you have me do?"

"Ibestor will rest. There is little more to be done with him, correct?"

"Yes." She shivered in the pre-dawn chill, pulled the blankets tighter around her.

"There will be others. What I wish to accomplish – we need more than three." He said with deliberate thoughtfulness. She frowned.

"You can do anything, my lord. Achieve any goal you wish." She hesitated, brow furrowing as she considered. "This is a...large-scale goal?"

"I refuse to be hunted another day." He lifted a hand to trace the column of her throat. Her pulse began to flutter under his fingers. "I have new plans, more immediate ones to be fulfilled before the others can be pursued. There are too many people in the world who oppose me, who would take me from you."

"I see." Her eyes took on a haunted look. Then it faded, firm resolution taking its place. "The Mancers would kill you. They don't understand that you meant for more."

"So," he began, his voice dropping an octave as he let his hand slip from her neck to her shoulder beneath the covers. She shivered again, for a reason other than the cold. "The Mancers are numerous enough, wide-spread enough, that I cannot do this with just you and Ibestor. I need others. When we find them, it will be your task to make them mine." He locked his dark gaze with hers. "I trust no one else, Nerisse."

She flushed in pleasure at the implication of his words. He had spoken the truth; he trusted no one completely. The Shadows had a measure of that trust, as did Nerisse, because they had proven themselves loyal. Yet they were still tools in his eyes – his tools, his possessions, nothing more.

Tools could break if mishandled.

"I will devote myself to the study of this issue. They will be other mages?" Her breath caught as his hand slid down to cover one breast. It was the promise of reward, this little byplay. She always responded to it.

"Yes." He thought for a moment, seeing renewed desire in Nerisse's eyes, in the subtle color rising under her skin. "There may be others, non-mages, but we will start with mages of at least equal power."

He let his hand fall away as Ibestor broke through the brush to enter their encampment. Slung over his shoulder was an unconscious child of perhaps eleven or twelve. At his approach, Nerisse closed the gap in her blankets Ba'tvian had made.

"I will see what can be done, my lord."

"Good."

Ba'tvian rose to inspect his latest gift for his blood mage informant. The limp body wasn't marred. He felt her skull for any lumps, felt her pulse to test its strength. She was very much alive and untouched. Curious, he glanced at the Shadows that had trailed after the barbarian.

She fainted. The contempt in the answering creature's voice amused him.

Witnesses? He kept his query mental out of reflex; he disliked giving them verbal orders in front of others. Too often, those orders dealt with his companions.

None. Ibestor left only bodies.

Satisfied, he took the girl, ordered the man to sleep. As he hunkered down next to a tree to rest, Ba'tvian turned to see Nerisse rising from the bedroll to dress. Unlike him, she had slept nude. She blushed when she caught him looking. He held his gaze steady, more out of show of dominance than out of a wish to see her body. Nerisse would have a different interpretation. She dropped her gaze, a faint smile touching her lips. Without a word, she donned a winter dress made for travel.

As she covered herself, a ball of dark orange light appeared, zinging through the trees to stop in front of Ba'tvian. He shifted the girl to his shoulder, mirroring Ibestor's method of carrying her. Securing her with one hand, he closed his free hand over the glowing mage sending.

You are early. I look forward to our meeting with interest. The words sounded in his mind, along with a sense of time. Red would meet him in an hour, two hours at the outside, as he was already engaged in something. Ba'tvian chafed at the wait. He was no one's lackey, yet was forced to acknowledge that neither was Red. Their agreement was one between peers. Not equals, Ba'tvian thought, aware of the other blood mage's seniority, the measure of power age and experience had garnered him. His hand tightened.

One day, I will be more than his peer, more than his equal. One day, he will see me for what I am. Or what he would become.

Red called him the Master of Shadows. His followers called him their lord. It was more than time he showed his enemies how worthy he was of both titles.

"Will you need me to help mask your gating, my lord?"

Nerisse's query broke through his reverie. He unclenched his fist, revealing that the mage sending had dissipated. He forced himself to relax, containing the intensity he felt as he answered her.

"Yes."

To open a gate or portal between one place and another was equivalent to sounding a trumpet through the magical world. Every mage's arcane signature was unique, flavoring their magic as seasoning, food components, or cooking methods did multi-course meals. They were embedded everything a mage did, telling anyone who saw the work the identity of the craftsman. Large works such as a gate would broadcast that signature to anyone nearby – or those looking for an outlaw blood mage.

Nerisse, however, was Elvanarae. The elven race had bonds with the earth that could mask the broadcast, in some cases muting it altogether. It was another reason that Ba'tvian valued her.

He gestured at the packs.

"Eat first, but do it quickly. I will be gone for most of this day and you have much to do."

She gave him an almost shy smile, looking much as she had when he'd first met her at the Trinity two years before.

"As my lord Ba'tvian wishes."

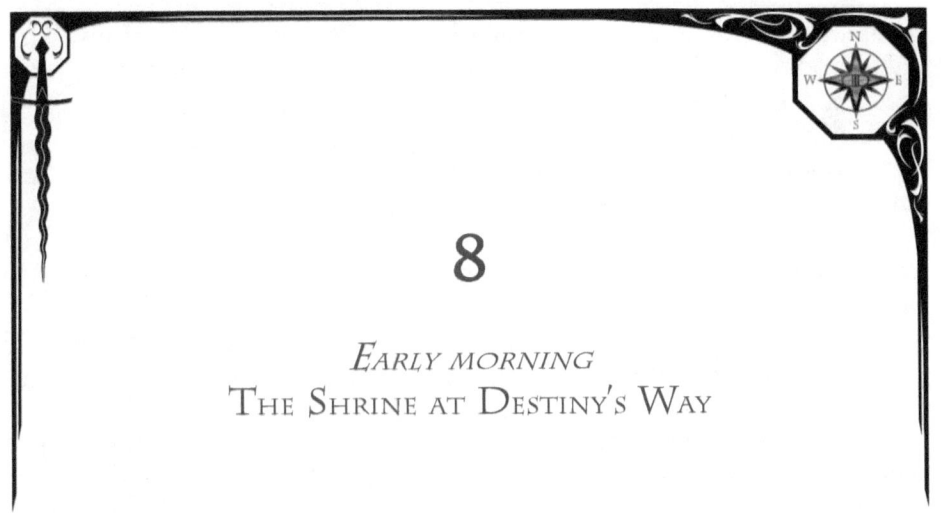

8

ABSOL Omine went through a series of stretches in his room, testing each muscle carefully. There were twinges, a faint burning ache along the healed ribs. It meant that the weeks he'd spent recuperating from his injuries were ending, something he was thankful for.

The inability to act in the aftermath of Timbrel's death had been torture. Though he had not been close to the other Mancer, they'd been friendly. The only things he could do was spread the word about Nerisse's involvement with Ba'tvian, conduct more research on their enemies, and begin I'k'Nole's Mancer education.

His ward was making good progress there, he mused as he completed the exercises. The boy was a quick learner, possessing a near perfect memory for technique and facts. He also seemed just as determined as Absol to enter the field. The lad was fearless, though not reckless. He had a good head on his shoulders, a strong sense of morality. Absol was also learning that his ward possessed a stubborn streak a mile wide.

I'k'Nole had made up his mind to be a Mancer, to put an end to people like Ba'tvian Delthanurk. He was doing everything in his power to get there, even if it meant training in the rain with a farmer's scarecrow as his dummy target. His dedication was paying off.

Eleven years old yet already well-schooled in swordsmanship for his age. The boy needs a regular sparring partner to improve his skill further. It's about time to consider sending him to the Guild House.

It was something he'd have to discuss with the Master Abbot,

Dannon, I'k'Nole's other guardian. At the Guild House in Chalbrooke, their ward would be able to get the extra training he needed. If he kept up his current pace, he would be dispatched to the field before he reached the age of eighteen. Absol felt some trepidation about that. Mancers who excelled too fast tended to make more mistakes. In this line of work, mistakes killed.

I could take him as my partner for the first few years, make sure he survives. It was an easy decision to make. I'k'Nole had dropped a few hints that he wanted to intern with him.

Finished with the stretches, he gathered his gear. There was enough time for him to go through a few practice moves. They were due to spar when the boy was done with his chores.

He made his way from the shrine barracks to an area out by the stables. Passing through the shrine kitchens, he paused long enough to snag a bit food – a slab of bread topped with slices of hard cheese – and a mug of steaming tea. He broke his fast as he went, finishing the food by the time he reached his destination.

He noticed the two benches – additions from his last stay. The monks would sometimes come out here to watch practice bouts in between tasks, giving encouragement to the trainee, keeping up a conversation with the trainer. This morning, Dannon sat waiting for him.

"Good to see you." Absol set his mug on the empty seat next to his friend. Drawing a weighted practice sword, he made a few slow passes with it as he continued. "I take it I'k'Nole is almost done with his chores?"

"He's finished." Dannon gave him a wry smile. "Boy's out in the paddock with your horse. He decided to use the spare time he had to give him a bit of exercise."

"He's always been fond of that horse." The boy had named him Brown soon after I'k'Nole had been found, Absol recalled. "Is there anything else going on?"

"We might want to consider sending him to the Mancer Guild. Between the two of us and our respective duties, there's little more that he'll be able to learn here."

"I was just thinking that this morning, actually." He smiled at his friend. "It's nice to know that we're of like minds on this."

Dannon nodded.

"When do you want to send him?"

"I was planning to leave in a week's time." Absol paused, considering. "I can send a message, get him enrolled before we leave. The last report I received was that Ba'tvian was headed east. I can drop I'k'Nole off with the Guild before picking up the hunt from there."

"So that's settled." Dannon looked over in the pasture beyond the practice area. Absol followed his gaze. I'k'Nole was riding Brown back to the stables, waving at them in greeting. They each lifted a hand to return the gesture.

"Time to get to work," the Mancer murmured. For today, at least, the future held promise.

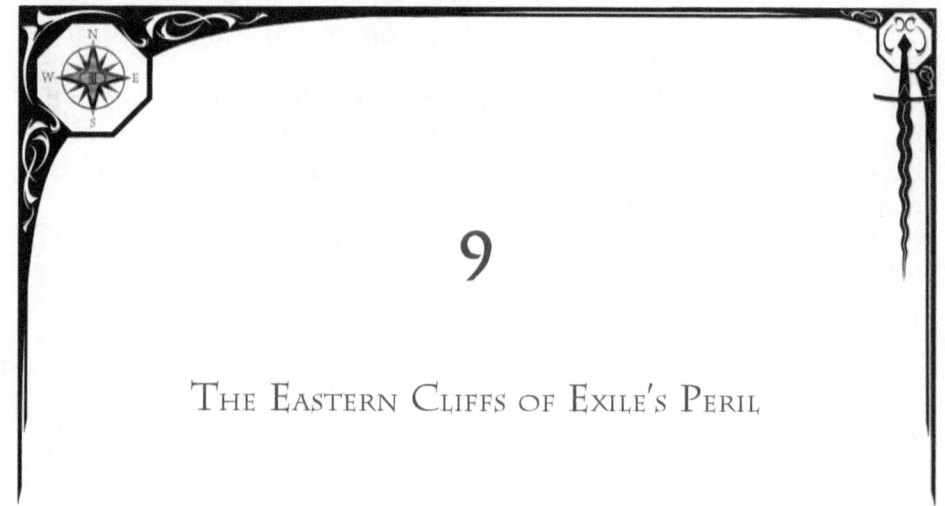

9

The Eastern Cliffs of Exile's Peril

BA'TVIAN stepped through the portal onto the barren cliffs. With him came an escort of the Shadows that had claimed him for their own. As the portal closed at their backs, he set the girl down with care. A sacrifice for someone else could not be abused or blemished. He touched her forehead, touched her mind with his in a way that Nerisse had shown him, sending the child into a deep slumber. Satisfied that she wouldn't wake or seek escape, he walked to the cliff's edge, staring out over the water.

There was no land on the horizon, nothing to hold his interest. The sky above was overcast, the clouds gray with moisture, and a cool breeze swept over the seascape. As his cloak responded to the wind, he thought of the plans he'd made, the things he had told Nerisse. He remembered, too, the boon that Red owed him for delivering two lives instead of the one required by their contract.

Ba'tvian felt the gate energies gather, announcing the arrival of another mage. He directed the dark creatures to guard the girl, then turned to face the newcomer. The portal flashed into being, giving him a glimpse of a study heaped with books, mirrors on floor stands, a desk laden with papers and scrolls. Red stepped through, the gate winking out behind him.

"Shadow Master," the mage greeted. Red had not changed in the time the two had done business together. He dressed in black clothing of high quality, his skin a pale ivory, his hair and trimmed beard the rich color of blood. His eyes, though, drew Ba'tvian's attention. They were golden, with a hint of crimson around the pupils – as they had always been.

Ba'tvian's own were a brown so dark they looked black. Yet recently he noticed a subtle change around his own pupils: a ring of crimson that matched Red's. He made a mental note to visit his hidden cache of books to research the effect.

"Red." He gestured at the girl asleep on the ground a few feet away. "The price of our bargain."

Red walked over to her, Ba'tvian's escort slipping away to allow him passage. He inspected the offering as one might one a horse up for auction. Straightening, he gave Ba'tvian a slight smile and a nod of acceptance.

"As always, you find victims worthy of our mutual esteem."

"There is a boon owed." The younger mage's words were careful stated. Ba'tvian was wary enough of Red's magic that he wouldn't make a demand, yet too conscious of his own standing to make a request.

Red's eyebrow rose, his lips curving a bit more. There was no humor or condescension in his expression, just mild interest.

"So there is. What would you have of me, Master of Shadows?"

Be careful of what you say, lord. The warning slid into his mind like the hiss of wind. *This one is worthy of caution.*

He sent a mental acknowledgment but did not respond. His full attention on Red, he chose his words with care.

"The Mancers have been more active of late. I find that it may be in our best interest if they were eliminated." As Red's expression cooled, Ba'tvian continued. "I have plans for their Guild House. It would be the first step in causing their downfall, one that I and mine will undertake. However, I find that while I have the power necessary, I cannot be everywhere. I will need others. Are there any blood mages in the region of Chalbrooke that might join in the endeavor? Putting me in contact with them would cancel the boon owed."

"You speak of starting a war." The older mage's face held no censure. He seemed to be considering be the possibilities. "One that I cannot overtly join."

"I am not asking you to." He wouldn't have even if he'd thought the mage would be open to such a thing. It would have put Ba'tvian's leadership at risk. "I am more inclined to leave our current…relationship the way it is."

"Yet you wish for others to join you."

"I am sensible enough to understand that a venture of this magnitude would be foolish to undertake alone. Yet I would not jeopardize our contract. It has proven too useful for me to put it in harm's way." Ba'tvian paused, waiting as the Red continued to mull over the matter. Even if the older mage did not participate directly, there was risk in his contacting others. Perhaps it was time to sweeten the pot. "I am willing to provide additional compensate for the hazards you may encounter. Two victims by the next full moon, in return for the contact of blood mages in the Chalbrooke area."

Red gave a slow nod.

"Very well. I know of several. Allow me the time to speak with them. I will inform you if they agree to meet with you, as well as when and where."

"If they do not?" Ba'tvian pressed.

"Then the boon will stand as owed."

The younger mage inclined his head to the elder one in a sign of agreement.

"I will continue towards Chalbrooke and await your mage sending." His smile was cold as he inclined his head in farewell. "Red."

The blood mage copied the gesture.

"Until then, Master of Shadows."

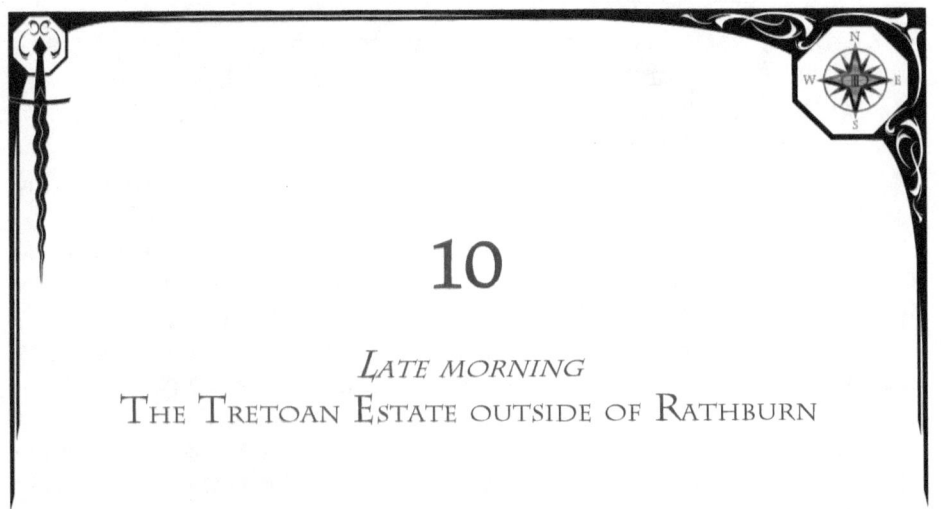

10

IN the spacious kitchen of the Tretoan household, Prialla Filoche scowled at the new maid she was supervising. The tall, beauteous blonde was losing patience with the girl. She did a haphazard job when cleaning, didn't heed detailed instructions, and couldn't seem to remember where anything was. As it was, the dishes that the girl was supposed to wash were rinsed at best. Most of them still had traces of food on them.

As a senior servant herself, Prialla had little tolerance for incompetence. As a practicing blood mage, however, she deemed the girl an excellent sacrificial candidate. Her homely looks had not caught the attention of the any of male servants. Her lack-wit work ethic would make it less likely that she would be missed if she disappeared. Prialla was all in favor of her disappearing, yet first she had to deal with the matter at hand.

Prialla glared at the girl, gesturing at the result of her efforts.

"Do it again. Properly. If I find one bit of filth on any of these dishes, that will be the end of you. Is that clear?"

She nodded, expression glum. Behind her, the rest of the kitchen staff busied themselves with their tasks. No one looked up or uttered a word. Prialla may have been a servant in the household, but they all well aware that she well regarded by the family they served. That she was the lord's bastard daughter as well as the chatelaine's assistant made them even more wary of incurring her wrath.

Whatever her mood, Prialla was not a woman who would go unnoticed. She made an impact, even when dressed in the humble, conservative servant's frock, and took command when at work. No one crossed her. While she might berate them as they went about their duties, the worst of her disciplinary action didn't occur during the work day; it was done on her time off. Her reputation for vindictiveness outside of the job was justified.

No one present in the kitchen wanted to be associated with the current object of her displeasure.

As the maid turned back to the dishes, Prialla's blue eyes flicked over everyone else in the room. Finding nothing else to address, she turned on her heel, leaving the kitchen for her half-brother's study. The well-appointed, if somewhat austere, room was where she and her cohorts usually gathered. Raptu Carthier was already there with his boyhood friend, her half-brother Halvark Tretoan.

She maintained the image of fierce authority as she strode through the house. She didn't let it fall until the study door closed behind her.

"Problems, my sweet?"

She glowered at Raptu as he lounged on a couch, the fire dancing in the hearth across from him. He was handsome, in a tarnished soul sort of way. The light reflecting in his whiskey brown eyes gave his features a wicked cast – something that she always found attractive. Her irritation began to fade. As it did, her expression slid into a pout.

"The newest hire will have to go. She's a complete idiot." Prialla spied a tray of finger foods on the coffee table. She snatched a pastry as she took a seat beside him. "Where is my brother?"

"A courier came with some message or other for him. He'll be back soon." He gave her a rakish smile, reaching over to tug at a curl that had escaped the no-nonsense bun she wore when working. "Halvark wants to play again."

She gave an unladylike snort. By 'play' Raptu meant their illicit blood practices. They'd been on the lookout for a suitable victim for a while now.

"*You* are the one wanting to play," she corrected, prompting a chuckle from him. "We can take that useless twit." She bit into the pastry, tasting the warm filling of cheese and onion. "She's ripe for dismissal. It would be simple to intercept her on her way back to wherever she came from."

"It's a good thing that the old man is off on that business trip if we're to take someone from the household again." He released her hair. "Remember what happened last time."

"I do." She sniffed. "My overbearing father isn't sleeping with this one, doesn't even know that she's been working here. We'll be safe enough."

The thought of Lord Tretoan had her scowling again. He'd become increasingly disapproving of the trio in recent months. They'd had to curtail their activities, tow her father's abhorrent line, play the obedient offspring of nobility. Even she, a bastard child, was expected to comport herself in a conventional, lady-like manner. One day, they'd have to do something about him. With the old man out of the way, Halvark would be in control of the estate, the purse strings, everything – and she had a measure of influence over her half-brother. The truth of that eased her displeasure.

The door latch rattled. Prialla set what was left of her snack back on the tray as she stood, her movements quick. The door opened to admit Halvark. Once it was locked, she resumed her former position, finishing off the pastry.

"Our...friend has called in his favor," he announced, throwing the written missive down on the table. The dark look on his face told them that they wouldn't like what it said.

The man Halvark referred to was another blood mage, one that had helped them cover up the sacrificial murder of Lord Tretoan's mistress a few years ago. Red, as they called him, had done it in exchange for future favor, one that would benefit everyone involved. That condition had outlined in a contract that all of them had signed in blood.

Prialla picked up the message, unfolding it to read. With a curse, she handed it to Raptu, taking to her feet to pace the room. Her thoughts whirled.

"Destroy the Mancer Guild House? That's the favor?" Raptu crumbled the note and flung it in the fireplace. The flames embraced the offering, rendering it to ash within seconds. "He's crazy."

"He recommended joining forces with the blood mage Ba'tvian Delthanurk for the task." Halvark brooded. "We don't know where he is, or if he can be trusted. Even if we're able to gain his aid, we're still risking everything. My father is suspicious enough as it is. If he were to find out..."

He let the sentence hand in the air like a bad omen.

"We signed that contract," Prialla reminded them. "We have to honor it. We're blood-bound."

"I told you we should never have signed that." Raptu's face was thunderous. "We should have just killed him," he continued, referring to Red.

"But we did sign it. Now we are stuck with it." Halvark glared at his sister. "It was your idea to accept it, as I recall."

"As it was your fault that we were in that fix to begin with, killing our father's whore." She met his furious gaze with one of her own. "So don't start with me, *brother.*"

"What do you propose we do now?" Raptu interjected before the argument could get underway. Halvark turned to the fire with a muttered oath. Prialla took a deep breath.

"We have time. There was no deadline given in the message. We have time to think, to plan. To cover our tracks so that the old man doesn't find out." She let that sink in. As it did, the tension in the room eased. "Let me contact Red. I can get him to help us track down Ba'tvian Delthanurk *without,*" she emphasized as Halvark opened his mouth to protest, "getting us further in debt to him. Since he made the recommendation, he should know how to get in touch with him."

"And then?" Her brother's tone racked over her nerves. Prialla gave him a cool look.

"I'll negotiate with Ba'tvian. Between all of us, we should be able to do something – discredit the guild in some way perhaps. To destroy something doesn't mean we have to physically tear it down."

"That's more plausible." Raptu's grudging acknowledgment earned a dark look from his friend. "Would you rather raise an army under our fathers' noses, Halvark? I wouldn't."

"We'd never keep it secret," Prialla pointed out.

"Fine." His capitulation was less than enthusiastic. "Just understand, *sister,* that I will not be party to bearing the burden of any more favors once this is done."

"Agreed."

"We'll have to come up with a reason for Prialla's absence." Raptu picked up another tidbit from the tray. "It's bound to cause questions."

"I'll take care of it." For the first time since the discussion begun, Halvark relaxed. "I can send her on a buying trip. I'll think of something suitable. With my father away on business and not due back for several weeks, we won't have to worry about explanations."

"Good." Satisfied, Prialla smoothed the front of her servant's frock. "On that note, I'll leave the planning to you while I get back to work. I'll contact Red later tonight." Prialla started for the door, then paused with her hand on the latch. She turned back to her brother. "We'll need to deal with our dear father soon. Perhaps even my mother. She's been asking some pointed questions lately; I wouldn't put it past the bastard to have recruited her to spy on us."

Halvark's mouth thinned in irritation. Still, he nodded. "We will need to deal with them upon his return. If I must kill my father, sister, then you must kill your mother. Let's not take any chances, shall we?"

Her stomach clenched at the thought. She didn't hate her mother, yet life would be so much easier without her poking around. There was also another benefit, she thought. Her mother was aging, the beauty that had caught Lord Tretoan's eye was fading. The woman was a reminder of what Prialla may one day become – a washed out female with sagging looks and a worn out body that no man wanted.

I will never be like that. She suppressed a shudder. *I will find a way to stay young, beautiful, desirable.*

Yes, getting rid of the reminder of what the future might hold for her was an excellent idea.

"Don't forget to fire that twit, my sweet. We'll have that rite before you leave." Raptu smiled at his friend. "You and I will just have to pick up our playmate after she's dismissed."

As they began to plan for the girl's capture, Prialla left to speak with the chatelaine.

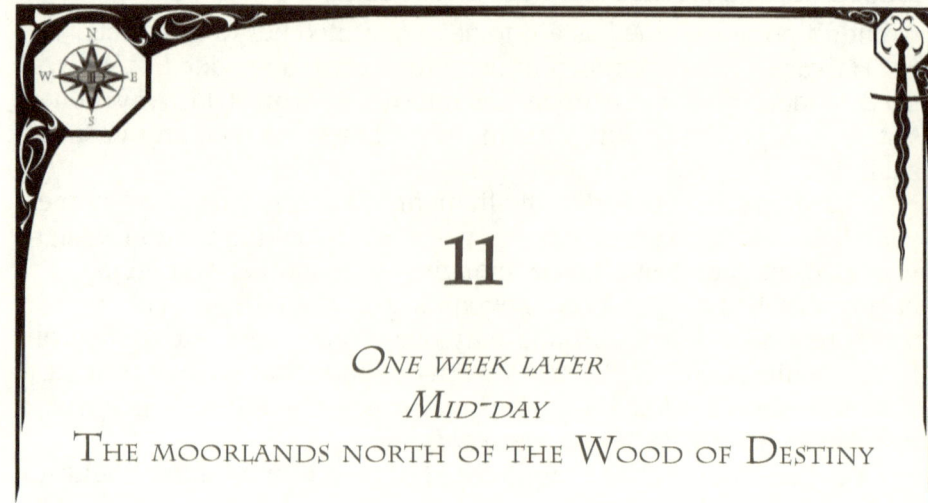

11

NERISSE studied the infrastructure of Ibestor's mind, aware that Ba'tvian shadowed her every move. He was getting better at it. She didn't noticed him as she checked the changes she'd made to the barbarian's mental processes. They had adjusted well to the modifications. Yet checking on the work she'd done Ibestor was not the point of this particular excursion. They were here so she could illustrate to her lord the results of the task he'd given her a week before.

Well? Ba'tvian's telepathic sending sounded clear in her own thoughts, segregated from the rest of the world.

Do you see this? She 'pointed' a mental finger at a thought pattern. It presented itself as a silver web tinged with red along the edges. *This spun out on its own from the loyalty compulsion we put in place.*

What is it? What does it mean?

That he's accepted the compulsion as being natural. She experienced a warm glow of success. This was something that she hadn't anticipated. *It's because he didn't have a fully developed personality. This pattern indicates that he not only sees you as his leader, his lord, but as someone who has to be served, honored, and protected. He doesn't question it.* She 'touched' a section of the web. *This part is how he views me.*

And how does he see you?

As yours. Her cheeks blushed. Ba'tvian ignored her reaction, waiting with a trace of impatience for the rest. *He sees me as ranking higher than him, yet lower than you.* It took her a moment to find the words to describe how the barbarian regarded her. *He doesn't see me as a person. I don't think he sees people as people. You are the top-predator in the pack, so to speak, not someone to be challenged. I am your property, and he respects that claim.*

Ba'tvian mulled over her explanation as she moved to another structure. This one resembled a forest of thin pillars of red growing around a central, glowing spark. That spark consisted of basic instinct, the raw elements of a human mind. The area around it should have been filled with things representing personality components, emotional ties, things that shaped a man. Instead, the pillars pulsed with influence. She'd built each one with meticulous precision, filling them with Ba'tvian.

Her lord hadn't allowed her to source his mind for that. She'd used her own feelings about him, her knowledge of his past, his ambitions, his beliefs. After she had given him the keys to Ibestor's mind, he'd gone in after her to add to the pillars. His influence pulsed in those structures in vibrant shades of crimson.

These are rooted deep, she observed. *There's no way for him to rip them out, even if he wanted to.*

You believe this needs to be replicated in a mage of greater skill?

Yes. She'd wanted to show him what they needed to strive for. *It will take longer to achieve with someone of a strong mind, a more developed personality.* Her psychic presence beckoned him to follow her as she moved to another part of the barbarian's mind, this time the center for sleep. *Do you see this?*

He studied it. *The mind is not as strong here.*

That wasn't precisely true. The mind was just more vulnerable in sleep. That Ibestor was an individual without the innate weaknesses presented with an empathic ability was key. Nerisse would not be able take over a mage in the same way she had the healer some time ago. Yet the window of opportunity present by the mind in a sleep-state was essential to the methods she was developing.

I can make a drug that would make this part of the mind more vulnerable while it rests, she explained. *The drug would not influence the mage's waking abilities so would go unnoticed.* She'd spent the last week testing it on Ibestor, probing the effects for flaws. *I would like to test it on a lesser mage, someone more easily overcome, to make sure it works without discovery.*

We may not have that option. Ba'tvian's cool answer was considering. Mages, as common as they were in Orthanor, were not found in the places the two ended up in.

It can be bypassed. There would be more risk involved, though not enough to be insurmountable. *If the effects are felt I can feign sickness, mimic the symptoms so that it can be attributed to something mundane, explainable, such as food poisoning.*

Good. Come out.

She retreated from the altered mind, opening her physical eyes to meet her lord's unreadable gaze. Back in her own body, seated on the ground beside the two men, she was light-headed. As the image of the inside of Ibestor's subconsciousness faded from her mental sight, he narrowed his eyes.

"Your color is off."

"Perhaps I need to eat something." She couldn't remember how much food she'd consumed that morning. They had risen early, leaving behind the wilderness at dawn. Their trek took them across the moorlands that stretched from the Relds in the west to the Port City of Edon in the east. She'd asked for a respite, wanting to use the opportunity to show him what she had figured out. Now the weariness of their travels settled on her.

"We broke our fast earlier than usual." She looked up at the sun, gauged the time. A few hours had lapsed, at least. It was no wonder she was tired. Still, the fatigue was lay heavier on her than she might have expected. "I didn't realize it would take up so much time, lord. I'm sorry."

Ba'tvian didn't respond to her last comment, just flicked a glance at Ibestor. They'd sent him into slumber for this little demonstration. Seeing that he was as deep in slumber as he had been when they'd started, he rose to his feet. He crossed over to where their things were, delved into one of her satchels to produce a packet of journey bread and jerked meat. He came back to thrust it at her.

"Eat. It serves no one if you sicken."

"Yes, lord." She opened the packet to nibble at the food. As she ate, she focused inward, trying to determine what else, if anything, might be wrong.

Her energy levels were lower than normal. Otherwise, she seemed fine. There was little reason for the energy levels, her innate power reservoirs, to be low, though. She wasn't maintaining anything other than what she normally did: her personal shields. The earth bond as psychic tie that she didn't need to fuel; the earth did that itself.

Perhaps it was a fluke. She would give it time to correct itself before telling him about it. They needed to keep moving east.

Ba'tvian had plans, things he'd shared with her, goals that were important to him. She couldn't be the one to slow him down or, worse, prevent him from doing what he needed to do. At least they were riding now, not traveling on foot. That would help.

Nerisse finished her food packet as she watched her lord rouse Ibestor. Together, they began to replace the bags on the mounts. They'd left them saddled, taking most of the packs off for the duration of their rest. It helped the beasts last longer. The sun's heat tended to be trapped under the gear the mounts wore yet Ba'tvian had refused to allow the saddles to be removed for the break. Her lover wanted the mounts ready in case they were forced to run. They wouldn't have the time to saddle them and their packs could be replaced.

Ibestor worked without a word, fastening bags to his mount while her lover did the same with his own. She folded the packet's wax paper, stuffed it into her belt pouch, then moved to gather her things.

As the last satchel was lashed to her saddle, she spoke.

"We're a few days travel north of the Wood, aren't we?"

"No. The Wood of Destiny may be in sight later today. Ibestor's beasts make better time than anticipated." Ba'tvian always knew where they were. It was the Shadows, she thought. They kept him informed about many things; locations would be one of them. Her lord mounted up, turning in his saddle to study her as she did the same. "Your color is still off."

"My energy levels are low." She took up the slack in her reins. "I am well enough to ride."

He goaded his beast over so that he could reach over, closing his hand loosely around her throat. His dark eyes bore into hers.

"You will tell me if you worsen."

She nodded. He released her.

"Ibestor," he called over his shoulder. "It is time to leave."

Interlude 2

The apothecary in Rathburn

LABIYAL sat in the back room of the apothecary. It was, he mused, a rather unassuming little shop. It sold cooking spices, medicinal herbs, potions, lotions, and various items that catered to the needs of alchemists, true chemists, healers, doctors, exotic chefs. Many of the spices sold there had uses in medicine, or cosmetic properties. The sheer volume of the shop's selections was understated in the front, where the patrons could peruse the items were in the highest demand.

Yet in the back room, where the rest of the stock was kept, it was apparent just how unique the apothecary was.

Sitting at a small wooden table in the middle of the room, Labiyal's eyes roamed the shelves, the bins, the baskets, the cabinets that lined the walls. Most of it was medicinal, alchemic, or the more expensive cosmetics. One had to be an expert in black or blood magic to see the true intent of some things stored here. Vials of blood, powdered organs, sheaves of skin – animal or human – no normal apothecary would have these things for sale. That this one did was due to Labiyal's whim; he owned it under one of his aliases.

Through the closed door he could hear the faint jangle of the door's bell as someone entered the store front. His hand slipped into a breast pocket to retrieve the small mirror he kept there. Prialla Filoche, dressed in the winter attire of a servant of the Tretoan Estate, entered the shop. He noted with approval that her countenance was subdued; she tended too often to be striking in the way she conducted herself. Tactics for gaining attention had no place in a meeting such as this. She spoke with the proprietor, who engaged her in verbal dance of coded phrases. It mattered little that the reason for her coming was common knowledge between them, or that they did business on semi-regular basis. Labiyal had certain rules in place. His rules were always observed.

Finally, she was invited to the back.

He replaced the mirror before reaching down to the bag that lay on the floor beside him. The half-daemon retrieved a small draw-string pouch of green velvet, setting it on the table in front of him. The door opened. His man bowed Prialla into the room, then departed without a word.

"Red." She greeted him with a small smile. "Thank you for agreeing to meet."

He waved her to take the seat opposite him, waiting for her get settled before replying.

"I am sorry that I could not do so sooner."

"Yes, well, we all have our own business to attend to." She tilted her head to one side. The movement was habitual rather than coquettish. Prialla, for all that she used seduction and wiles to manipulate others, had never tried to use it on him. "We received your note, which we burned after reading. As you can imagine, it is quite a…daunting task you've set for us."

"One that I believe, with Ba'tvian's aid, you are capable of."

"Hmm." She narrowed her eyes, just a bit. *A h,* he thought. This was the reason for the meeting; he'd anticipated correctly. "How do we know that Ba'tvian will be open to working with us? He might have as much reason to act against the Mancers, perhaps more reason than we do. That does not mean he would be willing to join with us."

"Ba'tvian Delthanurk," he began, "is a man tired of being hunted. You will find that him more than willing. A word of caution, however, my dear Prialla. Ba'tvian is by no means someone that will be led. He is a rising power, one to be reckoned with."

"Is this a way for you to curry favor with him then?" She gave him a shrewd look. "Give him tools with which to defeat the Mancers, solving a problem for him, while gaining you more room with which to work?"

"It is business." Labiyal returned her look with a cool curve of his lips. "Ba'tvian was already looking to move against the Mancers' Guild. He has paid his blood coin; now I must deliver on my end. Calling in the debt you three owed me seemed to be the way to fulfill the bargain. The mutual benefits of it, should he succeed, cannot be understated."

"Do you think he will succeed?" Her voice betrayed her doubt.

"Meet with Ba'tvian. You will have the answer to that once you do." He slid the pouch across the table to her. "This will guide your way."

"He's not anywhere near here." She opened the sack, brought out an ornate metal object. Prialla turned it over in her hands, running a finger over the hinge she found. "Ensorcelled?"

"Yes, keyed to you alone." He met her lovely blue eyes with his golden ones when she looked up. "Ba'tvian is traveling to Chalbrooke. He is coming from the north and west, bringing with him two companions who have proven themselves useful. His speed of travel has been very good. It will not take you long to find him."

"How does this work?" She held up the circular item she'd been given.

He instructed her to open it, explaining the effect of the magic imbued in the metal and glass of the thing. Once he was satisfied that she knew how to use it, he concluded the meeting.

"Ba'tvian will be notified that you are coming. Do not lose my trinket, Prialla. I will want it back."

"Of course." She tucked it discreetly into a slit in the seam between her bodice and her skirt. The hidden pocket gave no evidence that it was there, let alone contained anything. "I will contact you once I have returned."

"No. Ba'tvian will see to its return." He rose to his feet as she did. "Let us, for the nonce, keep our meetings as few as possible. We both have public facades that should not be compromised or suspected."

"Until we meet again, then."

Labiyal opened the door, let her out. As he closed it behind her, he allowed himself a pleased smile. This maneuvering had been much easier than he'd thought it would be. That was due to Ba'tvian. The boy's ambition, his hatred, his drive to be free ensured that he had made the request. If he had not, Labiyal, or Red, would have had to concoct a rather complicated story to unite the cast.

It is much better this way.

More, it reinforced Ba'tvian's position, the role he would play, in the eyes of his king. The boy...wasn't a boy anymore. Killing the Mancers one by one was an indication of his maturation. Wiping them out would make him worthy of much more.

His life, his goals, his ambitions, are ours. He will pave the way

to an unfettered future, as I have always intended.
   That purpose lived within Ba'tvian Delthanurk's blood.

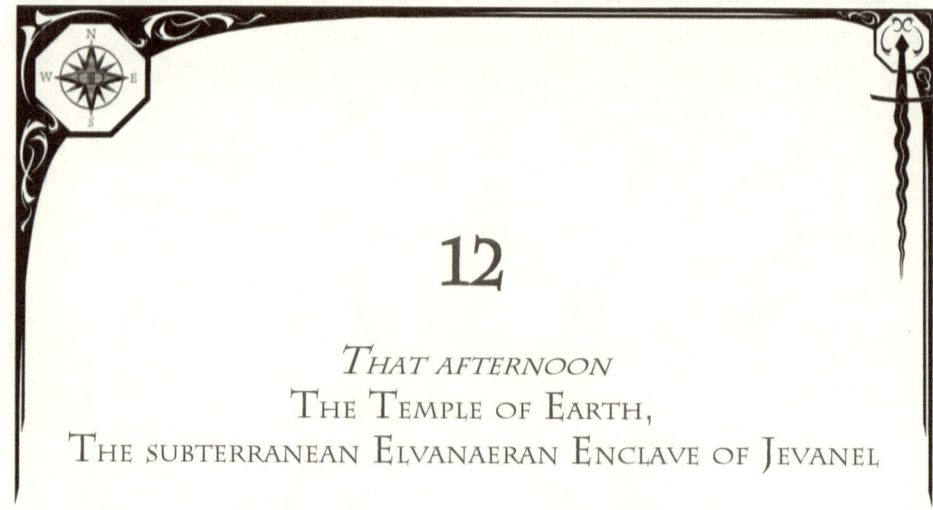

12

SAERLAN watched from a large balcony on the back of the temple complex as another group of Elvanarae was led onto the Rebirthing Grounds. Each of the five citizens was dressed in a loose shroud, accompanied by a white-robed member of the priesthood as they began the final phase of the cleansing rites. In one of the many grottos within the Rebirthing Grounds, they would be buried by the priests who would then watch over them.

Like the myriad others who'd come before them, they had spent three days immersed in prayer, ritual baths, and fasting. As night touch the land above the cavern in which Jevanel was set, they had their first meal. Then they were lead to Rebirthing Grounds to lay in a shallow grave. Their faces were left exposed to the air. As their overseers sang songs to the earth, they would sleep through the rest of the night. The earth would claim their past associations as it would the body upon death. When the people rose the next day, they would be without taint. They would be free to live, to laugh, to love without the burden of evil.

The High Priest let his gaze fall away from the group. He let his eyes drift over the glowing crystals embedded in the rock that illuminated the grottos, the mossy loam that covered the Grounds, the jagged mineral formations that grew in all living caves. From where he stood, he couldn't see the city that climbed up from the floor of the huge cavern they called the 'earth's womb'. Behind the Temple of Earth, there was only the Rebirth Grounds in the center, the Pyre Crypts to the far left, and the Cleansing Pools to the far right. Between each hung a 'curtain' of stone, a natural phenomenon that served to divide the sections.

In the still air was sorrow, fear, bewilderment.

Nerisse's descent into dark arts had come as a horrific shock to everyone. Saerlan felt the echoes of his own confused grief within the spirit of each person he spoke to. The rites, at least, gave them comfort, if not answers.

With a sigh, Saerlan turned away from the Grounds to walk along the length of balcony. The platform was three stories up from the ground, running from one end of the complex to the other. As he passed the stone curtain hanging between the Pyre Crypts and the Rebirthing Grounds, he tried not to think of the unpleasant task ahead of him.

Blood mages were rare among his kind. They were so in tune with the earth that they couldn't bear to harm it in any way. Blood magic hurt the earth the most. The darkness of it, the pain, the fear, the stolen life force – it cut through the earth's spirit as sharply as a knife.

It had to do with Einlienn, with its creator, Saerlan recalled, choosing to dwell on the teachings of his faith. The Elvanarae believed that the father of their race had forged the world, walked among his people. Xera had given them everything – a home, knowledge, compassion, provision. Their histories described that long ago era as a golden age, a time of tranquil happiness. Then evil had slipped into the world, leaving Xera dead, their people imperiled.

Their father hadn't been lost, however. Xera's spirit had merged with Einlienn. His spirit, though changed, continued to guide them to this day. They were taught that this was the reason for the earth bond. They were told that this was why black and blood magery were a poison to the world they lived in; both were born of the same evil that had slain their glorious patriarch. Saerlan reached the end of the balcony, taking the stairs down to the ground level. He wondered if that was reason enough for the earth to sever the bond it held with Nerisse.

As High Priest, it was his duty to complete her ostracism. She was not here in person to punish, so he was left with just a single option. As his sandaled feet touched the soil of the Pyre Crypts, he left off the thoughts of history to concentrate on what had to be done.

He walked down the path lined with the bowls of pyre rock. The grayish-white material burned with a low blue-green flame that cast its surroundings in an eerie light. Off the path, the bare soil was strewn with ashes – the remains of their dead. Luminous mushrooms, thick green moss, and tiny white star-shaped flowers called *Illiuss* grew around rock formations. They represented hope, life, and love for deceased, for those who still lived.

As Saerlan continued down the path, the ashy soil gave way markers. These were columns of carved stone that rose from the floor. Each belonged to one of the families of Jevanel. Upon the death of a family member, a carving was added to the column. If there was no room left, another segment of fashioned stone was set on the top. The dimensions of the columns varied, with just three or four tall enough to touch the ceiling of the cavern.

Having spent the majority of his life underground, he wondered if walking through a forest would feel like it did when he passed through the markers. They crowded path on either side, looming over him though they stood straight. Eventually, they came to an end with the path. Before him lay a broad hollow in the earth, like a shallow bowl, lined with the white residue of spent pyre rock, the gray powder of ash. Here is where the pyres were built. They were left to burn under the vigil of the priesthood until the fire went out. Anything that was left of the deceased, such as bone fragments or burial accoutrements, were tucked in niches carved into the cave walls.

Saerlan paced to the center of the hollow. From the belt of his robes, he drew a silver knife as he knelt in the place of death. With one hand, he dug a hole in the ground, going deep enough to reach through the layers of pyre detritus to the true earth. Then he prayed, his murmurings filling the cavern, echoing back to him, as he pricked a finger with the knife and let the blood well up.

Daughter of the earth, we knew her as Nerisse se li Astorae. Let her pass from your spirit as she has broken all covenants. She has wrought pain, shed blood, caused death. She has sought power through means outlawed by all...

The bead of blood dripped into the exposed soil. It was the symbolic bleeding of his heart.

...Sever the bond that holds her to you, allow her to fade from the grief she has caused into the death she deserves.

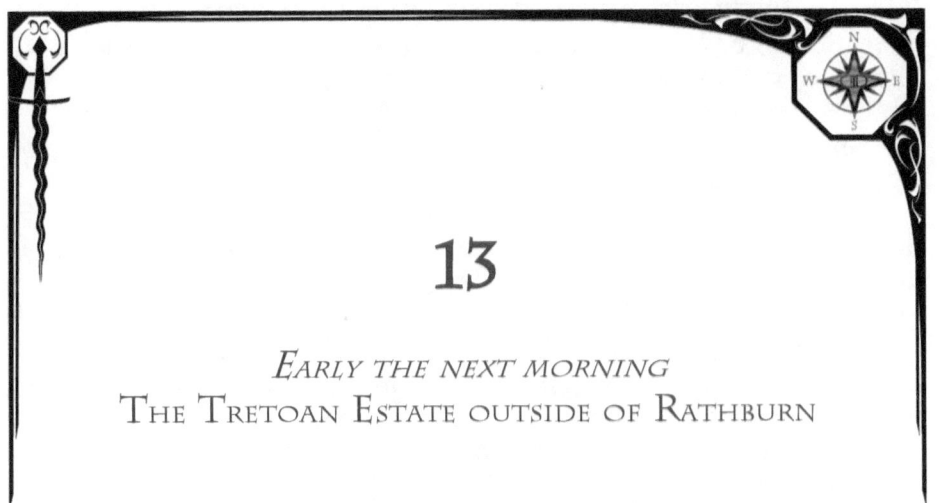

13

PRIALLA regarded the horse that Raptu had procured for her. The stables his father maintained were much larger than the ones her own sire kept, with a wider range in the types of mounts. This one was a gelding built for travel, and trained to fight back when necessary. The horse was not a war-mount. It wasn't large enough to carry a rider in plate armor, nor was it aggressive enough for the battlefield.

She stood in the Carthier stable with her half-brother, watching their friend deal with the horse inside its stall. Though the building was filled to capacity with equine residents, the stable-hands were nowhere in sight. It amused her. Raptu had a reputation for making sport of anyone who gave him reason. Most of his family's servants avoided him whenever possible.

"This is one of the horses we use for single couriers," Raptu explained with a negligent air as he tied her bags to the saddle. His family had made part of their fortune by providing messenger services. They employed low-level mages to provide mage-sendings for those who could afford the rates for quick responses. For those who could not, they provided a more inexpensive service of letter delivery by rider, provided that the destination was in the same region. The family's contacts did not extend to the western or southern parts of Orthanor, and only to limited areas in the northern wilderness.

With her mage-born senses, Prialla could see the sullen crimson lines that woven in and around the horse's body. It had been Red's suggestion, to make the journey faster. The spells they'd cast used a great deal of power; they wouldn't be repeating this any time soon. If the power cost wasn't enough of a drawback, there was an unfortunate side effect that was. It would kill the horse in the end.

She had five days to locate Ba'tvian Delthanurk before the animal keeled over. She hoped to do it in no more than three.

"Masquerading as a male messenger is the best idea in this whole farce," Halvark muttered from beside her. He was still unconvinced as to the wisdom of their bargain with Red. "There are bandits in the outlying regions, Prialla."

"I am aware." Her words were cool, confident, despite her trepidation. She wasn't experienced in combat. "I have enough magic to deter them."

Or frighten them enough to allow my escape.

She gave her garb one last critical look as Raptu finished with her horse and led it out of its stall. She was dressed in the riding leathers of a Carthier courier, her breasts bound so that she appeared flat-chested. Her golden hair was stuff up in the cap she wore, her face devoid of any trace of makeup. Up close, it was still hard to hide the fact that she was female; her face was too feminine. Yet at a distance, she could be mistaken as a slim boy.

Prialla tugged the cap's brim a little lower on her brow, then smiled. The uniform alone be enough to allow her passage unmolested along the major roads until she left the area of Carthier's influence.

"Do you have the thing he gave you?" Halvark asked, breaking through her reverie.

"Of course." She slipped a hand into her breast pocket, palming the small, circular mirror the blood mage had given her at their meeting. She brought it out, holding it up for her brother to see.

It was a mirror with a hinged lid and frame of engraved steel. She flipped up the lid to reveal the unblemished surface of the mirror. The glass held a subtle glow. It brightened after a moment, then showed a view of the land as it might be seen if one were flying above it. It should the Carthier estate sprawling over the earth with the Chal-Edon Trade Route running through it. The route was a long one, running from the northern wilderness to the city-state of Edon, before turning south to pass through Chalbrooke. Rathburn sat at its terminus to the west of their location.

A spot the size of a pin's head glowed red in the estate, about where the stable was situated. A yellow spot of the same size appeared on the road leading toward Rathburn, where the frame met the glass of the mirror. Halvark frowned.

"The red is you?"

"Yes. The yellow indicates the direction in which I must go." She glanced over at Raptu as moved closer to peer at the object she held.

"An interesting artifact." He took it from her, studying it with an avaricious gleam in his eye. "The bastard will want this back, won't he?"

She nodded.

"If it's returned damaged, he'll expect repayment." She reclaimed the mirror, snapping the lid shut to put back in her pocket. "He didn't say what kind of repayment and I don't believe that I wish to find out."

"I wonder if it can be replicated," Raptu mused. "He used blood to make it. It tastes of iron to the arcane senses." He was the only mage Prialla had ever heard of who 'tasted' magic.

She felt her lips curve as they began to discuss the possibilities. Her brother's somewhat reluctant interest in the mirror broadened her smile. He liked toys as much as Raptu did, and would enjoy the challenges presented in copying this one.

"Have either of you thought about our other little problem?"

"Yes." Halvark broke off the discussion with a frown. "It would be best to have a scapegoat. Staging an accident would leave too many questions. A random murder, however..." He glanced at his friend.

"With Ba'tvian to blame," Raptu continued, "may deflect any suspicion from us."

"We'll work out the details later. In the meantime, I'll leave you two to your fun. Try not to kill too many people while I'm gone." She said it lightly, but meant every word. They had a tendency to be...unrestrained when she wasn't with them. "I might get jealous."

Raptu flashed her a wicked grin as her brother scowled.

"Give us a kiss, then, my sweet."

She did so, bestowing her favor on both of them with equal parts of lust, affection, and camaraderie. She'd miss them while she was gone. While she had no illusions as to how or why she manipulated them, they were her friends, the only family she cared to claim. Not even her mother held the same importance to her as these two men did – no matter how difficult they might be.

She led the gelding out of the building before mounting up. With one last admonishment for them to behave while she was away,

Prialla rode out of the estate stable-yard.

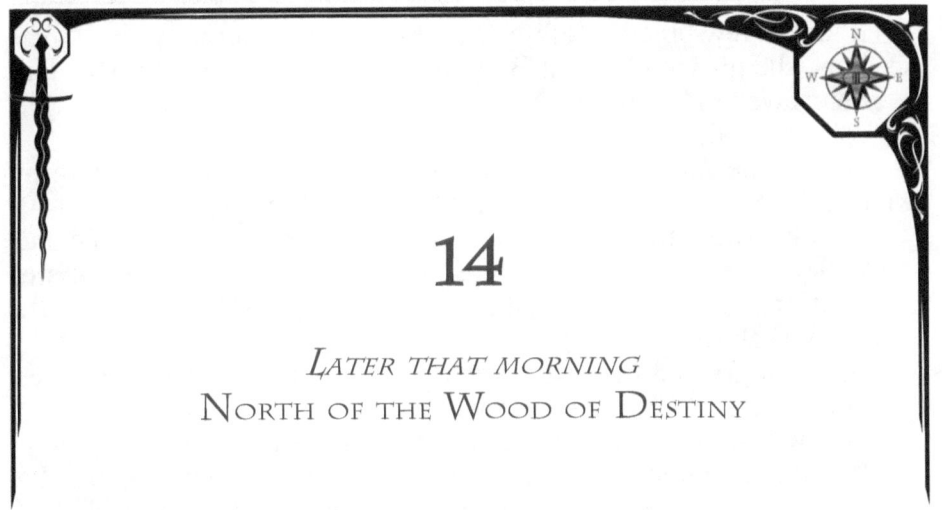

14

NERISSE stared at another vast expanse of woods as Ba'tvian led them nearer. They halted several hundred yards away, the sun plodding on to its noon-day zenith in the clear skies above them. She stayed in the saddle as her lord slid off his mount to stand in the snow-crusted moorland.

She was exhausted. Fatigue had become a hallmark of their journey for her, the weariness bone-deep in a way it hadn't been in the two years she'd spent with Ba'tvian. She didn't know what was causing it; the healer's herbal and her own meager knowledge of medicine had failed her.

It was worse today. The fatigue now included a nagging headache, a touch of nausea. She was so distracted by it that it took her much longer than it should have to notice the reason for their stop.

There was music in the air. It was harp-song, with a lyrical accompaniment. It almost sounded like children singing in a language that teased at primal knowledge deep within her. The inherent vitality paired with the music intrigued her. Beside her, Ba'tvian cocked his head, listening, as the misshapen creature beside him snuffled at the grass.

"This is the Wood of Destiny."

His sudden statement startled Nerisse, causing her to shift in her seat and overbalance. She grabbed the saddle horn with one hand, clutching at the cantle with the other as she let the momentum of her slide carry her off the beast. Her hands, she saw, were pale, more gray than the normal slate blue.

It took a few breaths before she was certain of her balance. Once she was, she glanced back at Ba'tvian to find him watching her. His eyes narrowed in harsh scrutiny.

"Are you ill, Nerisse?"

"I..." She faltered in the face of his demand. "I am unsure of what ails me. It is no sickness that I have ever heard of."

It took more effort than she'd anticipated to release the saddle and walk the few steps to stand before him. By the time she got there, she was trembling. Weak, she thought. She felt so weak. He despised weakness.

Ba'tvian gripped her arms, keeping his hold firm. His dark eyes bored into hers. "What is wrong with you?"

"I don't know." Her voice cracked, her body shook.

Cursing, he pulled her against him. Grateful for the support, she let her head fall onto his shoulder. He rarely allowed any kind of embrace, so she reveled in it even as she took comfort from it. Something black flickered at the edge of her vision. The Shadowed Ones were moving around them, encircling them. The largest broke from the others to slither forward. When it spoke, the words sounded in her mind, surprising her. It was not usual for her to hear them when they spoke to Ba'tvian.

What is the matter, lord?

She felt him tense, sensed a slight suspicion shading his thoughts. That alarmed her. He was shielded; she shouldn't be privy to his emotions. If her empathic shields were failing, then it was something beyond ordinary illness. Before she could voice the concern, Ba'tvian gave his telepathic reply.

Something is wrong with Nerisse. She says it is not true illness.

The creature blinked leprous white eyes, swinging its salamander-like head to stare at the elf. It glided closer, nudging her calf with its nose before turning back to its master.

Her ties to the earth are fading.

It didn't sink in at first, the meaning of those words. It didn't make sense. A permanent psychic tie didn't just fade. She'd had it from the day of her birth, would until the day she died. It was the same with all Elvanarae. The earth bond was a vital part of her existence; it was as important as breathing.

"How quickly?" The hard tone of Ba'tvian's voice reflected his concern.

There is time yet. She needs to reconnect with the earth or she will perish.

Death was not an acceptable outcome. She wouldn't leave her lord alone when he needed her. He needed her skills, her belief in him. Without her...he'd fail without her...

Her lord could not fail.

"Nerisse." He called her attention back to him. Dazed as well as weak, she looked up at him, saw his mouth tighten. "Your people – can they interfere with your link to the earth?"

"My people?" She frowned, confused. Why would they? "I..." Then she remembered. Timbrel Jodrek, the Mancer they'd slain in the wilderness had recognized her. He had gotten off a mage sending before they'd captured and killed him. Blood mages were anathema everywhere, yet the Elvanarae had a way of dealing with such lawbreakers, a method she'd forgotten about.

"Yes, they could." The words came out in a whisper. "They would. They wouldn't understand."

"Understand what?"

"That I...need to be with you. That you are a great lord." She flushed, ducking her gaze. He didn't care for gushy emotion or declarations of love. "They would see you as the Mancers do, would label me the same. I would be ostracized."

"What does that mean?" He closed a hand around her throat, used his thumb to nudge her chin up. "What will the Elvanarae do to you?"

"It's a long process." She felt sad, young, fragile, and alone. Yet she wasn't the girl she'd been when she'd left Jevanel for the Trinity. She was the woman her lord had made her. She took a deep breath, dispelling the sensation of frailty as she straightened from him. Her hand remained on his shoulder to steady her. The fatigue – that hated weakness – wouldn't allow to abandon his support. "The first thing they will do is the shunning. No one acknowledges the existence of the outcast. That's already taken place. The second phase is the isolation, the cutting of ties – the social ties, the familial ties. Then the earth bond is severed. Unless I'm present, they have to do it from afar, which takes more power, more time. Usually, it's the last step."

"I need to know what this will do to you, Nerisse. By how much will this diminish you?"

He sounded grim, concerned. Of course he would, she thought. He was her lord, her lover. He cared.

"I might survive, for a time," she murmured, focusing inward. "I forsook my family, my people, when I left with you. Their loss... I've mourned it. I had the earth bond...with you, with that, I had all I needed…"

She let her voice trail off as her focus slipped. She was so weary now. The future that lay ahead for her just made it worse.

"Do you regret coming with me? Regret what I've given you?" He pulled her flush against him, his grip dimly painful. He sounded angry, his eyes lit with baleful sparks of red.

They were beautiful. It was an inane thought. Still, it was striking how the glints of his power were like crimson stars set against black velvet.

"No, I can't regret you, Ba'tvian." That came out as definitive, despite her tired voice. His hold on her loosened. "I've missed home, but that's all. I realized a long time ago – at the moment I found you outside the Docking Cavern at the Trinity –that I couldn't go back."

She wasn't sure if her answer pleased him. His intensity was hard to decipher.

"What will the loss of the earth do to you?"

Fear and sorrow flooded her heart. Tears pricked at her eyes; she fought not to shed them.

"I'll grow weak. I may go mad." Forcing herself to meet his gaze, she told him the last truth. "My death will be a slow one."

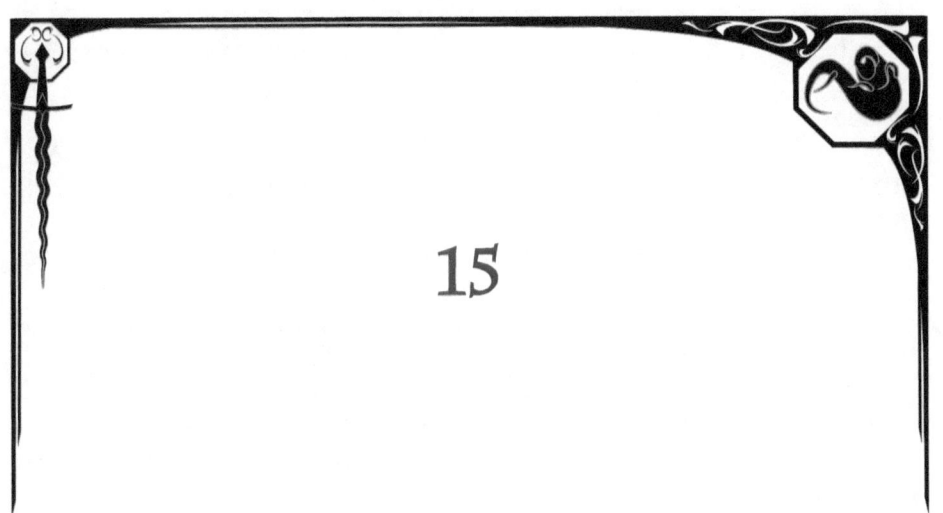

15

"**T**HAT is not acceptable." Ba'tvian refused to be robbed of one of his most powerful assets. That anyone would dare attempt it riled a cold fury within him.

I will not be stripped. I will not be diminished. I will not be made as the dirt beneath their feet.

He took a breath, then another. There was a lesson here, and he would be the one to teach it, to use it. A glimmer of an idea began to form in the back of his mind, one that might break his valued tool if mishandled. "We will find a solution for this, Nerisse."

"Once it is done, there is no way around it." She sounded resigned, tired. It infuriated him. He gripped her hair, forced her to look up at him. Her dull gaze met his furious one.

"Giving up, Nerisse? Do I mean so little to you that you would allow them kill you?"

Her eyes widened, her dull silver irises flickering with emotion.

"No, lord, you're everything to me." Tears gathered, yet did not fall. She was well aware how he hated weeping. "Everything."

"You will not let them take you from me. You will fight this. I will help you fight this."

She lost her battle with her tears. He gentled his hold on her, looking away as she wiped the moisture from her face. He focused on the Wood as he concentrated on his thoughts.

He needed Nerisse. His plans were such that he couldn't operate efficiently without her. The elven chit might be tiresome at times yet the burden of dealing with her was worth the rewards. Her loyalty was without question, her own need of him the perfect motivation to keep her working for him. If she died, it would be years – decades – before he found another to replace her.

He would not let her die.

If a reversal was impossible, then they had to prevent the… process from completing. Here, his ignorance of her race reared its head. The Elvanarae were a mystery to him.

"How do we," he hesitated for the barest of moments, "protect you? How do we stop this?"

"The priesthood oversees it, though any Elvanarae can complete the ritual, given enough time and effort." She smoothed his cloak hem as against his chest. Though he disliked the familiarity of the gesture, she didn't seem to be aware of what she was doing. She was thinking, which was more important. "My bond…it takes a great deal of persuasion for the earth to let it go."

"Can you persuade it to maintain it instead?"

"I can try."

"Shed blood for it." He bent down, spoke into her ear. "Your blood, Nerisse. It may be more accepting of you if you bleed for it."

She nodded. Blood held power; blood given willingly held a kind of purity that stolen blood did not.

"May I try this now, lord?" She glanced around at their surroundings. "I realize this is open, but…"

"Yes. Ibestor and I will safeguard us."

As Nerisse staggered over to her mount for what she would need, he became aware that the music had ceased. The Wood stood silent, watchful. Waiting.

"What do you wait for? Her or me?" Ba'tvian's murmured question received no answer. He hadn't expected one. Yet as he studied the Wood, he could have sworn it looked back, listening to what he'd said, watching for what he'd do. He glanced down at the Shadow still at his side. It responded to the unspoken query.

It waits for you to fail.

"It will be disappointed." He turned his back on the Wood to see Nerisse kneeling on the ground. She'd pulled at the grass until she had a patch of bare earth in front of her. With her ritual knife, she slit her palm, let her blood drip into the soil. As she prayed, as she bled, a hint of color seeped back into her countenance. Ba'tvian allowed himself a grim smile.

"They will all be disappointed."

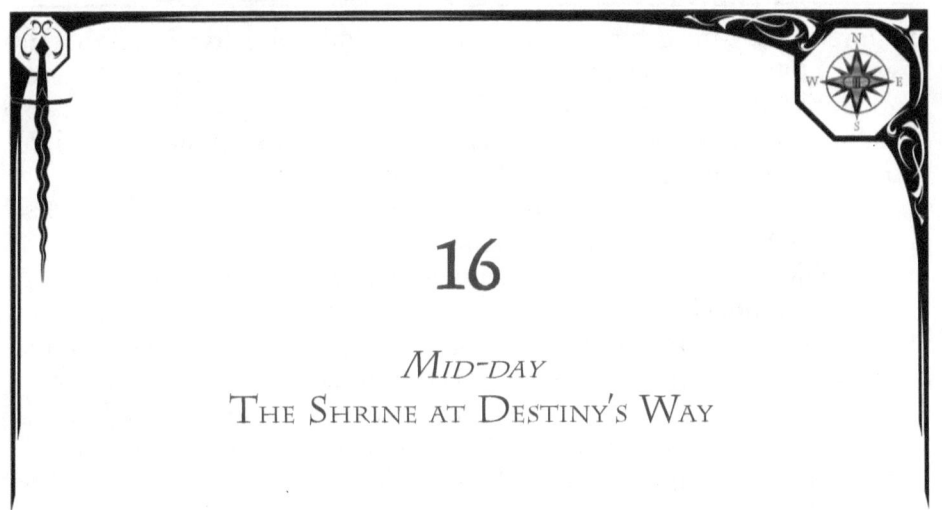

16

A BSOL Omine was washing up in preparation for the noon meal when he received the mage sending. The glowing ball of light was bright orange, carrying the signature of the Mancer Guild Master Zerik Mancerson. In the tradition of their order, he had abandoned his surname in favor of one that reflected the solidarity of the order when he'd become head of the Guild. If Absol had any interest in handling the politics that went with the position he would have claimed it years ago.

He'd sent a request to enroll I'k'Nole a week before, was expecting a response from the Guild. He hadn't expected one from the Guild Master. He grabbed up a towel to wipe his face and torso dry before cupping the sending in his hand. Zerik's voice sounded in his head as the message played out.

We accept your protégé, Absol Omine. It is well that you will bring him yourself as we must meet with you. There is a task that we believe would best be completed by you. Bring with you all that you have on the Monster of Menie. We will speak more on this when you arrive. Additionally, a new policy has been instated: all Mancers must notify the Guild of their location daily. More Mancers are missing, and we have found out much too late to act.

That was not good news. He felt tension build in his gut, a dreaded weight. Who was missing? Did he know them? How many more would he have to mourn? Timbrel had been killed a little more than a month ago. How many could that bastard murder in that time?

Too many.

The ball pulsed in his palm, an indication that a response was required. He forced himself to relax, to dismiss the dread he felt. He touched the sending telepathically, poured in his acknowledgement of summons, that he was at Destiny's Way, that he planned to leave for Chalbrooke the following day. He released it, watching it fade into nothing before it hit the wall of his room.

He turned back to the water basin, used the towel to mop up what little mess he'd made when washing. Setting it aside, he pulled on a fresh tunic and left to join the others in the small dining hall.

Dannon and I'k'Nole were there before him. Other monks sat at tables around the room. Out of respect, they tended to leave Dannon and Absol to their own space unless invited to join. Given what today's meal conversation was likely to be, Absol found himself grateful for the practice. Most of the monks tended to be apprehensive about Ba'tvian Delthanurk; the lives they lived here were too sheltered.

The Mancer took his seat – the only place setting with just a mug of tea – beside his old friend. He accepted a wooden trencher of meat, cheese, and mashed root vegetables from the Master Abbot. I'k'Nole cut a thick slab of bread from the loaf set in the center of the table. He offered it to Absol, cut another slab for Dannon, then himself.

"I'k'Nole has been accepted at the Guild." Absol saw the flash of excitement in the lad's violet eyes before he composed himself. He smiled to himself, amused at the lad's restraint as he piled various food items on his bread. "It also seems that I meet with the Guild seniors. We will have to leave in the morning." With a sigh, he looked at Dannon. "I'm sorry for the lack of notice."

"Ah, well…" Dannon shook his head, his mouth curving in a rueful smile. "It had to be sometime." He turned to I'k'Nole. "You'd best do us proud, lad."

"Yes, sir." I'k'Nole was solemn, his eyes flickering with momentary sadness. "I'll miss you."

"Your home will always be here." Dannon's statement left no room for argument or doubt. He gave Absol a stern look. "That goes for you as well, my friend."

"Yes." The monks at the shrine, his ward – they were the closest things to family he had.

"We'll get you packed up tonight, lad. Don't worry about what you can't take with you. We'll keep it safe here until you return." That said, the abbot changed the subject. "So what is the meeting about? Or can you say?"

Absol grunted as he swallowed a forkful of vegetables.

"Ba'tvian. It appears that the Guild is ready to concede that the way things are being done is getting us nowhere." He sipped his tea, found it strong. "We've lost more Mancers in the north. From what Timbrel was able to send us before he died, Ba'tvian is now the leader of three."

Dannon frowned. I'k'Nole continued eating, though he remained alert, attentive. The Mancer approved.

"That's not usual. Blood mages tend to be loners, unless they have an apprentice," the abbot mused, almost to himself. Though the number of Ba'tvian's group was not news, he seemed to be giving it more thought than he had previously.

"More unusual is that the third mage is a barbarian from the mountains. For whatever reason Ba'tvian has for it, we cannot discount that might be recruiting more blood mages." Absol took a moment to consume a portion of laden bread. "The real question is: what is he trying to do?"

"It could be chance that caused him to recruit the barbarian," Dannon suggested.

"True enough." Absol shook his head. "Most of what we have is speculation. It is unusual for blood mages to work together. There's too much ego, too much striving for power. Ba'tvian's plenty arrogant, and seems to have no tolerance for anyone else leading the way. I'm not sure what role Nerisse plays for him. The barbarian..." He paused, drinking from his mug as he contemplated. "Muscle, maybe. A lackey. Nerisse, though, doesn't strike me as someone who would be a mere minion."

"She was a priestess, wasn't she?" I'k'Nole's question was quiet, thoughtful.

"She was intended to be." The Mancer tried to think along that line. Finally, he continued. "I'm not sure of what import it might be."

"She could provide a different knowledge base. Take monks, for instance. They're educated in things like medicine. They can make healing potions. What if she's does that for him? He'd never get sick so bad that he'd have to find a hole to hide in for a while. She might also be his bait. People trust the monks; wouldn't they trust her?"

The lad had a point.

"I don't know enough about her training before she went to the Trinity. Still, what you say is as good a possibility as any."

They lapsed into quiet consideration of the matter as they finished their meal. As I'k'Nole cleared the table, Absol let it go. Dwelling on it served little purpose. They'd think themselves into circles if they kept it up. He waited for the boy to deposit the dishes in the kitchen and return.

"Let's see what gear we can find for you, lad." Absol rose from the table motioning the boy to follow him and Dannon as they exited the dining hall. "It'll take us a fortnight to get to Chalbrooke so we'll be camping along the way."

17

PRIALLA rode as if the legions of Hell were after her. Her muscles ached, her mind was tired. Her hands were cramping from gripping on the saddle horn and reins for so long. The horse underneath her was barely lathered. Its body hummed with magic.

She was in the middle of the moorlands now. Flat, frosted with a thin coating of snow, dotted with trees and shrubs, the moors stretch in every direction. It was easy to get lost out here where there were no roads, no signposts, no anything to direct an inexperienced traveler. It made her thankful that Red had given her the little mirror as a guide.

She'd been riding in a straight line since leaving Rathburn. It was perhaps more than time to check her navigation. Though her muscles protested, she shifted her weight in the saddle, easing back as she pulled on the reins. The equine slowed, from the preternatural all out run to a more controlled gallop, then to a canter, a trot, a walk. The animal was restless, tossing its head with the need to move. She kept it reined in tight, fished the mirror from her breast pocket.

Flicking it open with her thumb, she pursed her lips as she studied the display. She was still headed the right way, though it looked as if she now needed to angle southward. Prialla turned her mount's nose in accordance, then closed the mirror, put it away – and saw a rider in the distance.

Despite herself, her heart thudded hard in her chest. The horseman was coming her way. He wore a black cloak – a lot of travelers did – but as that was also part of a Mancer's gear. Heart beginning to pound, she wove concealing spells around her horse.

She didn't want him to notice the blood magic they'd used on her mount. Mancers, Red had told them years ago, were all mages to one degree or another. Each of them had been trained to detect forbidden magery.

Prialla kept her steed at a walk as she finished layering the spells to mask the magery. She didn't try to avoid the rider as he approached; it was too late for that. Instead, she studied him, tensing as she spotted the fist-sized cloak clasp that every Mancer wore. It bore the Guild's seal.

She fought the urge to flee, to tug at her cap, or fidget in the saddle. Instead, she forced herself relax, breathed deep as he drew to stop a dozen feet away. She followed suit with a nod of greeting.

"Afternoon, messire," she said, pitching her voice so that it might be mistaken for a boy's light tenor.

"Afternoon." The man's rich baritone was contemplative. He shoved his hood back to reveal a scarred face, friendly green eyes, and a wealth of curly auburn hair that came down to his shoulders. He studied the coat of arms emblazoned on her saddle skirt, then smiled. "Carthier courier. It's a bit far west for you, is it not?"

As an adventurous boy on the verge of manhood might, she bobbed her, gave a rueful grin.

"It is at that. Me lord Carthier's son wanted a message delivered to a lady in Menie and asked for a volunteer." She shrugged, offered a cheeky smile. "He's doubled the pay plus expenses. No worries, lord Mancer, I know the way." With a glance at the seal he wore, she hesitated before asking, "Is there anything bad about? Are you hunting here?"

"No, lad." His tone was reassuring. "Not that I've seen. There's a blood mage ranging far north of here that I've heard, though. Avoid groups of three, two men and an Elvanaeran woman. We've people tracking them in this region."

She widened her eyes, frowned in trepidation.

"I'll keep that in mind, messire. My thanks for the warning." She bit her lip, thought a moment. "Haven't run into bandits or anything between here and Rathburn, lord. It's been smooth riding for me."

"Good enough. I'll not keep you any longer, lad. Fair riding."

"Clear roads."

With that final exchange, the each goaded their steeds to resume their course. She fought the urge to look behind her; her shoulder blades itched, as if she could feel him staring after her suspiciously.

Stay in character. Don't act wary, or skittish. Don't let him see your fear.

She kept the horse at a walk, counted to two hundred, then moved her mount around a dense clump of high grass. Using the new angle to peer back without being obvious about it, she watched him disappear behind a small stand of trees in the distance.

She kicked the horse into its enhanced run, putting as much distance as possible between herself and the Mancer.

18

NERISSE swayed in her saddle as the beast came to a halt. Darkness had descended an hour before. They'd kept on as Ba'tvian hadn't been satisfied with the lack of cover for their camp. Nowhe'd found something that satisfied his requirements.

The moon was nearly full overhead, the skies almost clear of clouds. Moonlight lit the moors in monochrome hues. The illumination was enough for her to see they'd stopped in front of a small copse of trees. Ba'tvian dismounted, narrowing his eyes at her while Ibestor mimicked his action.

"Take the mounts." He spoke to the barbarian though his gaze never left her. "Nerisse, you need to get off."

Too fatigued to feel the usual self-recrimination for having to be told to do something she should have otherwise done, she slid off the saddle. Ba'tvian handed his reins to Ibestor, then grabbed her wrist to lead her into the trees.

There were just nine trees in the stand, sprouting from the moors in a rough circle. There was enough in the way of bushes, ferns, and tall grasses to mask a campsite if they were careful. The tree roots made the ground hard, lumpy; sleeping here would not be comfortable. Her lord led her to the tree nearest the center before releasing her. She braced herself against the rough trunk as he inspected the area. Ferns covered half of the ground beneath trees, thick enough to be used as padding for their bedrolls. He beat them down, using his booted feet and a long knife. While he did so, Ibestor brought the beasts into the coppice to begin unload their packs. He handed the two bedrolls to Ba'tvian who laid them out;

Ibestor didn't use a bedroll. He would sleep under the furs that clothed him, propped up against a tree.

An exhausted Nerisse allowed herself to be led to her bedding, sinking down on it. Still standing, Ba'tvian stared down at her.

"Your earth bond?"

"It's stable." Her voice reflected her weariness. "It's not a permanent solution."

She'd bled a great deal for that stability. Between the cost of almost losing the bond and the expense of reinstating it, she was in no shape to do much of anything. Even if she recovered within short order, she had no idea how long the reprieve would last. Her people would know that the bond wasn't severed. It was just a matter of time before they tried it again.

They'll try again, as many times as it takes until it is gone beyond all hope of reclaiming.

To make matters worse, the earth was reluctant to take her back. That pained her, hurt more than anything could have, save losing Ba'tvian. Like everyone else, the earth didn't understand.

"Understand what?"

She blinked at him, not realizing that she'd spoken aloud.

"The earth doesn't understand." Nerisse sighed, shivering a little in the cold night air. As she shifted a little so could she pull the blankets around her for warmth, she tried to explain. "Because it doesn't understand, it…won't fight to keep me." She tried not to sound as discouraged as she felt. "My people will be able to persuade it to release me again."

"You will not be able to bleed for it every time they do."

She shook her head.

"No." She fell silent, mulling it over as he continued to watch, to wait. At last, she spoke her thoughts. "Any of the Elvanarae can sever the bond."

"So you said." His voice, his expression was inscrutable. Looking into his eyes, she spied a faint glowing ring of crimson around the pupils. She'd seen the same phenomenon a few times before.

"You are the most important person in my life." She said it softly, half-expecting to see disapproval over the declaration. When it didn't come, she went on. "Not even the earth is as vital to me. If I am to survive, to stay with you, to aid you in your greatness, I must have that tie to the earth. I cannot live without it. To keep it, to keep you, they must die." Weary sorrow filled her. If there was pain, it drowned in her fatigue. No, she thought, there had never been another choice. Yet even as she realized it, she had to ask, "Must they?"

"Yes," Batvian answered. His eyes glinted with that crimson light she was seeing more often now. "They must die."

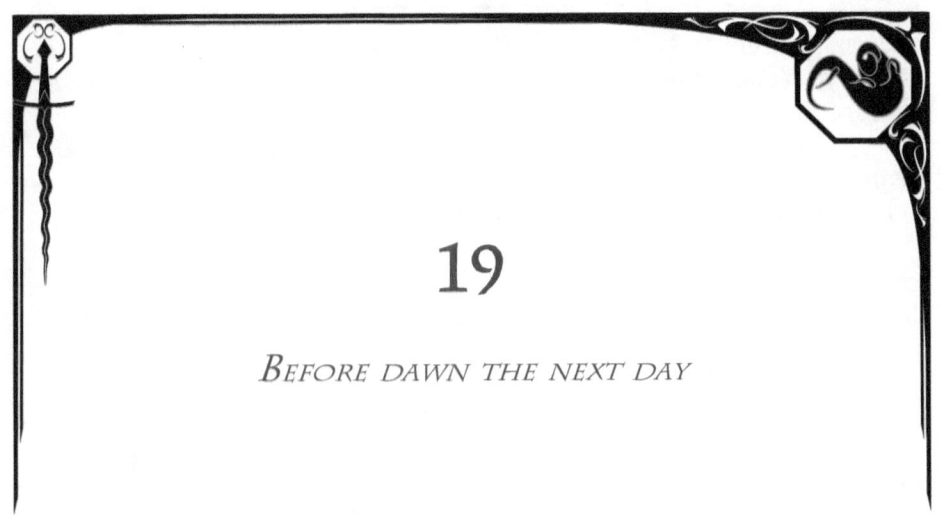

19

Before dawn the next day

BA'TVIAN woke to the nudge of his followers. The Shadow slipped back a foot or so as he stiffened, let his awareness sweep through the immediate area. Finding nothing amiss, he turned narrowed eyes to the creature.

A rider comes, lord. It blinked dull, glowing white eyes at him. *A blood mage.*

How far out? When will this rider arrive here?

Soon. The mount is fast, bespelled. It shifted restlessly. *The mage bears something belonging to the one you call Red.*

Good.

He rose, checked on his companions. Nerisse was deep in sleep. Ibestor snored as he lay slumped against the tree trunk. Their mounts were quiet, docile. He thought of Red, perceptions, and the title his Shadowed Ones used with him. Then there was the elven chit. He roused the barbarian. The unkempt man snorted awake, relaxing when he realized it was Bat'vian.

"We have a visitor. Whether they are friend or foe has not been determined. You will guard Nerisse, keep her safe while I deal with the newcomer."

Ibestor nodded, then got up to resettle closer to Nerisse's bedroll. After a moment, he turned his head towards their steeds, making a huffing noise. They stirred, shuffling through the undergrowth to surround the sleeping woman. Ba'tvian gave a silent order for a handful of his followers to join them.

The ailing elf is still important to you.

The telepathic sibilant whisper could have been from any one of the dark creatures. It was difficult to tell whether the speaker disapproved or was just making an observation. Ba'tvian addressed it regardless.

Her skills are important to me. She can alter the mind where I cannot. Replacing her would be an inconvenience. I would prefer not to do so unless there is no other choice.

There was a thoughtful pause. As he looked around their campsite, he saw them, all his Shadows gathered around him. Their leprous eyes glinted in the gloom. He could feel the weight of expectation, of something owed.

And when her skills are no longer needed?

He considered them. They'd believed in him first, given their loyalty to him before anyone else. They would serve a man of strength, intelligence, ambition. Emotional attachments was not what they expected of their master; they were chinks in a leader's armor. Yet Nerisse needed the seeming of caring, the little lies that coaxed her to stay, to obey, to please. That was her weakness, one he exploited.

The Shadowed Ones were trying to determine if he was weak.

He wasn't offended by it. The undefined pact that lay between them was something he'd become conscious of gradually. They were his to do with as he chose provided that he was the strong lord that they required him to be. They had been patient, giving him two years to grow, to gain power, to makes his plans. Now, as the third year started, he had to prove himself.

When she is no longer necessary, she will share the fate of any tool that has outlived its usefulness. He cocked his head, considering. *She will fight to remain useful. Failure for her means a worse fate than failure for you.*

Yes. The tone was satisfactory.

Escort the rider in. He paused, then turned to the largest of his followers. *Can we get spies in Jevanel?*

The Womb of the Earth is a holy place. We have not been there for millennia.

Test the boundaries.

He watched them scatter, a small group staying clustered with Ibestor and Nerisse. He walked out of the coppice, more of his followers trailing at his heels. Ba'tvian used a wisp of power to gather the night-born darkness around him. It wasn't true concealment; it just made him harder to detect. That done, he waited for the person Red had found for him.

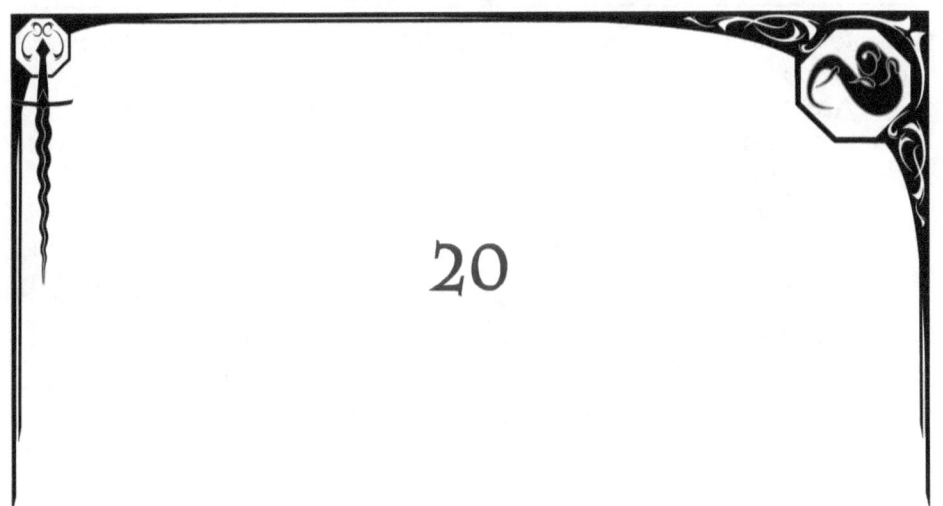

20

PRIALLA wondered how much farther she had to go. She was tired, yet the little mirror indicated that Ba'tvian Delthanurk was close at hand, so she had kept going. Perhaps that was foolish. It might have been better to rest, then face the man they called the Monster of Menie. She'd be warmer wrapped in the blanket she'd brought. Still in the saddle, she was forced to rely on her riding leathers to ward off the cold.

I'm not there yet. It's still possible for me to get a little sleep before we meet.

She began to slow the galloping horse, when the beast planted his hooves in the ground and skidded to a halt so abrupt that she almost lost her seat. She lurched forward in the saddle, the horn catching her in the abdomen as the mount danced in place. Swearing, she scrambled upright, clutching reins as the nervous animal gave a whinny of distress. What was spooking the damn horse?

Something flickered in the gloom of the moors. Several somethings.

Her eyes widened as she saw them. She'd heard of the Shadowed Ones. Every blood mage did eventually. The more extravagant mages, the one who indulged a bit too often than was safe, might even glimpse them during or after a rite. They fed off the dead, were fueled by un-harvested power. They were supposed to be rare, things of darkness and spirit flitting through the world like scavenging ghosts.

The moorlands held what looked like a hundred of them. Some were transparent, ethereal; the majority had true substance. The frost

-crusted grass rustled, bending beneath them as they slithered forward to encircle her.

"Are you hunting me, then?" The question came out in a whisper. The tales said they scavenged the dead, yet there were whispers of them seeking living prey.

Our lord waits.

The words slid through her mental shields as easily as the wind through air. She started at the hissing voice, sensed a condescending amusement at her discomfort. It made her grit her teeth.

"Is this lord of yours the one called Ba'tvian Delthanurk?"

Yes. You are expected. Do not try our patience.

She lifted her chin with a bravado she didn't feel as she replied.

"You are spooking my horse. If you wish me to continue on, you will need to give us room."

Hisses greeted her statement, but the circle did widen. In front of her, they opened a corridor for passage. Keeping a tight rein of her skittish mount, she urged the gelding into a canter. Around her, the creatures flowed over the landscape.

They reached their destination a short time later, as the colors of dawn began to touch the horizon. She halted her horse not far from a stand of trees, one of several dotting the moorlands. The serpentine, almost lizard-like things that had escorted her milled around it. A larger bit of darkness broke away from the twilight silhouette of the trees. Upright, it approached, becoming more defined as it moved.

It was a man, cloaked and hooded. He wore clothing of the northern trappers, a plain black scarf wrapped around the bottom half of his face. It was his eyes that drew her attention – intense, dark, powerful eyes that glowed crimson in the gloom. She met that gaze, felt her breath hitch at the impact. It wasn't sexual. It was pure power.

For the first time, she began to believe that Red was might be right. This Ba'tvian might well be able to destroy the Mancer Order.

Instinct told her that he wouldn't respond to her usual methods of manipulation. There was something about him that gave the impression that manipulating him would be a fatal mistake. She needed to be cautious and use her other, more mundane skills to come out on top of this encounter. So she remained mounted because it was a point of control, as well as a statement that she wasn't going to be a lackey. It was also to her advantage. If this meeting devolved into a confrontation, it gave her the advantage of flight. If bargaining became part of the proceedings, it gave her the upper-hand, psychologically.

"I am Prialla Filochen," she began, keeping her voice smooth, calm, cool. "I believe our mutual associate, Red, may have mentioned me."

He nodded, saying nothing.

"I, along with my two associates in Rathburn, have interests concerning the fall of the Chalbrooke Mancer Guild House. We were told that you were of like mind." Caught by his gaze, by his silence, she fought the compulsion to just tell him everything. Not even Red, a more powerful, older blood mage, made her want to say whatever came to mind.

"We do not expect payment, nor do we expect to pay you. It was our understanding that this shared ambition would be enough reason to work together on this matter." If that wasn't the case, Halvark would hold her responsible for their predicament. "If this is not truth, then it may be best we not enter into this venture."

He regarded her, letting the quiet build. When he replied, his words were a gauntlet thrown down in challenge.

"I am no one's servant. I will not be ordered, I will not be commanded. This venture, as you call it, is a goal I share, yet I am content to achieve my aim in my own time, on my own terms. You have come to me. If your need is great, you must be willing to pay for it."

Prialla's temper flashed. She kept it bottled as she tried to recall what Red had told her of this arrangement. It was precious little. Red had given them a few months to complete this task. She didn't think that Ba'tvian Delthanurk, if this man was indeed him, would act on his own in that time frame. He would might wait, if only to spite them for not getting what he wanted, whatever that was.

What choice do I have?

"A new bargain requires the feedback of my associates before we consent. What terms do you propose?" It would be best to get the details before passing on this news. She hoped it wasn't something impossible.

"A trade of favors. The destruction of Mancer Guild House in exchange for aid in another matter. Do any among you possess the ability to gate?"

"Yes." Halvark had been experimenting with it, with mixed results. "We will need to know more about this 'other matter'."

"One of my companions has a task she must complete for me. She will require transportation to the western coast and back. While that is underway, I will fulfill my end of this bargain." He glanced at the horizon, as if to gauge the time. "Message your associates. If we are agreed, then we will meet to discuss further details. You have until mid-morning to return an answer."

With that, he left, melting back into the darkness. The creatures that called him lord lingered. Wary of them, she prepared a mage sending and braced for the argument with her half-brother that was sure to follow.

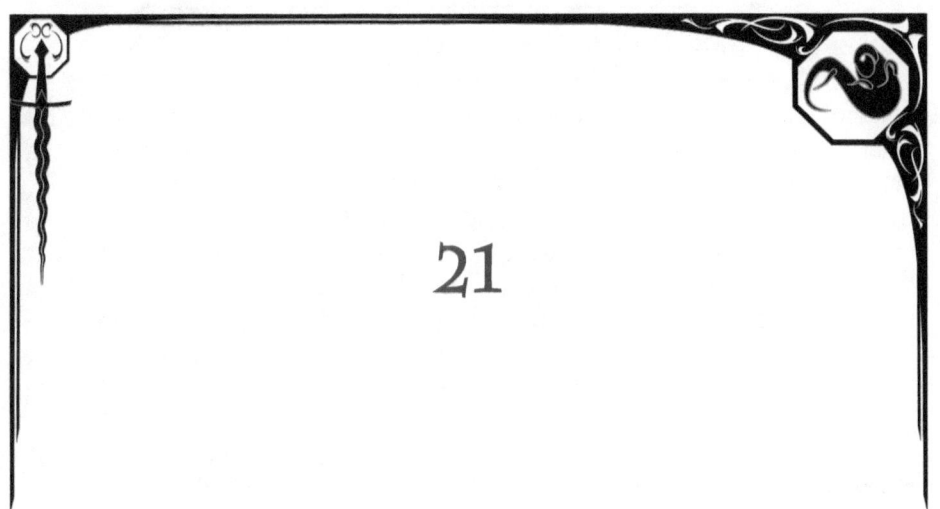

21

B A'TVIAN observed the woman dressed as a young man from the sanctuary of the trees. Beside him, the largest of his Shadows also trained its gaze on Prialla. He sent a tendril of thought to it.

Tell me of her.

We have tasted her thoughts. The woman is a high-ranking servant as well as a blood mage. She is not as well-trained as she could be. She is indebted to the one called Red, and has little choice but to meet your demand. It slid to arrange itself in a loose coil around his feet. *You are sending away the tool that is so important. We do not understand.*

Nerisse will return. Before she leaves, she will make them mine. It was Nerisse's purpose now. She knew what he required. She would do everything in her power to give it to him. *This woman – Prialla – how susceptible will she be to my tool?*

Shades of approval colored the creature's response.

Not as susceptible as the men. It looked up at him with a lazy blink of its white orbs. *Her triad includes her half-brother and his friend. She is promiscuous with both.*

He didn't care for incest. In this case, however, it gave him more to work with. Prialla was linked to both men through sex, and yet again to one of them by blood. If he won over the men, she could be influenced through the bonds with them. It was a somewhat complicated aspect of sympathetic magic that people exposed themselves to without thinking of the consequences. Using the magic in that way was forbidden.

Ba'tvian forbade himself nothing.

Her half-brother is Halvark Tretoan.

He gave his follower a sharp look, contempt rising. His Shadowed Ones told him of many things; he was aware of the aristocratic Tretoan family that ruled the city-state of Rathburn. This made Prialla the bastard daughter of the current lord ruler.

He hated nobility. He despised their superior attitudes, the way the world catered to them, the wealth that made their lives soft, their minds weak. They had societal influence, could impact economics, the perceptions of the populace if they were intelligent enough. Yet they lacked the *real* power – magic, the joy of blood, death, and stolen life.

With an iron-clad grip, he throttled back the contempt. He would make use of the opportunity presented. They would learn that an aristocratic lineage meant nothing. Power, ambition, will – those were what made a man great.

There is other news, lord.

He glanced down at the Shadow, expectant.

Absol Omine has left Destiny's Way. There is a boy with him. They are headed east.

What is their destination?

We do not know.

Ba'tvian thought a moment. It might be too much to hope for that Omine was headed to Chalbrooke. Even if that were true, he wouldn't arrive for a few weeks yet. His bargain, if accepted, would not allow him much time, if any, before his attack. Omine would have to wait.

Watch him. Do we have anyone in Destiny's Way when Omine is not in residence?

No. It wasn't a pleasing answer, though he had anticipated it. *We avoid it. The On'Desae monks are strong there as is the Wood.*

The Wood…it was another thing that needed to be addressed. He disliked anything that barred the way of his Shadows. For now, though, he concentrated on the more immediate future.

When he was finished, Chalbrooke – and the Mancers – would shudder in his wake.

22

PRIALLA leaned against the horse as it shifted, ill at ease. She hated waiting. More, she hated knowing that she would owe Halvark if he agreed to this bargain of Ba'tvian's. Her only consolation was that the favor entailed escorting another woman, not a man. If the chit was pretty enough, getting Halvark to agree to the escort service wouldn't be too difficult. He was a gentleman at heart. An arrogant, sometimes shallow gentleman, but a gentleman nonetheless.

Well, when it came women with a certain elegance, anyway.

The sun peeked over the horizon. The temperature was still cold. Her leathers didn't seem to ward off the chill anymore now that she wasn't moving. After sending off her mage message to her half-brother, she'd fumbled with her saddlebags, pulling out the blanket she'd brought. She was exhausted, achy from the hard ride. As much as she craved sleep, she couldn't allow herself to rest. Ba'tvian, along with his unknown companions, posed a potential threat to the unwary.

Time crawled along as she stood with her mount. The sun was still hauling itself up above the horizon when a speck of orange light appeared in the distance, closing in fast. She straightened, suppressing a groan as she placed a hand on the horse's flank for balance. When the ball of light neared, she lifted a hand to receive it, curling her fingers around it.

Halvark's response was acidic.

Of course, he would want something that you cannot provide on your own. You will owe me a debt, dearest sister. Rest assured that the payment will be steep. I will have terms of my own for my part in this bargain you've struck. He's stated he needs transportation only – that's all I'm agreeing to. We'll discuss this further when you return. Alert us as to when we should expect you.

She allowed herself a trickle of relief. There had been a very real chance that he would have refused. She looked down at herself, still wrapped in the blanket, and decided that warmth was more important than appearance at this point. Gathering her aplomb, she looked around the moors. The land was empty of people, yet she made out the silhouetted shapes of the Shadowed Ones still surrounding her in the dawning light.

"We will agree to your master's terms. If I can speak with him...?"

"Good."

Startled, Prialla's head snapped around to face the stand of trees several yards away. Ba'tvian was striding toward her. Behind him, she could see movement as his companions – a blue-skinned woman and – was that a barbarian? – broke down their camp. Ba'tvian stopped in front of her, his intense, dark eyes piercing.

"Come. I will introduce you to the others, and you can rest while we pack."

His offer pragmatic, she thought. Practical. Prialla imagined she looked as if she was about to fall down; she felt as if she might. Falling out of the saddle would serve neither of them well. So when he turned on his heel to lead the way back to the coppice, she followed, pulling the horse along behind her.

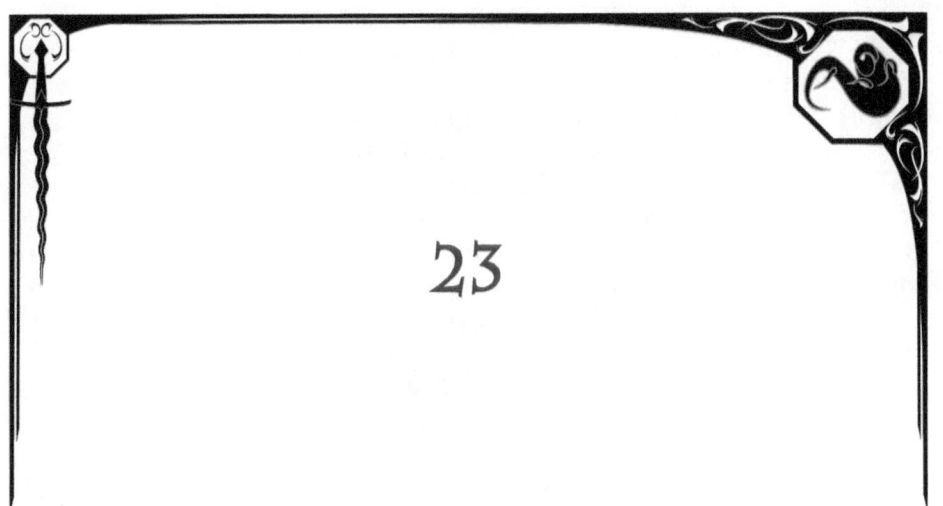

23

NERISSE felt better than she had in the last few days. She remained weak, though that would pass. Still, it was wonderful to be able to move about, dealing with the bedroll, gathering her things, and not tremble from the exertion.

She tried not to mind the woman, Prialla Filochen, her lord had brought into their encampment. The blonde was beautiful, holding herself with a confidence that Nerisse envied. Though she appeared fatigued, it was evident that she could continue on if necessary. She had that air of inner strength about her. The elf speculated on the woman for a moment. It was better than dwelling on the other thing she had to do.

Ba'tvian had told her a little of agreement. It would mean that he would not be with her while she…carried out her task. She'd experienced a flutter of near-panic at that. How could she do something so monumental as this without him? He had forestalled her fears by stating that she would not be alone, that he was providing her with resources and protection.

If there is need, I will come, he'd said. *But do not fail me, Nerisse. You are necessary to me.*

She took the memory of those words and entwined them around her heart. He needed her. He wouldn't abandon her.

Nerisse.

She gave no outward sign of having heard him, just sent an acknowledgement of his telepathic contact.

Can you get through her shields?

Of course, that was her purpose. She'd almost forgotten, she'd been so caught up in her own issues. Cautious, she turned her attention to Prialla. Her shields were solid, yet seemed to be built with only telepaths in mind. Empaths made contact on a different psychic level from telepaths. She studied the protections with her mind's eye as she closed up her packs.

My access will be limited. I can read her, though the type of shielding she is using prohibits me from making significant alterations. If her mind can be opened up a little more, I can set something in place to make the desired changes over time. It will be less noticeable to her.

She let him mull it over. As she waited, she thought it might be prudent to seal her packs. Her lord didn't trust the people would be meeting; there was no reason why she should, either. So she drew on enough power to bespell the packs shut. The magic working wasn't complicated, yet it would deter most mages from poking into them.

I think I have a way. Link with me and stay close to my mind. I will give you the access you need.

Extending out with her awareness, she settled into Ba'tvian's mind just below the surface, in a pocket of his consciousness that he held reserved for her. As she rode his mind, her physical body picked up her bags to carry over to their mounts. She and Ibestor began loading the beasts as Ba'tvian approached Prialla. He spoke to her without preamble as Nerisse listened as she split her attention between tasks.

"The sooner we get started, the better. Can you gate?"

Prialla shook her head.

"We have training, but not at that level," she replied. "Halvark has gated successfully for short distances. I have not yet tried my hand at it."

"Then I will gate us." Ba'tvian made the statement as if doing so would be of little effort to him. "Nerisse will conceal it from others in the area. All I will need is an in-depth memory of a place to gate to."

Oh, that is perfect, my lord. Nerisse let her approval seep into his mind. What he spoke of was truth – gating required a thorough, psychic knowledge of the place one was, and the place that was their destination. Ba'tvian had never been to Rathburn; he would need to get that knowledge from Prialla.

"I'm afraid that I don't understand." Prialla's words were careful.

Nerisse sensed Ba'tvian's spurt of impatient derision at the woman's ignorance, felt him hold it back as he explained the intricacies of gating. While he did so, the elf and the barbarian finished up with the mounts. Ibestor led them to stand across from the woman's horse. It snorted, rolling its eyes at the beasts, jerking back on the reins that held it in place. Exasperated, Nerisse extended a tendril of awareness into its mind to soothe it until it stood still under the trees. She glanced over at Prialla, saw her mouth thin with displeasure. Realizing that the woman was going to balk, the elf used her empathy to smooth the way.

It's just a memory. He will only receive what you give him. This shouldn't compromise you in any way if you take care.

She released the wordless sending to "drift" to the woman, then observed as it trickled into her consciousness like water through sand. If Ba'tvian took notice of what she was doing, he said nothing, nor did he look her way. Instead, he gave Prialla time to think it over.

Minutes passed. By now, the sun had risen above the horizon to shine down on the frosted moorlands. Ibestor stood beside her, his gaze curious as he, along everyone else, watched Prialla. For her part, Nerisse used the time to build a tiny psychic artifice, hiding it within her awarenesss. That done, she shrouded her mind with Ba'tvian's presence.

"Very well. A single memory." Prialla focused, then dropped her outer shields to allow Ba'tvian to link with her.

The moment he did, Nerisse slipped inside, timing her entry to coincide with the passing of the memory. Once there, she used Prialla's own mind to mask hers. Working quickly, she found the site within Prialla's mind she needed, and planted the artifice. As she double-checked its moorings and camouflage, Ba'tvian questioned the woman on the memory, distracting her from the invasion. Satisfied with the placement, the elf slipped back the way she had come.

She remained with Ba'tvian until he broke the connection with the woman. As her lover turned to her, she retreated behind her own shielding, gave him a slight nod.

"Come," he intoned. "We are leaving."

24

PRIALLA felt strange, disconnected from what was happening. It was probably due to her fatigue, the cold, the strain of being in the company of people she didn't trust.

She couldn't wait to get home.

Standing next to her mount once again, she leaned on the gelding. The animal was much calmer than it had been. Perhaps the weird creatures Ba'tvian and his people rode reassured it, though they made Prialla uneasy. The animals' eyes were empty. Not docile, but mindless. She suppressed a shudder.

At least, the others were more normal. Ibestor, the barbarian, seemed like a devoted dog. His arcane signature ran through their beasts, along with the fainter flare of Ba'tvian's own. Nerisse, the Elvanaeran girl the Mancers had believed dead for so long, was as Prialla had expected: submissive, subservient. Her love for her master, as well as loyalty to him, was as plain as the sun shone in the sky.

A victim. Cool exasperation and contempt welled up in the blonde. *A powerful victim. That's what love makes us. Fondness is admissible, perhaps, but we have to be able to override affection with expediency. In our world, there is no such thing as absolute trust.*

Ba'tvian was perhaps the most surprising of the group. His leadership was without question; even the Shadowed Ones obeyed him. His intensity reminded her of religious zealots, yet he spouted no rhetoric on his beliefs. Aside from that intensity, the only other sign of his power was his eyes, the way they glinted crimson. Nothing gave her an idea of how much magic he had at his beck.

Then he began building the gate.

When Halvark did it, she could sense, in a vague fashion, the shaping of power. The portal remained invisible until complete. Once it flared into being with their destination displayed in the center, as if the gate was a window in time and space. That was not the case here. The power rose in a red mist from the dark creatures around them, streaming towards the blood mage. He poured it into the form being constructed, the flow of magic visible to the naked eye. The glowing mesh of crimson lines built up in layers to become a solid framework.

Unlike Halvark's attempts, Ba'tvian's signature was not being broadcasted out into the surrounding area. Instead, Prialla sensed the psychic presence of soil, trees, and mineral rock. She puzzled over it as she glanced at the others. Nerisse stood with eyes closed, her slate blue skin a shade paler than before. Hairs raised on the back of her neck. That was her, she realized. Nerisse was masking Ba'tvian's work.

The portal didn't flare up as Halvark's did when completed. It stabilized with a subtle pulse of power, igniting with transparent flames that licked the frame. The center lightened, displaying the small garden behind one of the tenant cottages at the Tretoan Estate. Ba'tvian turned back to Prialla, inclined his head, stepped back. She tightened her grip on the gelding's reins. She did not want to go first, yet it made sense for it to be her.

The gate showed the back of the cottage, her friends exiting the rear door to meet them. Feigning a confidence she didn't feel, she strode through the gate as if she did it every day. The horse followed her, hesitating at the portal itself before stepping through. Once on the other side, she had to fight the urge to sag in relief at nothing having gone wrong. She moved away from the gate as Ibestor, then Nerisse lead their mounts to the other side. Ba'tvian brought up the rear, collapsing the portal behind him.

Raptu took the reins from her, patting the steed's neck as he looked over the newcomers. Beside her, Halvark was frowning. Prialla made the introductions.

"Halvark is the mage with gating capability," she added, laying a hand on her half-brother's shoulder.

"Is something wrong with Nerisse?" Halvark's question surprised her. She looked over at the elf, saw that she hadn't regained her color.

"I am well," the Elvanaeran replied quietly.

"She masked our journey here." Ba'tvian's cool statement was simple. There was nothing to indicate that Nerisse's condition was anything to worry about. His eyes narrowed at the nobleman as if he saw something that he didn't care for. Prialla touched Raptu's mind with her own.

I don't think the boys will get along well.

"The cottage has a small stable on the south side. We'll deal with the beasts." Raptu pretended not to notice the slight tension beginning to build. "Then you tell us more about this task Halvark will be providing transport for."

"We will also discuss Chalbrooke and the Mancer activity in the area," Ba'tvian agreed.

As the newcomers followed Raptu to the stables, Prialla let herself relax.

"They can stay in the cottage. Everyone else knows to keep away from it in any case." Her half-brother regarded her, gaze keen. "You look as if you haven't slept. Did you not rest at all?"

She shook her head.

"No." Sighing, she leaned into him as he brought an arm around her. "A word of warning, brother-mine. I got the distinct impression that Ba'tvian believes Nerisse to be his alone. She appears to love him, is loyal to him, may do anything he asks of her. I don't know what it is that she has to do for him that would require long distance travel. Whatever it is, it won't be pleasant." She paused, thinking back to what had been said at the camp about their bargain. "She wasn't happy to learn that someone else would be taking her to – wherever it is she needs to go."

"Because it will be me, or is it because he won't be going with her?" Halvark's query was shrewd. It made her smile.

"The latter, I believe." She shrugged. "She may be needy, or at the very least insecure."

Prialla was certain in her conclusions; she possessed a knack for reading people. Nerisse was an open book to her. Even so, Ba'tvian was much more difficult to read.

"Anyway," Prialla steered the conversation back to her initial point. "Let's not antagonize him. He's powerful; the portal cost him nothing to build. We'll repay our debt to Red, fulfill our end of the bargain to Ba'tvian. After that, we'll go our separate ways. I would much prefer we do so without making an enemy of Ba'tvian Delthanurk."

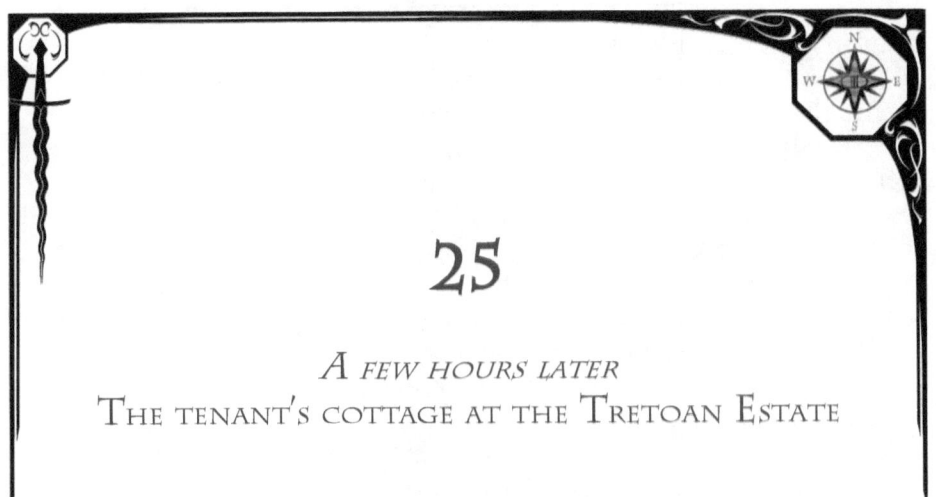

25

N ERISSE brushed out her hair while her lord prowled the bedroom they'd been given. The dwelling was a simple one, possessing a wooden floor, plastered walls, and no windows. There was a small kitchen area just off the main room, with bedrooms ranging the back end. It was quaint, furnishings minimal. Save for its austerity and the basement below, it reminded her of the healer's cabin outside of Piete Town.

Especially the silent screaming.

Inaudible to non-Empaths, the shrieks of pain, fear, and death echoed in the walls, the floors. They rose up from the cellar to fill her ears, to nag at her shields. It was so pervasive that she could almost smell the blood, taste the branding of flesh, feel the violation of body, of mind. There was so much empathic residue here that she'd have gone crazed without the medicinal draught. With it in effect, the screams were sensed as a kind of muffled noise, a faint din that echoed in her head.

Her companions didn't hear it. Ibestor, who had decided to remain in the stables, seemed oblivious to the haunting of their quarters. Her lord was more concerned with the way their new allies conducted there rites than how the psychic echoes may affect people.

"They waste power here." It was the latest of many mutterings criticizing their new allies. His tone held contempt, disgust. "There is no cleansing, no wiping of arcane signatures, no masking of the site. There's enough psychic noise embedded in this building to alert any Mancer who passed by within a half mile of it."

"You can sense it? I had thought it was only me." She ceased brushing, putting her utensil away.

"The floor *resonates* with power." He spat the words. "If we are to use them for the long term, there will have to be changes."

"I will help with that." Her soft voice was firm. In this, she was certain of her ability. "They will have to be educated by you, yet I can make them listen, make them heed your instructions. They will be yours, my lord."

He whirled to face her, his dark eyes blazing with crimson energy. He reached her in three strides, closing a rough hand around her throat as his gaze bore into hers.

"Halvark would have you if he could," he declared, voice harsh. "Would you let him?"

"No." Taken aback, eyes wide in surprise, she blurted out her response. "No, I am yours – only yours. There is no one else for me, there never will be." Had she done something, said anything that might indicate that she was willing to consider the advances of another? Her mind whirled, frantic, as she tried to recall and failed. "What have I done that you would question my faithfulness, lord?"

His grip gentled, his thumb stroking along her jugular. The anger in his eyes banked, fading a little.

"You have done nothing." He played his fingers along the column of her neck. She let herself be soothed by the motion. "I do not trust him. I certainly do not trust him with you." He fell quiet, studying her as he analyzed the problem. "I will send Ibestor with you."

"Your Shadows?"

"That goes without saying." He let his hand slip to her collarbone, his gaze never leaving hers. "Were you able to do anything during our meeting with the men?"

She nodded.

"Raptu is more open than the other two. I was able to infiltrate him. I did the same with him that I did with Prialla. He…" She let her voice trail off as she searched for the right words to describe him. "He is reckless by nature; it's reflected in his shielding. His approach to magery seems haphazard. It's not that he doesn't care about the outcome; it's that he enjoys everything it takes to get that outcome too much. In terms of power, it makes him weaker."

"What of Halvark?"

"His protections are more thorough. I think, of the three of them, he is the most studious. I wasn't able to do anything without alerting him." She hesitated, then continued. "He's extremely wary. He shares the leadership role with Prialla in their triad and he may feel threatened by you."

"So he should be." His tone was matter-of-fact. She couldn't tell if her observation pleased him. "He will not retain that leadership for long."

"No, lord. Yet I do believe it is one reason why he is so closed off. If he accompanies me to Jevanel, I may be able to do more than the gradual alterations I have in place for his companions."

He narrowed his eyes at her, sliding his hand lower on her torso. Her breath caught. When he spoke, his voice was a warning whisper.

"Make no mistake, Nerisse. Should he ever touch you, should I find that you allowed it in any way, what I do to him will be nothing compared to what I do to you."

She shivered, refusing to give in the niggling fear that sought to take root inside her. Instead, she lifted her hand to his face, trailing her fingertips along his cheek. Her words, full of bravado, were a fierce vow.

"I will kill him, to your glory, before that ever happens."

Interlude 3

Labiyal Biyalban smiled.

Sitting at his desk in the study amid the array of mirror stands, he sat in satisfaction as one of the silvered-glass ovals showed Nerisse's image giving her oath to Ba'tvian Delthanurk. He'd chosen well there. Ba'tvian was turning out to be as skillful a manipulator as his sire was, making the most of his tools – and Labiyal had provided one that wasn't easily broken.

That was important. A man could be an excellent strategist, a powerful mage, yet he was only as good as the tools and resources he used. If Nerisse had possessed a weak spine, was any less devout, or lacked the level of ability needed, she would not have helped Ba'tvian get this far. The boy, now a grown man, would not have shown the promise he did.

Then Labiyal would have needed to take direct action. That was fraught with risks he would rather not pursue. Worse, if the little failures had been noticed by Biyal or others who reported to their king, Labiyal's life may have been forfeit. His continued existence hinged on the fulfillment of Hell's words, the future Hell dictated in the *Helkorix Noxim*.

The prophesied Child of Einlienn would not fail his king.

With that in mind, he flicked his gaze another of the mirrors. The glass flared to life, showing the three blood mages he'd cultivated. Prialla slept in a chair while Halvark and Raptu debated over what needed to be done next. The group was already becoming influenced by Nerisse. Even through the mirror, knowing what he did of her work, he could detect the minute traces of change in them. Halvark bore the least sign of alteration. That would not be the case for long.

Yet there was a factor that needed to be addressed, a possible threat to the taking of their loyalty. As a third mirror lit up, Labiyal leaned back in his chair.

In the glass, a raven perched on the roof rail of a coach. Its eyes glinted a sulfurous yellow. Around it was the bustling street of Chalbrooke's business district. There were tall stone buildings, painted windows and wooden signs declaring the names of the shops or offices. The cobblestone-paved road was rife with middle class citizens, horse-drawn carriages, and the occasional mounted aristocrat.

The bird angled its head as if able to see through the mirror's view to Labiyal. It couldn't, yet the Chained One residing in the raven's form would sense the attention, hear the words spoken.

"The time is coming for the Lord Tretoan to play his role. Ensure that he arrives home safely." The order came with a slight pulse of power, enough to use the mirror as the relay. The raven bobbed its head as the words reached its mind.

He released the mirror's magic. The scene faded, the glass going dark.

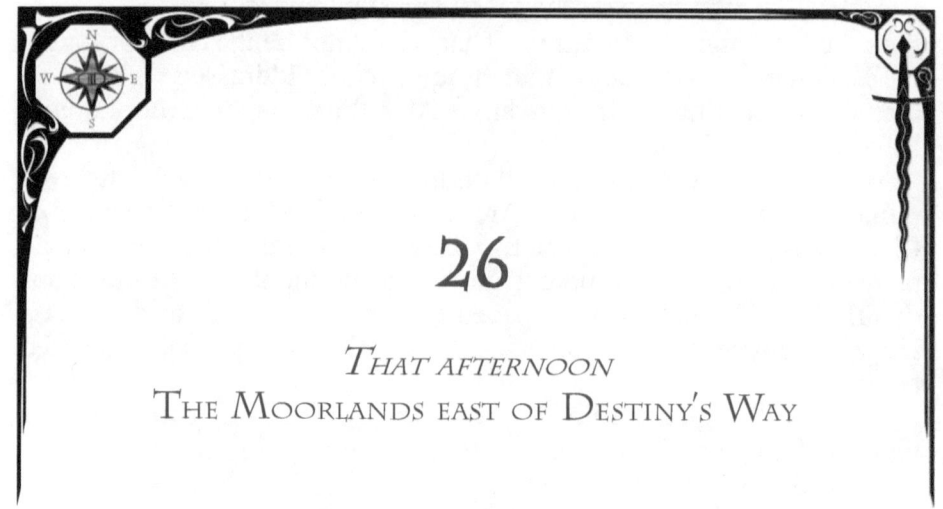

26

ABSOL rode with I'k'Nole through the moorlands, the Wood of Destiny still visible on their left as they headed east toward Chalbrooke. They had started out just after dawn, the Mancer astride his horse Brown, the boy mounted on a placid piebald horse borrowed from the monks. The morning had passed in companionable quiet. Their lunch break, and the afternoon up to this point, had not.

He cast a tolerant, amused glance at the boy riding beside him. Normally reserved in the company of others, he had relaxed into the chatter any child might exhibit around someone they admired. The Mancer could no longer claim ignorance of the village gossip or events, and the boy's reiteration of rumors came with intelligent commentary. The observant I'k'Nole was perhaps more insightful that he was given credit for.

"Brother Filtan said that travelers are more wary than ever before," the child continued. "He told me that one of pilgrims said that he felt safer at staying at shrines or temples than hostelries or inns when going from one city to another." There was a thoughtful pause before those vivid, violet eyes of his turned to Absol. "Is it safer?"

"Not really. There is an illusory sense of security to be in a holy place when there are evil people out in world."

"Like the blood mages."

"Yes." The Mancer nodded. "However, some blood mages believe that religious sites are protected in some way. Others have what Dannon calls 'a crisis of spirit' where they believe themselves damned, feel some degree of guilt for what they have done. They will avoid religious sites in order not to be confronted by the deities that own them, or by their own wrong-doing."

I'k'Nole considered that for a bit.

"But they can still walk in and kill people. Master Dannon says that the sanctity of a shrine or temple is dependent on the devotion and intentions of those who serve it. Even then the patron deity may not interfere. He said it was because of the free will clause."

"I tend to agree with him." The free will clause, as the abbot liked to call it, was something that he debated with others over many times. Absol could recite from memory: that free will, once given, meant the right to dictate the future for mankind had been given up. It was why the gods didn't walk Einlienn, why people were allowed to do bad things. That was gist, anyway. "Regardless of that, most people, when faced with something they cannot control, cannot defend against, cannot even see, will seek what comfort they can find. The shrines are no less safe than the hostelries, so there is no harm done in letting them stay there."

"Will we stay at a shrine or hostelry?"

"No. We'll make better time riding through the countryside than if we took the roads."

They lapsed into quiet for a few minutes. When I'k'Nole broke it, he sounded a little apprehensive.

"Do you think we'll encounter the blood mage Ba'tvian? He's headed south east, isn't he?"

The Mancer frowned. Much as he wanted to assure the lad that they wouldn't, I'k'Nole needed to be prepared for the possibility.

"I hope we don't. There is no guarantee of that." He leaned over in the saddle to grip the boy's shoulder in a bolstering gesture. "If we do, I don't want you to stay, or to fight. You run. Run as if the daemons of Hell are at your heels. You head for the Wood of Destiny. The Wood has a mind of its own; it may offer you some protection."

"What about you?" His violet eyes were anxious.

"Don't worry about me." Absol made his voice firm. "Don't wait for me, either. You run, and leave Ba'tvian to me."

"Because you're the Mancer." I'k'Nole's expression was troubled, his tone resigned. "That's what Mancer's do. You slay the monsters."

"Yes, lad. That's what we do." He studied the boy's face. "Having second thoughts about becoming one of us?"

The anxiety in I'k'Nole gave way to iron-clad determination. In that moment, his eyes seemed far older than his eleven years. So, too, were his words.

"Monsters prey on what's good in the world. If there is no one to slay them, then all the good is lost." He took a deep breath. "I'd be a fool not to fear the monsters, but if I can protect the good, I want to. I will be a Mancer."

I will make you proud.

The unspoken subtext was there in the child's words. Absol might have worried over them if it hadn't been for the look in his eyes. This boy, who in another life, a different world, might have been his son, understood. It wasn't just the dangers, or the honor. He saw the responsibility, the duty.

Deep within his own soul, he could hear an answer to the subtext:

I know you will.

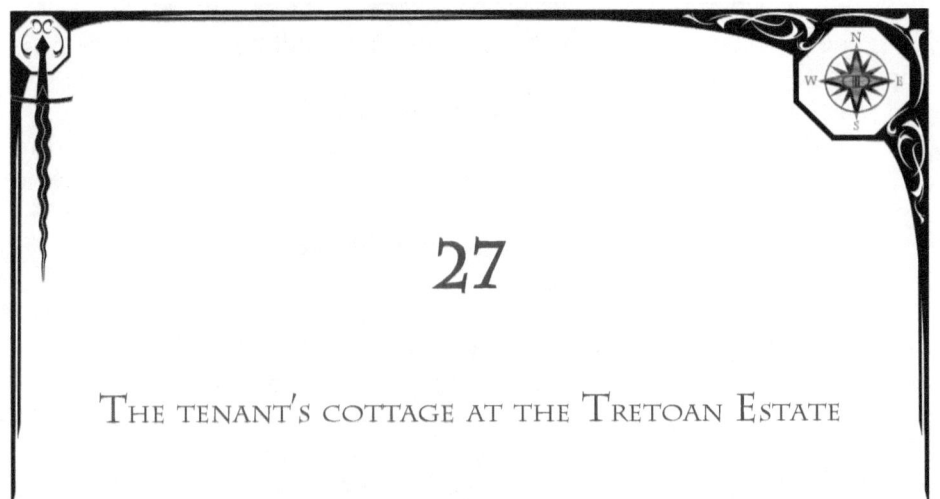

27

THE TENANT'S COTTAGE AT THE TRETOAN ESTATE

B A'TVIAN stood in front of the fireplace of the main room in the cabin. He'd shed most of his outer garb. He now wore a hooded dark brown jerkin with his scarf still wrapped around the lower half of his face. The concealment of his face was a deliberate choice, not habit. It was an intimidation trick, one that gave him the advantage of keeping his features less readable by others.

Logs broke, shifting on the grating within the fire place as they burned. Beneath his feet, the boards of the floor pulsed with un-harvested power. That would be the second order of business seen to tonight. The first, would be the outlining of what needed to be done.

He'd given that a great deal of thought. Their initial discussion had told him two things of import: that Mancers traveled through the area often, that their usual method of dealing with them was to veer away from them. For all their noble status, they hid from the enemy. Hiding was weak.

Flight wasn't that much better. Bat'vian had to admit that his two years on the run could be seen as cowardice. It hadn't been. He'd run so that he could learn, build up power, strategize. He'd run to survive. Without the resources that Prialla and cohorts possessed, there'd been no other choice for him.

They come, lord.

The sibilant whisper slid into his thoughts. He sent an acknowledgement back to his spy. The Shadows that had come with him were ghosting through the estate, had been feeding him information throughout the day. Several were tailing Halvark, Raptu, and Prialla.

There was a knock on the cottage front door. He turned as it opened to admit their hosts.

Nerisse, Ibestor, he ordered telepathically, *come.*

"I trust you've rested well?" Prialla asked. No longer sporting riding leathers, she was garbed in a serviceable gray dress. She graced him with the smile of a hostess – quick, automatic, a lip service to courtesy. He gave a slow nod.

"You said that you would have a plan for us," Halvark began. "Do you?"

He took a moment to lock eyes with the noble. He didn't care for the man's tone or for his genteel appearance. Ba'tvian wasn't noble born yet he was no man's servant. His allies would do well to remember that. He conveyed that message with his eyes, let them speak for him, saw that the message had been received. He drew the quiet moment out, then cut Halvark off when he opened his mouth to speak.

"Yes, I have a plan." He didn't shift his gaze as his traveling companions entered the room. Even so, he was aware that Nerisse came to sit on the couch closest to him, that Ibestor placed himself between the elf and the others. "According to your information, the Mancers have not faced a blood mage of any skill or power in or around Rathburn or Chalbrooke in living memory. My understanding is that they do not encounter anything dark until well away from this area. It is a kind of safe zone for them."

"Right." Raptu slumped lazily into a chair, his words half-mocking, half-amused. "We'll shatter that safety for them."

Ba'tvian ignored the remark.

"You know where the Guild House and yet do not know much about the activity there."

"No." Halvark frowned, impatience leeching into his expression. "We've been over this."

"Have any of you been there?"

"I'm afraid not." Prialla shrugged, linking a casual arm with her brother. She stroked a hand along his forearm.

"Very well, then." He wasn't pleased. He would, however, make do. "We will need to watch it. I want to be familiar with the area in which it resides. We need to verify if any Mancers stay outside the Guild House when in town. This will take a few days."

"It is easier said than accomplished." Halvark's tone held the chill of pessimism. "It's risky."

"Blood magery is not without risk." Ba'tvian's voice was cool.

"You've taken a great deal of risk with this place already." He indicated the cottage with a minute gesture. "It reeks of unused power. A Mancer with any kind of sensitivity would be able to hear the screams locked within the walls. The only reason you haven't been discovered is that none have passed within a half mile of it." Halvark flushed with anger. Ba'tvian kept his tone even, matter-of-fact. "It is, however, something that can be remedied. The power can be harvested and used. You," he inclined his head to the red-faced noble, "will be able to use it to fuel the gate. I will show you how."

He paused, letting that sink in a moment. There was interest in their eyes now, along with wariness. Halvark, as the evidentiary spokesperson for the trio, broke the quiet. "For what price?"

"None." Ba'tvian gave a dismissive flick of his wrist, a deliberately careless motion. "If we are to succeed in this, it is important that every command all resources available to them." *You are of little use to me elsewise.* He kept that to himself. "The cottage will have to be cleansed. If you wish to continue your practice without attention, you do well keep up with the lessons I shall give you."

"That's...generous of you." This came from Raptu, who studied him with narrowed eyes. Ba'tvian turned his attention to him for the first time since his arrival.

"It is not generosity. If you are caught, if you fail in any way, it will be my head on the chopping block." His response held the chill of winter. "I have no death wish."

"None of us do." Nerisse's voice was serene. It had a soothing effect on the others, a subtle thing that Ba'tvian noticed, yet doubted anyone else did. The levels of wary suspicion gradually dropped.

"The power in this cottage will answer more readily to you three as you were the ones to release it in the first place." It was a lie. Stolen power was never easy to tame to hand no matter who had done the stealing. "We will harvest it, we will cleanse this place, then Halvark will take Nerisse and Ibestor to lands around Jevanel."

"I've never been there." Halvark scowled. "How am I to gate there if I've never been?"

"I will provide you with what you need for us to make the journey." Nerisse continued to use that quiet, calming inflection. Ba'tvian approved. Her provision would also give her an opportunity to get inside his shields if done right. "It will suffice."

"And we'll scout around the Guild House." Raptu snorted. "I'd love to know how you're going to pull that off without being noticed. Isn't your face gracing wanted posters in all the taverns by now?"

"There is always a way." Ba'tvian sent out a silent call. "With care, with wit, and with power." As he spoke, his Shadows came. They crept into view, gliding over the floor. They'd been feeding on the residue of haphazard rites, on the lingering death, the rotting blood on the basement floor below. It showed in their energy, the dull glow of their eyes, the definition of their forms. They gathered around their lord as the noble trio swore. Ba'tvian gathered his power around him, let his new allies glimpse the depths of it. He addressed them just a hint of his usual arrogance:

"Follow my instructions, and we will all succeed."

28

Late that evening

BEHIND the cottage, Nerisse watched Halvark build the gate that would take them to Jevanel. Her lord had spent hours instructing them on the most efficient ways to clean up a rite, to harvest the fruits of it. He had worked with the nobleman to refine his technique, had lent him power so that he could witness Halvark's skill before they made the transition.

He would not risk her.

Prialla and Raptu stood nearby, holding the reins to the horse that Halvark would be taking with him. Ibestor and Nerisse did the same with their mounts. Ba'tvian held himself apart from everyone, studying the arcane construction underway. As they waited, she felt her lord's mind touch hers.

What were you able to do with him?

That he would ask so soon did not surprise her. *Not much. He's very much alert for intrusion. Without someone else to distract him, I cannot accomplish much. However, I did manage to make a hatchway. It's a small opening, and he'll notice it if I use it while he's awake. I will be able to do more once he sleeps.*

What of you? Your earth bond.

I am well. That he asked warmed her. *A bit fatigued. The bond is strained yet should hold me.*

I will be most displeased if this does not go well. I will not lose you, Nerisse.

She understood. Nerves skittered through her blood. Still, she took a deep breath, caught her lord's eye, gave him a faint reassuring smile.

I will not fail you.

The gate, initially a framework of orange lines of power, flared into being. The portal in the center went dark, then lightened to reveal a snow-crusted tree line of pine. Beyond it lay a meadow, and farther out were barren fields.

A few of the Shadows will go with you from here. You will be joined by others upon arrival. His telepathic sending held a dark undertone. *Do not forget, Nerisse, to whom you belong.*

I cannot forget. I will never forget.

He gave her a terse nod – as much, she thought, in acknowledgement of her words as in permission to go. Halvark had stepped aside, giving her room to pass through the gate. She led her beast through it, knew that Ibestor followed right behind her.

The air was much colder here than on the Tretoan Estate. It had her shivering as she hurried to clear the way for her companions. The moment she was out of the way, she traded her light cloak for the embroidered heavy winter cloak that Ba'tvian had given her some months ago. Ibestor didn't seem to register the temperature. Halvark did.

He hissed, gritting his teeth as he turned back to the portal to dismiss it. That done, he was quick to search his pack for his own cloak.

As he did so, Nerisse studied the sky through the tree branches above them. It was close to midnight, or just after. If her memory was correct, her father's fields lay within two miles of the main entrance to Jevanel, yet her family's private entryway should be close by. It would resemble a stone hovel, a place where someone might store farming tools. It did serve that purpose. In the back of it, though, where a cellar trapdoor would be, was the way in.

No one would be using it now; winter laid the fields fallow until the spring thaw. Everything would be locked up. The locks would not be a problem. Ba'tvian had taught her how to pick locks when the need arose. What concerned her was what would come after the door was open.

They've already cut me off, cast me out. The pain of it was a faint twinge in the region of her heart. She couldn't let herself dwell on them, her family. She couldn't remember their love for her, the tenderness they'd shown her. Tears burned in her eyes regardless.

She gripped the saddle horn of her mount, squeezed her eyes shut and tried to dismiss the tears. She didn't want to cry in front of a man she didn't know.

"Nerisse?"

She heard the frown in Halvark's voice. His hand touched her shoulder. A warning hiss sounded. She stepped to the side, away from him, as he jerked his hand back. Rubbing her eyes clear of the unshed tears, she looked at him to see him staring at one of the larger Shadows under Ba'tvian's command. It had wedged itself between them, its eye glowing leprous white, its posture agitated.

"My lord sent them with us. They view me as his," she explained, grateful to have something else to think about for a moment.

"It was not my intention to encroach on his claim." Halvark's gaze never left the Shadow. The creature stopped it's hissing, twitched its tail, yet didn't move out from between them. The noble left off his stare to regard Nerisse.

"What upsets you?"

She sighed. So much for her reprieve.

"The past upsets me." She glanced at the fields that lay beyond the trees. "My past."

"You're from here, are you not?" He followed her glance. "Did they abuse you in some way?"

"Abuse...no. Not in the way you mean." She petted her beast's neck. "Killing is not abuse." What to tell him? How to say it? She tried to think of what Ba'tvian would do, how he would handle it. He would, she realized, tell the truth as he saw it. "They would see me dead because I love him. They have tried once already."

I have to remember that. My family, my people, the ones I loved – they tried to kill me. I can't lose sight of that.

The moment she did, she would die. She would be useless to her chosen lord.

"Then why are we here?" He didn't understand – that was clear in his voice. "What are we supposed to do?"

"To stop them." She turned to him. In his eyes, she saw what Ba'tvian had seen: compassion, a gentleman's need to aid a lady in distress, curiosity, and attraction. There was also knowledge there. She wasn't his, and he would respect that.

He didn't see her as less than him, she realized. He believed her to be noble born, though the Elvanarae had no aristocrats. She supposed that different rules applied to her.

But not to our lord. It was a sly whisper teasing at the recesses of her mind. *Everyone knows that our lord was born in the dirt, a serf so poor he might as well have been a slave.*

No. She steeled herself. Her lord would have that same respect. He would have more. Her lord was not the dirt beneath everyone else's feet.

"How are we supposed to do that?"

"I have to find a way." She let her eyes track back to the fields she'd played in as a child, then helped harvest once she'd grown older. The earth provided for them, her father had said. If you needed it, it would provide it. The germ of an idea took hold. It was so simple really.

There would be a price. Something like this could not be wrought without consequence. She would have to bear that burden, whatever it might be. Nerisse wasn't weak; she would take it on. She'd find a way to cope.

The earth would help her with that. The earth always did.

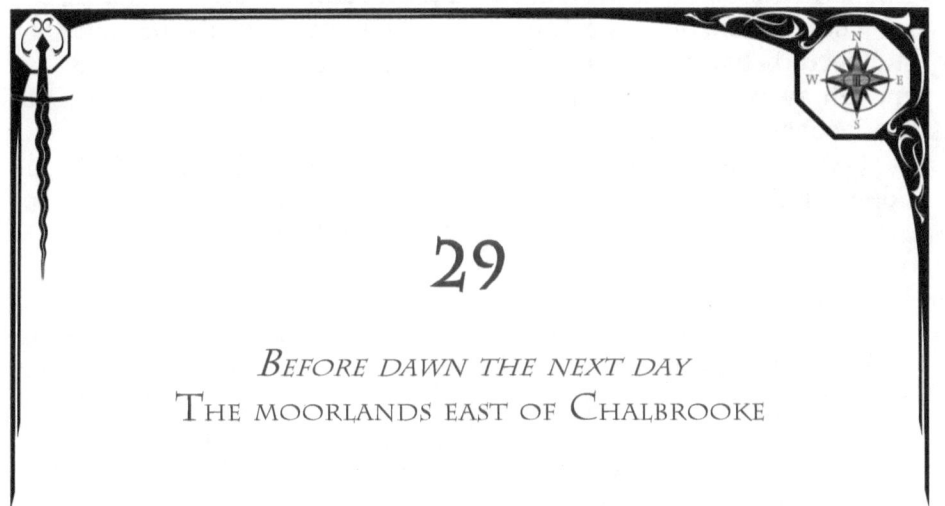

29

PRIALLA and Raptu rode through a portal onto the dark moorlands outside Chalbrooke. Prialla's horse stumbled on the uneven ground, pitching her forward in the saddle. She kept her seat while cursing the animal, its ancestry, even the origin of its species. Raptu chuckled.

"Keep it up, my sweet, and no man will believe you to be a noblewoman." He flashed her a wide, mocking grin.

"Oh, shove off." In ill-humor, she glared at her companion as he laughed at her. "As if the night-time guards will accept our story with your smug demeanor."

"They might." His words confident, Raptu studied her dress. The elegant gown she wore had been well-prepared. There were tears, mud splatter – not too much, she thought as she glanced down at the skirts. Just enough to indicate that she'd been on foot along the road at some point. There were plenty of grass stains, though they weren't visible in the pre-dawn light.

His eyes dipped to her skewed neckline as she tossed her head, muttered another curse on her beleaguered mount.

"You certainly look the part of the damsel in distress."

Raptu's pronouncement prompted a small smile of satisfaction from her.

"Good. Now, if you can keep up with the harried act you demonstrated earlier, we'll be fine." She hoped. She had doubts. Chalbrooke guards weren't stupid, after all. Stil, with him dressed in clothing as tattered and dirty as hers, they might pass muster at the city gates. Might.

They fell silent as they guided their mounts towards the road that stretched between Chalbrooke and Rathburn. The city was far enough away that they'd have to gallop hard to get there before the sun reached its zenith.

Once all eight hooves were firmly on the packed dirt of the Chal-Edon Trade Route, Raptu gave her a sly grin. She knew that expression. It meant mischief. For him, mischief included bloodshed or sex.

"I'll race you, my sweet."

"For what stakes?" Racing – they could do that without giving anything else away. Prialla held up a hand before he could answer. "No killing. Not yet. We'll have time to play in the blood later."

"Spoil sport." His mock-chiding tone had her responding with a level stare. He chuckled. "How about this, then? If I win, I get to flip your skirts before we contact Ba'tvian."

"If I win," she countered, "you'll be obedient to my every command for the rest of the day."

"Done." He smiled. "See how well we play together? Now, my sweet..." He let the sentence trail off as they each readied themselves. They dug their heels in simultaneously.

Side by side, they took off at a dead run.

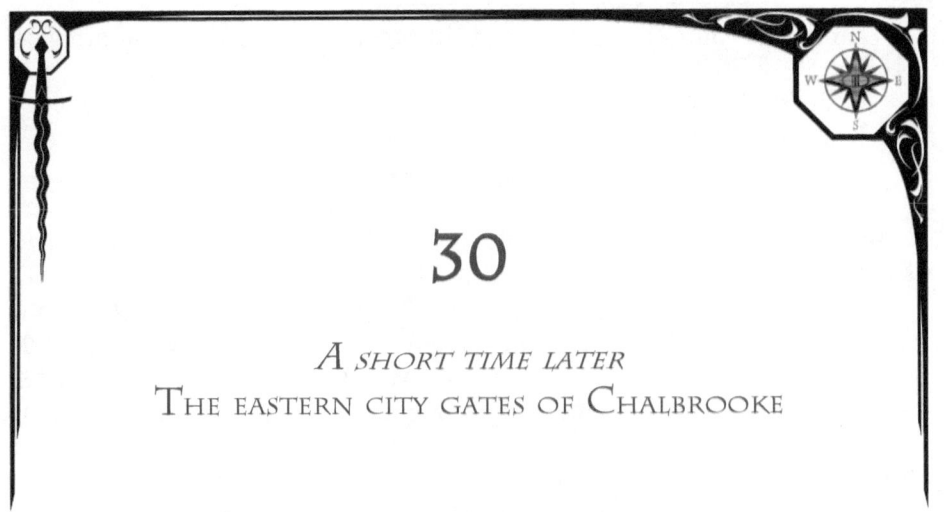

30

A SHORT TIME LATER
THE EASTERN CITY GATES OF CHALBROOKE

THE night-time guards were nearing the end of their shift. The horizon had lightened, though the sun was in hiding. The pair, Ezil Ormonson and Kale Hornbush, stationed outside the gates judged it to be another hour or so before they could head to the tavern for a hot meal.

There'd been no incidents as during shift. They'd spent several hours playing mental games of logic or sharing bits of gossip. It kept them awake while not violating the mandate that remain standing at their posts. Whoever lost the most games in one night bought the morning meal at the tavern. Tonight, Kale had been the winner, much to Ezil's chagrin.

"We could play another game," Kale offered. Like all city guards, he wore chainmail, a surcoat sporting the city's emblem in white on a field of blue, and a conical helmet that left the face bare save for a nose piece that descended from the helmet's brow.

"What would be the point?" Ezil tamped the butt of his spear on the ground as he groaned in defeat. "You're ahead by four. I'll win tomorrow night."

"Looks like someone's coming on the road." Kale inclined his head at a dark speck that was just visible in the dawning light.

They watched it for a moment, saw it grow, resolve into two separate specks.

"Coming in fast," Ezil observed. He frowned, straightening off the wall he'd been leaning on as he readied his spear. His partner did the same. "Riders. You think it's only the two of them?"

"Looks like it."

Moments later, there was a bit more light, and the new arrivals were clearly visible.

"Man and woman. Nobles? The woman's wearing a blue gown." Kale shook his head in answer.

"No guards. Nobles travel with an entourage."

"At this speed?" Ezil was doubtful. Fast travel like this was for couriers, or it indicated trouble. "You may be wrong there, my friend."

"We'll know shortly, won't we?" Kale stepped forward, hand raised, as the riders pulled up at the gate. Their horses were lathered, head's dropping in exhaustion. The riders weren't in much better shape. They wore the finery of aristocrats; it had not fared well in their travels. They were in such a state of disarray, that Kale found himself too stunned to speak. His friend stepped forward.

"Lord, lady, what happened? Are you hurt?" Ezil took hold of the lady's bridle. "Were you attacked?"

"Bandits." The noble – a young man by the look of him – gasped it out wearily. "We were attacked just before evening yesterday. When they – the bandits – attacked, our coach was run off the road and overturned. We managed to get out and grab the horses while our guards kept the bandits busy…but…" He faltered.

"They died so that we could get away." The lady concluded in a sad, tired voice. "We rode through the night to get here. Can we please go in? I – we need to rest, and our horses need care."

"Of course." Kale hurried over to the gate portcullis, called to the guards inside to open it. As he did so, Ezil gave them instructions to file a report with the Merchants' Guild.

"They maintain the road. They will see to it that someone deals with the bandits," he advised. "Do you have lodgings?"

"Yes, yes, we're well set, thank you." The lord gave him a wan smile as the portcullis lifted. "If we can cool down the horses, give them some water…?"

"There's a side courtyard just inside the walls." Kale stepped towards the gate to point the way. "We use it primarily for trade goods inspections. There's a water trough for the horses, plenty of room to walk them cool."

"Thank you." The lady gave them a grateful smile, brushing her loose, tousled blond hair out of her eyes. "You've been so kind."

The nobles dismounted, leading their weary mounts on foot. As they disappeared into the city, the guards resumed their posts. The portcullis lowered once more.

"Well," Ezil said, a tad smug. "That's a point for me. You were wrong about them."

"I'm still ahead by three."

"We forgot to get their names for the logbook." He grimaced over the realization. Their captain would not be happy with them.

"Another point for me, then, as I recognized the man. He's Raptu Carthier, heir of Lord Carthier of Rathburn." Now it was Kale's turn to be smug. "Comes to Chalbrooke on business often enough. The Carthiers have that courier business and the old lord is of the mind that his children should do some work, not just lay about on his largess."

"So you're still ahead by four." Ezil sighed. "Wonder who the woman was."

"That I couldn't tell you," Kale admitted, "The captain will be satisfied with what we've got, though. Tavern's serving beef stew tonight."

"Beef's expensive." His friend gave him a mournful look. "At least we just got paid."

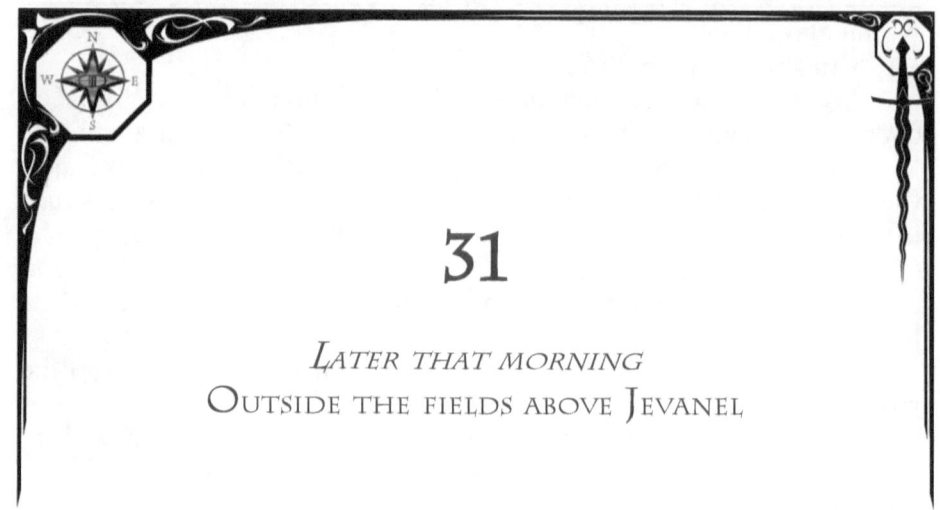

31

NERISSE knelt on the snow-crusted ground as Halvark watched on, one hand on a large, moving leather sack on the ground beside him. Ibestor and several Shadows stood on guard a few feet away. Though largest of the dark creatures observed her movements, the others gave their attention to the fields that lay out of sight beyond the trees. With the winter sun climbing high, there was some activity in the fields. She'd forgotten about the snow blooms that her people sometimes cultivated. Though they wouldn't produce their berries until spring, they were planted in the late fall and tended through the coldest part of the year.

Her father had never grown them. The plants preferred more northern climes than this so would only grow here during the years when the winter was harsh. This year's winter had been longer than normal. It was part of the earth's seasonal cycle, her father said. It was manageable so long as one paid attention to it.

Yet the crops of snow blooms meant workers during the daylight hours. They would have to wait until nightfall to do anything. The more they waited, the riskier their situation became. The earth was already uneasy. Her pleas for it to keep silent would not hold it for long.

Ba'tvian had anticipated this, though. His knack for forethought and planning was one of the reasons he would succeed. They'd discussed what she would need to do. It meant more blood – more of *her* blood. So, kneeling, she used her hands to dig through the snow, past the layers of dead grass, to the soil below. She created a hollow in ground, murmuring prayers in her native tongue as she did so.

Her gut clenched. Even with the draught that dulled her empathy, her emotions, what she was about to do made bile rise within her throat. She fought nausea as she slashed her palm, letting the blood drip into the exposed soil. Halvark knelt down, opened the large sack. It was a bear cub the size of a thirty pound dog. Ibestor had found the bear den earlier, stealing the cub when she'd requested a sacrifice.

The cub's muzzle and feet were bound with strips of cloth. Still, it wriggled, mewed, rolled eyes that were impossibly young. Seeing the fear in them, Nerisse almost broke. She needed to do this. She didn't want to.

"I need you. You are mine."

Her lord's sharp words echoed in her mind, cutting through the reluctance, the grief, the pity.

"I will not lose you. If the earth would take you from me, then you must bind it to me. If the Elvanarae would see you dead, then you must show them no mercy." His eyes, so dark, sparking with crimson light, bored into hers, into her soul, as he'd spoken. As he'd commanded. *"You will do this for me, to my glory. Won't you, Nerisse?"*

Yes, she thought. She'd said yes, given him her promise.

"Lay it over the hollow." It, she had to think of the cub as an 'it', just as she had to think of her people, her blood-kin, as 'them'.

As Halvark positioned the sacrifice, she heard the murmuring, the worry, the growing anxiety from the earth. What was she doing? Why was she doing it? She absorbed the earth's communication, gripping the bond she shared with it tightly. As the cut on her palm bled, she gestured to Halvark. He wrestled with the bear a moment, yanked its head back to give her access to its throat. She took a moment, bracing herself as she began to chant in her native tongue.

I am your daughter. Through me, through my relationship, my love, you have a son – Ba'tvian Delthanurk is your son. You must accept your son, your daughter. You must protect us. By the blood I shed, the blood I give – She raised her ritual knife, slitting the both jugulars of the cub. *– the blood I take, I hold you to this, I bind you to this. You will fulfill your obligation,, your promise, to me, and to him.*

She repeated the chant, drawing on the power unleashed by the death to forge chains for the earth. It would be effective for a little while, just for this area. She hoped it would be enough.

She'd closed her eyes at some point. When she opened them, still chanting the binding-spell, she could see the Shadows. They were everywhere – hundreds of them scattered throughout the alpine forest, clustered around them. They glowed with the crimson light of blood magic. Each of them bore Ba'tvian's arcane signature.

How many, she wondered. How many were used as vessels for his power? How many assisted her? Aid her they did, the red lines of power they harbored arced from their bodies to the blood soaked hollow. They intertwined with the chains she had forged, made them stronger, longer, far reaching.

The largest Shadow slithered to his side, ran its tongue along her skirt-clad thigh.

Finish it, it hissed into her mind. *To our lord's glory.*

"I bind you, earth to daughter, daughter to son, earth to son." Her words rang hollow with power. "I bind you to Ba'tvian Delthanurk, my lord, your master."

In the echoes of those words, she plunged her knife into the hollow as the earth shuddered.

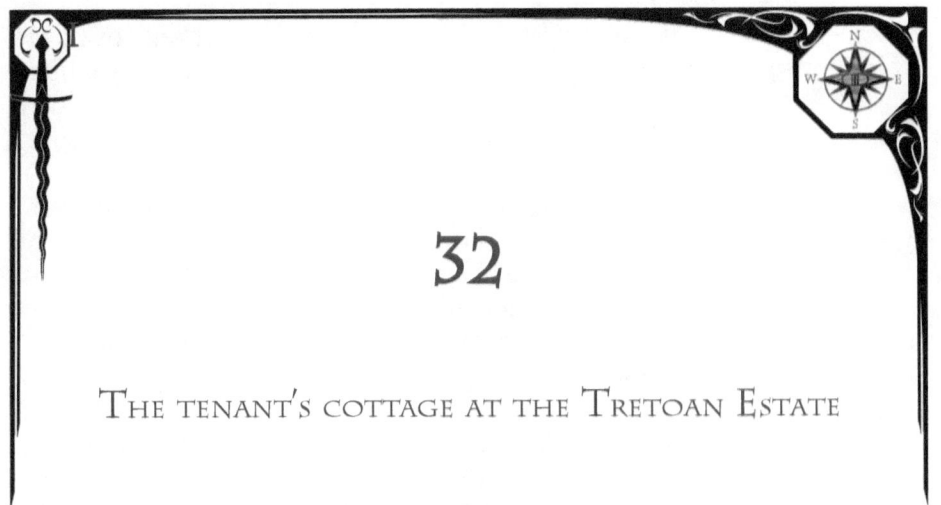

32

IN the basement of the cottage, Ba'tvian jerked in reaction. All the breath left his body as he sensed something – a tie – settle into place deep within him. His attending Shadowed Ones swarmed around him in excitement. They had caught the change as well.

Breathing deep, he explored the new bond. It led to the earth, splintering off to connect him with Nerisse as well. Through it, he was dimly aware of her exhaustion, the weakness of blood-loss. There was nausea, a sickness at heart. She needed rest, some emotional bolstering before she completed the rest.

He debated contacting Halvark. The noble was with her, might be willing to give her support. No. He needed to appear strong, confident. He could not afford to be thought of as worried or concerned about Nerisse. She would pull through. His followers would see to that.

As if to confirm the thought, his Shadows brushed against his legs in what most would term affection. They felt no such thing. They were like himself in that regard. What that gesture represented was a cold, devoted loyalty.

He resumed what he'd been doing: cleansing the basement. He had shown the trio how to do this, how to wipe their tracks clean at ritual sites. Yet there so much had been left lingering for so long, that it needed repeated, thorough cleansings to wash the signatures away. The work was tedious, simple enough that he could turn part of his attention to other things.

If this venture succeeded, if Nerisse was right about the work she'd done, then they would be using the Tretoan Estate as a base of sorts. It would mean getting rid of the current lord, perhaps even the neighboring Lord Carthier. As he checked for any traces of tainted power in his surroundings, he considered that. Not yet, he decided. He needed them locked in place under him before he started stripping away their other connections.

He'd done the same with Nerisse. Her devotion was his reward for his patience there. He had time. He could afford to wait. The Mancers, however, were another ken.

Finished at last, he inspected his work. He found no lingering taint in the structure of the basement. To make sure of his findings, he ordered his ethereal followers go over every inch. As they did so, a mage-sending came winging its way into the basement, gliding up to him as a pink spark. He caught it in one hand, using the contact to trigger the message within. Prialla and Raptu had arrived in Chalbrooke, their plan to gain entrance without guards or suspicion successful. They'd acquired suitable lodgings near their target and Raptu was now out in the city scouting. Included in Prialla's sending were images of the room – what he needed to gate there directly.

There was one aspect of this that he'd failed to anticipate. Nerisse was not there to mask his arcane signature or gating activity. He didn't know how she accomplished it, just that she used the earth in some way to…but he was now tied to the earth as well, wasn't he?

He mulled it over as his creatures reported back to him: they'd found the basement to be clean. Selecting the most powerful Shadows from the throng around him, he crouched down for a conference. By the time it ended, he'd bound them to him, to the earth. They were intelligent, had evolved enough to work some small magics independently of him. They would serve to mask his signature as he worked.

With the arrangements made, he began to build his gate.

33

The Inn of the Golden Stag in Chalbrooke

PRIALLA felt the tingling sensation that was the prelude to a gate forming. It was faint – faint enough that she almost missed it. If she hadn't been expecting Ba'tvian to gate directly into the sitting room, she would have. It intrigued her. She'd been under the impression that he needed Nerisse to mask the portal.

Anxiety bloomed in her stomach, taking her by surprise. She'd never been nervous about seduction – and that was part of the plan here. It was why Raptu wasn't there with her, what she, Raptu, and Halvark had discussed soon after the three of them had left their new allies in the cottage. Sex was one of the best weapons in her arsenal; using it might give them more of an edge in their dealings. Still, Ba'tvian had shown no interest prior to this. Was he that devoted to Nerisse, she wondered, that fixated?

With the elf was off doing whatever at Jevanel with Halvark and the barbarian, Prialla had an opportunity to test that theory.

She watched the crimson lines of magic trace themselves into the lattice work of the gate's frame. As the opening flared into being, she caught a glimpse of the basement where they held their rituals. Then Ba'tvian stepped through, escorted by dozens of the black creatures he called his own.

The Shadowed Ones unnerved her. She'd die before she let that show, yet her skin crawled as they inspected the suite of rooms they'd rented. Ba'tvian paid them no attention.

"Where is the Guild House?"

Straight to business. With a mental shrug, she answered, "Two blocks down the street. The Guild House entrance is on the opposite side of the road, but the property surrounds the round-about at the end. The back of the main building butts up against the city wall."

"Is all of it stone?" He spotted the window that faced the street below, moved to it. He twitched the heavy drapes aside to peer out at the Guild House.

"It's difficult to tell. Everything in the front looks to be stone." Prialla, dressed elegantly in a slim wine colored gown bought that morning, joined him at the window. "Raptu hasn't reported back yet. I don't expect him to for a few more hours."

"What is he doing?"

"Taking care of some business. His family has offices in Chalbrooke; business was as a good a reason to be in the city as any other. He is also making a few purchases to replace what we...lost during our misadventure on the road." Her lips curved. "There are plenty of rumors that you're heading in this general direction; he's using them as an excuse to ask questions."

"Not too many. We do not wish to tip our hand."

"He knows how far he can go." She'd won their race by a head. He'd honor their bet and obey the restrictions she'd set. "He's on a leash."

"Good."

He continued to stare out the window, his gaze brooding. She shifted a little, let her body brush up against his. When he didn't react, she laid a hand on his bicep, let her fingers play along his forearm. It wasn't as subtle as she would have preferred, yet he'd ignored subtlety up to this point.

He slid his narrowed gaze from the street view to her. She met his eyes, saw the red glow in them. In a sudden move that left her gasping, he had a hand around her throat, squeezing just enough to have her stumble back a step.

"What is it that you want, Prialla?" His voice was soft, his eyes burning. "Don't lie to me."

His hold loosened enough to allow her to speak without straining. Something brushed against her calves – one of his creatures. She allowed herself a shudder, then took a deep breath.

"Power is something everyone wants." Her words were cool, calm. "Why should I be different?"

"Sex will not gain you power with me."

She saw that now. This, she decided, was not the time to bargain for an edge in their dealings. Her mind spun with possible angles, ways to route this situation back onto even ground.

"What will?" Let him think that power was all she was after. It wasn't a lie.

"Loyalty." He ran a thumb over the column of her throat. Perhaps he wasn't so indifferent to her after all.

"Loyalty's earned," she countered. "You haven't done that yet."

"Loyalty can also be bought." His eyes never left hers as he drew a small knife from his belt. "What price would you set for yours, Prialla?"

"What have you to offer me?" She let her gaze drop to the knife. Her heartbeat sped up.

"A true desire." He brought the knife up, ran his bare thumb over the blade, then down the edge. Blood welled up from the shallow cut. "You desire youth, beauty, a kind of immortality."

She stared at him. How had he known? Not even her cohorts, the only people she was close to, were aware of her innermost fears. Aging, the loss of beauty. The lines that came with the years robbing the planes of a pretty face of their smoothness, their appeal. How many times had she seen herself in her mother, witnessed the way that time had treated the woman?

Still holding the knife, Ba'tvian slid his cut thumb over her face. She went motionless as the blade caught the light, as the blood smeared over her cheek. He murmured something too low for her to catch, felt her skin warm with magic. He released her, stepped back with a single word.

"Look."

With a hand to her face, she left the sitting room for the vanity mirror in her bedroom. She studied herself in the silvered glass, leaning against the vanity.

Her skin held a subtle glow – a pale light that illuminated from within. Her eyes were a brighter blue, the minute lines that time had formed on her face had been smoothed over. Color, a healthy rose, tinted her cheeks, her eyelids. A deeper vermilion stained her lips. Beauty without makeup, youth without looking immature.

She whirled around to find him standing in the doorway.

"How? How did you do this?" Eager avarice caused a tremor in her voice.

"I can teach you, for that price."

She fell silent, considering. She wanted this, so much did she want this...

"I can't betray them – Halvark, Raptu." They were hers. She didn't abandon what was hers. Yet she turned back to see herself in the mirror. To take in the subtle changes in her appearance. He'd done that, she thought, with just a smear of blood.

"Will they stand with you?" His words were devoid of judgment. When she faced him once more, she couldn't read him. He just waited there, dressed in the trapper's gear he'd worn when they'd first met.

"In time." She took a deep breath, let her thoughts race in her head. She would persuade them. Of course, she would. "Yes."

"Then there's no betrayal, is there?" He crossed the room, gently turned her to the mirror again. "Blood is power." He whispered it into her ear. "However it is shed doesn't matter. In the end, blood will give you the means to obtain what you need."

She shivered. Staring at her reflection, at what she could have, Prialla made her choice.

"For this I will follow you." She touched her cheek again. "For this I will give you loyalty."

"Seal the bargain – with blood for me." She watched as he ran his hand down her arms. "With sex for you."

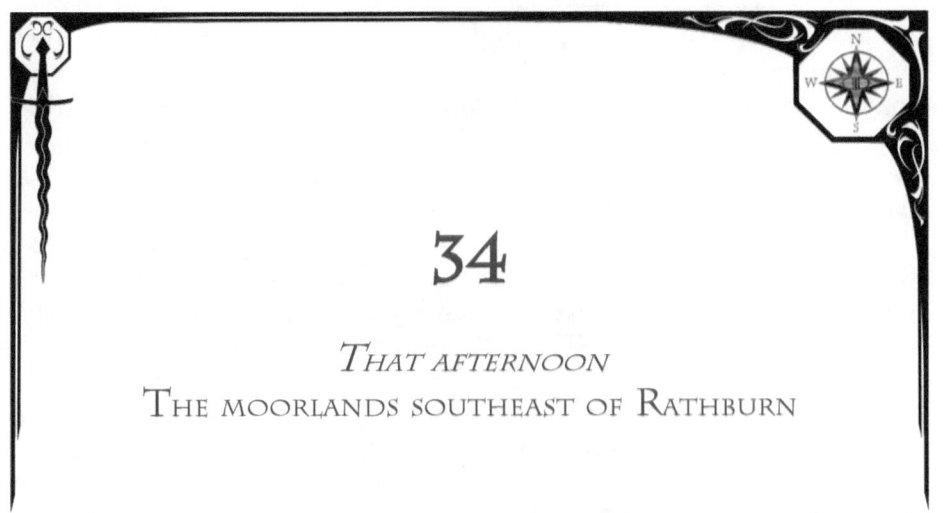

34

ABSOL Omine rode in the quiet beside his ward. The Wood of Destiny now lay at their backs. Before them, the moors stretched out, a rolling expanse of grasslands dotted with shrubs and trees.

It was peaceful through here. With I'k'Nole snoozing in the saddle – and how Absol envied the lad that ability – the only sounds were those of the horses as they waded through the uneven sea of long grass. The temperature was dropping again as the sun began its descent. Night was on its way, bringing the frost it would sprinkle over the moorlands.

He let his mind roam as he guided them closer to Chalbrooke. There wasn't anything else to do on journeys like this. It was just as well as there was plenty for him to think about.

Ba'tvian Delthanurk headed southeast. Was it a random direction or did he have a destination in mind? The last update he'd received indicated that he'd left the Northern Wilderness a few days ago. Several Mancers trailed him from the north, yet they'd lost his trail once he'd entered the moors north of the Wood.

Given how open the terrain was, it surprised Absol. There was so little to hide behind – a few shrubs, maybe the odd tiny stand of trees. One thing might explain it: Ba'tvian had learned how to create portals, an ability possessed by adept and sage level mages. Before he was murdered by his former prodigy, Master Oknare of the Trinity had revealed that Ba'tvian would be an adept once his training was complete.

Gating –using a portal – made the most sense as the blood mage wasn't alone. He traveled with companions now: an unidentified barbarian and the elven lady Nerisse se li Astorae. Nerisse, at least, may not be a problem for much longer. He'd received confirmation from the High Priest of her people that the casting-out ceremonies were underway. Those rites would sever the girl's bond with the earth. Death would occur soon after that.

How soon remained to be seen. According to High Priest Saerlan, it varied from person to person. His message also relayed the task's difficulty; Nerisse's bond was much stronger than the majority of her peoples'. The earth seemed reluctant to let her go.

It begged the question why. From what Absol understood, the practice blood magery would prompt the earth to withdraw from the practitioner. What was it about Nerisse that kept the earth attentive? Had she been duped, blinded to immorality of her actions? Did the Monster of Menie have a hold over her, one that coerced her into being loyal, into participating in his sacrifices? There had to be more to it.

I'k'Nole's theory of love being her motivation had some merit. It didn't explain everything, though. Her empathy, for instance. How could she get around her empathy long enough to complete a ceremony? An Empath didn't just close off her ability as one might a room in their house. She would be forced to experience everything done to the victims, living it as they did. Another question surfaced on the heels of the last: what would Ba'tvian do with an Empath?

What was he after?

That was the answer everyone wanted. For more than two years, he'd run, killing as he went, avoiding Mancers like the plague. Yet a few months before there'd been a change in his tactics. He'd hunted down a Mancer, baited him, killed him. Timbrel Jodrek hadn't been the first Mancer to fall to Ba'tvian's knife – a more inexperienced Mancer had gone down two years ago near Glasten Port. That death had all the signs of an impulse killing.

The more recent deaths were of a different ken.

Perhaps that was it. Perhaps the goal he had in mind now was to kill every Mancer he could find. There was a problem with that, however. He hadn't taken out the Mancers on his trail.

Had he been aware of them? His movements appeared to indicate that he'd known. He'd steered clear of traps, altered directions without any discernible reason.

That in turn led him back to his own hypothesis of a Daemon Lord aiding the blood mage. Yet...the more he thought about it, the less likely it seemed. To his knowledge, Daemon Lords bore little patience with their puppets. They desired quick results, demanding much more than they gave in return. Then there were the Shadowed Ones. No record that he or Dannon could locate stated that the Daemon Lords used the Shadows. If the texts were to be believed, most Daemon Lords regarded them as near mindless animals, spiritual scavengers, lacking the wits to be a servant of any kind.

The Mancer annals held them in a different light: predatory, cunning, with the capacity to learn. They avoided Chalbrooke, for instance. There were always Mancers in the city, though their numbers were few enough that no permanent posts had been erected anywhere else. Yet once, long ago, that hadn't been the case. Absol's Order had hunted them down, the younger members cutting their teeth on them in the moors. Soon after the Guild House had been established, the Shadows vanished from the area as if they'd never been.

Absol was certain they communicated with each other. He'd witnessed them act alone as well as cooperatively. They congregated around death – at battlefields, disasters, any event that dealt huge casualties – and would travel for miles to find it. Still, they'd never been led by anyone.

Now they followed Ba'tvian around like devoted pups. His kills consisted of one person, perhaps two, at a time, a far cry from the mass slaughter that usually attracted them. It was a mystery, one of many connected to the blood mage.

Absol wished the Mancers knew more. With a sigh, he sent a mage sending off to the Guild House asking about the blood mage or the Shadows' in the area. Odds were low that they would impart anything new. Still…still one could hope.

Even as the world drowned in darkness and fog, there was always hope.

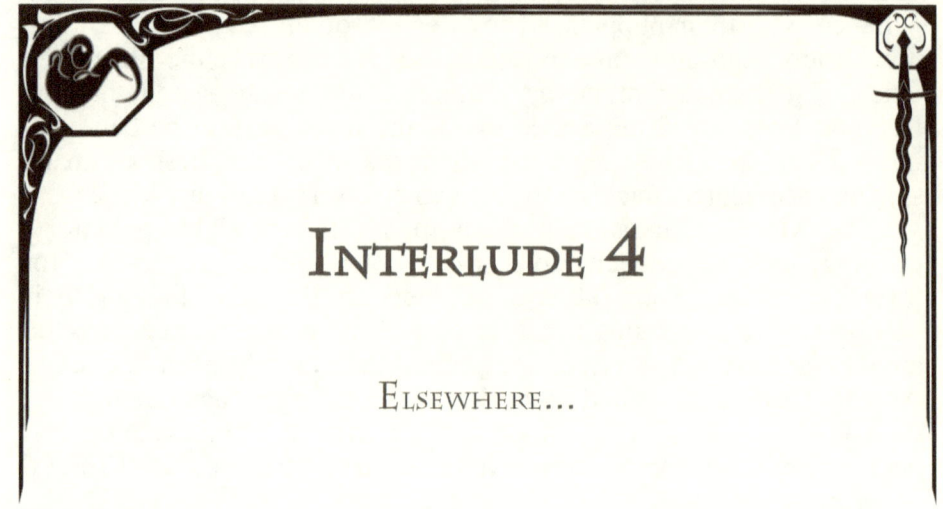

Interlude 4

LABIYAL Biyalban allowed himself a slow smile of pleasure as he sat at the desk in study and watched Prialla succumb in the tabletop mirror. Ba'tvian was developing manipulative skills similar to his own. Given enough time, his skill might well rival Labiyal's.

He leaned back in his chair, contemplating the progress made, the steps yet to be taken. Around him, mounted on floor stands, was the array of mirrors he used. All but one displayed a scene conveyed by the linked minds of his spies – birds, rodents, the single Chained One at his command. The blank mirror, its frame black, austere, was covered. It served as a reminder of whom he served, of his purpose on Einlienn.

Ba'tvian was not quite ready for what needed to happen. That would come soon enough. In the meantime, his immediate ambitions would whet the appetites of Daemon Lord Biyal and their king.

Unless he had other plans, ones that Labiyal had no inkling of that conflicted with the daemon goals.

It was a real possibility. As a daemon half-blood, Labiyal possessed a knack reading the intentions and desires of other races, humans in particular. Yet Ba'tvian's mind was becoming increasingly opaque to him. It seemed that the boy's – man's, he corrected – mixed heritage was coming into play there, an unexpected outcome. The ties between them, those hidden links chaining Ba'tvian to his fate, should have been enough to allow Labiyal to see into his mind regardless of his ancestry. They were failing, which meant he'd missed something.

He tugged a line of magic, cut off the sound coming from the mirror as he rose. The scene continued to play out as he walked through the half circle of mirrors. He pulled out a battered leather tome, flipped it open as he made his way back to his seat.

It was an old text on associative magics, a rare volume written not by a mortal blood mage but the daemons. He browsed through the passages, looking for anything that might hint at the blockage. It told him nothing new.

There was, however, a remedy: blood. If he could obtain a vial of Ba'tvian's bloodhe would be better able to bypass the protections building up around his mind. It was not an easy solution. Ba'tvian was a careful blood mage.

Very careful.

Labiyal closed the book, glancing at the glass. Things had moved on from the sex his...protégé had engaged in. It would be best to wait, he decided. There was a tenuous level of trust between them, one dark mage to another. The fragile trust would be used to found something far stronger in the near future: a true alliance. This project would require several, and an ally had the right to make certain demands – things that were not covered in their current contract. The benefits of blood did not, at present, outweigh the potential of trust. So he would wait, he would see, and if the opportunity presented itself, he would take advantage.

Until then, he would do as he'd always done: pull the strings from behind the scenes.

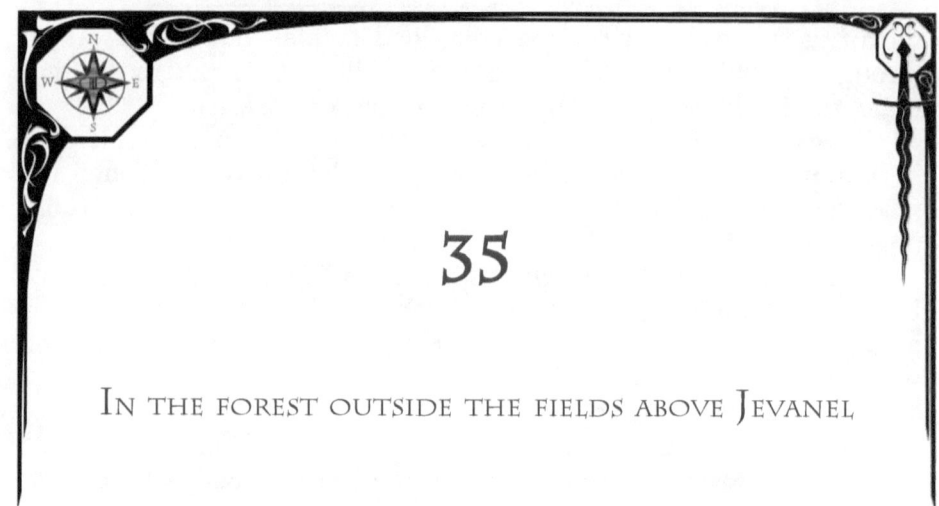

35

IN THE FOREST OUTSIDE THE FIELDS ABOVE JEVANEL

NERISSE woke to find herself settled on her bedroll. Confused, disoriented, she took a moment to take in her surroundings. Her last memory had been of weaving chains through the earth, of the Shadows joining Ba'tvian's power to hers, then…nothing. There was nothing.

What had happened?

Beside her bedding, the largest of the creatures her lord had sent with her stirred from its resting place. It seemed lethargic, its dull white eyes lacking the usual faint glow. Its body was as substantial as early morning mist. It looked much the same way as she felt. She levered herself up to view the camp. Its fellow Shadows were in the same state.

"Nerisse?"

She turned her head to see Halvark kneeling on her other side. His handsome face was stoic. There was no sign of fatigue on him. Unlike her, he had not channeled power into the rite or binding; his role had only been to restrain the sacrifice.

"I passed out." Self-conscious, she touched a hand to her face, pushed strands of her alabaster hair away from it. In her mind was the echo of Ba'tvian's words to her.

"Yes." He passed her a flask of water. "Will you be able to do your task tonight?"

Her task. Halvark was aware that they needed to prevent her people from killing her. He didn't know what she had to do to achieve that goal, she realized as she took the flask to drink. He would need to, wouldn't he?

She considered. What she had done that morning gave them reprieve. Between her efforts and those of the Shadows, she was able to do more than she'd intended. Even now, as she looked down at the ground she sat on, she could see the flecks of blood-born power embedded in the earth. As she stared at them, it came to her – what she would do, how she would do it. She looked back up at Halvark.

"I think so. With more rest, I think I can do it tonight." She sipped more water, let her gaze unfocus. "I'll need more power," she murmured. "Strength. I have to do this, for Ba'tvian."

"He is that important to you?"

The question had her blinking.

"Yes. Of course he is." Did this man – this veritable stranger – doubt her loyalty to her lord? If he did, if he *could,* what did Ba'tvian think of her? "He's given me everything. How could I not love him?"

He didn't give a reply to her response. He gave her a scrutinizing look, as if he didn't truly understand what she meant yet wouldn't admit his own ignorance. His understanding wasn't necessary, she thought, quelling a flash of frustration. His help was.

"How will you complete your task?"

She took a deep breath and told him. He stared. Around them, the Shadows stirred, began to glide nearer. When one brushed up against her thigh, she suppressed a reactionary shudder. Halvark already thought her weak; she couldn't lend any weight to that supposition.

I have to be strong.

"To do this," she went on, "I need something from you."

"What would that be?" Wariness shown in his eyes, in his closed expression. She pretended not to notice it.

"Power. Can you feed me? I can draw what I need, refresh my own magic stores by nightfall. It may be enough, it may not be. I don't know. If I can't – if I can't do this, then I'll die. I'll go mad, die, and likely take others with me when I do." She met Halvark's eyes. That grave truth was mirrored in her own. "My failure here could be the death of all of us, because you're here with me. If they break me..." She let the sentence hang.

He frowned, studied her with suspicious blue eyes. She sensed his psychic probing of her mind, allowed it so that he find the truth of her words. Not the whole truth, perhaps, yet still the truth. His mouth thinned in irritation.

"He knew it would come down to this." Bitterness edged his aristocratic voice. "Didn't he?"

"It was always a possibility," she admitted. There was no point in lying. "If you and yours hadn't come to us over the Mancer Guild, it would have been Ba'tvian in your place right now."

He scowled but nodded.

"Fine. I'll lend you what I have. However, I want something in return." A Shadow hissed in disapproval. Halvark glared at the thing. "I want one of you to take the blame for killing two people. The old Lord Tretoan and Prialla's bitch of mother have to go. To secure the estate, we need someone to take the blame."

Relief bloomed in her chest. She'd been afraid that he would demand something more personal. She looked down at the largest of the Shadows, hesitated a moment, then spoke to it telepathically.

Will Lord Ba'tvian be agreeable to this?

It blinked its dull white eyes at her. *Our master will make use of the opportunity. Give the lordling what he wants.*

Nerisse raised her gaze to Halvark's. She nodded.

"We accept the exchange."

"I will hold you to your word. Do you want what I have now?" He offered a hand. She took it, linking with him. As he opened a channel to feed the magic to her, she saw her chance. The psychic construct that she'd had readied was slipped inside the breach, settled into place as she feigned a fumbling grasp on their link to distract him.

"I'm sorry," she murmured, letting a trace of fatigue into her voice. "I'm a bit more tired than I realized."

"Don't worry about it." They completed the transfer. "Will you draw from – what his name?"

"Ibestor. Yes, I'll draw from him tonight." She glanced over at the barbarian who sat at the base of a tree, watching them with disinterest. "We will need to rest. Ibestor, you will stand guard."

The barbarian's eyes sharpened as he grunted. He got to his feet, then went to check on the animals. She was familiar with his habits by now. Once he was finished, he would wander around the perimeter of the camp before settling down again. He had a strange way of warding a place, laying down lines of power that served no other purpose than to alert him of an intruder. Yet the lines were faint, just noticeable to mage-born senses. They were like hair-fine, barbed threads, strung out as one walked.

The Elvanarae would never see it, or recognize what it was when they did.

Nerisse dug into a pack for a food packet. As she nibbled, her eyes fell on the Shadow. She opened her mind to it again.

Are you reporting to our lord? When it didn't reply, she continued. *Will you tell him that I managed to get inside Halvark's shields? The seed should be well rooted by the time we return to him.*

She sensed the creature's assent, its approval. Anything that furthered Ba'tvian's ambitions gained the Shadows' support.

She finished eating, stowing the waxed paper in the pack before settling back onto her bedding. Closing her eyes, she willed herself to sleep. She prayed that her dreams would not be drenched in the blood she had to spill.

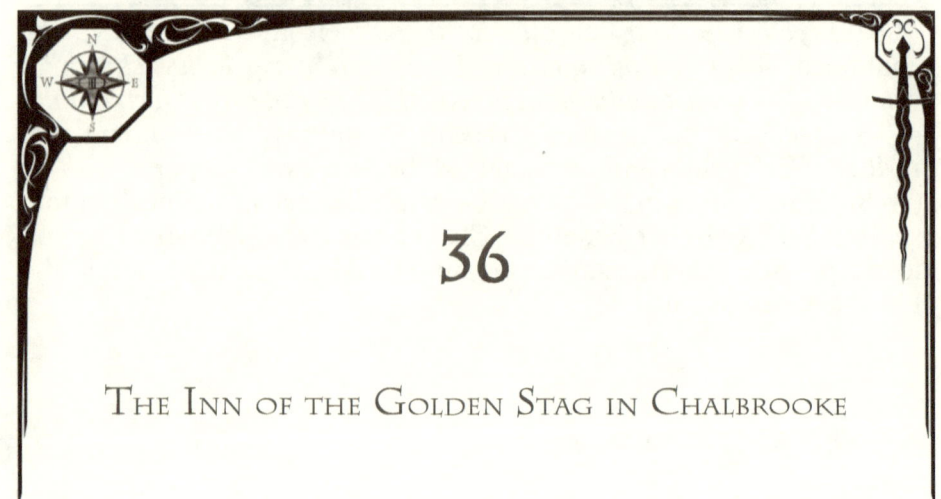

36

The Inn of the Golden Stag in Chalbrooke

B A'TVIAN remained in the third floor suite as Prialla conversed with the innkeeper in the tavern area on the ground floor. All around the sitting room, on every surface save the ceiling, his creatures crowded in. The atmosphere was a mixture of anticipation, wariness, and expectation as they delivered their reports to him.

Chalbrooke, it seemed, had been free of the Shadowed Ones for so long that most Mancers didn't bother looking for them there. The city was considered a safe haven from their enemies. That laxness was a gift that the blood mage took full advantage of. His followers scouted the city, ghosting Mancers. A few were dispatched to certain sites to spy until their purpose in Chalbrooke had been served. The city entrances had been among the assigned positions.

Many Mancers have entered the city today. The gate guards have noticed.

"Did they take note of the reason?" Though the reason would change their fate, it could impact the timeline Ba'tvian had been working on. The question was answered by another of his followers.

They come because of you, lord. It seemed pleased by the notion. *There was talk in front of the Guild where two Mancers met on their way in. The Guild Masters wish to destroy you.*

Ba'tvian allowed himself a cold smile of satisfaction. They feared him. Fear was another form of power.

"Were any of you able to get inside the Guild?"

Yes.

"Show me."

Thoughts, memory, observations began to flit through his mind.

He absorbed them, channeled them, then began to strategize. Ba'tvian had cleared off the table in the sitting room to use as a platform for a transparent, three-dimensional rendering of the Guild and the properties surrounding it. His allies stopped just inside the room, staring at it as he finished it.

It was something new. Others had done it – that had been recorded in the mage books he'd stolen from the Trinity two years ago. This was the first time he'd used the technique. The structures were shaded in the colors of blood, making the details difficult to see. With a bit of concentration, he managed to change the hues, tone down the transparency so that they became clearer.

He picked out the buildings of the compound. The training galleries and armory were located to the left of the gate; the stables lay to the right. Between them was the open courtyard with the main part of the fortified structure behind it. The great hall was at the center. To the right of that, were the main barracks. The hall's left were the administration offices, then the kitchens and dining areas. The barracks and the offices were four floors high; all other sections were no more than two.

The wall separating the Guild House from the city was manned. There was one guard at the gate, several roaming sentries that checked the grounds. According to his ethereal spies, the armory and kitchens were deserted at night. The stables always had grooms on hand. Few people tended to be awake in the main building until the early morning.

Overall, though, the security was lax. Ba'tvian felt the disgust well up. They'd grown too complacent in Chalbrooke. He could think of several ways for a small party to overtake the lot of them.

By the time Prialla returned to the suite with Raptu at her heels, he'd refined his tactics to his satisfaction. He straightened, beckoning them forward.

"Well?"

"Dinner will be sent up shortly." Prialla studied the arcane mapping on the table, fascinated.

"A few travelers have been telling tales of black ghosts on the moors." Raptu sprawled on a settee. "The Merchant's Guild will be passing that information along to the Mancers soon, if they haven't already. Most people know that things like that are unnatural."

Ba'tvian's eyes narrowed. He flicked a glance at the Shadows surrounding him.

All of you are to remain unseen until we commence with the attack.

He received a universal acknowledgement. A few of the larger creatures slipped away to ensure their brethren outside the city knew of their lord's edict. The order may have been too little, too late. Conscious of the possibility, Ba'tvian reconsidered the timing of his plans.

"We will strike tonight." He met their eyes, felt his own begin glow with anticipation as he outlined his strategy. He fielded a few questions, made assurances. "I will gate you out first. After my Shadowed Ones have cleared the Guild, I will follow."

"You are making light of their numbers," Raptu observed with a frown. "You're certain that the three of us will be enough?"

Ba'tvian gave him a cool look, then gestured. In response to the wordless command, his followers converged on the lordling. They swarmed up his legs, his torso, wrapping themselves around him with a quick agility that was astonishing to behold. Prialla gasped in surprise as Raptu cried out in dismay. He stumbled, falling to the floor as Ba'tvian gave the command to release him. They did so. Their master stepped forward to offer the fallen man a hand up.

After a wary look, Raptu took it.

"Their numbers," the blood mage stated with finality, "will not matter. You are unhurt?"

"No, I'm not hurt." Raptu scowled, brushing himself off as Prialla stepped forward to straighten his clothes. "Fine, then. We are set?"

At Ba'tvian's nod, Prialla glanced down at herself, pursed her lips.

"Perhaps not altogether." Prialla smiled at Raptu. "I hope you bought me something suitable to wear while you were out. A gown won't do for this event."

"Of course, my sweet. I have just the thing for each of us: good lightweight leather armor and serviceable clothing." He smirked. "The tale of our 'troubles' on the road came in handy once again. I even managed to pick up some weaponry without gaining undue attention. It's all waiting to be unpacked in the foyer."

"We will eat." Hunger would be an unwelcome distraction. Ba'tvian's gaze returned to the mage-wrought replica of the Mancers' Guild. "Then we will tear it down."

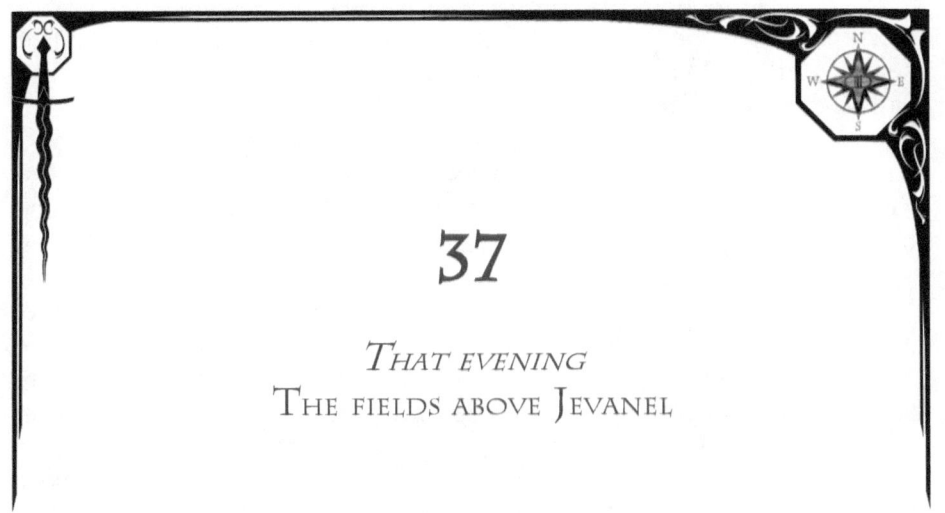

37

THAT EVENING
THE FIELDS ABOVE JEVANEL

N ERISSE led the way to her family's entry shed. Around them, most of the fields lay fallow with only a handful planted with snow bloom plants. Overhead, the moon shone bright, rendering the landscape in shades of gray. They traveled on foot, their mounts having been left in the woods. Once this was done, they wouldn't have the power to gate far; so their beasts had to remain safe.

She refused to think of what lay ahead – had done so it all day, taking refuge in the medicinal draught that blocked her empathy. Planning it had been one thing, an exercise in strategy and magic, or that's how she'd managed to look at it. Yet now, as the time drew near...

One step at a time, she thought. She had to do it one step at a time, or she'd never go through with it. The first step was to get the shed, to go through the door. After that...after that...

The enormity of the task, of what it meant, weighed down on her. Her heart beat a little faster with every stride she took. Her mind flashed with another memory with every moment that passed.

From early childhood, to her sixteenth year, each memory of love, understanding, caring, cascaded through her mind. Her mother's laughter, her father's smile. Her own small hands tending to new seedlings. Her family having dinner, the conversation light and carefree. The benevolence of the High Priest, her awe at being chosen for the Temple. Her first ritual cleansing, the first time she'd heard the murmuring of the earth...

Stop.

The sibilant word broke through. She blinked, halting on the worn path between plots, just yards away from their destination. Her heart thudded loud in her ears, her breathing came short, fast. Halvark gripped her shoulder, and she jerked away in reaction.

"Don't!" Her cry come out as a hissed whisper. Nerisse raised a hand to her face, felt the wet tracks of tears. She held out a hand to forestall her companions as she wiped the tears away. She took deep breaths, waiting for her pulse to calm, for her mind to clear. "I need – just give me a moment."

Halvark glanced back at Ibestor who watched her, impassive. Seeing no help from that quarter, he turned his back to her. The Shadows, however, circled her, closed in a little. One brushed up against her boot, causing her to step away. Another of them hissed in warning, but they gave her more room.

"I can't." The whispered words were out before she realized they were there to be said. More tears stung at her eyes. "I can't be the one."

You must. The Shadow's voice was insistent.

He commands it, spoke another.

He is our lord. Do you not love him?

If you loved him, came a contemptuous voice, *you would sacrifice all.*

We have.

Will you?

"I – " She loved him, of course she did. Yet – her family – could she do this? Did she really have to?

They will kill you.

He needs you.

His command stands. What will you do, elf?

Yes, what will you do?

The voices slid in and out of her mind. They taunted, preying on her fears.

She is weak, unworthy.

Our lord is deserving of so much more.

She could give the order if she cannot do this herself, yet all she does is stand there, dithering.

Useless.

She does not love our lord.

"I do, I do love him." She'd closed her eyes – when had she closed her eyes? When had she covered her ears? It didn't stop them from speaking. It didn't stop her from hearing.

You must prove your loyalty.

They will kill you, then our lord.

Give the order if you cannot spill the blood.
Give the order.
Give the order.

The mantra continued as she opened her eyes, lowered her hands. She didn't have to do it herself. She swallowed, found her mouth dry.

"Are they – how many are in the house?" Don't think of who they are. That was the trick, what she needed to remember. It wasn't who. It was what.

Our brethren say there are two.

"Ibestor." The name came out tremulous. Hating that sign of weakness, she tried again. "Ibestor." It came out stronger. The barbarian ambled forward, cocked his head, as Halvark turned back to her, face inscrutable. She licked her lips, then motioned to the shed. "Go inside. There are two in the house below. Kill them."

"Wait." Halvark's interjection had them both looking at him. "We need power, correct, Nerisse?"

"Yes." Was he going to suggest they –

"Then allow me to go with him. Ba'tvian demonstrated something at the cottage, a way draw the life-force of a dying thing to power an arcane working. I can do that here." He gave her an empty smile. "You and the Shadows can scout ahead."

Her mouth trembled. The whispering started again, the insidious voices echoing in the back of her mind. She gave a jerky nod, and they faded away.

"Take them to the storage room in the back of the kitchen." It wasn't near the corridor that led from the surface entrance through the house to the front door that opened onto the streets of Jevanel. She wouldn't have to see them. "It's a cellar. There are thick walls." Earthen walls. She hoped she wouldn't have to hear them. "It should be quieter."

Nerisse reached out with psychic hands to tighten the chains holding the earth surrounding them. As she did so, she watched the men go on ahead. The shed, a sturdy little building built of rough-hewn logs, was unlocked. The door was opened, then shut. She bowed her head, began to murmur to the earth, telling it to drown the screams, to hold the noise from Elvanaeran ears. She kept at it until a Shadow nudged her leg.

They have begun. We must go.

Grief crushed her heart like a steel-clad daemon's fist. One sob escaped before she could suppress it and had her doubling over as she fought for control. Later. She had to hold it until later. When she was done, she could grieve, she could scream. She'd let the world know of her anguish, her pain – later.

With a tear trickling down her face, Nerisse followed the Shadows as they streamed into the shed. She went home as her parents' blood began to soak the stone below.

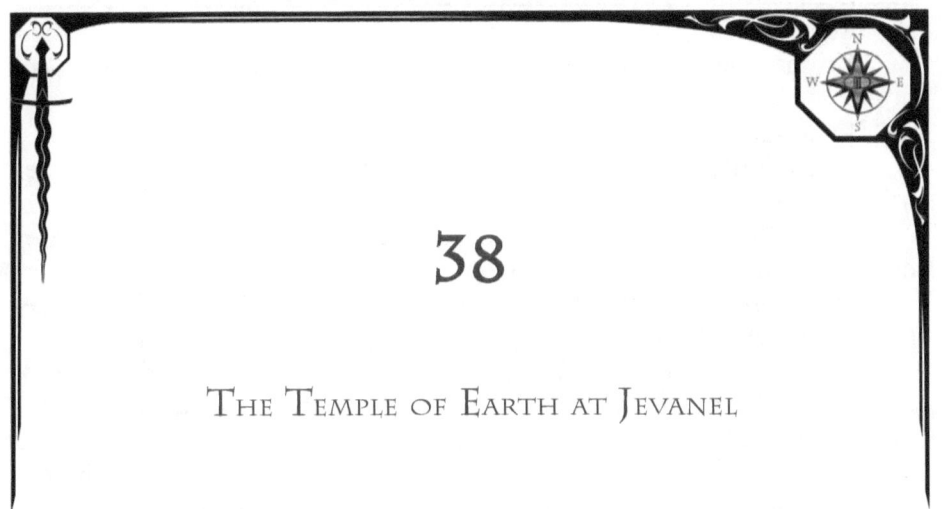

38

THE TEMPLE OF EARTH AT JEVANEL

SAERLAN couldn't sleep. He felt uneasy, oddly alone in his rooms. He'd never been alone. The earth was a constant, comforting presence in his mind. Yet tonight, the earth seemed withdrawn. Silent.

Unable to settle, he rose from his simple bed, searched for his sandals and robe. Dressed, he left his austere chambers to wander the corridors. He was restless; a walk would help calm his mind. There'd been so much going on in the last few months that it was little wonder he was affected. The cleansings, the grieving, the severance...they'd had to reassure their people, bolster the Astorae family. It hadn't been just the loss of a daughter, but the loss of a priestess. Added to that, the manner of her leaving was hard to accept.

As he left his suite, he saw a neophyte priest in the corridor. Garbed in the light blue robe of a novice, he was one of several that had joined their ranks in recent weeks. The boy's name escaped him; he hadn't spent much time with the new members of their faith's order. There'd been too much to do, too little time to do it in.

"Good evening, High One." The novice's shy greeting was soft. "I hope I did not disturb you."

"No, young one, you did not. Are you unable to rest?"

He nodded.

"I thought a walk might help." His expression became rueful. "I'm afraid that I'd lost my way for a bit. I am still learning the halls of the Temple and got turned around."

Understanding, Saerlan gave him a reassuring pat on the

shoulder.

"I remember getting lost in my first days. Do you have your way now?"

He nodded again.

"Then you'd best get back to your rooms before the novice master misses you."

"Yes, High One." He turned to go, yet hesitated. "The earth does not seem happy to me. Am I mistaken?"

The High Priest caught the notes of anxiety in the boy's voice, recalled what he'd been sensing through the day and evening.

"I am unsure. I, too, have sensed something amiss, and will look into it. In the meantime, you need to go to bed, to rest. Tomorrow may bring the answers to tonight's questions."

He stood in the corridor until the sound of the neophyte's footsteps had dwindled away. Turning, he headed for the back of the Temple, to the Rebirthing Grounds where he felt closest to the earth. If the earth was unhappy, there was a reason for it. That reason was likely somewhere in Jevanel.

He just needed to persuade the earth to tell him what it was.

39

The Inn of the Golden Staf in Chalbrooke

PRIALLA led the way, dressed once again as a young man in the gear Raptu had provided. She avoided the tavern patrons as she wound her way through the back halls of the inn toward the alley entrance. Behind her, Raptu followed closely. Ba'tvian had already left, taking his creatures with him.

He'd said something about taking care of the lighting. Candle-lanterns mounted on the building front and atop short poles illuminated the streets of Chalbrooke. As the lantern casings were locked, she wasn't sure how he was going to snuff the candles within them. Was he going to accost the lantern-lighter who maintained this street, steal the key? Or would he use magery?

She stepped out into the chilled air of the alleyway behind the inn, and saw that she needn't have worried. The mouth of the lane was dark. Raptu slung an arm around her shoulders as they came out onto the street, where pools of moonlight illuminated the cobblestone road. They weren't the only ones out in the night air. Though most of the city slept, there were guildsmen off-duty guards, and party-goers out on the streets traveling from one destination to another.

Not all the lanterns had been snuffed. Pinpricks of flickering flame, like fireflies in the night, were scattered along the street. They kept a casual pace, murmuring about inconsequential things as they walked. Ahead of them, the Mancers' Guild sat at the end of the street, a walled monolith squatting in the shadow of the higher city wall butting up behind it.

"Do you see them, those freakish things of his?"

Raptu's question was hissed low in her ear. She scanned their surroundings as discreetly as she could manage.

"No." That didn't mean they weren't there. The damn things could be hard to spot when they wanted to be. "How many Mancers do you think are out right now?"

"He would say too many. I say not enough." She could hear the scowl in his voice. "He's more confident about this scheme of his than I am."

Prialla was not as sanguine about it, either. The two fell silent as they drew closer. Nerves skittered through her blood, fluttered in her stomach. The guild entrance, a set of two iron lattice doors, stood in grim silence in the two-story high wall that fronted the property. A single point of light moved behind the door – a handheld lantern carried by whoever manned the gate.

They were not a dozen steps away when she began to doubt if Ba'tvian was where he was supposed to be. He'd said that he would be in position at the gate. Maybe – perhaps he'd done as he had out on the moors, used the darkness to conceal his presence. The Shadows seemed deeper, thicker here.

Don't dither, Prialla. I am here.

She just managed to mask her surprise at his telepathic voice. Taking a deep breath, she forced herself to relax, caught Raptu's eye, gave him a subtle nod. His arm fell away. He stepped forward to rap on the doors.

"Good evening, lord." He used the customary mode of address for a Mancer, as the lantern on the other side swung toward them. It illuminated the face of a young man garbed in a Mancer's usual leather gear and black cloak. The guild's seal emblazoned on the cloak broach glinted in the yellow-orange light. "My friend and I have come into the city today and we saw some…things along our way that we thought unusual. Someone in the tavern said we might come here to find out more about them. Black things, slithering through the grass like snakes or lizards. We didn't get too close to them, though I could make out white eyes."

"You couldn't miss them," Prialla muttered her addition. "The eyes glowed."

The Mancer gave them a narrowed stare, frowning at the description.

"Where did you see them?"

"We were on the Chal-Edon, between Rathburn and Chalbrooke." He looked thoughtful as if judging the distance. "Perhaps an hour's journey from here at a steady trot. Do you know what they might be?"

"There are a few possibilities," the other man replied. He seemed concerned over the news. "We've heard rumors of such sightings though little more than that. Would you mind coming in, speaking one of the guild masters? I'm certain that they will be interested in hearing a first-hand accounting."

Perfect. Prialla had hoped it would be this easy.

"Yes, we can do that." At Raptu's assent, the Mancer brought out a ring of keys, chose one of the larger ones on it to unlock the door. He opened it, stepped aside to let them in.

Ba'tvian's creatures struck.

They swarmed like angry ants moving at the speed of stooping falcon. Though she had seen their quick agility demonstrated earlier, this was faster, this was worse. They didn't just cover him. They wrapped around his body, his throat, squeezed. He opened his mouth – a reflexive reaction – and one of the smaller Shadows crawled inside. He choked, eyes wide, collapsed to his knees.

She watched in fascination as he struggled to crawl away.

"Get inside."

The order jolted her. She hurried to obey it. Behind her, Ba'tvian passed through the gate with Raptu bringing up the rear. He bent down to retrieve the fallen ring of keys, then closed and locked the door. Ba'tvian drew his sword – another provision by Raptu. His pets re-doubled their efforts. The Mancer's limbs gave out as he gurgled. He fell on his side, body convulsing. Blood shone like ebon oil in the moonlight, trickling out from around the thing that wriggled its way down his throat. The wide eyes glazed over, the convulsions stilled. As the creatures released their hold on the body, Ba'tvian used his sword to slice into the torso, utilized its length to crack the sternum, spread the rib cage.

Reaching inside with a gloved hand, he tore out the heart. He murmured an incantation as he squeezed the organ, dripping the blood in a complex pattern on the ground. The blood flared red, the droplets joining into thin lines.

"Won't they sense this?" It was common knowledge that most Mancers were also mages to one degree or another. Prialla peered around them. She saw no one. It didn't reassure her. "What is it for?"

"They won't sense it. I've seen to that." Ba'tvian finished his ritual, setting the organ aflame then letting go of it. It hit the center of the diagram causing the whole thing to light up in a burst of arcane energy. "As to what it's for, it will serve as a focus for the rest of tonight's work. It will also call more of my Shadows here."

He looked from one to the other.

"My followers tell me that there are only a handful of Mancers in the courtyards and stables. The rest of them are in the main hall or barracks." He reminded them of their assignments as his Shadowed Ones began to group themselves into escorts for each of them. "They know what to do. Go for the quick kill, keep the noise to a minimum, and don't waste time. Stealth and speed are vital."

He glanced across the courtyard at the Guild House itself. Lights burned in a few of the windows and in the lanterns bracketing the front entrance. He felt his blood quicken with anticipation.

"We will meet in the barracks." Ba'tvian's smile was ice cold. "We will slaughter them like sheep."

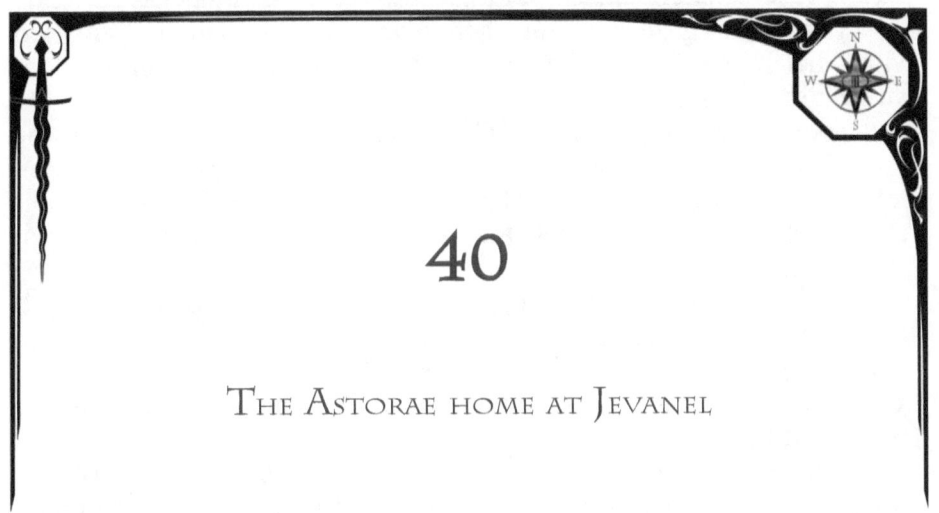

40

THE ASTORAE HOME AT JEVANEL

NERISSE felt adrift on the sea of what she'd begun. It was surreal, being home after all this time, after all that had happened. She wandered the corridors of the place where she'd grown up in, found her feet taking her to her old room. It was a mistake. She *knew* it was a mistake yet she couldn't help it. She had to see it.

The door swung open at her touch. She stepped inside the pitch-black room, reaching up to a shrouded fixture next to the entryway without a thought. She uncovered the glass globe, filled with the luminous fungi her people used for indoor lighting, and let the cloth fall from her fingers. The white light spilled into the room. It was empty.

There was no furniture, no possessions, not even a speck of dust.

It was a slap in the face, a punch in the gut. Ba'tvian had been right, she thought, as the tears burned in her eyes. He'd been right. They didn't love her. If they had, they would have kept the room, kept something of her.

Grief turned to pain. Pain morphed into anger. Anger was better. It would get her through everything else she needed to do.

"They can cut me out of their lives," she whispered, willing the tears away. "But they can't kill me. I won't let them kill me. Ba'tvian needs me too much."

She turned on her heel, left the room without a backward glance. When Halvark stepped out into the corridor her voice was cool, controlled.

"It's done?"

"Yes." His gaze bore into her, searching. Apparently satisfied with what he saw, he looked behind him to find Ibestor in the door way leading into the kitchen.

"Then we're finished here. Come with me." She headed for the front entrance of the house, stepped out onto the worn path that ran between the rows of homes. That dream-like quality settled over her again, though it didn't touch the anger she held tight in her heart. The city hadn't changed.

The underground cavern that cradled Jevanel was vast. It wasn't dark. The same fungi that lit her room grew on the ceiling, the fungal colonies glowing like clusters of stars. The beauty of their display was lost on Nerisse as she marched down the lane towards the Temple of Earth.

If anyone saw them as they made their way through the city, she didn't care. She rode her anger all the way to the Temple's common entrance. It lacked a door. The Temple of Earth welcomed anyone who came looking for guidance, reassurance, or peace of mind.

Like the city, the Temple remained as she remembered it. The sheer, austere façade was imposing, running from the cavern floor to the rocky surface overhead. The arcade spanning the forefront of its second level stood vacant, the Supplicants' Garden surrounding the entry ways at its base was devoid of people. There was a tension in the air, an uneasiness that felt like grease in the mind. It came from the earth.

The earth had no choice but to accept what was to come. Hurt, resentful, grieving, Nerisse was not willing to sympathize or back down. How could they? How could they judge her lord, judge her, then do everything they could to hurt them both?

She let the waves of her emotions carry her into the Temple. She barely noticed the Shadows gathering around her, didn't register their growing excitement, or notice that she'd drawn the ritual blade Ba'tvian had given her for their rites. When the corridor led to another hall, she made the turn without thinking, and collided with a neophyte.

She reacted on instinct. The blade rammed point-first into his gut. Withdrawing it, she slashed it across his throat as he doubled over. Her lord's pets pounced on him as he gurgled, slurping up the blood as it spilled out from the wounds.

Shocked and shaking over her own actions, Nerisse stumbled back, looked away. Her breath, coming hard, fast, shuddered in her breast.

His was an easy death. However cruel, no matter how much it

sickened that small part of her that retained what little innocence she still had, there would be worse yet to come. She needed there to be.

She looked at her companions. Both watched with a strange, horrified fascination as the Shadows began to feed in earnest. She ignored the sounds of flesh being consumed, turning her back on them so she wouldn't have to see.

"The novice quarters are this way." She gestured towards a side corridor, then indicated the direction she'd been heading in. "The main altar is in that direction. The novices aren't allowed to lock their rooms. Fetch me two, and bring them to the altar."

They nodded. She hurried past the feast in progress, refused to look down at it. By the time the others came back with the sacrifices, altar needed to be ready. She would use her own blood to re-consecrate it –

– to Ba'tvian's glory.

41

THE MANCERS' GUILD IN CHALBROOKE

B A'TVIAN entered the stables, his followers creeping in around him. They glided silently in the dark, dispersing to find the grooms that lived in the lofts. In the stalls, horses snorted and shifted uneasily. He walked to the nearest one, grabbed the bridle, and murmured low to the beast as he stroked its nose. As it settled down, as more of his creatures slipped in among the other horses, he ceased petting.

Drawing a blade, he slit the animal's throat. In the other stalls, the horses reacted to the smell of blood, neighing, kicking, rearing. The Shadows swarmed up their bodies, causing massive panic in the stables as they entered through the mouths, the nostrils. The larger ones began to chew their way into the bellies to get at the softer tissue.

His own victim tried to scream, tried to jerk away. Crimson liquid seeped; He hauled on the bridle, driving the knife through the horse's eye into the brain. It collapsed, blood spurting from its neck wound. He ignored the death throes, dipped his fingers into the blood to draw on the floor of the aisle that run through the middle of the building.

Above him, he could hear thumps, muffled yells, a strangled screech. He continued to layout his diagram with calm, precise strokes of his wet fingers.

The lines of blood glowed.

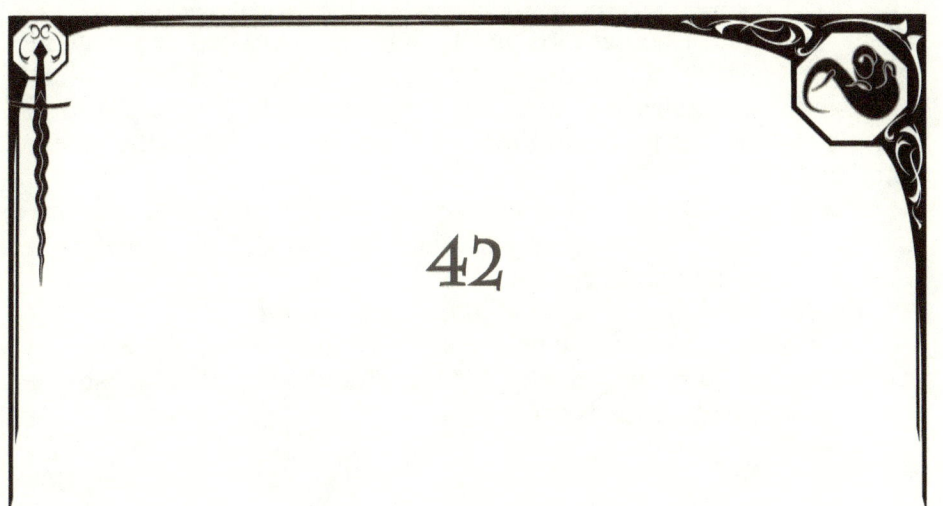

42

PRIALLA followed Raptu along the wall. Ba'tvian's things surged on ahead, spotting a roaming sentry before they did, overtaking him with a quickness that stunned. By the time they reached the man, he was a twitching, bloodied corpse.

She was forced to admit that they were efficient. She paused long enough harvest some of the life force the sentry's death released, then sought out the entrance to the armory building. They'd bypassed the one that led into the courtyard; it was too open. Instead, they rounded to the back of the building where the practice targets and outdoor sparring areas were set up. The rear door was bare of lanterns, cast in darkness by the moon. When they tried the door, they found it locked.

Raptu brought out a set of lock picks. As he worked, Prialla kept watch for any other patrols. She glimpsed one just as the Shadows attacked. She heard nothing as he staggered, clawed, twisted, collapsed. Another movement caught her attention, this one along the top of the wall that surrounded the Guild property. More ethereal creatures were slithering over the wall, joining their brethren or darting off towards the stables. By the time Raptu opened the door, the things had tripled in number.

Without a word, they split up as they entered the armory. Ba'tvian had been very specific about they needed to find, what they had to do.

Prialla opened the first door she came to, conjuring a small mage light so she could see. Barrels of practice swords lined one side, while crossbows hung from the wall opposite. It was the wrong room. She didn't bother closing the door as she exited and began to go through each. She found more rooms full of weapons, a small workshop for repairing or making things that didn't require a forge. With only three more to go on her side of the building, she entered another room.

There were shelves filled with small, corked caskets of oil, spare lanterns, torches, rope, sacks of feathers for fletching and other miscellaneous items. She smiled.

Raptu, I've found it. Second to last door on the left.

Sensing his acknowledgement, she picked up a casket. She drew a knife, pared away the wax sealing the cork. She worked the stopper out, then stepped into the corridor.

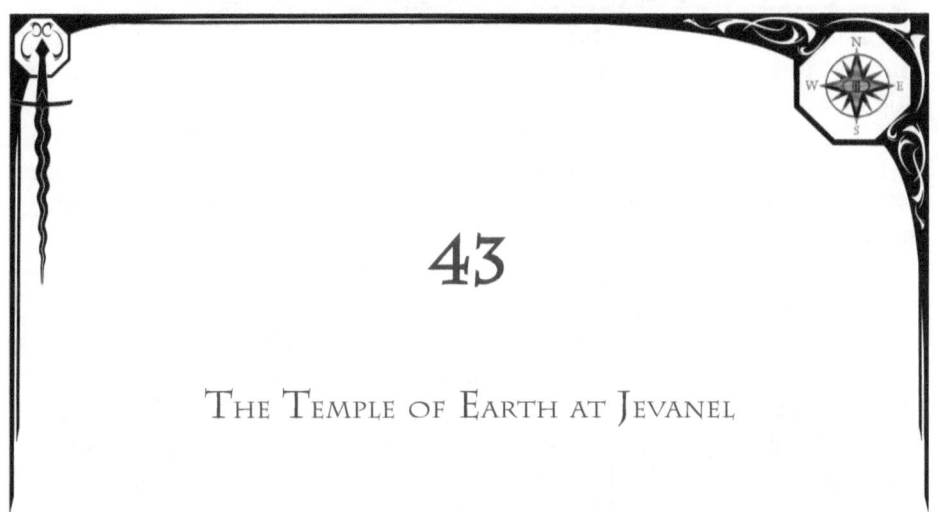

43

THE TEMPLE OF EARTH AT JEVANEL

NERISSE watched her blood pool on the altar, saw it seep into the polished surface as she finished her whispered incantation. Crimson dripped over the edge, down the sides, droplets of it hitting the floor. Her voice faded to a dry rasp with the last syllable. A metallic clinking noise sounded on the raised dais to signal the she'd dropped her ritual knife. She swayed in place a moment, then pitched forward as her legs gave out. She fell against the stone, her torso landing in the red liquid. Blood – her blood – soaked the front of her winter dress.

Her head spun with the loss of it. The scent roiled her stomach.

She had prepared for this. Breathing through clenched teeth, she levered herself up, pushed away from the altar. She kept one hand braced on it, leaning over slowed to reach for her bag and the medicines she'd concocted. She sipped from two flasks – one for the shock, the other clarity of mind – then brought out bandages, ointment. She tended to the wounds she'd made on her wrists with exaggerated care.

Done, her mind clearing of the light-headed fog, she studied the altar. There was only thing left to cement its new purpose. As if cued, Halvark stepped into the hall. Behind him, he dragged two unconscious acolytes.

So young. It struck her hard, their youth. How old were they? One could have been her age, the other no more than fifteen. Elvanaran boys dedicated to the priesthood – and they would die before realizing their potential.

Halvark dropped the larger at the bottom of the steps leading up the altar. Hefting the smaller of the two, he carried him up to place him on the stone. Nerisse stared, blank-eyed, at the sacrifice. Must she do this? Wasn't there another way?

Too late. It's too late. I can't turn back now. All chances to walk away from this are long gone. I knew that – didn't I know that? When I chose Ba'tvian – chose love – didn't I know that there would be no return?

She couldn't remember. In the end, it didn't matter. It was her reality now. The time for such choices was over.

"Hold him down." Her voice sounded hollow, raw. Halvark obeyed without a word. At the far end of hall, Ibestor dragged more unconscious victims into the room. She paid neither man heed as she took up the knife she'd dropped. The blade struck, sharp and quick, cutting through the belly, under the ribcage. As she fought to get at his heart, the boy slipped into death, oblivious.

Nerisse's tears mingled with the blood that spilled forth.

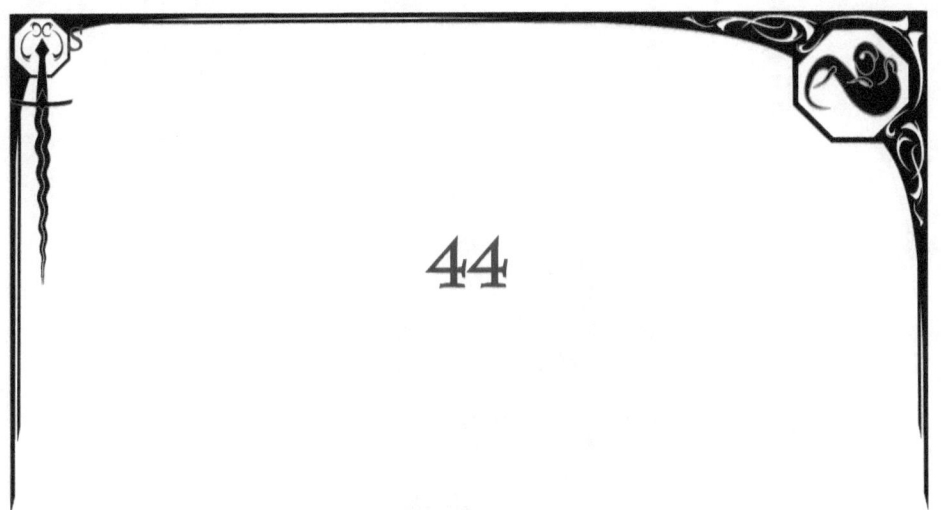

44

SAERLAN wondered into the Rebirthing Grounds. He spoke to no one as he trod the path that wound past the grottos grown over with moss and luminous mushrooms. Most grottos were occupied with priests overseeing the final steps of spiritual cleansing. They exchanged wordless nods when they saw one another. The High Priest's brethren were tired, weary. There had been so many vigils it was little wonder that his people were feeling the weight of their burden.

Yet as he turned to go back the way he'd come, he found that his night-time walk had done little good. Unease still plagued him. He prayed as he began the journey back, asking the earth to reveal what was wrong. Though he received no answer, he continued to try.

When he reached the stone curtains that separated the Grounds from the rest of the Temple complex he heard the earth groan. The cavern trembled. Power flared, an ethereal teasing at the very edge of his arcane awareness. The world stilled.

He took off running for the Temple's main hall.

45

The Mancers' Guild in Chalbrooke

B A'TVIAN finished the rite. Death lay all around him, the charnel smell of it a foul perfume that permeated every nook and cranny of the building. He stood in a state of heightened senses, eyes closed, arms spread with hands fisted, as he concentrated on the rhythmic beat of magic that vibrated the air. He wove it into a simple spell, something he could trigger from elsewhere. He laid it over the mangers. From there it would spread out on its own.

Behind him, the stable door opened to admit a skulking Raptu and Prialla. He felt his comrades stop just inside the door, detecting their surprise, their excitement. Their unease.

His Shadowed Ones clung to every surface. Some were piled on others. Over half the number present had traveled from far off to answer his summons, to partake in the bounty he'd promised them. All focused their attention on him, their glowing eyes pulsing in time with the power. They'd feasted, grown, strengthened.

He had given them a boon. They had earned it through loyalty. They would also repay it ten-fold should they stray from him. He'd gifted them power to use on their own. It would fade before the night was over yet while they had it, they could use it for anything they desired – so long as it promoted Ba'tvian's own ambitions.

Their approval was a caress in his mind. He open his hands, felt the residual magic being absorbed through his palms as he lowered them and turned to face his companions.

"Was it necessary to kill the horses?" Raptu asked. "Not that the nags the Mancers use are of much val…" His voice trailed off as Ba'tvian opened his eyes. He wondered what the noble saw in them.

He sees you, lord. For the first time, he sees you as you truly are. The dark, sibilant hiss in his mind was pleased. He gave them a cold smile.

"Come with me." He led them down the center aisle to the far end of the stables, past the blood-spattered stalls, the half-eaten equine carcasses. The Shadows followed in their wake. "You found the oil."

"And did as instructed," Prialla confirmed in a quiet tone.

"Good."

They exited the building, entering a covered breezeway constructed between the stables and the right wing of the Guild House. They paused at the barracks door. Ba'tvian gestured for his oldest followers to enter first. They did so, their ethereal bodies slipping through the creaks around the sturdy door.

He could see them in his mind's eye. They scattered through the halls, ascending to the upper floors, seeking occupied rooms, late night roamers – anyone who lived. When they found their targets, there was no mercy. Deaths were quick, messy. Once a kill was made, most moved on in search of the next. Ba'tvian gave them enough time to clear at least the first floor before he led the others inside.

All of them had studied the layout. The Guild's heart lay in the left wing. Without speaking, they split up again as they left the barracks to cross the great hall into that heart. The place was as quiet as a tomb.

Raptu took the stairs to the top-floor; Prialla laid claim to the ground level. Ba'tvian had plans for the library that lay on the second floor – and the still office he'd spied while at the gate. The Shadowed Ones went with them.

Almost as an after-thought, Ba'tvian triggered the spell he'd set in the stable at the end of the rite. Seen only by the dead that lay there, the straw began to burn.

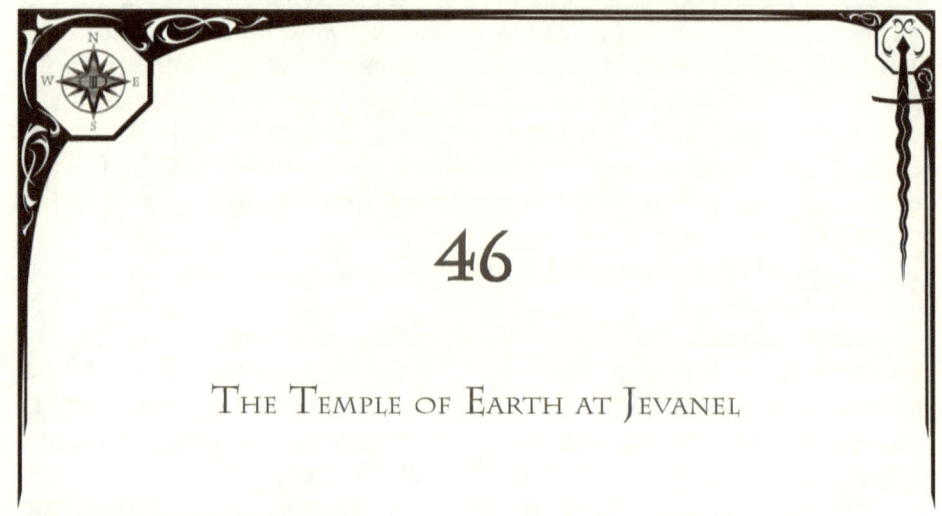

46

The Temple of Earth at Jevanel

NERISSE, her hands unsteady, gestured for Ibestor to take the body off the altar. Halvark replaced it with another. As they worked, she invested the stolen life force into the stone. The power drained out of her like the blood draining out of the victims. Her stomach clenched again. She gripped the altar for balance as the room took a slow spin. She waited for the nausea to pass before beginning again.

After the first two, she ceased seeing the faces of the sacrifices. It helped somewhat to think of them as animals, something already dead or dying. Keeping them unconscious served to reinforce the illusion. Of course, if they'd been awake, able to feel what she was doing, then she wouldn't need so many of them. Fear, terror, despair – their emotions would have multiplied the power harvested by a factor of one and a half.

Wet warmth landed the back of her hand. It was amazing, a miracle, that she still had tears to shed. They'd started to fall with the first victim, and had yet to stop.

How much time had passed? She didn't think it had been very much. Ba'tvian had told her once that a practiced blood mage could ritually dispatch a victim in the time it took to count to thirty. He'd claimed that he'd done as many as forty-seven in the span of less than half an hour. She wasn't as practiced as he was. Her knowledge of anatomy sped up the process, but her meager medical training was a poor substitute for skill.

This was the sixth, she thought, plying the knife in a way that no longer required her concentration. Familiar with the routine now, her hands moved of their own volition. If they trembled, she didn't notice.

There was a muted sound at the far end of the hall. In the recesses of her awareness, she could sense the silent cry of the earth. It was leaden with grief, with fear. A warning. *For whom? For me?* She looked up as she plunged her hand into the now open body cavity.

She saw the horrified face of the High Priest.

Guilt, fear, desperation – it all swirled in her mind. She stumbled back, the room spinning wildly. Squeezing her eyes shut to forestall nausea the motion brought, she whimpered. She heard a shout, felt the harsh spark of power in the air as whispers filled her ears. She clamped bloody hands over them, falling to her knees with a sob.

Finish it.

Kill him now.

He would kill you, kill our master…

He must die before you do.

Our master has such faith in you…

Will you shame him?

Do you not love our lord?

"Yes, I love him." Tears spilling in earnest, the whispering now a roar in her mind, she fought for control. She labored to rise to her feet.

When she opened her eyes again, the world was a dream-like in her vision. The knife was still in her hand. The body on the altar still breathed, unaware of its mortal wound. Corpses draped over the stairs leading up to the dais like macabre ornaments. Halvark and Ibestor had abandoned their posts on either side of the sacrifice. They now held a struggling Saerlan.

Nerisse ignored the man she had once loved like a favorite uncle as she approached the altar once more to finish what she'd started. He tried to speak to her, calling out. She couldn't understand him. His voice was a muffled din, drowned out by the hissing of Ba'tvian's followers.

The edges of her sight feathered now. Shock, blood-loss, extreme fatigue – that's what it meant. She didn't have much more time before a collapse, even with the magic to keep her going. She delved into the body cavity again. Her fingers found the slow-beating heart, gripped it. Her other hand worked the knife in, cutting through the arteries that tethered it. She pulled it out, raised it up, murmured without sound the chant required. The heart burned as she stepped back, gesturing to the elven shell on the stone.

Halvark came forward to yank it off. Ibestor dragged up the still screaming High Priest to take its place.

His death cries echoed in the empty Temple, unheard by those outside its walls.

47

The Mancers' Guild in Chalbrooke

BA'TVIAN found the office he was looking for. The door was ajar, the light spilling out into the hall like a beacon. On this floor, it was the only one occupied. He didn't bother with subterfuge.

He pushed the door wide, stepping into the light. His sword was held low at his; the blade caught the golden light. Candles burned in the large lantern that hung in the middle of the room. A smaller, older man, sat behind the desk, dressed in a much lighter version of the Mancer's trademark gear with gray streaking his golden hair. He looked up, puzzlement and consternation defining his face as he rose from his seat.

"Who are you?" he demanded. His hand crept to the short sword strapped to his side as his doe-brown eyes narrowed. "What are you doing here?"

"I'm surprised you don't recognize me. Are you not Zerick Mancerson, head of the Guild?" Ba'tvian's voice was mocking as he advanced. "You've searched for me, hunted me. I thought it was time for us to meet, put an end to the game."

"Game?" He shifted, keeping the desk between him and the blood mage while maneuvering the chair out of his way. "What game? Who are you?"

The loud words carried into the hall like a clarion. There was no one to hear them.

"Pity. Not what I expected from someone who had lived this long in your profession." Ba'tvian gathered his power. His followers, half-seen shapes against the stone and wood, flitted into place. "But then, you're not much of a mage, are you? No arcane talent to speak of."

He bared his teeth in a feral grin, raised his sword. Crimson flame flickered along its length.

"Look behind you."

The Mancer didn't. He kept focused on him, side-stepping around the desk. Ba'tvian shoved the chair towards the man, reversing his path to intercept him before he reached the door. Their blades clashed in a shower of sparks. Ba'tvian, unskilled a swordsman as he was, used his strength and height to his advantage. The Mancer was forced back as the blood mage kicked out.

The man gave a startled yell as a creature struck his calf, sinking its teeth deep in the muscle. It twisted, tearing the flesh. Ba'tvian kneed the man in the crotch, driving his sword down on his opponent's blade. The Mancer fell to his knees. His sword, still raised, was the only thing preventing the flaming weapon from cutting into him.

"Allow me to introduce myself." Quick as a viper, the blood mage wrenched his sword up, drove it in low as another of his Shadows bit into the man's side. The metal length rammed into the torso up its cross guard. The Mancer dropped his weapon to clutch at the hilt. Eyes holding a cruel glow, he yanked his victim's head back with one hand.

"I am Lord Ba'tvian Delthanurk, blood mage and Dark Adept. You and your order have grown weak, Mancer. Weak to fall so easily." The hand that grasped the sword withdrew it. "Die knowing that I have destroyed you. Your Guild may linger on its death bed, yet it, too, will follow you into darkness."

With that promise, he cut off his head.

He studied the headless corpse as it toppled over, as the dark things swarmed over it. He dropped the head into the resultant chaos, then left the room.

It had been indulgent, he thought. That little speech had been nothing but indulgence. Still, he had earned it, had he not?

Yes, lord. The mental hiss was echoed by a chorus of others.

He made his way to the library. He pushed open the doors to find more of his loyal ones piling books in the center of the room. There were two heaps, one much smaller than the other. He scanned the contents of each, nodded in satisfaction. Using some of the death energy he'd gathered, he created a portal to his own library, a secret cavern on the Skeleton Coast. The vigilant guards of this treasured possession came through the gate to carry the newest acquisitions back with them. They were also Shadowed Ones, ordered to this duty more than two years before. He touched each as they returned to their posting, transferring a little of the bounty he had taken for himself to them. When the last of the smaller pile had vanished through the portal, he closed it.

With the gate dismissed, he sent his mind seeking. He had no link to Raptu, so could not speak with him directly. Instead, he found one of the Shadows escorting him.

Where is Raptu?

The third floor, lord. The fourth was empty. The third held two. It sent images of a gruesome slaying, then more of a fight in progress. *He will finish here soon.*

End the fight. We are almost done here. He contacted Prialla. With her loyalty given, with the sex they'd sealed their bargain with, he had a link to her mind now. *Are you finished?*

Yes. The ground level of the administration section and dining hall were clear. There were three in the kitchens. There were taken out quickly.

I am done, though Raptu is not. Find the oil stores.

I'm ahead of you there. He felt her smile in his mind as he dropped the link.

He laid another spell over the books, then left the floor. He checked with his followers. A handful remained alive, cornered in the barracks. They would die soon enough.

By the time he found Prialla, Raptu had joined her. The excited grin on his face was the only indication of his success that Ba'tvian needed. He gestured them to come with him, leading the way out of the Guild House.

They stepped out into the courtyard. Wisps of smoke were escaping the stables. Ba'tvian watched them curl into the night air as his creatures touched his awareness to report in. He murmured an order. Moments later, Shadows poured out of every opening in the Guild. Raising one hand, he created another portal.

"I am given to understand that there are two at the Tretoan estate that are in need of killing."

"Yes." Prialla raised her brows at his soft statement. "They aren't a part of our agreement with you."

"They are a part of Nerisse's agreement with Halvark." Ba'tvian felt the magic flare, saw the basement coalesce in the gate's center. "I will honor the bargain struck, taking public credit for their deaths. You and Raptu will take them tonight. I will join you when I am done here."

He faced them.

"Make it a full rite, using one at a time. I will return in time enough for the second. Go."

Raptu passed through the portal first. Prialla hesitated a moment. Ba'tvian reached out, touched her cheek, smearing blood over the skin. The faint lines in her face melted away.

"I will teach you, just as I have promised."

She nodded, then followed their comrade. The portal closed after her. Left in a courtyard filled with Shadowed Ones, Ba'tvian turned back to the Guild House. Together, he and his loyal ones triggered their spells.

The compound exploded into a hellish inferno.

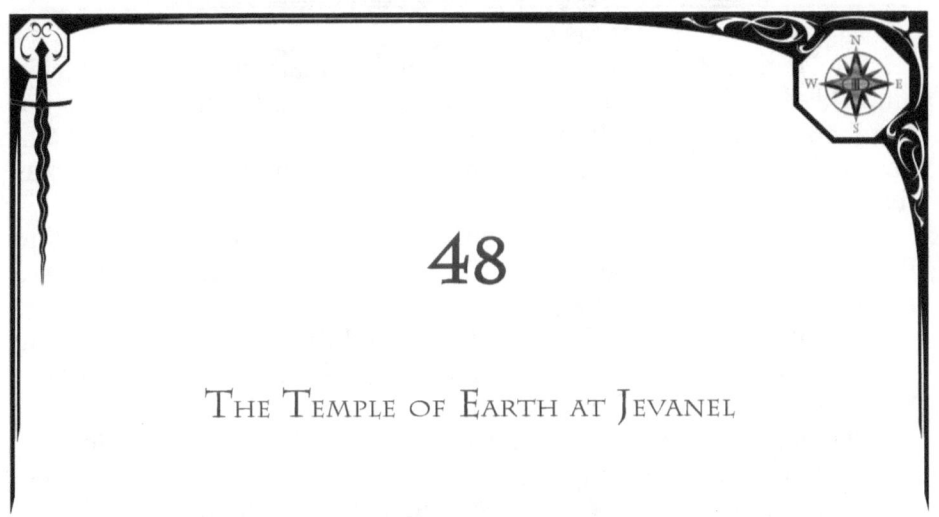

48

THE TEMPLE OF EARTH AT JEVANEL

NERISSE retched on the floor. She had lost the fight with sickness this time.

No more. I don't have to...do anymore...

Thirteen, combined with the harvested energies of the previous kills, were all that she'd needed. She didn't bother getting up from where she lay, half-sprawled. She just scooted over to lean her back against the altar in an upright position. Eyes closed, she sought for the chains she'd forged around the earth of this region. Her mental hands found them, fumbled to grip them tight.

Focus...focus...

Her concentration wavered. She was approaching the end of her strength. It didn't help that the draught she'd taken earlier had lost its effect. Around her, the hall echoed with voices. Accusing voices... damning words...they battered her shields.

They know in death what they did not in life...

That's what her teachers had always maintained. Did the slain linger? Were they the ones calling to her?

Do not listen.

Do as you promised our lord.

You must succeed...

You must prove yourself...

The Shadows' whispers drowned out the phantom echoes. She used them as a shield while she painstakingly wrought new links, fresh chains, with the power she'd stolen. Engrossed in the task, she didn't register the hand on her shoulder until moments after new energy began to pour into her.

Halvark. He'd kept his word.

She locked the chains in place, joining them together in a web embedded in the earth until she held the end of only one. Exhaustion weighed her down, made her sluggish. As she held that final chain, her body was numb. Its response to her mental commands was feeble.

"Ibestor...carry me." She didn't feel him pick her up. Cradled in the barbarian's arms, her eyes still closed, her voice faint, she spoke again. "Halvark...the gate."

Moments passed. How many she couldn't tell. She was drifting now, anchored in place by the chain she still held and the whispers of her lord's followers in her ears.

"Done." Halvark's pronouncement was muffled to her senses.

"Leave...must leave..." Mustering the last of her strength, she pulled on the chain. She passed into the unconsciousness as they fled, as death fed death. The Earth's Womb, the cavern that housed her once beloved city of Jevanel, began to collapse in on itself.

The screaming voices hounded her in her dreams.

49

The Mancers' Guild in Chalbrooke

B A'TVIAN stepped outside the front gate into the street. There was a crowd gathering, a bucket brigade being mustered to contain the fire. The citizens of Chalbrooke stood between him and the Inn of the Golden Stag.

Well, there was more than one way to deal with that.

Using the link Nerisse had gifted him with, he drew upon the earth, forcing his mind into it. He felt the pavement, the stone of the wall behind him, the structures of the buildings along the road. He sensed the dim beating of people's hearts. The blood mage poured raw power into the stones of the wall, the road, taking care not to be caught up in the havoc he was about to unleash. As he did so, he sent his Shadows into the crowd.

They came as a black wave, surging towards the people, ripping into them as they panicked. The screams, the pain, the fear – if the creatures didn't get them, they fell to each other, being trampled by the mob in its effort to escape. Ba'tvian fueled himself with all of it, rode the exhilaration, the ecstasy. It was perhaps the finest pleasure he had ever experienced.

He laughed as he spent the last vestige of stolen power to burst the paving and stone. The Guild wall erupted, flaming rocks trailing smoke flying up into the air to arc over the crowd. They smashed into the buildings, setting their wooden structures on fire. The street exploded under the crowd. Many of the people fell to the onslaught of stone and Shadow.

It was fresh death, new glory. Yet he could not bask in it, much as he wanted to. He conjured a portal beside, spoke to the crowd. He used a tiny bit of his personal stores of magic to carry his voice through the city.

"This is the fate of all who challenge Ba'tvian Delthanurk."

He stepped through the portal as the words reverberated through the streets.

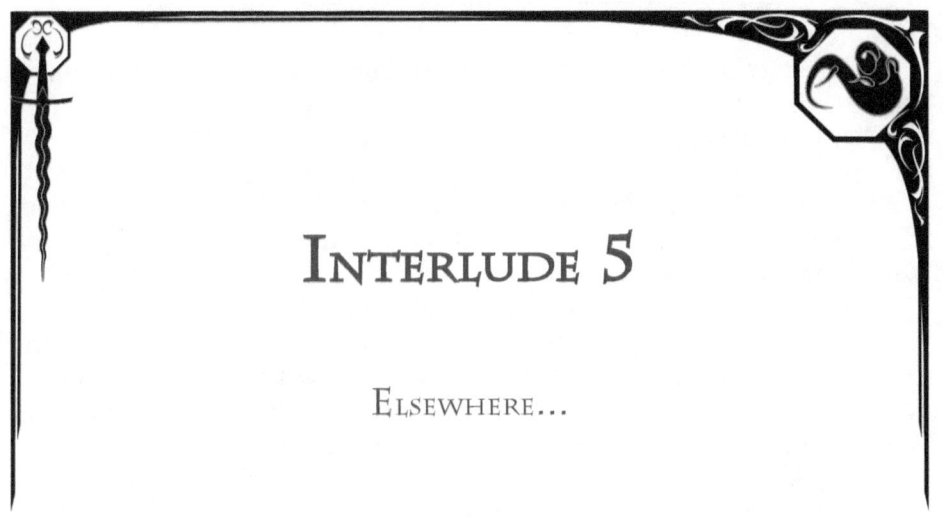

INTERLUDE 5

ELSEWHERE...

LABIYAL Biyalban watched the display in the large mirror from behind desk. Seated to his left was his sire, the Daemon Lord Biyal. The Daemon smiled, swirling wine in his goblet. As the blood mage made his exit, the view panned slowly over the crowds, through the Chalbrooke. The panic had spread wide – in no small part due to the Shadows that swarmed in the streets. Already, some citizens were in flight, heading out of city-state.

"Your pet is showing his potential," he stated, pleased. "Our king will be happy to hear of his progress."

"He still has more to do before he achieves our goals." Labiyal flicked a finger at the enchanted silvered glass. The image of the destruction in Chalbrooke slide away to be replaced by one of a cottage basement in Rathburn. Two cloaked figures where hauling a pair of struggling, bound prisoners into the room from the stairwell.

"Who are these twain?" Biyal sipped his wine, narrowing his eyes.

"My pet has acquired new minions." The half-Daemon observed them for a moment. "He has bound them to him. The others will be bound in due time. They will aid him in our endeavors much in the same way as the renegade priestess does."

"Ah." The older male frowned. "This…reliance on others may prove to be a weakness."

Labiyal's lips curved.

"It isn't reliance so much as manipulation and domination. Should any of his tools fail, he will find a way to make use of their failure before replacing them. Ba'tvian Delthanurk is nothing if not resourceful."

"These two – the Shadows follow them, as well?" Biyal gestured at the dark creatures that crept about the room in the mirror.

"No. Their presence is Ba'tvian's doing."

The rite began. The subject of their conversation joined them. Labiyal flicked a finger again to shift the image to someplace else. The view soared and swooped a bit – the result of using the Chained One in raven form for spying here.

Just off the trade route that ran through the eastern moorlands, two riders rode through the countryside: a young boy and a Mancer. Approaching from the west along the road, a carriage with a mounted escort slowed to halt as they drew near. A horseman hailed the riders. Though the mirror conveyed no sound, the expression of the Mancer Absol Omine was clear.

"He seems quite upset. Who is the boy?"

"A foundling. Omine stumbled upon him in the ruins of the Spirlan Forest after the Great Earthquake." Labiyal narrowed his eyes at the child. He had little information on him yet could surmise the reason for his presence on the moors. "Apparently, he is to follow in the man's footsteps. New Mancers are trained at the Guild House – or were."

"One day," Biyal intoned, glaring at the group discussing the recent events in the glass, "there will be no one willing to tread that path."

"It is Ba'tvian's aim to make it so."

Again, the scene in the mirror changed. A galleon plowed through the sea, its ebon sails filled with the winds summoned by its captain. The man stood beside the helm, a hand resting on the hilt of his cutlass. He bore the weathered complexion and sharp face of a Dithume, one the long-lived human races. He was speaking with two others, identical twins who bore a resemblance to the ship's captain.

"More of your toys?" Biyal raised an eyebrow. "What is their significance?"

"You shall see, sire." Labiyal watched the pirate ship with satisfaction. "You, and all of Einlienn, shall see."

DESCENT
INTO
DARKNESS

PART 5

HIS
REVENGE

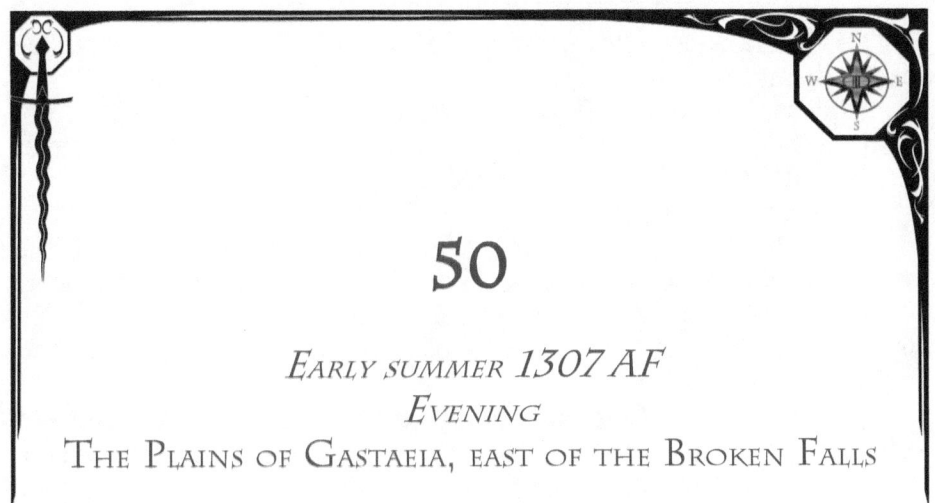

50

Early summer 1307 AF
Evening
The Plains of Gastaeia, east of the Broken Falls

BLOOD sprayed as Ba'tvian Delthanurk sliced the knife across the throat of a Mancer. The man was already bloody, beaten, scraped over – the results of his fellow blood mage Raptu Carthier's method of transport: dragging him behind a horse. Half-dead, he was hardly worth the effort of a ritual. So Ba'tvian ended him, then rewarded his Shadows.

This one is yours.

The blood mage straightened from his kneeling position, letting the head fall back the ground, sidestepping his loyal ones as they swarmed the still warm corpse. Turning his back on the wet sounds of rending flesh and cracking bone, he scanned his surroundings.

He didn't look like the callow youth from three years before. At the start, he had been slim, fit, non-descript. The years spent on the run had hardened his body, made the muscles lean, the features of his face sharp. Glimmers of crimson could be seen in the depths of his eyes.

Now those eyes searched the surrounding plains. When all they saw was the inky black of night his mind stretched out, searching for minds that shouldn't be there. When he found none, he strode back to the cold camp set up twenty feet away. There, his adepts waited for him.

Adepts.

As the world measured a mage, the rank of adept was defined by the amount of power a mage could control. For him, and those that followed him, the label of adept was not a true denotion of their rank. A few of his cohorts – Raptu Carthier, for one – would never ascend higher than a Master level mage. Yet that was what the populace called them: Dark Adepts.

It pleased Ba'tvian. It was an acknowledgement of power, if not skill or knowledge. That recognition mattered, as did the fear that flavored it. Regardless of that success, he refused to grow lax.

Because it wasn't enough. Not nearly enough.

Once, he'd thought to simply wipe out his enemies, prove to the world he was a power to be reckoned with. Butchering Mancers would achieve that. Yet, once attained, there needed to be something more. If there wasn't, he stood to lose everything he had fought for, killed for.

Because while Orthanor might be the largest continent on Einlienn, it wasn't the most populous, wasn't the most powerful. Somewhere in the world was someone else greater. They could undermine him, throw him down. Worse, they might not even take notice of what he'd accomplished.

He refused to be forgotten, brushed away like the dust from one's feet.

Ba'tvian walked past Ibestor as he tended to his strange beasts, entering the camp proper. Halvark Tretoan, the blond nobleman he'd recruited, looked up from where he was digging a shallow pit in the ground. With a mute nod of acknowledgement, he turned back to his task. Ba'tvian found the elven Nerisse se li Astorae seated on a bedroll close to where his own laid, saw the rolls of the other three on the opposite side of the pit Halvark was digging. Ibestor, he was well aware, would sleep with his creations.

"Where are Raptu and Prialla?" He posed the question to all in the camp, yet watched the girl he'd seduced away from her people with a keen eye. A year ago, those same people had tried to take her from him. The price they – and Nerisse – had paid for that mistake had been high.

"They are gathering straw grass for kindling, my lord." It was Nerisse se li Astorae who answered his question, her voice as soft as velvet. She hesitated as their eyes met, then dropped her gaze. He followed her line of sight, saw the herbal cradled in her lap. The elf opened the book, summoning a ball of light to illuminate the pages. "There is rat root growing in the area. I'd like to harvest some in the morning, if you see no reason to leave right away."

He took his time giving her an answer. The ties that bound Nerisse to him were emotional, augmented by a practice of punishment and reward. She had not presented him with problems of late, though she had also not done much to warrant favor.

"What is the rat root for?"

A faint blush stained the slate blue of her cheeks.

"It is a female medicine." She flicked her silver eyes up at him, then glanced off into the darkness to the east of their camp. "We both could make use of it."

He narrowed his eyes at the neutrality in her tone. He'd become increasingly aware of a growing antagonism between Nerisse and Prialla Filoche, suspected what had founded it. Prialla may be discreet but she did enjoy twisting the knife in someone she didn't care for – and she didn't care for Nerisse.

"She's so insecure, so emotional, Ba'tvian. Why do you drag her around with you?"

The question had come after one of their ruts far from the camp they'd made. As they both dealt with their clothing, he looked at her with eyes gone black. The Shadows that escorted him everywhere paused in their ceaseless drifting around them, as if anticipating the order to pounce.

"Nerisse is useful to me in ways you barely comprehend, Prialla. Her loyalty to me irrevocable, her skills beyond price. In return she asks for little more than the illusions I give her."

Prialla had given a disdainful sniff. "It makes her weak."

"It makes her mine." *The statement was carved in stone. "Know this: should your pettiness ever cost me her servitude, your fate will be far worse than the one we gave your benighted whore of a mother."*

Unlike the other female in their party, Nerisse held her tongue, never questioning him on why they needed Prialla. That she was willing to persevere in silence was reason enough to give way on her request. Safety was not a concern at present; they weren't being actively hunted at the moment. They could afford the time she wanted.

He gave the elf a nod of permission. She smiled at him from where she sat on her bedroll.

"It's almost the full moon," she murmured. "When do you go?"

"Tonight."

Many things had changed since the fall of the Mancers' Guild. His regular meetings with the blood mage he called Red was one of the most significant. No longer was Ba'tvian bound to provide a sacrifice for every cycle of the moon. Instead, the two of them had agreed to an informal alliance. It was a logical step. Their long term goals were the same: the eradication of the Mancers. Yet Ba'tvian's ambitions were growing beyond that and one day that fragile alliance based on the exchange of information for death would fall apart.

No blood mage of power ever trusted another.

For now, however, they could work together. Ba'tvian had stated in their last meeting that he needed mages with certain skills. Red had indicated that he might have a few on a line for him. He need only wait until midnight to find out.

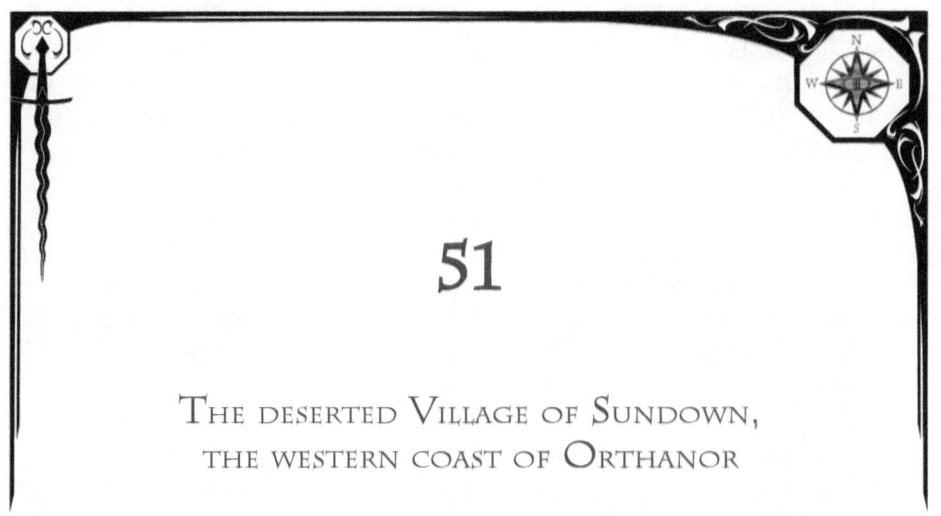

51

IN the dead of night, Absol Omine walked down the overgrown lane that led to the village square. The fishing huts he passed were worn, weathered by the salty air, and washed in the silvery gray light of the moon. The thatch on the roofs were rotting; some collapsed inward. The plaster covering the mud brick walls was cracking, crumbling. To the Mancer, it looked more like a graveyard's parody of a village. Yet there were no graves here. No bodies. Absol had seen to it that those who'd died here were buried elsewhere, in a spot farther up the coast overlooking the sea.

Their agony echoed around him.

Whether the not-quite-noise was real or imagined, Absol closed his ears to it and glanced at his apprentice. Now twelve years of age, I'k'Nole walked beside him, a solemn expression on a face that looked more ageless than young. Neither of them wore the attire most associated with Mancers. The black cloaks had been switched out for brown, the light chain mail that Absol wore was more in keeping with a traveling mercenary's gear. The boy didn't wear chain. Instead, he sported leather. If didn't fit very well. When I'k'Nole had made it clear that he was going with his mentor to Destiny's Way, it was all they'd been to find.

The Mancer sometimes forgot just how much I'k'Nole had grown in the past year. He'd seen the death at the Guild, heard the stories of Ba'tvian's transgressions, witnessed first-hand the kind of damage the evil man wrought. He understood the monsters in their world in a way most boys of his age wouldn't – and he didn't glorify any of what they did as Mancers. Still, this was the path he chose.

The breeze picked up, rustling the stunted weeds along the ground. Nothing else stirred within sight. Absol kept scanning their surroundings as they walked in silence.

Once he had hoped never to return here. Tonight, with the moon hiding behind the clouds above, he'd returned – not because the remains of the village would tell him of Ba'tvian Delthanurk, but because he was certain the blood mage was nowhere near the site of his second confirmed human sacrifice. It was a safe place with no other settlements for miles. That was why he would meet his remaining brethren here.

Mage sendings had gone out to everyone he thought might still be alive. They, in turn, and forwarded the message to others. He relied on his reputation within their order to bring them – provided that they still lived.

Things needed to change. Mancers needed to change. If they didn't, if they continued to work solo, they would die.

Ba'tvian would hunt them down like animals to be tortured and slain.

I'k'Nole's harsh, indrawn breath caught his attention. The boy's jaw was set, his violet eyes resolute. There were shades of darkness in them tonight, as if he was aware of the direction of Absol's thoughts. When he saw his mentor looking at him, he broke the eerie quiet around them.

"He killed here. He killed them all, right here." It wasn't a question or guess. There was knowledge in those eyes. *Ancient eyes*. That had been Absol's first thought when he'd found the boy wandering through what remained of the Spirlan Forest.

"Yes, he did." He waited, wanting to see what his ward would say.

"He stole pieces of them." Sorrow seeped into the striking violet of those eyes, muting the hue. "Now they can never leave."

"What do you mean, 'they can never leave'?" Frowning, he studied the boy. Many things about the child had come to light since the attack at Chalbrooke; a strange sensitivity was one of them. I'k'Nole could sense death, fresh or old. The boy had led them to several bodies buried in the rubble of the Guild House.

When Absol had mentioned it to Master Abbott Dannon the last time they'd passed through Destiny's Way, his old friend had looked thoughtful.

"It explains a few things then. I'k'Nole has somehow managed to

either attend, or alert someone else to attend, every death in the shrine. Animals mostly, yet he was there when Brother Milon was dying. He knew before I did, came to my door in the middle of the night so that I could give the final rites."

According to the shrine's records, a few others had developed the ability to sense death. Most of them had been either healers or On'Desae monks. I'k'Nole was not a healer, nor did he feel called to serve the One as a monk.

"I'll be a warrior against the dark." Eyes burning bright with hope and resolve out of a nine year old's face. "I'll be a Mancer like you."

Such a strong commitment from someone so young.

With the echo of memory reverberating in his mind, he watched as I'k'Nole's brow wrinkled in concentration.

"Well...you said that Shadows eat people?" he said, finally.

Absol nodded.

"And blood mages steal life force to use as magic?"

He nodded again.

"Ba'tvian took more than the life."

There were rumors that the more powerful blood mages could steal pieces of a person's mind or soul. He had never seen evidence of it – wasn't aware of what signs, if any, there would be.

"How can you tell?"

"I don't know." Now the boy looked apologetic. "I just do. A soul has to be whole to move on. They can't. This place..." He looked around them as they came into the village square. "It's like I can hear them. They're whimpering, kind of like old Marsterson's dog," he explained, referring to the canine that has lost its paw in a fight with another dog. "They're not whole. It's like something's missing from them and they can't leave until they find it again."

"Your apprentice is very astute."

They looked up to see another Mancer approaching from the opposite direction. He was dressed much the same as they were, with nothing to suggest that he was Mancer. Blonde hair going gray, the line around his brown eyes pronounced, he looked as if he'd aged a decade since Absol had last seen him two years before.

"Veln," Absol greeted as he placed a hand on his ward's shoulder. "This is I'k'Nole."

Veln Greenmeadow nodded to them both.

"So what does this place tell you?" Absol inquired. Veln was not a sensitive in the same way that his ward appeared to be. He was a mage with a knack for finding ghosts then laying them to rest.

"It tells me that it's haunted." The man's frank gaze met Absol's. "I can do nothing for the spirits here. They're too far gone to do anything other than gibber." He looked I'k'Nole over. "We'll need to see to his mage training as soon as possible. If he's picking up on things such as this, he's ready for it."

"I've begun his instruction but my abilities are limited. I can only take him so far."

"Perhaps I can help there." Veln gave a wry smile. "If I know you – and I do – you'll be wanting to keep us together. We haven't done well alone or in pairs, though that's our traditional practice. That provides ample opportunity for me take over some aspects of his education."

They paused as another of their brethren joined them in the square. One greeting turned into several as more Mancers wound their way through the huts to stand in the village center. Together they waited, hoping to see more come in. When none did, Veln bowed his head, his voice breaking through the quiet murmur of conversation between the rest.

"Palin Fernick is dead. He was struck down two months ago." His words brought on a moment of absolute silence.

"Geralle Bennin was killed three months ago in the moors," came a melancholy report from one of the others. "They'd fed her to the Shadows."

More death confirmations followed as Absol listened, appalled. So many dead, over thirty in the past year. After the Guild's fall, they'd scattered, kept in touch as much as they were able. Yet eight months prior, the mage sendings, letters, the occasional face-to-face contacts – had slowed. For some Mancers, they'd stopped altogether.

Prior to the meet, Absol had estimated sixty Mancers remained roaming Orthanor. Eleven had managed to meet in Sundown. With the litany of thirty-two dead, that left seventeen unaccounted for.

"We can't go it alone any longer." His voice was quiet. Everyone turned to look at him. "That's too many lost. If any of us needed proof that Ba'tvian Delthanurk was hunting Mancers, we have that answer."

Nods met his words.

"What do you suggest?" This from one of the younger Mancers. "We cannot just abandon our duty in favor of hiding." There were murmured agreements.

"We need to consolidate our forces. They'll find us eventually, yet if we band together we have a better chance of surviving." Absol looked at the group of men and women, praying that this wasn't all that was left. "We live in dark times. When we go, there will be no one to stand between the people and Ba'tvian, except for the armies of the ruling lords."

"Some of the lords won't a lift a finger to help their people." Veln's voice dripped with disgust. "The corruption in the city states is spreading like a disease. They might even negotiate with Ba'tvian giving him payment in the form sacrifices or money so that he'll leave them alone – or worse, consolidate their political power for them."

"Fear is his best weapon," said another Mancer, her features shadowed by her cloak's drawn up hood. Based on her voice, Absol identified her as Celina Behr, one of the few women who had lived long enough to achieve senior status in the Guild. "Rumor is almost as strong a tool. Do you know what happened to Jevanel?"

"The city has fallen," Veln answered, his countenance grim. "It lies entombed in the earth."

"They did worse than that. They bound the dead to the spot." She shuddered. "I've been there, to where their surface fields used to be. The land has sunken in and you don't need mage-born sensitivity to hear the Elvanarae screaming from down below."

"You hear them?" Absol considered the village, wondered if the same had occurred at the underground city. He was not familiar with the details of the fall of Jevanel, only that the cavern that contained the elven city had collapsed in on itself. There were conflicting rumors as to who was responsible for the disaster – Ba'vian Delthanurk or the once-intended earth priestess he'd corrupted, Nerisse se li Astorae.

She nodded.

"More, I saw one. It was a woman. She wandered the shallow valley where the crops used to be, wailing and weeping. She looked..." There was an audible swallow. "She looked as if she'd been cut open. Blood stained the gown she wore. There was a gaping hole in her chest where the heart should have been. Her head – one side of it was caved in." Another shudder. "I couldn't stay. The sight of her chilled my blood. I took off. Later, I learned that I wasn't the first to have seen her, or others like her. The nearest settlements whisper of what happen at there, of what the Elvanarae have become. Now they avoid the place. They say it is cursed."

Silence stretched for a long moment after she'd finished speaking.

"We can't allow that to happen again." This came from one of the men, though Absol couldn't tell which one. "Omine has the right of it. We stay together, we make a stand."

"But not foolishly." Absol was adamant. "We hide, we prepare, then we let Ba'tvian come to us on the battleground we choose."

"What of our duties?" This came from one of the younger Mancers, one Absol did not know. "The people will suffer if whole swathes of Orthanor is not patrolled."

"They are suffering now." Absol shook his head, his bleak face resolute. "If we few here tonight are all that it left, we could continue our patrols in any case. What we can do is spread word, gather resources, recruit others. Once we are ready, we choose our battlefield."

"Where do we hide? We can't go to ground the cities or villages, can we?"

"No." Veln's reply was thoughtful as he rubbed his chin, narrowing his gaze on Absol. "Still, there's one place that even Shadows avoid, isn't there?"

"The Wood of Destiny." I'k'Nole spoke for the first time. His tone was somber, firm in a way that adults seldom expected from an unblooded boy. "Destiny's Way and the Wood have always been free of evil."

"We can melt into the Wood if necessary," Absol put in. "We'll need to figure out who is still out there, see if we can get word to them."

As the discussion turned to who might still be alive, Absol noticed that I'k'Nole watched, listening. It struck him that the look in the boy's eyes wasn't just ageless.

It was the look of man grown.

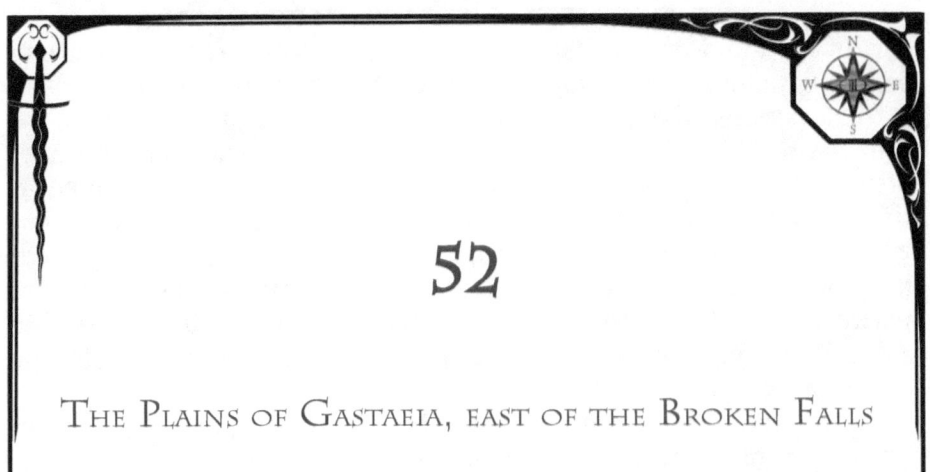

52

THE PLAINS OF GASTAEIA, EAST OF THE BROKEN FALLS

IT was time.

Ba'tvian closed his gloved fingers around the ruddy orange spark that was Red's mage sending. The older blood mage wanted him to meet a pair of possible tools. He gave Nerisse's mind a psychic nudge to wake her from her doze as he turned to Raptu, who was standing the first watch.

"I have a meeting. Nerisse goes with me." Raptu nodded as Ba'tvian gave a silent directive to his pets to keep an eye on his cohorts in his absence. Just because they were bound to him didn't mean that he trusted them. Prialla, especially, possessed enough ambition to one day challenge him if the roots of the compulsions planted in her mind had not grown enough.

One year was too short a time for that kind of growing entrenchment.

Impatient, he waited for his most loyal follower. The elven chit was quick to gather herself so he was not left waiting long. With her trailing after him, he stalked off into the gloom them. It wasn't until they were out of sight of the camp that he paused to erect the arcane portal.

They left the camp once everyone else had settled in for the night. Raptu took the first watch, idly oiling the knives he favored for their rites as he gazed out into the dark. Shadows flitted out there, unseen in the gloom as their chosen lord and his companion walked a fair distance away before constructing the arcane portal.

Nerisse stayed silent as he worked. He knew this bit of magery so well by now that he didn't need all of his attention for it. Leaving part of his mind on the task, his mind touched the creatures that had come with them, conveying what he wanted of them without words.

Instructions given, Ba'tvian laid the last line of power into the framework and triggered the magic that would allow them to travel great distances in moments. Light flared blood red, then shifted to fiery white as the image of the familiar sea side locale faded into view at the center of the doorway he'd created. They stepped through the portal onto the sandy cliffs of Exile's Peril, the barren island where the civilizations of Orthanor sent their criminals. Shadows streamed through in their wake before the portal went black, winking out from existence.

Red, stood there in his elegant ebon attire, two men at his side. The older man's name, a pseudonym they'd agreed upon ages ago, came from his hair; it was the color of fresh blood. Ba'tvian gave a nod of greeting to the man with pale skin, then studied the ones he'd come to meet.

They were identical twins. Each sported the same ocean deep blue eyes, sun-streaked nutmeg hair, weathered golden skin, and aquiline features that marked them as Dithume. Their garb wasn't customary for their race. Dusty brown, the cloaks were a tad threadbare yet of decent quality, the leather jerkins and trews creased from use.

Dithume... Ba'tvian searched his memory for details on the race. Weather workers, sailors, deep sea fishermen – islanders for the most -part. They could live for several hundred years. Their homeland lay somewhere to the southeast or Orthanor, an archipelago he barely remembered. He had never heard of their race producing blood mages. Still, when he viewed them with his psychic eye, he could see the rusty hue that stained the mind shields of most users of blood-born power.

"Well come, Master of Shadows." Red inclined his head at Ba'tvian, flicked his gaze to Nerisse. "Lady." She gave a gracious nod, yet said nothing. "You are looking for people of a certain... bent. These twain are Lakit and Tavor Jeste. They are looking for a place to be." Stepping to the side, he gave them a half bow. "I will leave you to negotiate terms. Shadow Master, we will meet again for our usual exchange in a day or two."

Ba'tvian gave him a curt nod, waiting until the blood mage walked down the cliffs to the portal he had standing by. Meanwhile, his pets began to circle the men whose eyes tracked their movements. The twins remained still, their expressions evidencing mild curiosity more than anything else. Wanting a better look at them, he conjured a ball of light, setting it to hang in the air above the newcomers while he remained in the dark.

"Why do you need a place to be?" Ba'tvian broke the silence, wondering if they ran from something. He was not yet ready to take on new people with baggage that might hinder him.

"We've recently fled Exile's Port." The one on the left answered, naming the port city that hosted the island's main prison.

Ba'tvian had never been there. He'd heard that it was difficult to break out of. Even if one succeeded, there was still the rocky desert of the island's interior to pass through, or the sea to somehow traverse, before any prisoner could deem himself free. Most attempts failed, either killed by guards during the escape, or dying in the desert for lack of food, water, and shelter from the sand storms that raged there.

"You are?"

"Lakit."

"What were you incarcerated for?" He was beginning to see minute differences in the twins. Lakit had a small crescent shaped scar at the tail end of his right eyebrow; it was a few shades lighter than the rest of his skin. Tavor lacked any facial defects.

"We destroyed crops over in Nilbre," Tavor answered, turning his attention back to Ba'tvian.

"Why?" He did not want people given too much to impulse. Raptu's tendency toward that impulsive behavior was tempered by Prialla's attention and wit; these two had no one to balance them.

"We were run out of town." Tavor returned Ba'tvian's gaze with an empty one of his own. "Blood mages aren't welcome visitors to most places." It was a statement with which he could relate.

"It is why a blood mage should never give himself away." He held the other man's eyes steadily. "What led to your discovery?"

"A traveling Dithume. Someone who knew us, knew what we were." Tavor gave a slight shrug of his shoulders. "We were fine until he raised the alarm."

"He met with an accident soon after." Lakit continued to watch the hypnotic slithering of Ba'tvian's pets. "We made our escape as he died."

"How did you destroy the crops?" This came from Nerisse. The detached quality of her voice told him that most of her concentration wasn't on the conversation.

"We manipulated weather patterns in the area, encouraged certain insect vermin to flourish." Lakit shrugged. "The region is now afflicted with famine and pestilence. People are dying. One village has lost almost all of its original populace to the famine, which is why we were marked for execution at the Port."

"Creating droughts..." It was a skill set that Ba'tvian could use. "Yet you were caught."

"Bad luck. The man we'd killed wasn't the only Dithume in the area. The other was a weather-worker. He decided to investigate the aberrant weather patterns we'd woven to bring on the drought." Lakit's expression took on a disgusted cast. "We should have been more subtle."

Ba'tvian sent a mental command to his pets to crowd the twins a bit more. He wanted them distracted until Nerisse finished what she was doing.

"How did you escape?"

"I found a nest of sand worms, called them to me." Tavor turned his head to follow the path of Shadow that had brushed against his leg. "They bore through the grout in the prison cell floor."

"Tavor has an affinity for those kinds of creatures – insects, pests, the small things that most people regard as detrimental." Lakit cocked his head at another ethereal creature as it slithered up to him. "It's his primary strength, as his weather magic is marginal at best. My weather magic is very strong. What are these?"

"Shadows. They are mine." Ba'tvian considered the abilities. "How did you come to be here with Red?"

"We met him years ago, just before the Great Earthquake, and owed him a favor." Tavor spoke this time. "He aided in our escape. When the sand worms weakened the floor of our cells, they'd created a tunnel we could crawl through. It ran under the prison, came up in the desert out of sight of the city walls. Red was waiting for us there."

"He said he was calling in his favor." Lakit gave another shrug. "Thus we are here, speaking to you. He mentioned that you might be willing to aid us somehow in exchange for something."

"What aid do you seek?"

"We have no wish to be executed." Lakit glanced at his twin, who nodded. "We are given to understand that we are now to be killed on sight. A place to lie low for while might be all the aid we need."

"I have such a place. Using it, however, requires loyalty," Ba'tvian replied, tone low. "Give it to me, obey my commands, and you will not only be free from execution, you may have your revenge if you wish it."

The twins switched their attention from the winding lizard-like threading around them to Ba'tvian.

"We are not interested in slavery." Tavor's voice was quiet. "Or indentured servitude."

"I am proposing neither." He let his power glimmer in his eyes. "I seek an alliance of sorts, one that is mutually beneficial. I have plans for Einlienn. To see them succeed, I require allies I can trust." A lie; he would never trust them. "My plans, my goals. Work alongside me, and you will reap the rewards of my ambition."

"We need to know more before deciding," Lakit replied.

He chose his words with care, giving them just enough information for them to be able to glimpse what the future held. He needed to convey more than the promise of that future, though. It was vital that his ambitions be feasible. If they believed they were not, he would one day have to kill both of them.

"A moment." Lakit and his brother turned to walk off out of hearing range to discuss the proposal. Ba'tvian looked at Nerisse.

"Tavor's shields are much weaker than Lakit's," she replied to his unspoken query. She kept her voice low, lest the wind carry it to other ears. "I was able to get in, plant a few of the compulsions. His mind...there's a lack of emotion in it. Not like with Ibestor, but an inability to connect on an emotional level with anyone save his twin."

"What does that mean for us?"

"It means that we cannot use emotion to conceal what we do with his mind. He's not simple in his thinking." She brushed a few strands of white hair out of her face. "I have to be cautious. As with Halvark, what I seeded in his mind won't take root immediately."

Halvark Tretoan, he recalled, had required Nerisse to use every bit of trickery and subterfuge in order for his mental guards to relax. Once they had, she'd succeeded in making the subtle alterations to his mind, then hiding them from the mage. Halvark was still unaware of the changes in his mind. There was no doubt that she would have similar results now.

"Good enough." He was willing to invest the extra time as needed at this early stage. "What of Lakit?"

"His shields are stronger, yet I was still able to get in. His mind has more emotional capability than his twin's, though it appears that his ability to connect on that level with others is degrading. It may be a side effect of his link with Tavor's mind."

"They're linked?" Intrigued, he glanced at the silhouettes of the men. "I suppose that such a bond might be expected between twins."

"Yes." Nerisse gave a little sigh. When his gaze returned to her face, he saw what he had missed under the moonlight earlier: the paleness of her slate blue skin, the dark rings under her eyes.

"Are you well?" His voice was flat, harsh. If she fell ill now…

"Yes. I'm just tired. Sojourning in the minds of two who might detect me at any moment is wearing, especially after a hard day's ride." She met his eyes without flinching. "I do not lie to you, my lord. My earth bond is strong, my health good. I just need rest."

He studied her, eyes narrowed.

"You've been tired more and more of late, Nerisse." His voice was soft, dangerous. He did not appreciate being lied to, least of all by her.

"My sleep has been troubled in recent weeks." She dropped her gaze. "I had no wish to burden you with it."

He reached out, grasped her chin. Tilting her face up, he saw the shame in her eyes, the kind that told him that she believed her problem to be a sign of weakness. Nerisse had become more concerned about appearing weak since Prialla had joined them.

"What troubles your sleep?"

"Dreams." It was a reluctant whisper, one followed by vehemence. "I do *not* regret what I did to be with you. Some part of me might regret the necessity, yet not the result. You are my lord; I won't be parted from you."

"You will tell me if these dreams become too much." She nodded. He relaxed as he released her. "You were able to seed Lakit's mind as well?"

She nodded. He returned his gaze to the men, thinking. It was almost time to return to the Tretoan Estate. It had to be maintained if it was to remain useful, both as a base and as a source of income.

There was a hunt to finish; the Mancer they'd caught earlier had been partnered with another. He'd managed to slip away from them. He mulled it over, decided to send the three nobles back to the estates to oversee things there. In the meantime, he would take the twins, Nerisse, and Ibestor to finish out their hunt. Prialla could be trusted to keep a tight rein on the men she considered her own. It would, of course, mean an interruption in their private lessons – the ones where experimented with magery to alter the effects of age.

The 'noble three', as he tended to think of them despite the fact that Prialla wasn't an aristocrat, would also need something to do. Raptu, in particular, needed instructions to carry out. Without them, he tended toward reckless behavior, the kind that could land them all in trouble.

Then, there was the matter of Raptu's family. There had been reasons to keep them around. At present, the family, convinced by their heir's skillful story-telling, believed them to be exploring a mercantile venture. Keen as he was on business, Lord Carthier was happy to believe that his son held the same interest and was supplying financial support for this expedition.

The cost of that patronage, though, was becoming burdensome. Reports had to be sent back to the family. The practice was risky. It could give their location away to their enemies, made them keep track of a multitude of lies. More, the time was fast approaching the point where the Carthiers would begin to question the lack of profits or contracts.

It may be time to have Raptu prove his loyalty as the others have. He would give it further consideration.

"We will not leave the current camp until midmorning." He made the statement absently as he strategized. "You will rest. Prialla can harvest the rat root you want."

"Thank you."

The words were almost too low to hear as the twins walked to back to them. His Shadows drifted in their wake, a few gliding ahead to circle their master and Nerisse. When the men stopped in front of them, the dark creatures began to gather around all four, gliding in lazy circuits as they waited. Lakit spoke.

"We will agree to one year of conditional service in return for a safe haven, with our agreement to be re-evaluated at that time. We will also retain the right to reject unreasonable demands."

Unreasonable was a matter of perspective. His arsenal included an elven mage who could alter minds and a blonde seductress who could wrap any man around her little finger. He was sure that he could get what he wanted when the time came.

"Three years." One wouldn't be enough for his plans. Though the compulsions might bear fruit within that time, he didn't want to rely on them alone.

The twins looked at each other.

"Two years," Tavor proposed. "And we want a contract written to that affect."

"Done." He began to gather his power in preparation for building another portal. "Nerisse will draw up the contract – to be signed in blood," he stipulated, "in the morning. For now, we will return to the mainland. Coming with us would make things more convenient. Do you agree?"

They nodded as one. He left them to Nerisse and his pets while he built the portal. His mind was ablaze with possibilities. Long-term plans for long-term havoc. Their talents would prove useful indeed.

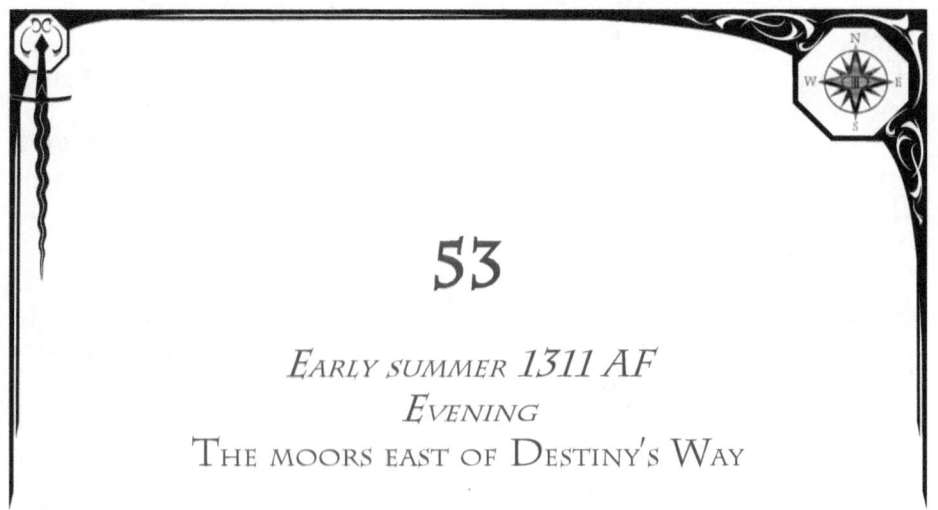

53

A stray cow was being run to ground.

The bovine bawled out in terror as it ran, only to pull up short as it thrash its horned head at something in the tall grass. It lunged from side to side, looking for a way out. The grass rippled as the things pursuing the animal closed in. It bellowed again, kicking in panic.

Absol Omine rode hard for the cow, his horse lathered and snorting. I'k'Nole Kar'k'Eige kept pace beside him, his sword already in hand. He caught his apprentice's eye, signaled their strategy as they bore down the distressed bovine. The animal was screaming now, half-collapsed on the ground. As the Mancers swept to either side, leaning down in their saddles to brandish their sword blades, they heard the wet tearing of flesh.

The Shadows were eating their prey alive.

Absol sliced through as many as he could reach. He was certain that he killed at least two; by the psychic shrieks ringing in his mind, he knew I'k'Nole had scored well. Swinging his mount around to pass again on the opposite side, he glimpsed a flicker of violet. I'k'Nole's sword was engulfed in a strange translucent purple flame. Anything it touched burned away. It didn't leave much behind.

Omine didn't have time to wonder at it. He cut into a few at the cow's hindquarters before turning the horse for a third round. This time, the Shadows abandoned their meal.

They surged toward Absol, biting at his horse's legs, causing it to buck as it ran. Hooves kicked out, the steel shoes cutting into the ebony bodies. His apprentice rode by him, arcing his sword as if throwing something from the tip. A trailing wave of amethyst fire landed on several of the creatures. They writhed, some of them of skittering into their fellows in their efforts to escape the flame, spreading their plight to the rest.

Absol's horse bolted through the opening. Fighting to control the equine, the elder Mancer missed what happened next. A flash of violet lit the moors, vanishing a moment later.

That's the last of them.

The young male voice the sounded in the older man's mind as he continued to struggle with the horse. Not a mage able to communicate mind-to-mind very well himself, he responded aloud, letting his sword drop to the ground as he wrestled with the reins.

"If that – blast – cow isn't dead – dumb animal – see to it." From what he'd seen, the bovine was beyond salvation.

In the end, Absol let the bloody horse run off most of its fear. By the time he'd regained control of his mount there was no trace of the cow or its predators. All that remained was a blackened, bare area, as if something had burned for long time. Yet there was no smell of fire, no heat from the as on the ground.

Absol halted his mount beside I'k'Nole's, then slid out of the saddle. He took in the charring, gave his protégé considering glance, then summoned a mage light so he could see how bad off the horse's legs were.

"Neat trick," he said. The forelegs bore superficial bite wounds. Moving to the hind legs, he continued. "You're coming much further along in your studies on magic."

"Yes, sir."

"You've only been learning for about four years," the older man observed, noting a deep gash on a fetlock. "I'm well aware that channeling power has been part of your studies but since when did you learn how to do all of that?"

After that fateful meeting in the ruins of Sundown, Veln Greenmeadow had taken over his apprentice's arcane education. The other man was better qualified than Absol to teach a mage showing signs of both sensitivity and magic. For his part, Absol used his contacts at the Trinity College of Magery to acquire copies of mage texts to supplement the lessons. The tomes were necessary. In some ways I'k'Nole was outstripping Veln – even if, the older man thought, the lad used unorthodox of methods.

The boy had encountered a few issues when it came to the traditional patterns of instruction. Absol's apprentice couldn't seem to follow the lessons as outline in the text. He floundered, the spells breaking apart halfway through their completion. Yet if left alone long enough, I'k'Nole would devise unconventional ways to achieve the same results, though he was unable to explain it in terms anyone else comprehended. The biggest drawback was that none of them understood how his magic worked. The patterns of his magic were barely visible to them on the psychic plane – which led to far more questions than Absol was comfortable contemplating.

Veln and Dannon had theories that they would discuss at length. Absol, never an apt student of magic himself, preferred to leave the debates to them. Instead, he chose to trust in the boy he'd come to think of as his own.

"Well, um…" I'k'Nole's expression turned sheepish. "I've been trying various things. The fire trick was something that I figured out how to do yesterday. I wasn't sure how it would work in a fight." He gave a rueful smile.

"A little forewarning would have been nice. I suppose you also can't tell me how you did it?"

"No, sir. I just sort of…thought about I wanted and it happened."

Absol winced. Working magic without defined restrictions was a good way to get killed – or worse.

"The help is appreciated. Next time, though, think about some protective measures for yourself in case things don't work out. The last thing we want is for you to end up like the Shadows did tonight." He rose to delve into a saddlebag. Bringing out medical supplies, he began to treat the horse's injuries. "What was that light at the end?"

"I – ah – I'm not sure." This time he sounded chagrined. "After you bolted – "

"The horse bolted, the idiot beast," Absol corrected mildly. He continued to bandage the worst of the bites.

"Right. After that, they converged on me. They leapt at me – jumped up like dogs to snap at any part of my body they could get to. I panicked, and…it happened."

Concerned, the older man's head came up. "Are you hurt?"

"No." The youth shook his head, his ebon hair falling into his violet eyes.

Absol narrowed his gaze, directing his mage light toward the boy to see for himself. The leather armor and light cloak bore no bloodstains, tears, scrapes, or scratches.

"Panic," he said after a moment of silence, "is the most useless – the most dangerous – reaction to have in a fight."

"Yes, sir." I'k'Nole's voice was subdued.

"It helps the enemy; though, that doesn't appear to be the case this time. Be careful not to panic again." He waited for a nod, before going on. "Where are you practicing?"

As if he needed to ask. He knew where his protégé went.

"The Wood. No one goes there."

The Mancer grunted. Most people went stark raving mad if they spent a fraction of the time I'k'Nole did in the Wood of Destiny. They couldn't handle the music, the whispers, or the visions. Absol walked there on occasion, but was certain to stay within hearing range of the Wood's eerie song for less than a half an hour. I'k'Nole had been among the trees for as a long as a day and night.

"You always were a strange boy." He fastened the last bandage and straightened. "Practice more on that technique. See if you can replicate what you did. It might come in useful later. Otherwise…"

He strode over to clasp a gloved hand on his apprentice's shoulder.

"Well done."

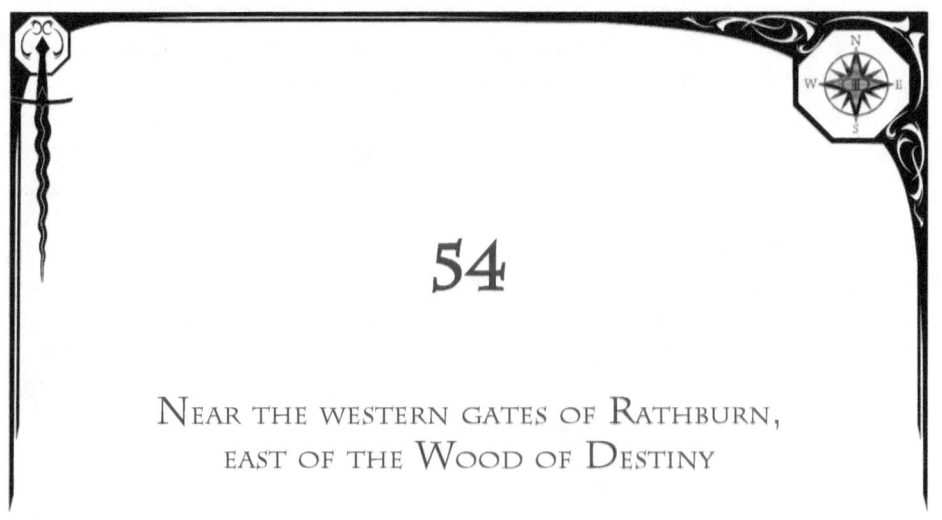

54

VELN Greenmeadow rode through a moonless night on his way to a place he'd once called home.

Most Mancers were raised in the order, sourced from orphanages or street urchins. They trained for years in combat and magic, seldom knowing any other trade. Veln had been different. He'd grown up in a family that had loved him.

Veln had begun his adult life by following in his father's footsteps. A member of the Rathburn Watch, his father had lived a hard life enforcing the law, cracking the heads of the unlawful. He'd taught his son everything he needed to know in order to do the same – until some lowlife instigated a tavern-wide brawl one rainy night. The violence of the fight had left three watchmen dead, two injured, and a young watchman with a vendetta.

Two months were spent tracking down the guttersnipes that had done for his father. After finding them there'd been no need for restraints or a jail cell. Even a grave hadn't been necessary. A short trip to the river had taken care of what remained of them.

Lawmen frowned on what they saw as murder. Veln hadn't stayed long enough to be connected with the bodies when they surfaced. Guilt was another factor in his decision at the time. As justified as he might have been, vigilantism outside the law he'd been taught to honor always. So he'd quit the Watch, gone to Chalbrooke where he'd run into a Mancer who was out recruiting. Though they ordinarily took on recruits much younger than Veln's twenty-two years, they'd given him a chance because of his background. A third of his Mancer training had already been completed, leaving just magic and lore. He'd possessed an aptitude for both.

The rest was history.

In the years since, the two murders he'd committed had slipped from memory. No one in the Rathburn now seemed to remember it or care. Still, Veln seldom returned to the city he had once called home. One reason was his duties. Another was his guilt.

One day, he supposed, he'd get over it.

He shook off the past as the rough stone walls of Rathburn came into view. Torches lit the gate, one mounted on each side of the western gate. The portcullis glinted in the firelight. Above the gate was one of two guard houses; the second was just inside the city. As Veln drew his mount to a halt in front of the city entrance, he peered up at the sentry who leaned out of the window above.

"It's late to be traveling the moors, especially in these times," the man called down. "I'll need your name and purpose before we let you in."

"Veln Greenmeadow is my name. Captain Reg Morrin of the Watch requested I come for a visit." He patted the left breast of his leather jerkin. "I've his letter if you need to see it."

"Just a moment." He ducked back inside the guard house to shout an order to his counterpart below. Muffled voices sounded on the other side of the gate before the portcullis began to rise with a clatter. The second sentry stepped into the torchlight, waving at Veln to ride on through.

Once inside the city walls, Veln dismounted. Reaching under his jerkin to the tunic pocket beneath, he pulled out the letter and proffered it to the guard. The man skimmed over the letter, then handed it back with a nod.

"We've been expecting you, lord," he intoned, using the customary address for Mancers. "Welcome to Rathburn."

"Sir, if you must, or just Veln will do," he replied, with a nod of acknowledgment for the courtesy. "I would appreciate it if you forgot that I am a Mancer. I have no wish to tip off anyone in the area" – Ba'tvian Delthanurk in particular, though he kept that to himself – "that I am here, let alone at the Captain's behest."

"Yes, sir." The sentry gave a solemn salute. "Good hunting."

"Thank you." Veln returned the salute, then remounted to set off to his destination for the night: the Guard Arm Tavern & Inn. Above him, the sky rumbled. He hoped to find the tavern before the clouds opened up.

It didn't used to rain so much when I served here. Aside from the weather, Rathburn had changed little over the fifteen years since he'd lived there last. The buildings looked rather dreary, the streets dark. Pinpoints of light came from the lanterns or torches marking the entryways to various establishments. On this side of town, there weren't many businesses or merchants; most of it was residential. A few of the larger residences would let out rooms but meals would have to be secured elsewhere, and they didn't take tenants during the dead of night. Late comers to the city resorted to the central district or the wharves. The shipping district where the wharves were located offered the cheapest rooms. The accommodations, however, left a great deal to be desired. The city center, where the Watch House and city offices stood, was a better bet. Side roads spanning out from the center held several taverns or inns. Of those, the least expensive was the Guard Arm; it was the reason it the city's lawmen favored it.

The streets were quiet, save from the *clop-clop* of his horse's shod hooves on the cobble pavers. From what he could recall, night-time traffic was scarce. The Watch would sometimes see drunkards or party-goers in the better parts of town, street-walkers and sotted dockworkers down by the wharves. Yet by the time Veln reached his destination, not a single soul. The lack of life was almost eerie.

Entering the courtyard of the tavern, he saw that the glass-encased oil lamp by the door was still on; it the Guard Arm's indicator of whether or not rooms were available. Pleased to have beaten the rain, he dismounted to lead his horse to the stables that butted up against the tavern's right side. He knocked on the stable door before opening it. A yawning stable-hand was climbing down from the loft above.

"Evenin', messire," the boy mumbled. Veln took in the sleepy face as he approached, judged him to be about twelve or so. "Can I help you?"

"What's the rate for one room and one horse?"

"Three coppers a night or a quarter silver a week. That gets you a porridge breakfast, but no other meals. A half silver gets you two meals a day, too." The child reached up to stroke muzzle of Veln's horse. "I can hold your horse while you settle up inside."

"Very well." Veln dug out a quarter copper, showed it to the boy. "Don't unsaddle him until I get back. Keep out of the packs; they're trapped against tampering. If all's well when I get back you get this."

He brightened at the prospect. Veln gave him the reins, patted his gelding's neck, then left for the tavern. He found the owner at the bar, haggling down the weekly rate to one quarter silver and four coppers before he returned to the stables to untack his mount.

An hour later, with his belongings stowed in his room, the horse taken care of, and nothing else to do until morning, Veln ventured into the tavern for a late meal. There wasn't much left at this time of night. He made do with bread drenched with stew drippings. He'd eaten better, but it certainly wasn't flavorless, or close to the horrid stuff it would have been if *he* had been the cook.

Veln Greenmeadow was a lot of things. A decent cook wasn't one of them.

As he sat in the tavern in which his father had died, he found himself thinking of how much was still the same since he'd last patrolled the streets here. Workmen and watchmen alike flocked to the taverns after their shifts, washing down the miseries of the day with a few mugs of ale before heading home. He recognized them by their garments; he didn't see any faces that he knew from before. Regardless of who, or what, they were, they still chewed over rumors, still sang horribly when drunk, still made passes at the barmaids. Even the ale, watery stuff that foamed like the churning sea, was the same.

After the first sip of his, Veln decided that he'd stick to water. It tasted of the brine it resembled, something he'd forgotten since his last visit. Unused to it as he was, he would be sick if he drank too much of it. Given the people he expected to meet at this tavern, he didn't care to be vomiting all over the floor when they walked in.

"Welladay! If it isn't you."

Veln smiled, turning in the seat he'd appropriated at the bar. He faced a gray bearded oldster about the age his father would have been had he lived. He wore the uniform and great coat of the Watch. With a broad grin, he greeted the old, bedraggled lawman with a warm clasping of hands.

"Welladay, indeed, Jimnel. How's the wife?"

"Jolly, old, and fat." Jimnel Elfren, an aging sergeant, gave a raspy chuckle. "She hasn't changed much since you were here last. Just passing through?"

"Visiting. Thought I might catch a few of my old mates if I waited here long enough." He lifted his tankard. "Can I buy you a pint, old friend?"

"That's an offer I won't turn down." He eased onto a stool as Veln signaled the tavern keeper manning the bar. "So what brings you back into our area now that your mum's passed on?"

"I'm in town to see an old friend." He glossed over the truth. He didn't want rumors flying around just yet. "While I was here, I thought I'd check on my old mates at the Watch House."

"Hmm." A second mug of ale was plunked down on the table. Jimnel took it up for a thoughtful sip. When he spoke, he kept his voice low. "I know the Captain sent for you. Truth, we weren't sure if you were still alive, what with the Monster of Menie roaming around and that bad business at Chalbrooke. Haven't heard of or seen much of your order since your guild house burned to the ground."

"It's been tense. We're still out there, just keeping a low profile," he confided. "We don't know how stale the information is, but last we heard, Ba'tvian Delthanurk was in the area around Rathburn."

"If that's the case, then it may explain the goings on around here. I wish you luck, my young friend. That's one I've no wish to meet in this lifetime, or any other."

They drank for a moment, or rather, Jimnel drank and Veln pretended to. The ale, he thought, was quite vile.

"How are things here?" the Mancer asked in normal tone of voice.

"Tense, as you say. We've got a murderer in Rathburn, a sadistic bastard, too. He's leaving bodies left and right. Not all of them low-lifes, either." He brooded a moment. "One of the corporals lost a sister to the bastard. She was raped, carved up. Pieces were missing."

Veln laid a comforting hand on the older man's shoulder.

"All of them were like that?"

Jimnel nodded.

"Most of them were women – girls, really." He sighed. "A few men, some boys. Over half of the ones we've found were middle-class. People of service: maids, washerwomen, cooks – they'd either plied that trade or were aspiring to."

"Aspirants?" Veln frowned. "Were they promised job someplace or an interview for one?"

"A few were. Can't say more than that at this point. We're still prodding in the bushes for the partridge we know is there." He gave Veln a steady look. "If you happen to hear of anything unusual, I'd appreciate it if you passed it on. These killings have everyone afraid, and we've been hard pressed to find the culprit."

"I'll keep an eye out, Jimnel." Veln tapped his friend's tankard with his own. "Once a watchman," he said, "always a watchman."

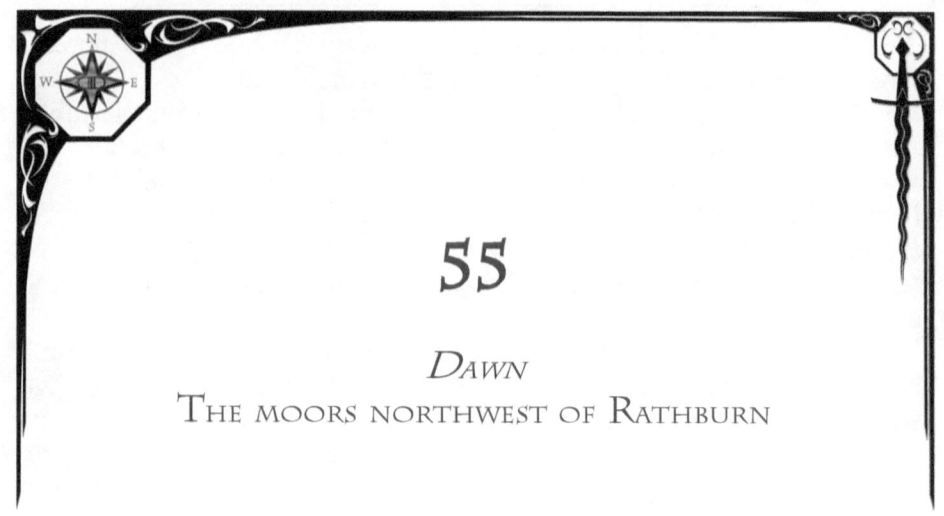

55

B A'TVIAN Delthanurk was racing on the moors, thin patches of ground-hugging fog scattered in his wake. Alongside him, Lord Raptu Carthier and the Jeste twins rode their mounts hard, his Shadows gliding over the ground ahead of the group. They were coming up fast on the desperate figure of a man atop a mule some ways ahead. His short sandy hair ruffled in the wind as he turned to look back. Desperation dominated his expression.

His mule couldn't keep up the pace; it was beginning to tire. The man wrestled with his pants, unfastening his belt to use a makeshift whip. He flailed it at the animal's rump.

Flank him, Ba'tvian ordered his pets. *Spare the mule.* Raptu had grown possessive of his equines since they'd quietly dispatched his immediate family a few years before. Ba;tvian could not care less about the animal or Raptu's attachment for them. Still, he saw no reason to chip the man's loyalty by letting the mule die.

And the man?

Capture him. He will be yours after I am done with him.

With that promise made, the creatures surged forward. Before they reached the rider, the mule brayed, sitting on its haunches as it skidded to a stop on the grass. The fleeing man catapulted over the animal's shoulder, screaming as he landed in the vicinity of whatever had spooked the mule. Freed from its rider, the mule lurched to the side, stumbling in its haste to get away. All around it, Shadows emerged out of the twilight gloom, eyes glowing a sickly white with excitement.

Raptu slowed his horse to a trot, then raised a hand. He muttered an incantation as he made an arcane gesture. The mule, having regained its feet, looked at him with its big ears pricked forward. Limbs shaking, it began to make its way toward its true owner.

Meanwhile, the twins had pulled up beside the fallen man and dismounted. They each grasped an arm to haul him up as Ba'tvian, still mounted, approached.

"Did you truly think that you could run?" Ba'tvian's voice was menacing. "Were you so deluded that you believed we would not follow?"

A whimper was his only answer.

"My dear Lord Ba'tvian," Raptu began as he, now on foot, led both his horse and the reclaimed mule over to join them. "My former seneschal may be deluded, but he is not altogether a fool. He'll have a reason for this foolhardy endeavor." His gaze slammed into the servant's, his teeth flashing white in a savage smile. "Won't you, Wilton?"

Anxious, the seneschal's eyes flicked from his master to his master's lord. Ba'tvian extended a mental touch to the largest of the Shadow's with them.

What is he thinking?

The creature crept over to the man, twining about his legs. Though restrained, Wilton's body jerked in reaction.

He is hoping that you will not discover what he has done. There was another beat of silence. *He is strangely skilled at blocking his thoughts. It is not true shielding. When may we have him?*

Ba'tvian answered his follower aloud.

"We will take him back to Raptu's estate. The rest of the household can witness my pets' feeding." His chill expression made it clear just what they would be feasting on.

Wilton's eyes bulged at the implication.

"No, please, I pray you, lord. Just kill me," he begged, voice cracking. "Kill me now."

"Mercy is earned," Ba'tvian countered. "Or bought. What do you have that would buy you mercy?"

"Your word." The man swallowed, flinching as the creature at his feet licked at his pants leg. "Your word that I die a quick death if what I say is of value to you."

"Tell us and we shall see." Raptu sounded almost bored. On either side of the man, Lakit and Tavor Jeste were stony in their silence. Ba'tvian waited.

"Th-the Rathburn Watch. Th-they know abo-about you. About the killings on the Carthier Estate."

"Do they?" Sounding intrigued, Raptu leaned forward, his face almost boyish in its eagerness. He eyes, however, glinted like cold agates. "Just how did they find out, old boy? Hmmm?"

He told them. The whisper ghosted into Ba'tvian's mind just as he came to the same conclusion. *He sent them words on paper.*

A letter. *Is there any way of stopping it from reaching its destination?*

The Shadow concentrated on the man. *His thoughts are blocked completely now.*

No, then. Cold fury burned in his gut. Strong as the urge was, he did not carve him up on the grass. The idiot would be an example. As for the letter, the Rathburn Watch would not discover anything should they search the Carthier estate. They had done their killing elsewhere.

"We will return." The blood mage's voice was low, intense. "Then we will...discuss what you have passed on to the Watch." As an afterthought, he added. "You were incorrect, by the way. No one has been killed on the grounds. It seems appropriate that you would volunteer to be the first."

The man called Wilton Lanne had been trembling. Now his ashen skin went sheet white, his eyes rolling back in head as he fainted.

"Now that is a man lacking spine," Raptu observed with disgust.

"The fool earned his fate, not his mercy." Ba'tvian's terse reply gave little indication of the anger welling within him.

The twins picked up their prisoner, slinging him over the back of Tavor's mount, just behind the saddle. Lakit pulled rope out of his saddle bags to secure Wilton to metal rings worked into the leather on either side of the cantle. As they did so Raptu tied the mule's reins to his own saddle and remounted.

"How much trouble are we in, do you think?" the lordling asked his liege. With the twins once again stride their horses, Ba'tvian turned his horse about as he answered.

"Uncertain. Prialla and Halvark have bribed certain officials in Rathburn before this. Those can be lured to our side." It was how they had gotten away with so much over the last five years. "We need to determine who isn't in our pocket."

The Watch Captain. He was not one of their paid officials, though there were a few under him that were. Not many, but a few –

enough to muddle most investigations. *Yet not this one. There are too many honest men attached to this one…*

The four rode in silence for a few moments. It wasn't long before Lakit broke it, speaking as he often did for his brother as well as himself.

"It is time we owned Rathburn, isn't it, Lord Ba'tvian?"

"Yes, it is."

And Halvark would be the key.

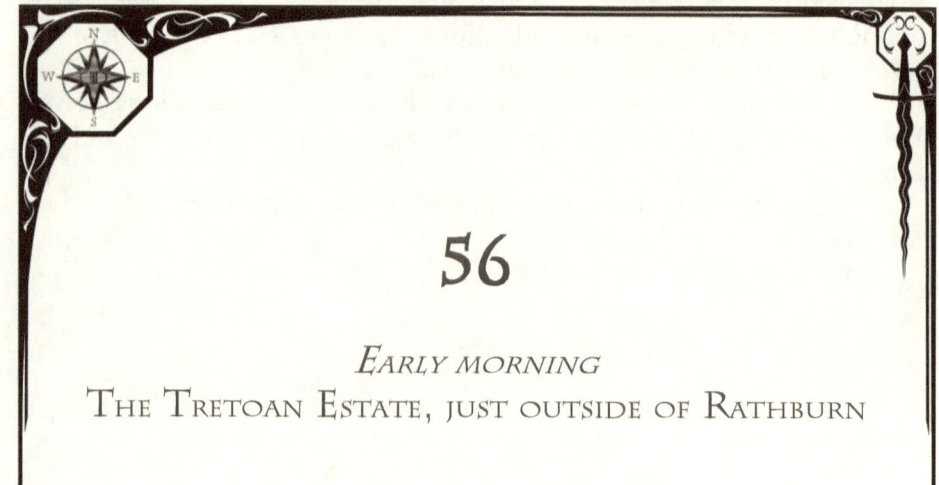

56

PRIALLA Filoche eased back in her chair as she stared at the balance listed in the account ledger on the desk in front of her. The amount was particularly good, perhaps the best ever. It had been, she thought, a stellar year for the estates in terms of crops and cattle – the mainstays of the Tretoan family. Raptu's estate had done a bit better, but then he also had the courier business to augment his coffers.

She supposed she had Ba'tvian to thank for the increased prosperity. He'd had the elven witch do something with the fields before each planting. Then Dithume twins followed his instructions regarding the weather. They managed to keep pestilence away from their lands and the weather decent, while using both to blight the crops and livestock of their competitors in the market. The result was profit.

Lots of profit.

What their leader proposed needed everything the estates could provide. The plans he'd shared were ambitious, hinging on their ability to generate the funds required, as well as to destroy or discredit the opposition. First, however, they needed to deal with the Mancers. The Guild House might lay in ruins within the citywalls of Chalbrooke, yet the order remained. They hadn't been able to estimate their numbers. Still, on this one thing they all – Dark Adepts as well as unallied blood mages – agreed upon: even one Mancer alive was too many.

Ba'tvian believed he knew where they'd gone to ground.

Regardless of that knowledge, he wanted more manpower before they dealt the killing blow.

"Mancers are mages. Strength will matter little if they have the numbers to overwhelm us."

He was correct, of course. She saw the logic in building a solid foundation, raising the funds, doing everything they could to find out more about the village people called Destiny's Way.

"We're almost ready." She tapped a slim finger on the column of figures penned in the ledger. "We have only to hire the swords we need."

Tretoan and Carthier would cover the expense. Their reward would be power. Hers would include ever-lasting beauty, maybe even immortality if she could figure out how. She smiled to herself. She would make sure that she received her due.

She raised a hand to her face, stroking a finger down one flawless cheek. The flesh was firm, the skin smooth. It should have been, given how much blood-born magic she spent on maintaining her beauty.

Rising, she walked to the window overlooking the courtyard two stories below her study. An elegant blonde dressed in the clothes befitting a well-bred lady, she looked like a modest noblewoman with an authoritative air about her. She wasn't an aristocrat. Illegitimate, with calloused hands used to hard work, Prialla was a blood mage who had craved a higher status in life. Officially, she was the chatelaine of her aristocratic half-brother Halvark Tretoan's manor home. Unofficially, she ruled the estate in the ways that mattered most.

That she wanted more was no secret. That she would get it was no question. Yet despite her greed – she was well aware of her own flaws – she refused to sacrifice her loyalties. Halvark and Raptu belonged to her as that girl Nerisse and Ibestor belonged Ba'tvian's. She needed her men with her, sharing in the bounty, until the end.

Movement caught her eye. She peered into the courtyard below, spying the tiny red spark that sailed across the grassy lawn, then shoot up the face of the manor. It slowed as it reached her study window, passing through the glass without a shimmer or crack. She cupped it in her hands, listening to her master's voice as it sounded in her mind.

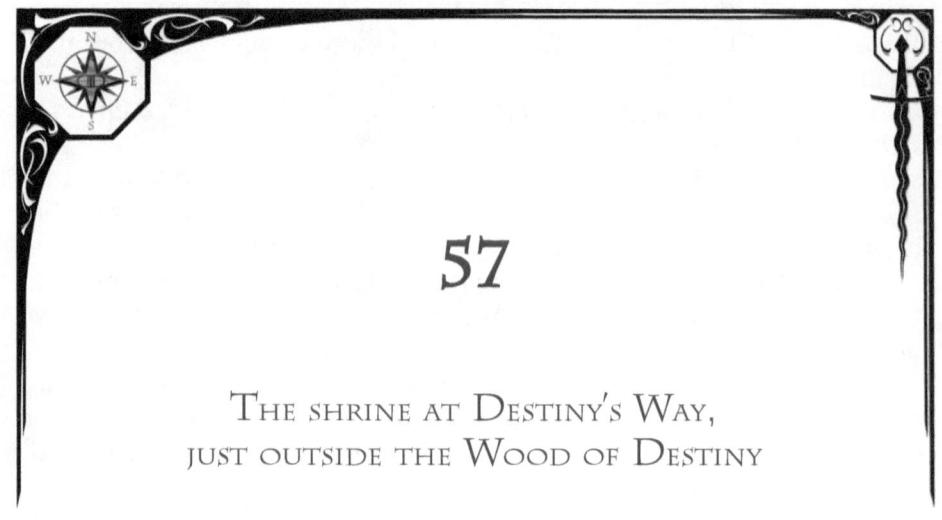

57

THE SHRINE AT DESTINY'S WAY,
JUST OUTSIDE THE WOOD OF DESTINY

A weary Absol Omine left the shrine stables, having tended to his horse after a long night of patrolling. At this point, he wanted only a bath and bed. Those would have to wait; he had to report to the abbot before he could have either. For that, though, he needed food to help him along until he could rest.

He entered the kitchens, then halted. The place was crowded with monks. The On'Desae Order was a self-sufficient one, not employing servants of any kind. Now they stoked fires, kneaded dough, tended simmering pots, and washed dishes.

One balding monk looked up from his task as Absol lingered in the doorway. With a wordless smile, he abandoned his bread dough to fetch a wheel of cheese as well as a small onion from the dry stores just off the kitchen. Returning to his worktable, he cut a generous wedge out of the wax-coated round, placing the piece on a plate before wrapping the rest in butcher paper. He halved the onion. After putting both halves on the plate he handed it to Absol.

"There's bread baking but none left from yesterday," he explained in a soft voice. "I'll bring you some when it's ready if you plan to eat in the hall."

"Thank you." Absol took the offering to the large room where the dining took place. It sat empty this early in the day. Depositing his simple meal on the table closest to the large hearth, he saw plenty of heavy mugs sitting on another. On the hooks over the low burning hearth were steaming kettles. He took a mug, poured what turned out to be tea into it just as he heard someone else enter behind him.

"Good morning, Absol."

"Late night, my friend." He turned to smile at Master Abbott Dannon. The abbot looked as refreshed as Absol felt tired. He held up the kettle. "Tea?"

"Yes." He fetched a mug, studying his old friend as the hot liquid was poured. "Saw I'k'Nole just a bit ago. The lad said you'd had another run in with Shadows out on the moors."

"They're getting closer to the village. They killed a stray cow before we finished them off." The Mancer sighed as they seated themselves at the table. Absol drew an eating knife from his belt, gesturing it at his breakfast in an unspoken offer to share.

"I've eaten, thank you. Besides, you look as if you need it more than I do." Dannon sipped at his tea. His nose wrinkled as he set the mug down, then rose. "By the One, that's strong. It tastes like I'm drinking the leaves themselves. I'll get us some honey, perhaps a bit of cream to tone it down."

Absol sliced up his cheese and onion to make a bread-less sandwich with the onion in the middle. Dannon returned with a few moments later, the fixings in hand along a couple of spoons. He set them down in the middle of the table before he began to doctor his tea. After he poured enough of each into his drink to satisfy him, he took a long swallow.

"Ba'tvian is aware that we're here, isn't he?" His face had a grim cast to it as he spoke. "Surely, he suspects. It was never a secret that the Order of On'Desae aided the Mancers in their endeavors."

"If he knew for certain, Dannon, he'd have found a way to attack by now." Absol ate as he willed the fog to clear from his brain. "Well, perhaps not. It would depend on how much he knows of our numbers. We've changed the game on him in the last couple of years."

"So you have." The monk took another sip as Absol carved more slices from the food on his plate. "We haven't heard a great deal about his activities. Last I heard he was hanging around Rathburn."

"I believe he's made that area his home territory. We're still trying to confirm who all he has with him at this point. The barbarian and Nerisse are all that we've identified. There are others – at least two or three – but we haven't been able to pinpoint who they are. Veln's poking around trying to get more information for us before we make our move."

"So there's nothing new." Dannon grunted. "Well, preparations continue. One of our farmers bought some livestock from over Goose-Bree way. I had him buy us a few more horses. The blacksmith has been busy shoeing them. We've enough grain, dried fruit, tubers, and salted meat to last us for a month or so."

"The shrine still needs defensive work."

"Too true, my friend. At least the doors for the front gate will be done soon." Dannon gave him a wry smile. The shrine's entrance hadn't had doors for longer than the village had stood. "None of us are experts in warfare, so we're doing the best we can. We've got those plans you've drawn up. Also, one of the brothers is digging through the library for more ideas. Our biggest issue, I think, is that we've little usable wood and no stone quarries. We have to source them from somewhere else."

"I suppose no one has thought of venturing into the Wood of Destiny in search of deadfall?" Absol wasn't stupid enough to suggest that they start chopping down trees there. The Wood was a strange place with a mind of its own. There were legends about people who'd harvested live trees. None of them ended well.

"No. There aren't many willing to go. Even you don't spend that long in the Wood," the abbot pointed out.

"I'k'Nole does. He doesn't appear to suffer any ill effects. I'll talk to him later about it. Has there been any word from the others?"

"Not as yet."

Absol sighed as he finished his meal. Half of his people were either out seeking clues to their enemy's whereabouts or attempting to gain recruits for their cause. They had found that most of the city-states wanted little to do with their venture. The ruling lords felt it was a conflict that did not touch them in any way. The people in the rural communities, however, were not so sanguine about Ba'tvian and his ilk running roughshod over the countryside. They were all too often his prey.

Though the villages were more supportive, there weren't many who could join their ranks. The farms had to be run, crops planted, herds tended. They gave what they could, often in the form of food or the odd livestock – older animals, well past their prime. It was something, at least.

"Did I'k'Nole do anymore of – well, whatever it is that he does?" Dannon asked as he left the table for the tea kettle.

"Yes." Absol frowned, then realized that he hadn't touched his mug. He took a large, almost absent swallow from it. Without honey or cream, the strong tea was bitter. The Mancer wasn't in a state to care overmuch about the taste. "He did some sort of fire trick. He can flick it off his sword blade. It burns the Shadows to nothing in short order, yet touches nothing around them. He also did something else; I didn't see what it was. There was a flash of light. The things are all gone when it faded."

"He's become quite the mage, hasn't he?" Dannon poured his tea, set the kettle on the table beside them. Sitting down, he reached for honey.

"He needs more training." Not for the first time, Absol wished they could afford to send his ward to the Trinity College of Magery. The teachers there would be able to school him with greater aptitude. The lad's mastery of his power was more intuitive, but their guidance and experience would be invaluable. With his knack for magic, his apprentice would likely be away just a year or two. "Not that conventional arcane methods work for him. He's been experimenting in the Wood."

"Is that safe?"

"I have no idea." Absol said it with tired resignation. "Dannon, that boy has magery in his bones. He seems to be aware on an instinctive level where the limits are – even if most spells he attempts fall to pieces half-way through. Still, your guess is as good as mine as to how safe it is for him to practice there. Still, the Wood seems to welcome him."

"Hmph." The monk dwelled on that for a moment, then let it go. "Knowing him, he'll do it even if we tell him not to. He's an obedient lad, but…"

"Not when it comes to magic or the Wood." Neither man had ever been able to keep the boy from wandering past the Wood's boundary, or from playing with the power within him. "He's sixteen – old enough to bear the brunt of his decisions."

"Ba'tvian was sixteen when he went to the bad."

The sobering statement had Absol looking at his friend, eyes sharp.

"Do you seriously believe that I'k'Nole – the boy who is so determined to slay every Shadow in the world – would join their forces?"

"No, no, my friend." The abbott sighed. "I'm sorry. He is mature for his age, skilled, and opposed to the blood mage's path. But the young make mistakes, Absol. I don't want him to do something that could cost him his life."

"I think we can trust him to make the right choices in this." Absol relaxed. "As for mistakes – life is full of them, old friend. There's no avoiding making a few along the way."

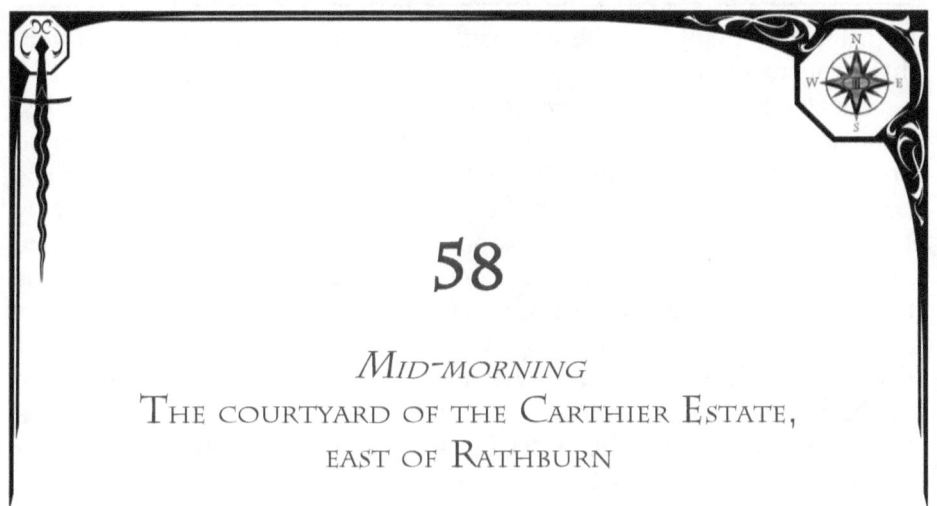

58

NERISSE se li Astorae walked into place with the Jeste twins, the front façade of the manor at her back. The household servants gathered by the larger of the two stables in the courtyard. Opposite them, Ba'tvian and Raptu stood with the former seneschal Wilton bound at their feet. The young Lord Carthier wore a stern expression, though those acquainted with him could see the glint in his eyes that bespoke his enjoyment. Unlike Raptu, Ba'tvian's expression was cool, distant. Only the red light of magic that glittered in his pupils gave away his anger.

She noted the absence of Prialla and Halvark. Both were likely attending to things at the Tretoan Manor, making sure that this… breakdown of obedience did not affect the household there. Given how Prialla ran the estate, Nerisse would have been surprised to find anyone willing to risk her wrath. The punishments were harsh, yet the rewards were many. She doled out each with a firm hand, while letting Halvark play the figurehead.

Raptu, she decided, needed to learn from his blonde playmate's example.

She didn't listen as Raptu described their prisoner's transgressions to the servant audience. They'd discussed the speech in depth before calling everyone together. Certain that Ba'tvian would keep the lordling on track, Nerisse devoted her attention to monitoring the psychic conditioning she and her lord had given the twins. They needed to be checked often. Their reactions to it were different from the others.

Ibestor had seemed to embrace it, his animalistic nature yearning to be accepted by a 'pack'. There had been no changes in his thought processes as they had already been what Ba'tvian required of him: a desire to be wanted, needing the security and guidance provided by someone he saw as stronger. Raptu, Halvark, and Prialla had slipped into the necessary modes of thought little by little, retaining the fullness of their personalities. Though still ambitious, they were more open to acknowledging the leadership of her chosen lord. Prialla's ambition was part of her motivation; they were also the core of the chains that bound her. Of those three, she was the one that Ba'tvian had wanted the most hold over, as she in turn held great influence over the other two.

Lakit and Tavor, however, had undergone notable changes in personality. Tavor had been almost completely without emotion when they had first met. He'd seldom spoke, often letting his twin do so for both of them. Where Lakit had led, he followed.

Tavor's twin had possessed emotions. She had observed that those emotions were waning at their initial meeting. Now they were on par with Tavor's. As they were now, both were obedient, quiet, retaining only enough personality to appear semi-normal when put in situations where they had to think for themselves. They had preferences, yet no real feelings about them; their likes and dislikes had become no more than habit.

They did – or rather, Lakit did – participate in conversation when the topic turned to their peculiar brand of mage-craft. The twins specialized in promoting famine and pestilence. Skilled as they were, the techniques they employed did not always show instantaneous results. It took them six months to a year or more to afflict a sizable area. They could not pin-point one small location without affecting the whole region in some way. There were other variables to be factored in: food stores, native climate, economy, even the type of terrain – all of it skewed the results.

Ba'tvian had been working with them to fine-tune their methods. He hadn't gone into detail with her, just advised her of the overall progress made. After all the work of the last few years, her lord wanted to be certain that they would stay.

Nerisse found nothing amiss in their minds. She retreated back behind her shields as Raptu announced the seneschal's punishment. It gave her enough forewarning to reinforce her protections as

Ba'tvian gave a negligent motion of one hand, signaling to the Shadows to take their meal.

She watched Ba'tvian as they converged on the struggling man, did her best to ignore the screams, the waves of terror. She concentrated so hard that she barely registered the stink of bowel, the spray of blood, the slick sounds of flesh being rent apart. It didn't stop her from feeling the pain or the death. Nausea welled up. She had to swallow hard several times to keep her gorge from down. The entire time, even as her temples began to pound in time with her heart, she never took her eyes off the man she loved.

Finally, the sounds of the Shadow's feasting diminished. Raptu addressed the cringing crowd, reminding them that it was their place to keep his secrets, to stay loyal, to not allow betrayal in their midst.

"We do not wish to make slaves of anyone," he said with a smile that was just a bit savage. "I also have no desire to go through the trouble of replacing any of you should you break my trust as he did." He waved at that ragged remains of Wilton. "Traitors are deserving of nothing less than this. Yet I am not a tyrant. Be assured that your fidelity will be rewarded…"

Though the seneschal's death throes had stopped, the echo of them throbbed inside her mind. Her head started to swim. She tuned out the spoken promises as her ears began to buzz. Blinking, striving not to faint, she ducked her head and began to breathe deep.

Nerisse.

The harsh voice came with the psychic equivalent of a slap. The blow hit her shields hard enough that they shook, disrupting her thoughts, her concentration. It was what she'd needed. The nausea leveled out, the lightheadedness retreated. Even the headache began to dull. She looked up to see Ba'tvian walking toward her. Behind him the crowd was breaking up. The servants streamed past her, pale and shaking, to resume their duties inside in the manor.

"Didn't you take your draught, Nerisse?" Ba'tvian's tone was disapproving. Her heart quivered in her chest at the sound.

"I did, my lord. It's losing its effect much more quickly than it used to." She rubbed at one temple, giving him a contrite look. "I'm sorry. Thank you for what you did."

He studied her, his eyes dark, cold. After a moment's hesitation, she felt obligated to explain further.

"I've exhausted the library looking for a way to augment the draught, or another way to block the empathy altogether. It's not a mage's or healer's library – not at Halvark's manor or here. I'm not sure where else to look."

"There's an apothecary in Rathburn. Take Ibestor."

She bowed her head. "Yes, my lord."

"Before you go, there's another task I need inform you of."

She raised her gaze, her eyes inquiring. Ba'tvian lifted a hand to her throat, played his fingers along its column. She took reassurance from the possessiveness in that gesture. It told her that he wasn't upset with her – always a concern when she faltered.

She hated letting him down.

"It seems I'm losing Shadows on the moors again. The signs are leading back to the village of Destiny's Way." Ba'tvian brushed a thumb along her jawline. "Absol Omine once used that village as a kind way-station, before the fall of the Chalbrooke guild house. If he, or another Mancer, is continuing the practice I want it confirmed."

"What would you have me do, my lord?" she asked in a soft voice.

"I need a spy. I want you to make one for me."

"A person? One we control." Nerisse chewed her bottom lip, thoughtful. Her skills in mind-manipulation had improved since the night she'd brought Ba'tvian a northern woman as a gift. Yet she'd always been close at hand to reinforce the work she'd done. This would push her capabilities to the limit unless...

Unless I rebuild the mental structure entirely. She'd never done it before.

"I need to know more about Destiny's Way. Then I'll need several people who wouldn't be out of place there."

His eyes narrowed. "Why several?"

"Altering the mind to meet our needs is a precarious endeavor, my lord. One misstep can break it past usefulness." She gave him a summation of what she intended.

"We don't need something elaborate, Nerisse. The spy is disposable once it has served its purpose." Hand still clasped loosely around her throat, he tugged her forward. "It just has to do the job we need it to do."

"I'll do my best for you."

Ba'tvian brought his lips to the point of almost touching hers.

"See that you do."

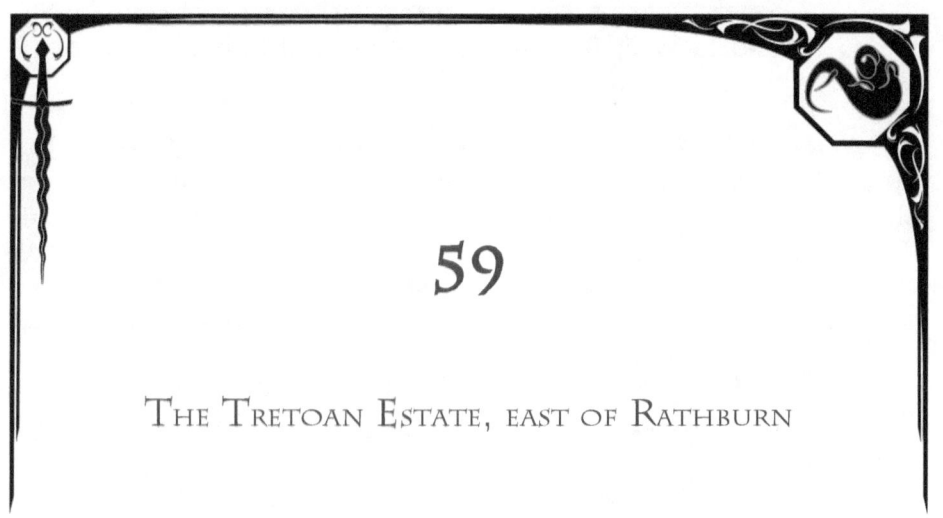

59

B A'TVIAN watched from the window of Prialla's study as a carriage wheeled to the front of the manor. The elven Nerisse, shrouded in her cloak from the rumbling sky overhead, climbed into the vehicle, followed by Ibestor. Beside him, Prialla stood witness with a critical gaze.

"A servant should have been sent to the apothecary. She's too recognizable with her white hair and blue skin," she stated.

"A servant would not have the knowledge needed to look for what she needs. Nerisse can handle potential problems."

He'd also had a brief word with Lakit. A weather-mage was another tool he was very pleased to have. The Dithume would see to it that Nerisse had few people to deal with.

"Why send the barbarian with her? If she doesn't attract attention then *he* will." Exasperated, she abandoned the window for one of the settees in the room. Ba'tvian said nothing as she lifted the lid off of a glass dish on the low table set between the couches and chose a honey crisp. "We have enough issues in the city as it is, Ba'tvian."

"She will not add to them."

Below, the carriage rolled through gates at a sedate pace, its windows obscured with drawn curtains. No, he thought. Nerisse would not add to their troubles. If anything, she would add to their arsenal.

One of his ever-present Shadows slithered up to his side. It curled around his feet, staring up at him with unblinking eyes of leprous white. He touched its mind with his own.

What is it?

You wished to learn more of the village by the Wood. The creature flicked the tip of its tail. Images spilled into his mind, showing him the community seated where the moors met the Wood. They were all from some distance away. *The Wood has influence there. We avoid it, as you know, yet our brethren have gone closer to it in recent weeks. It is a small farming village with an On'Desae shrine. There is no militia, no watch.*

Tell me of the shrine. There had been whispers of a link between the monastic order and the Mancers. Several books in the Tretoan library had also hinted at some sort of relationship. That, added to what he'd been able to glean of Absol Omine's movements, made the notion of the Mancers being based in Destiny's Way more plausible. Especially if the man was familiar with his pets' avoidance of the village.

The On'Desae are blessed. We do not go near them.

Ba'tvian nearly sneered at the word 'blessed'. He had long ago abandoned any semblance of religion. He reined in his condescencion, set it aside. In this instance, what he believed was not relevant; what the Shadows believed was.

Blessings will not help them. Do the monks aid Omine in any way?

The creature gave the mental equivalent of a shrug. *We have seen no evidence of it but we cannot enter the village.*

That will change.

There is a Power there.

Ba'tvian narrowed his eyes at the emphasis on the single word, the implication of something greater. There had been no mention of a Power before this. *Explain.*

The brethren we lost, began the dispassionate answer, *hunted a cow. They were killed by two Mancers.*

Yes. He curbed his irritation. He had been told this already.

One of them was Omine. The other was much younger. The Power came from him. Any of our ken near him was...destroyed.

Destroyed? It seemed an odd choice of word.

As if they never were.

He fell silent, thinking. The notion of absolute destruction intrigued him. At the same time, the act seemed such a waste. Anything that existed held some small trace of arcane energy that was released once the bonds holding it had been cut. That this ability lay with the enemy…

What do we know of this Power? In a younger man…a trainee, perhaps? A Mancer of adept or sage level potential was not something he'd counted on. None of the ones he'd heard of were above master. If this was true, then they could be facing a greater problem than the one in the Rathburn.

Very little.

I need more information about this individual. How dangerous is he? How committed? Weaknesses, vulnerabilities, anything that could be used against him – find them out. He switched to a different topic. *What is the mood of the household?*

He had little doubt that the Carthier servants had spread word of the seneschal's execution to the Tretoan help in short order. He had seen no reason to curb the communication there – provided it didn't go anywhere else. Gossip, he'd found, was yet another tool to be used.

Subdued. Shocked. Many are glad that it was not one of them that betrayed you.

Good. Yet he would still have Nerisse dip into their thoughts, see where their loyalties stood. He glanced out the window, toward the city hidden by the rises of the moors. *What of Rathburn?*

Uneasy. The Watch has been more visible of late. It closed its eyes in a slow blink. *There are rumors that the city officials will be ousted if bodies continue to be found. The Captain maintains a personal interest in the investigation.*

Alert me to any changes there. Follow the officials; their patterns of behavior may prove useful.

He allowed himself a small smile over the next bit of news the Shadow gave him. Dismissing his pet, he turned away from the window to take the seat of authority at Prialla's desk. She sat watching him as she nibbled another of the treats.

"It appears Tretoan's competitors in the cattle market are beset with illness."

"Oh?" Prialla made a show of finishing her morsel. "What illness?"

"Something their cattle hands are calling 'black tongue.' I understand that the tongue swells, turning black once it reaches a certain stage. The cattle afflicted with it have a great deal of trouble eating."

"Then our profits in that quarter seem assured." Her tone was cool. She selected another treat. "Tavor is certainly useful. What are we going to do about the situation in Rathburn?"

"Halvark and I need to discuss it. I want him to see how much pressure he can put on the investigation, perhaps see if he can somehow influence its outcome." He had a few ideas there. "Have we located a more suitable dumping ground?"

"My brother has come up with a few possibilities. I still say that we'd be better off burying the rubbish," she replied, referring to the bodies leftover from their rituals. "If it's done on our land, no one will find out about it."

"It's best not to leave one's skeletons in the closet at home to be found. If the Watch comes to call, they may look for burials." She grimaced as he continued. "I've set Nerisse to a task, one which will aid us in tracking the Mancers. It may mean more evidence to conceal. Isn't there a pond or lake not far from here?"

"A pond. It's one of the places Halvark had in mind." With an expression of studied casualness, she selected another honey crisp. "What are you having her do?"

"Making spies."

"You have the Shadows for that." Her off-hand dismissal wasn't just of the notion, but of Nerisse. This...tendency of hers was cropping up more frequently. Ba'tvian felt his temper begin to simmer.

This one does not like the elf. The creature's voice slipped into his thoughts as a whisper. *Her ambition will be her downfall.*

Has she made a move against Nerisse?

No, lord.

Unspoken was the affirmation that they would keep an eye on the situation. He let the mental connection drop, certain that his oldest followers would protect his interests. Prialla was a replaceable tool. All of them were, save perhaps Nerisse.

"Shadows can only listen. They cannot solicit information." He gave her a steady look as his tone taking on a withering edge. "Nerisse will succeed; she knows not to fail me. Her success will open more possibilities for us – and could give us an answer to the Rathburn issue. Do not," he warned, his voice dropping an octave, "underestimate her usefulness, Prialla."

"Hmph." She finished her treat. Then, apparently deciding that switching topics would be a good move before she angered him, she put on a more sultry expression. "And is there anything you'd like me to do? Aside from the accounts."

They'd discussed those earlier. Ba'tvian needed to decide where to go, and who to send, for mercenaries. He made a mental note to speak with Jeste twins later. As the most well-traveled, they might have the answers he sought.

"I'll need you to take a few of the others out to fetch what we need after Nerisse returns. In the meantime," he let his gaze drifted down her body, "there's time to...experiment. We'll use a cow. There's no sense wasting a human sacrifice on something that may not work."

Her face lit up in a luminous smile. She touched her fingertips to her face.

"You've devised a way to make the spell last longer?"

"Possibly."

"Then let's head out to the pastures." She rose, her enthusiasm making her imposing figure seem girlish. She moved to the door, tossing a winsome glance over her shoulder at him. "Come play with me, Ba'tvian. It'll be such fun."

INTERLUDE 6

ELSEWHERE...

SEATED at his desk with his mirrors on floor stands around him, Labiyal Biyalben finished writing his letter, detailing instructions for his staff. He was expecting a delivery from an associate, a slaver who raided the coast of Annia for the people he sold on the other continents. A few Labiyal would keep for his own uses. Others would be gifted to his imprisoned king. His sire Lord Biyal would see that they made the journey safely.

Hell appreciated such things. That Biyal reaped the rewards of that appreciation did not bother him. Labiyal himself saw the practice as one that prolonged his existence. If the king held him, or at least his connections, in some approval, he was less inclined to have him killed.

Setting his pen down, he folded the note, forgoing wax or seal. He spoke the name of manservant waiting just outside the door of his den. Power echoed in the word, guaranteeing that it would be heard by the one he called regardless where he was. A moment later, the door opened to admit the man, a bald male in his twenties wearing the discreet dark gray uniform that Labiyal assigned to all his staff.

"My directives should be explicit." He handed over the letter. His servant took it with a silent bow. "Not a mark on the merchandise, Nagun. They are not to be spoiled in any way."

"Have I permission to enforce this among any who may think otherwise?"

Labiyal's lips almost curved. Utterly loyal, Nagun always asked before acting.

"Yes. Try not to kill any of them. I could do with the entertainment upon my return. As to the rest, you are well versed in how to handle it."

Nagun bowed again, then left the room. Labiyal took care to tidy his desk before giving his attention to one of his many mirrors. The image glass, a sophisticated with pale skin, golden eyes, and hair the color of fresh blood, stared back at him. He considered his black clothing for a moment. It was elegant in an understated fashion, perhaps a tad too subtle for what he had in mind. He needed to find something more suitable to wear before appearing in Rathbun. His hair, too, was far too striking. Well, that was an easy remedy. The eyes were the most difficult to deal with. He couldn't change them. No half-daemon was able to. Still, there were tricks, little things that masked them with little or no magic required.

Considering of the task that lay ahead, he made a motion with one finger. The picture in the mirror changed, shifting from his reflection to a moorland pasture. Two people crouched over the carcass of an old cow, the man speaking to the woman as he gestured with his knife. Though no sound filtered through the glass Labiyal saw it was a lesson.

"Intelligent of you, Ba'tvian, dribbling out what you've learned." The corners of his mouth curved upward a fraction. Yes, Ba'tvian was like his blood sire, feeding his followers tidbits while strengthening his hold on them. "That will only get you so far with this one. You will have to change your tactics with her soon."

If the boy he'd watched become a man hadn't realized that, Labiyal would need to contrive a way to educate him. Prialla had the potential to break free of his control. As long as she believed there was something to be gained, she was willing to be his. Yet the moment she stopped being willing her mind would begin to strain at the web that Nerisse had spun in her consciousness. Given the strength of Prialla's mind, it would not be long before that web broke.

And then there is the other one…

The one that Ba'tvian depended on more than any other. Did he know how much he relied on Nerisse? Perhaps If he did, he must resent the necessity. But Nerisse was not a perfect tool. She had a problem, one that Labiyal had anticipated.

The mirror responded to the change in his thoughts, the display shifting to show an ill-kept desk with a messy pile of books on one

corner.   The room was dark, empty, yet laden with shelves of
ingredients. Stacked underneath the pile were the leather folders that
contained sheaves of medicinal recipes, pages that had fallen out of
their original volumes, entire books whose bindings had fallen apart.
In one, the third folder down, a red tipped page corner peeked out.
Good. His agent had placed it correctly. That folder contained the
more illicit concoctions. It would be one of the first the apothecary
would go through when the elf visited.

He stood, dismissing the image with a thought as he did so. He
needed to get on with his end of things if he wanted the Shadow
Master to succeed.

60

The Watch House in Rathburn

VELN rose early. He tended to his horse, listened to the rumors making the rounds at the tavern over breakfast. The stories – the ones he'd heard last night as well as this morning – weren't for the faint of heart or weak of stomach. Though they were vague, and most likely exaggerated, the Mancer could see why the Captain wanted him.

He trawled through the gossip until mid-morning, then ventured into the city center and the Watch House. In the distant past, the building had been a brothel. It had lasted until the madam running the place had retired at the ripe old age of seventy. As the story went, three of the brothels main girls had thought to succeed the old woman. Not liking any of them, or the brashness their rivalry incited, she had chosen to donate the building to the city.

That was the story. Per historical records, the Watch had shut down the brothel, confiscating the property. The old madame had flown the coop for greener pastures elsewhere. She'd been at least thirty years younger than the popular tale portrayed her.

Veln shook his head. *The things you remember when you return home...*

He found the foyer empty when he entered. If, he thought, one could call it a foyer; it was just a tiny space with a desk on one side, stairs on the other, and a corridor that started a bare five feet from the door. That corridor was bracketed on either side by four rooms. The grunts – the ones who patrolled, manned the gates, and kept the general peace – used two. The desks within those rooms were shared, used for end-of-shift paperwork. One room was for officers, who were priviledged enough to possess their own desks. The fourth room were for the hunters, those who pursued the killers, the large-haul thieves, the criminals that just wouldn't stop.

Veln hadn't made it past grunt. Sometimes he wondered how high he would have climbed if he'd stayed.

The Captain wasn't down that hall. His office was up the stairs, so Veln headed there. The second floor held the meeting rooms, along with several private offices belonging to the Watch and – Veln noted the placards on several doors – the tax collectors. Interesting. The tax people hadn't been there when he'd served.

He found the Captain's office at the far end of the corridor. The door was ajar. Knocking on the frame, he waited for an answer. He heard unintelligible muttering, then a grudging "come in". He pushed into the room, closing the door behind him after he'd stepped inside.

"Captain Morrin."

"The gate guards said that you'd made it in." A wiry man with steel gray hair and faded blue eyes, the Reg Morrin rose to shake his hand. The Captain gestured him toward a seat. The man looked older now, the creases in his face more like deep crags than wrinkles. Yet that seemed the only mark that age had left on him; he still bore himself with the military posture he'd gained in his youth. "Took you long enough to find my office. Did you forget where it was, Greenmeadow?"

Veln suppressed a grin.

"No, sir. I spent some time tapping the rumor mill."

"Hmmm." The Captain dug into his pocket to bring out a smoking pipe. He knocked the bowl against his palm in an idle motion. "Can't believe all that you hear, lad."

"Can't discount it entirely, either."

"Too true." Morrin gave a brusque nod. "So tell me what you think is going on. After you do, I'll tell you what you've got wrong."

Some things never change. Reg always treated each briefing like an object lesson.

Veln related the stories, what Jimnel had told him, then added, "Ba'tvian Delthanurk is thought to be based somewhere in the area, with at least two others: the Elvanaran lady Nerisse se li Astorae and a barbarian from the north. Both are blood mages."

"Yes, yes." The Captain waved a hand. "We do know of the Monster of Menie and his so-called Dark Adepts. He has anywhere from two to ten in his band."

Veln raised an eyebrow as he continued.

"Correct. We've confirmed two. There are indications that two or three others may have joined them. We don't know as to what or who they might be; the supposition comes from witness accounts of when the Mancer Guild was destroyed. However many there may be, a single blood mage with help is enough to account the victims I've heard about in Rathburn. I can't speculate the number of culprits, or even if there is a blood mage involved, without more evidence – or seeing the bodies."

Morrin's expression was thoughtful. Then he opened a desk drawer and took out a small leather bag. He spent some time carefully sifting some of the crumbled, brown contents into his pipe bowl, and used a small flint and steel to light it. He puffed on the stem.

"Well, you've learned a thing or two, haven't you." The Captain leaned back in his chair. "I think it's a group, no less than five. We don't have the means to keep bodies around here, so viewing them is out. We've got reports with sketches of what the healers found; there's three we use for this, none of them healer-born. The bodies were just dumped. We haven't found the killing ground yet."

"When did this start? I wasn't able to get a concise time-frame."

"Four years." He sucked on the pipe again, letting out a translucent stream of smoke before continuing. "Maybe more. I've done some digging through the files, gotten some answers from the guilds that monitor the roads. We'd get bodies occasionally along the Chal-Edon Trade Route, you see, close to the Rathburn end of it. Most put it down to some sadistic bandit or other. If we pair those deaths with the odd one or two that we'd get in town every few months, it *looks* as if there might have been at least one blood mage here for over a decade."

"That's a long time to be operating." Veln took a deep breath. "We didn't have enough to link them, or any reason to, did we?"

"No, lad. Not that I could see." Morrin sighed. "Maybe I want to see something so I do. It may be I've been working this case too long. Whether or not that theory is true, the deaths have increased over the last four years. We'd find the ones that no one cared about, the homeless ones, the lost ones, the strangers that come in from off the river. Then people started disappearing – the poor, working class, young people who had family to miss them. Some turned up dead. Others have never been found."

"Now they've gone up a social level," Veln murmured. "The middle class, though not the ones with money or prominence."

"Yes." Reg lowed his pipe, scowling at the smoke curling out of the hollowed cob. "The last one was Corporal Hagan's little sister."

"Jimnel mentioned."

"It's also gotten political." He puffed on the stem once more. "The city officials are hollering for this case to be closed. There's talk of forcing the higher ones out of office." He met Veln's gaze. "That includes me. People want answers. All I have are suspicions, hunches, and not enough evidence for a pin to stand on. It took two years for me to get wind of this mess, put a proper investigation together. It took another year to realize that there might be a blood mage connected to it, then damn near seven months to find you. That's far too much time."

"I'll do whatever I can, sir." He paused. "I think it might be better to keep the fact that I'm a Mancer to ourselves."

"The gate guards mentioned it. For the moment, you're a special constable on loan from Chalbrooke. You know a bit of the world, learned a few things. You're here to – what's the word – consult." The Captain smiled without humor.

"Of course."

"Let me get those sketches for you. Then you can tell me if I'm wrong or not."

Veln was sure he wasn't.

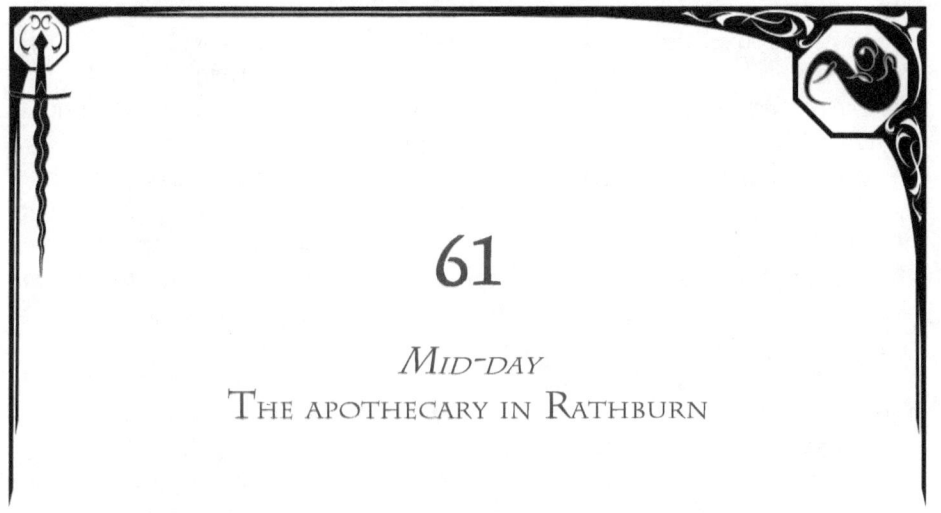

61

I T was raining.

The water came down in gusty sheets, drenching the city in dreariness. Hundreds of droplets spattered themselves on the window panes of the carriage as it was pulled down the cobblestone street. Nerisse had no trouble hearing through the small curtains that shielded her from onlookers outside.

She tweaked the fabric of the window closest to her. Rathburn was such a gray place, she thought. Smoke and smog from everyday living gave the buildings a dirty appearance. The clouds, the rain – they darkened the stains and cobblestones until they were almost black. She found the effect depressing.

Halvark had said once that Chalbrooke looked much the same, only the citizens there painted their homes in brighter colors. After the rain washed some of the grime off, the place had a cheerier ambience under the sun, yet during weather like this the colors looked muted, drab, worn. Rathburn's residential areas, by contrast, were monochrome. No amount of rain or sun could make them appear any better.

They should have called it the Gray City. With a sigh, she tugged the curtain back into place. The weather, coupled with her surroundings, might have lowered her spirits but she was still grateful for it. People didn't often come out in the rain if they could avoid it.

The carriage pulled to a stop in front of the apothecary shop they customarily used. She sat for a moment, studying Ibestor. Clad in rough trousers and shirt made of animal skins he refused to part with, the barbarian sat across from her, his strange, empty eyes staring back at her.

Once she'd wondered what kind of man he might have been had he not been born with magic. The northern barbarians abhorred it. When they'd found it in him, they'd chased the toddling Ibestor into the wastes they called the Ice Fields. His memories of that moment were very clear. The memories of what happened after, less so. They blurred, one into another, until the years were no more than residual images of one basic memory: cold, ice, snow, pain, hunger, the power that kept him alive...

"Stay close to me. Do not touch things. Do only what I instruct." Nerisse stated each order clearly, pausing after each one until he had given a nod of understanding. Ibestor's comprehension of speech had improved a great deal during his time with them, though he was still unable to speak. His mind was more like a more complex version of a dog's than a simple version of human's. The difference lay in instinct; Ibestor was very much in-touch with the most primal of his.

Nerisse pulled her hood up, making certain that her cloak was secured about her shoulders. She gathered her skirts to rise from her seat, stooping a bit as she opened the door. She exited as the carriage driver descended from his perch to check the horses. The elf instructed him to wait for their return, then led the way over the short distance between the street and the apothecary. Behind her, Ibestor trailed like an obedient pet.

The apothecary door opened without a sound. The owner of this place didn't have the need for bells or creaking hinges to make him aware of customers. Slipping inside, Nerisse halted to let her eyes adjust to the dim lighting.

The shop was warm, the humidity low. Herbs, spices, and oils scented the air. The comforting smell reminded her of the still room where she'd learned to make medicines as a girl; she'd often prepared things for the handful of friends she'd had back then. She's made gifts of lotions, soaps, teas, tonics – anything that could be used, really. Her mother had taught her how to make them. She'd been so proud, her mother, the first time she found Nerisse concocting things on her own...

Sudden tears stung her eyes. She blinked them away, breathing deep until she was certain none would spill down her cheeks.

She knew better. She *knew* how bitter the sweet memories of her childhood were. There could be no room for regret or sorrow, not when her people had forced her to choose between them and the man she loved.

The memories were forced aside as she moved through the aisles of wares, past the bins of ingredients towards the back counter. Then she froze. Someone stood there speaking with the shopkeeper.

She stepped back, motioning Ibestor to do the same. Nerisse used the shelves of jars to shield herself as she studied the man. He wore a great coat of gray wool, the emblem of the Rathburn Watch embroidered on the back between his shoulder blades. His broad-brimmed hat obscured his head.

She picked up a glass jar, turning it over in her hands as her mind raced. If the Watch suspected something...well, they did, didn't they? At least one of them did. Why else would they be here?

Think, Nerisse. Be certain before you act. Her lord would not appreciate it if she added to their troubles through carelessness.

Putting the jar back, she proceeded to walk away from the counter. She perused to the bins, playing the part of a patient woman waiting for the clerk to finish his current exchange. She made some show of inspecting the dried herbs as she sent out a psychic probe in the direction of the watchman.

His mind was that of a typical human male. The natural shields that most minds possessed were paper-thin; she passed through them easily to sample his surface thoughts. He was very intent, quite suspicious. Beneath it all was roiling emotional storm. Pain, grief, despair, anger – the feelings stewed in a simmering mess. She touched it, exerting a whisper of empathy to soothe the brewing violence of it. Not too much; she didn't want to risk exposure. It was just enough for it to settle more into the background, making it easier for her to sift through his mind.

The watchman – Olef Altheson – didn't like the apothecary, believed him to be illicit in his dealings. He was here to link a recent murder to the woman he saw as the most beautiful, as well as the most degenerate: Prialla Filoche. That connection may prove out another theory: that Halvark or Raptu were as involved as Prialla. All he needed was corroboration from the apothecary, perhaps a few others. Once he had that, he'd be able to persuade his superiors into a search.

The clerk was not cooperating, dancing around the answers the watchman desired. It made him angry, brash. A wealth of grief magnified his emotions ten-fold. He'd lost someone. The one he blamed for it was Prialla.

Nerisse paused. She hadn't gotten many of the details, yet what she'd found was enough for a decision. The man posed a danger to them, to Ba'tvian. She pulled out of his mind, redirecting her consciousness to Ibestor.

Capture this man. I need him unharmed.

She moved to the front door to ensure that no one else came inside. At the counter, Olef was so intent on the clerk that he didn't notice the barbarian stalk him from behind. The shopkeep, however, did. His eyes flicked over the man's shoulder as Ibestor approached. The watchman began to turn, following the apothecary's gaze – too late. Big, bulky, and immensely strong, the barbarian wrapped one large arm around the man's neck, the other around his torso. Then he squeezed.

The watchman's eyes bulged as he struggled, his mouth worked. His breath came out as hoarse whisper. The clerk backed away.

"All will be well, shopkeeper." Nerisse kept her tone serene, extending her empathy to smooth the way. She came up to the counter, watching Ibestor suffocate his prey until he passed out. "Let him go."

The man was dropped to the floor.

"Do you perchance have something with which to tie him?" she asked the apothecary. He was mousy man, she reflected. Still, he knew her. More, he knew who her master was. He would cooperate with her where he would not with the Watch.

"I – ah – yes." A bit apprehensive, he gestured toward the backroom. She nodded permission.

"Do not be long." The elf watched him go, then glimpsed something dark slither across the floor after him. The Shadows, it seemed, had followed her. They would report back to Ba'tvian before she could do so herself. She hoped that they would approve of her what she'd done. If not...her lord would not be pleased.

The shopkeeper came back quick enough to suit her. At her direction, he and Ibestor trussed up the watchman, then, with a few Shadows serving as lookouts, the barbarian carried him out to the carriage. He would guard the man until her return.

As the door closed after him, Nerisse turned back to the clerk. From a pocket sewn into the seam of her skirts, she brought out a folded piece of paper: the recipe for the tea she used to dampen her empathy.

"I need some advice," she began, "on ingredient substitution for a medicinal draught."

Still anxious, the apothecary studied the formula. His brow furrowed.

"An interesting affect." His nerves began to settle as he considered the matter. "I need my books. Come to the back room, lady, if you would please." He muttered to himself as they entered the room he used as both his still room and office. "As it happens, I saw something just this morning that might work. A different recipe altogether..."

Ba'tvian's Shadows trailed after them.

62

The Watch House in Rathburn

TWO watchmen, one a captain, the other a former corporal, studied a series of sketches in one of the rooms they used to lock up evidence. The pages were of good parchment, the ink used was of the kind that didn't smear or dissolve once dry. The pictures they had been used to portray were...

...*well, detailed certainly.* Veln fingered a familiar set of marks on the one in front of him. *Grotesque is something of an understatement.*

"There are runes here, the kinds used in blood rites." He tapped the page. "They are carved while the victim still lived. The slash marks, cuts, even sections hacked off –", he gestured toward another drawing, "– overlay the them. It's done afte death to hide the runes, or render them inert. This is the kind of thing that stains the world, leaving an imprint of everything the victim felt." He gave a sad shake of his head. Most these had been so young to endure that much. "It's as well you don't have any healer-born working on this. This would have made them sick."

"Blood magery." Morrin scowled, straightening from the table covered with the pictures. "Can you tell if it's that Delthanurk monster?"

"No. For that I'd have to see the bodies, identify the arcane patterns." He reached out to pick up another sheet. "Some of these have been eaten."

"Scavengers will eat anything." Frustrated, Morrin began to shuffle the papers back into their leather evidence case.

"How many eat bodies from the inside out?"

"Where'd you hear about that?" The Captain gave his former corporal a narrowed-eyed look.

"The Monster of Menie has...allies. Our lore calls them Shadows, a kind of daemon kin. No one really knows their origin. They feed on the dead, like scavengers, but they've also been known to attack the living. Ba'tvian uses them – for what, we're not sure. Still, wherever he is, these things are there." He went on to describe the Shadows. "Have there been any reports of black creatures? Lizard-like in apparence, of varying size, with white glowing eyes. They can be either substantial or ghost-like."

"About three I think, none in the city." The Captain frowned as he thought. "There could be more. I'll have to check to see if they've been reported farther out along the Chal-Edon."

"They tend to stay out of cities, for the most part." Veln helped to gather the papers, giving him to his one-time superior to put away. "How were the bodies handled?"

"Burned." The older man shook his head. "Hated to do it; burial is our custom, as you're aware. Still, I understand that fire is the best way to...deal with ritual victims."

"It is."

Morrin tied the flap of the case shut, then shoved it into the cabinet it had come from. Locking it, he pocketed the key as a knock sounded on the door. With a nod from the Captain, Veln opened it.

A nobleman stood there, one with a face that Greenmeadow recognized from years ago. His shoulder-length blond hair was tidy, his blue eyes veritable chips of ice. The expensive doublet and trouse were of a more practical cut than Veln remembered Lord Halvark Tretoan wearing.

Veln allowed him in with a slight bow, his skin tingling with awareness as the man passed. Something about him wasn't...quite right. He blinked in a slow, deliberate fashion, opening his mind to 'see' what ordinary eyes could not. An aura of hazy orange light surrounded Halvark. Hints of crimson flitted in the orange – unusual. The man's mind was well armored, the diamond hues of his shields hinting at not only strength but skill. Suspicion raised its wary head.

There were ways for a blood mage to mask his nature.

Trailing behind the aristocrat was another man. Balding, he sported a mustache so tiny that made the Mancer wonder why he bothered with it. The newcomer's verdant coat was edged with that scratchy gold trim that proclaimed status and wealth. Around his neck was the over-sized triangular pendant that was the mayoral badge of office.

A mayor as taken with his status as any noble. No wonder the Captain doesn't like him.

"My lord." While the Captain's greeting was polite, it somehow conveyed the idea that the interruption was wasting his time. "Mayor Yilsed."

"Captain Morrin," Yilsed began, "Lord Tretoan is requesting to help you in your investigation. The last one was due to start work at his estate, you see. He is keen to be of service."

The mayor's voice had that wheedling yet haughty quality that some of the newly rich had taken to affecting before he'd left Rathburn. He'd found it annoying back then. He still did.

"I am, Captain." Halvark's voice, on the other hand, was cool, confident. It spoke of a man with the authority. "This is not the first time we have had a servant disappear. If I can help prevent more such occurrences I will endeavor to do so." He gave a humorless smile. "I'm afraid that I am not, however, well-versed in investigative procedures. I will rely on you for guidance."

In other words, he wants to make a show of cooperation. Cynicism was an old trait that Veln had left behind with the Watch years ago. Being back in the saddle was resurrecting it. *I don't trust him.*

"I'm sure he will be an *asset* to your investigation." Yilsed wielded what he'd intended to be a subtle emphasis like a club. "Now I must run along to my duties. Please try to make some progress, will you?"

The little dandy sailed out of the room, leaving Morrin scowling. Though Veln was careful to keep his expression neutral, he shared Reg's sentiment. He had to wonder where the man had come from. How had he gotten into office? Given how irritating he was in person, he'd had to have bought his way into it.

"Apologies," Halvark said into the quiet. "I did not intend to make trouble for you or your investigation. The mayor is...ham-handed when it comes to things like this yet I was unsure as to how broach the subject with you myself. My household is very tense over this situation. Though we have openings for new servants, few are willing to venture out to the estate. I am afraid that until this killer is caught, I will be dealing with a staffing issue. If it goes on too long, it could impact the running of my properties. I am sure that you understand my position." He paused. "As I said, I have no wish to make this difficult."

"Yes, I understand."

And we've no choice in the matter. Veln remembered how the old Lord Tretoan had run things. He hadn't elected officials or worn a crown. Instead, he'd greased the wheels that ran the city administration with money, elbowing out anyone else with the same goals. He'd maintained a strangle hold on those finances, with a squeeze here or there to regulate results. The old man would have taught his son to do the same.

Yet the younger Tretoan had never shown much interest in the kind of political games his father had played in the city. Though Veln remembered him as a self-important, brash youth, the rumor mill indicated that the new lord had matured. He still lacked the dominant personality that his late sire had possessed. More, there had been little about him outside of discussions on whose cattle was faring the best this year. It begged a single question:

What are you really here for, Lord Halvark Tretoan?

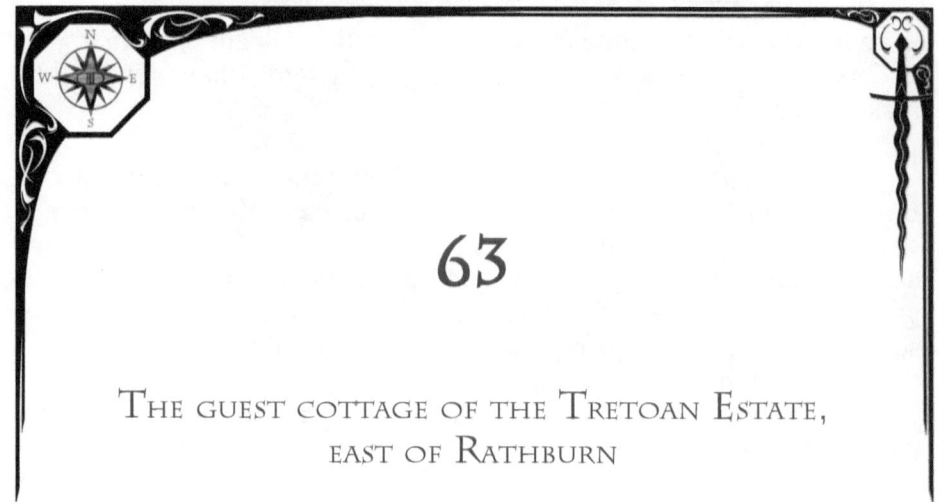

63

THE GUEST COTTAGE OF THE TRETOAN ESTATE,
EAST OF RATHBURN

"SHE did what?" The words came out like a whip, quick, harsh, brutal. Ba'tvian reined it in before his displeasure lashed out. Rage, no matter how entitled it might be, would not help. "Was she seen?"

No. The elf has not endangered her lord. The Shadow who was the bearer of this latest news blinked its white eyes. *She would not intentionally displease you.*

This morning he'd left Prialla after their experiment in the pasture, coming to the cottage basement to think. He'd intended to outline the next steps he needed to take. Now Nerisse, his most faithful follower, had dropped a new problem in his lap. However, the Shadow was correct. The chit would not risk his ire, which meant there had been a good reason for what she'd done.

"What led to this?" The blood mage kept his tone even. Temper prodding him into movement, he stalked around the room, thoughts racing. Old blood, old death permeated the air here, the echoes of pain stirring at the edges of his senses as he moved. A crimson glow began to light his gaze.

Patient, the Shadow ignored its master's temper as it described the incident in detail.

She spoke with the apothecary. He will not betray you. It gave a lazy flick of its tail. *We watched. We listened. No one is aware that the man is missing.*

"That will not last long." Still seething, he managed to calm his mind enough to begin strategizing. The elf had not, actually, made things worse; if they were quick to deal with the watchman, they could capitalize on the opportunity.

We tasted his mind. He is not expected to report back until tomorrow. It paused.

"Hmm." An idea began to take root in his mind. Its success would depend on Nerisse. Fitting, he thought, as she was the one bringing the man home with her.

Time might be an issue, though. Halvark was in town, learning more about the ongoing investigation. If he was with the Rathburn Watch, Ba'tvian couldn't risk sending a mage message. "We have one of the others keeping an eye on Halvark, correct?"

Yes, lord.

"Make sure that it knows about what Nerisse has done. If the situation gets to a point where he has to cover for it, he'll need to be informed." He stopped pacing to stab a glare at the Shadow next to him. "Not until. Halvark is no great actor."

It will be so. The creature glided over the basement floor with him as he resumed his stalking.

"Where is Nerisse now?"

She returns to you. It gave him a detached, curious look. *Will you punish her?*

The Shadows did not normally ask such a thing. It made him consider. She had not disobeyed him. She had not been disloyal. She'd been careful, taking advantage of an opportunity as it presented itself. Nerisse, he'd long ago learned, did not take risks, not with him. She knew how he viewed failure.

"No." He thought for a moment longer, then added, "She has done something that will prove useful. If she is unable to complete the tasks I demand..." He let the sentence hang. "We will see what she does."

64

PRIALLA met the witch at the door to the cellars. She kept her features cool, an expression she often wore around Nerisse. The servants hauled up the detritus of a bloodline that refused to let go of anything they deemed valuable. Clothing, trunks, furniture, rugs, tapestries, and paintings came past them in a stream to be deposited further down the hall. More servants took them away from there. The two woman stood off to the side, out of the way.

The blonde woman was not in the best of humor, despite the morning's entertainment, and the still evident youthfulness she perceived in her body. She resented being forced to cater to the elven twit. Worse, she hadn't been told what she was doing it for.

Probably so the stupid chit can get into someone's head.

The idea of it made her skin crawl. A mind could be manipulated, scarred, injured, broken. Anyone was capable of that. The elf didn't stop with that. She took a mind apart, rebuilding the pieces in such a way that the essence of what that person was, who he had been, was lost. Even the insane retained some sense of self. The mad experienced lucid moments when they knew their own identities. When the witch stuck her fingers into a person's awareness...

Hers was an ability their leader prized. None of the others possessed any comparable skills. Prialla, in the deepest recesses of her heart, feared it. She kept that fear locked away. No one, not even Halvark or Raptu, could see it.

No one saw it now. As the two women stood to one side to allow the footmen by with their cargo, she forced herself to look the Elvanaran in the face. Nerisse appeared serene – she always did. The girl might be naïve, weak, emotional in a way that Prialla never would be, but none of it reflected in peaceful façade she wore. It was one of the things Prialla hated most about her.

"Ba'tvian requested that the cellars be made available for your little project." Her voice was cool. She had no idea what they were going to do with all the old tosh. "He didn't give a reason."

"He set me a task to complete. I must make him a spy. I already have a patient to work with." Nerisse's expressing took on a subtle, inquisitive cast. "Did you wish the details of the process?"

"No." Prialla didn't want to think about what the witch was going to do down there. Still, the elf had reminded her of something from before Ba'tvian had taken her out to the pasture. The irritation eased. "What else do you need?"

"Two work tables, a sizeable cage, perhaps two cages," came the quiet reply. "One of the tables needs to be large enough to hold a man. He'll need to be strapped down. Chains, rope, or leather strips – whatever is easiest or closest to hand will do."

Prialla signaled one of the footman as he returned for another round of hauling. He detoured her way, bobbing his head politely when he stopped in front of her. She instructed him to make sure the necessary items were left below. At this point, she didn't care about potential value so long as it wasn't something that matched furniture in the rest of the house; the Tretoans could spare a few useless antiques.

She watched the servant leave, thought of the gossip this was going to generate below-stairs. Rumors traveled fast, spreading malcontent. Most of the staff were now implanted with compulsions to be discreet, yet Prialla wanted assurance. She glanced at Nerisse, gestured her farther away from the others.

"We don't want this spreading through the gossip mill," she began in a low voice. "*He* doesn't need the aggravation." Nor did she. Still, Ba'tvian was the lever to use with the witch. "Will the alterations you've made to them take care of that?"

"Yes, they will. The servants are not able to discuss anything that occurs on the estates with anyone save their superiors. There needn't be worry."

Prialla gave a brisk nod in return.

"Very well. This should be done an hour or so. Where did you put..." she recalled the term the witch had used, "...the patient?"

"The cottage basement. Ibestor can haul him to the cellars once this is finished. He'll be docile by then." The elf tucked a stray strand of white hair behind her ear.

"Ah. Is the barbarian still playing with animals? He requisitioned two of the old bulls last I heard." Halvark was not pleased. Still, the bulls were past their prime, no longer be useful for breeding.

"Yes. Ba'tvian wanted to see if he could make something more suited to war." Silver eyes flicked up to meet Prialla's azure gaze. "For future endeavors."

"I suppose anything that helps get rid of the Mancers is worth the cost of a bull or two." Prialla gave her a cool smile. "Go...do whatever it is you do. I'll send to you once it's finished."

65

MID-AFTERNOON
THE WATCH HOUSE IN RATHBURN

VELN pored over case notes in the file room while Captain Morrin and Lord Tretoan spoke in the office down the corridor. In the distance thunder grumbled. The weather had started out fine that morning. Now it soured. Rain was well on its way.

He finished reading through the folder in front of him. He'd found nothing new in it. The Mancer closed it back up to set it on the discard pile at one end of the table. Then he grabbed another file folder off the top of the stacked notes at the other end. It was thick, filled with sketches, abbreviated notations, cryptic reminders about leads or clues. As he sorted through the pages in search of the report he was certain was there, his thoughts wandered back to his encounter with Halvark.

Veln had been introduced as a special constable from Chalbrooke on loan to the Rathburn Watch to help with the investigation. While it wasn't true in this particular situation, it did happen on rare occasions. Sometimes a criminal fled a city to burrow in a hole found in a smaller town or village. Other times it was because the local enforcement didn't have the experience. All that Reg cared about was the plausibility.

So long as Halvark has no reason to make inquiries in Chalbrooke the story will hold.

He didn't think that the lord. Halvark had accepted the explanation, asking just a few questions to gauge the Mancer's supposed experience. Now he was being briefed on what they knew so far. If he knew his old superior, answers were also being pried from the aristocrat in the process.

Morrin possessed a knack for finagling answers out of officials. Greenmeadow hoped that it served him with the nobility. Though there hadn't been anything untoward about Tretoan, there was a nagging feeling in his gut that said something was off.

The report...

It was shuffled into the back of the file. Veln dismissed the previous train of thought, settling back in his chair to read through the notes. Voices sounded in the hall outside. He ignored them as he read through case summary.

> *...according to the family, the girl was on her way to the apothecary on Cobble Lane. She'd gone to get medicine for her ailing brother. The apothecary did not remember seeing her or selling the coughing syrup remedy that would have been used to treat the brother's illness...*

He mulled it over. There wasn't much to indicate a victim type, yet most of the other reports inferred that the victims were venturing into, through, or from a poor section of town. They had been on foot. Quite a few of them were known to use alleyway shortcuts. The Cobble Lane apothecary was the only one in that area, often selling medicinal concoctions at rates that were more affordable to the area's clientele. It made up for the reduced prices on the shop's sideline wares: magic and religious supplies. Nothing catering to a specific religion or order, Veln recalled. Just the general sort of thing: resin incense, herbal mixes for scattering on hearth fires, various oils, salts, soaps, chalks, charcoal, glassware, a small selection of more exotic accoutrements.

His family had patronized the shop. If they were running lean in the purse, the owner would sometimes barter or trade for goods. He'd swept the floors there many times as a boy when his mother was ill, nor had he been alone in doing so. The little shop was a touchstone for at least a quarter of the city's inhabitants.

Yet it kept popping up. Not too many times, given the number of victims spanning through the years, but just enough to stick in the mind. He wasn't the only one to have noticed it, either. The latest file belonged to Olef Altheson, the watchman whose sister had been the last victim found. He'd linked the apothecary, or its general location, to several of the dead, then linked it again to Prialla Filoche, the current chatelaine of the Tretoan Estate.

It's not a crime to buy things on the cheap.

Servants often did. Still, Veln decided that he'd have to find out a little more about Prialla.

"Greenmeadow!"

The Captain's bellow had the Mancer bolting upright, abandoning the case files to hurry down the hall. The office door was open. Inside, an elderly gray-clad woman stood clutching at her knitted shawl. Her curly hair was covered with an oversized white handkerchief, the cloth pleated in the manner used by washerwomen. Beside her, Halvark frowned, his gaze on the letter held in the Captain's hand.

Reg thrust the paper at him, a grim look in his eye.

"This was written by the seneschal of the Carthier Estate. He sent it to his mother," he nodded at the woman, "who brought it here."

Veln scanned the scrawled lines. Murders on Carthier land? Hidden by the lord himself. A description of a victim seen the author matched that of Claire Altheson. Yet all the investigative findings – the few that pointed in any direction – seemed to hint at Tretoan or Prialla. They needed to confirm the letter's allegations.

Reg turned to the woman. "Thank you for bringing this."

"My son doesn't lie, Captain." Her voice might have quavered but her eyes glinted with steel. "He'd not risk his position with a lie."

"We understand." Captain motioned to lead her out. "If you'll step this way, I want you tell me more about your son." Morrin would have those details by the time they made it to the front door, Veln knew. The woman would also get tuppence for her time.

When they were alone, Halvark held out a hand for the letter. Unable to think of a plausible explanation for not giving it to him, he complied. The man's face firmed like granite as he read it through. He gave it back, looking the Mancer in the eye.

"That's a serious accusation." Halvark paused, taking a deep breath. When he spoke again, there was a note of reluctance in his voice. "Lord Carthier is a dear friend to me and mine. I personally do not believe him capable of such heinous acts."

"Close friends often don't." Veln watched for any suspicious signs.

"You will, of course, need to verify it before he can be cleared. I believe I can persuade him to allow a search of his property to expedite this." He gave a slight nod, as if the decision had been finalized. "It is, as I have said, a serious matter. The sooner it is resolved, the less impact it will have on business, and the reputation of a good friend."

"Your assistance is appreciated. However, the Captain will not want him to be aware of the nature of our search." Veln said it as both a reminder and a warning. "We will need to consult with him."

"Of course. I will also refrain from mentioning the letter to Raptu." He gave a humorless smile. "I am unused to waiting for permission."

"As I am unused to working with a noble. We will both get through it, my lord."

Veln's gut told him not to trust the man before him. Perhaps, he thought, it would be best if he took a look at the estate first.

66

THE CELLARS OF THE TRETOAN ESTATE, EAST OF RATHBURN

B A'TVIAN descended into the cellar below the manor to find the room illuminated with wax candles. In the middle of the cleared space, stretched out on an old dining room table and bound with rope, was the lawman. Beside him, the Elvanaran woman was bent over his body, the fingertips of both her hands laid on his temples. Around them, his Shadows moved in lazy circles.

Something was not right with the scene. Tiny flames were everywhere, flickering as the wax ran. Heat was heavy in the air, as was the scent of animal fat. There was no darkness in the room, not even in the farthest corners. Eyes narrowed in thought, he came further inside to wait until she'd straightened from her task.

"You've been dreaming again." He said it with a neutrality that he did not feel. Her nightmares were of Jevanel, what she'd done there to prove her loyalty to, and love for, him. There was always the possibility that one day the guilt stemming from Jevanel would undermine her commitment to him.

She looked up, startled. Her silver eyes were unfocused. Then she blinked, and he could tell she was truly back from the mind she'd been wandering in. He waited to see if she had understood what he'd said.

"Yes. It never stopped. There's an herbal tea that aids with sleep; I've told you of it. I use it, so I do not go without rest." She sighed. "It doesn't stop the dreams, but it helps me sleep after them.

Has there been some sign that it's affecting me in my waking hours, my lord?"

He gestured to the room. "You've lit the cellar as bright as the day at noon. Are you afraid of the dark?"

"No, my lord." She hesitated. "Not really. I kept hearing things. The scurry of a mouse, the settling of the foundation. It was distracting. The candles are a comfort to me, allowing me to ignore such noises." Pursing her lips, she eyes the ones on the floor nearest her. "These are tallow candles; they're cheaper than the wax ones."

Though not completely satisfied with her answer, he let the subject drop. Light, it seemed, was now another privilege to grant, the dark a punishment to give. He tucked the notion away to be considered in more depth later.

"Tell me what you have done here, and to what end you've worked."

She smiled. It was a shy, girlish smile, the kind she wore when she was pleased with an accomplishment. She gestured him closer.

"I've been thinking about the – " Her eyes flicked to the stairs behind them and back. " – things we've done with the others. That's more long term than what we need here, but it occurred to me that I could use the same psychic constructs to achieve a more immediate effect. In addition to altering his thought patterns, we plant conditional triggers. Once a set of conditions are met, the construct activates, enforcing a behavior that we define. I can mask my work from him; this man isn't a mage of any kind. I also believe that I can fabricate false memories to cover the abduction and time spent away from the city."

"How long will this take?"

"Until morning." She tucked a lock of white hair behind her ear. "I'll need an hour more, perhaps two, to set everything in place, then perhaps half the night for it all to settle. This kind of working isn't permanent, as I said. It will last a few weeks at most before it begins to break down. Once that happens, he'll start to recall what happened to him. At that point, he'll be able to fight the compulsions to do as we've dictated."

"That's a reasonable time period for him to be gone." He paused, eyes narrowing. "What of his normal behavior? Will there be any change? We cannot afford for his family, his friends to notice that something is wrong with him."

"It shouldn't be an issue, my lord. The patterns I make will work around his normal ones, preserving and mimicking them while nudging him towards the goal we've set. This will continue until conditions warrant a compulsory change or the patterns break down." She paused, bit her bottom lip absently as she considered. "With his position in the Watch, and the investigation... We will need to ensure that he dies, if not by our hands, then by someone else's." She looked at the man on the table, a hint of sorrow in her eyes. "He won't give up, Ba'tvian. We took his sister."

Ah. Now he knew why the Shadows were pleased with her. His elven chit had been more forward in her design than he had anticipated.

"See it done, then." Leaning over the body, he cupped her cheek, then slid his hand down to her neck. "Can you can give him the behavior, the patterns, of the rituals for use later?"

She gave a cautious nod. "I can implant the knowledge. I cannot guarantee that he will be able to perform – "

"He will not have to." A summoning would remedy that. He already had a target entity in mind, one that could be hidden within its host. Leave that to me."

"Yes, my lord. Would you like to see what I've done thus far?"

"No." He ran a thumb along the column of her throat. "Unlike some others in our party, I know I can trust the quality of your work."

A blush of pleasure bloomed on her cheeks at his words.

"It may take a few days to get you the subjects you need for Destiny's Way."

"For that, we'll need the alterations to last quite a bit longer." She looked down at the man between them on the altar. "I think I'll need two days, perhaps three."

"Reasonable." He found his lips curving despite himself. She had served him well in this, proving that she was deserving of a reward. "Complete this, then join me at Raptu's. We need to go through the servants, finish winnowing out the liabilities. On the morrow...I'll find some time for you."

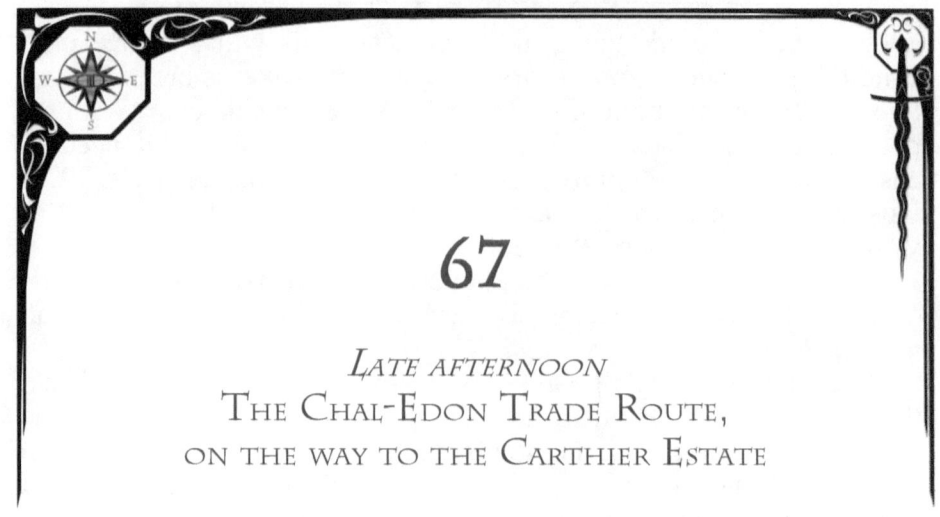

67

LATE AFTERNOON
THE CHAL-EDON TRADE ROUTE,
ON THE WAY TO THE CARTHIER ESTATE

*W*ILL *this rain never end?*

Veln rode along the Chal-Edon Trade Route alone while Captain Morrin worked with Lord Halvark to set up the search of Lord Raptu Carthier's estate. He wanted to take a preliminary – and unofficial – look over the property. Reg knew of the venture. Halvark did not.

It was not a pleasant day for riding. The weather was dreary and wet, the air unseasonably chilled.

The road took him past the property belonging to the Tretoan family. Rathburn abounded with rumors about the manor's chatelaine, Prialla Filoche. Some said she was the true power behind Lord Halvark. Others said she was working to undermine him, intending to claim the estate for herself. Both sets of rumors agreed upon that people who crossed Prialla tended to disappear. Only a few had turned up. By that time; they'd been dead so long that it was impossible to say what had killed them. Then one had to consider the mysterious circumstances surrounding the old lord's death...

Yet the Watch had their sights set on the Carthier holding, not the Tretoan one. The letter – the only piece of substantial evidence to link a noble to the murders – pointed in that direction. So that's where the lawmen would look. Veln doubted the place was clean of wrong-doing. Raptu Carthier was a close friend of Halvark Tretoan, and Prialla Filoche was sleeping with both men, according to the gossip.

Veln recalled the trio's reckless exploits when they were young. He remembered, too, what most of Rathburn had either forgotten about or had never known: Prialla had been the bastard daughter of Halvark's father. Even after she and her chambermaid-mother were dismissed from the household, Prialla had remained in contact with the two men to whom she was closest. They'd gotten into scrapes together, caused trouble among the locals, skipping out of gaol or fines when their fathers stepped in. Carthier had thought his son could do no wrong. Tretoan had been stern with both his offspring, to no avail. The trio had still run wild.

He wouldn't be surprised if they'd become involved with Ba'tvian Delthanurk.

His mount went past the marker that divided the lands between Tretoan and Carthier. Pastures straddled the road now. Horses grazed in vast herds, though Veln spotted a few mules, and even a burro grazing. He wondered what the horses were bred for. The Carthiers made their money from their courier services, also running a small, elite racing stable alongside their main business. He supposed which didn't matter as both utilized speed.

As the road crested a hill, Veln saw the fortified walls of the estate. Set close to the trade route, the open gate left the courtyard in clear view of any passerby. He made out the rooftops of the manor, noted that the architecture was newer than that of the Tretoan Estate. Tretoan's place, set farther back from the road, was larger, with towers built into the corners of the oversized house.

With the rain coming down, no sentries were visible atop the walls, no guardhouses or turrets. A small forest planted along the farthest side seemed the most covert point of entry. As he rode by, the place was strangely deserted. There was no activity anywhere. Peering back through gate as his horse carried onward he saw something he would have otherwise missed due to the angle: a blackened spot of ground, large enough to be seen despite the downpour.

He frowned as he continued down the road in search of a thick stand of trees. He found one just off the treeline of the small wood. After securing his horse out of sight, he took a grapnel and rope from a saddlebag, stashing a few other pieces of equipment about his person before he set off into the foliage. More trees butted against this side of the holding. He took advantage of them, climbing up one gnarled oak to get closer to the top of the wall. High enough to have a clear view of the courtyard, yet screened by the leaves, he waited, watching for signs of life. There were none.

His gaze was drawn back to the anomaly on the ground below. An eerie feeling came over him as he studied that dark stain. There was something not right about it. He needed to venture closer to discern what it was. Lightning flashed above him, followed by a roll of thunder. He readied the grapnel, swinging it as he waited for the next peal of sky-born sound. When it came, the thunder drowned out the metallic scrape of the metal hooks latching onto stone.

He swung off the tree branch to the wall, then began to climb. Pulling himself onto the catwalk, he crouched, waiting. Still nothing. Cautious, he moved to a better vantage point to scan the courtyard again.

Nearest to his position were large stables, presumably for courier mounts. An empty paddock stood beside the structure. A smaller stable with built-in carriage sheds sat across from its counterparts. He found the steps leading down from the walk at the end of the wall and descended, pausing to re-evaluate his surroundings often as he went. Once on the ground, he inspected the stable doors, discovered them locked. At least one groom or stable hand should be inside, though he was unable to verify that as the structure lacked windows.

He cast a wary eye over the manor house, caught the flash of lighting reflected in the glass there. If he could see the windows, then he would be visible once he stepped out in the open. Even as he thought it, the sky boomed. The rain became torrential.

Un able to see the house now, he dashed through the wet to the dark spot on the far side of the yard. As he drew nearer, the air around the stain felt heavy, almost oily. He crouched down, touching a finger to it. When he sniffed the muddied tip, it smelled of char. It was as he out his hand so the rain could rinse it clean that he heard weeping.

He froze.

It sounded like a woman in despair, conveying a loss so great it tore at his heart. He looked around, caught a flicker of movement by the carriage sheds, perhaps fifteen feet away. Not knowing if what he had seen as the source of crying, he rose slowly. With one hand on the hilt of the short sword belted at his waist, he approached whatever it was he had seen.

The sobbing grew louder.

As he got closer, he saw the flicker resolve into two ethereal forms. The first was an older man curled up in a fetal position on the ground, his body so gnawed upon that he was barely recognizable as human. His face had been mauled, his eyes gouged out, and his lipless mouth moved. He didn't utter a sound, just stared into nothing as he twitched.

Veln swallowed. He'd seen such ghosts at another place: the fishing village of Sundown. *Victim...Ba'tvian took him as a victim.* When he opened his senses to see any lingering arcane remnants of ritual, he saw the faint lines of power that bound the spirit to the blackened area in the yard. He shuddered at the implications.

Yet the man wasn't the one weeping. It was the female figure behind him.

Her form was faint, her face buried in her hands as she shuffled over the ground. She wore a kind of white or light gray gown, stained with something much darker. The simple garment paired with the translucent slate blue tint of her ghostly skin told him what she was.

What is the ghost of an Elvanaraen woman doing in Rathburn?

She continued to cry as she wandered past him. That was when he realized she was missing the back half of her head. Horrified, he watched as she turned toward the house. She ambled to the center of the courtyard, looked up at the manor, then gave a screaming wail.

It sounded as if hundreds screamed with her.

An unnatural chill spread through his blood. His heart hammered fast in his chest. Such grief, such *rage* filled the sound...

Muttering an oath under his breath, he raced back through the rain, running up where his grapnel waited as fast as he could. As he climbed over the top of the wall, he looked back. Below, the yard was empty of man or spirit, yet the wail echoed in his mind without end.

Shaken, he swung back to the tree, tugged his hook free, and shinnied down to the ground. He'd needed to get back to Rathburn. Absol Omine had to be told of what he'd found.

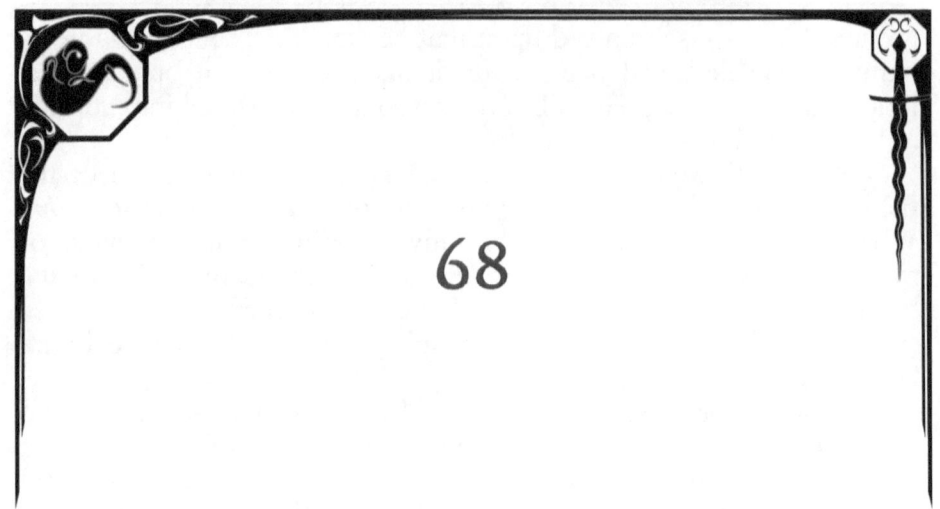

68

Ba'TVIAN watched the man move through the forest alongside the Carthier property. The image in the water bowl Nerisse was using showed only the barest hint of the rain outside, the colors coming through as muted shades, and the shadows beneath the trees were as a bright as day. The scrying spell followed the intruder back to his horse.

"It's coming to the end of its range," Nerisse murmured as the image began to dim.

"I've sent a Shadow to trail after him. Let it go for now." Ba'tvian paced to the window, staring at the dark patch in the courtyard. Behind him, he heard the water splash as Nerisse flicked her fingers the water to dismiss the magic. "What did he see when he looked at the charring?"

They had spotted the man on the catwalk before the rain had become heavy, and only then because Nerisse had been looking out the bay window of the drawing room. She had just arrived from Halvark's manor, resting on the window seat before sampling the thoughts of the Carthier servants.

The manor was quiet, filled with a nervous air with Ba'tvian in residence. The staff were doing their best to make themselves invisible, in the way that only servants could. He had taken advantage of it, going through mage sendings received from the others. The twins were off seeding more havoc in the fields of a rival in the grain market. Prialla and Raptu were scouting out drop-off locations for when their watchman spy would be set loose. There had been no word from Halvark as yet. There wouldn't be until he was free of the Watch.

"I'm not sure, my lord."

Hearing the frown in her voice, he glanced back at her.

"I could tell it scared him," she went on, joining him at the window to sit on the padded seat. "But I didn't see anything. Not a glimmer."

Ba'tvian studied her face, seeing the little things that indicated that she was hiding something: the way she wouldn't look directly at him, how her skin had taken on a hue more gray than blue, the subtle haunted look in the silver of her eyes. Leaning over her, he turned her head so their gazes met.

"What aren't you telling me, Nerisse?" His voice held a hard edge to it.

"I thought – " She gave him a helpless look. "I thought I heard a scream. The kind of sound a grief-stricken mother might give over the loss of her family. You didn't hear it." She sounded very certain that he hadn't.

Which was true. Considering her, what her abilities were, he ran a fingertip over her cheek.

"It was a woman?" he finally asked. "Not a man."

She hesitated, brow furrowing. "Perhaps a man. Some men can sound like women when they scream."

"An echo of the fool we executed, then." The empathic resonance was bound to linger. Nerisse's sensitivity might have been enough to pick it up from within the house. "The storm may have amplified the effect."

He'd found such instances documented in the books he'd stolen from the Trinity's Red Tower years ago. Whether it was true or not didn't matter. What did matter was that Nerisse accepted the possibility. She relaxed, color seeping back into her face.

"That makes sense. What will we do about the intruder?"

"It depends. We need to know what he is, first. If he's a part of the Rathburn Watch, then we'll arrange for an...accident. There's too much attention from them to risk a ritual killing."

"You don't believe he's a watchman." Now it was her turn to study him. He saw the realization dawn on her face. "You think he's a Mancer."

"I certainly hope he is."

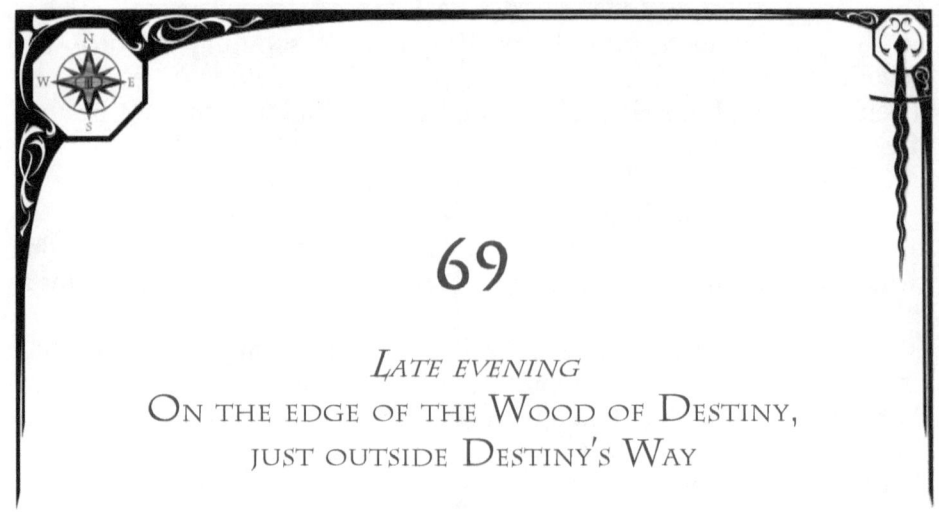

69

ABSOL could not sleep. He tossed and turned in his bed, his mind too restless to settle down. Thoughts of Veln's report from Rathburn kept running through his consciousness intermingled with memories.

He remembered meeting Dannon at the orphanage, how each had been inducted into their orders. He recalled finding I'k'Nole as a young boy wandering the ruined Spirlan Forest, and the way he'd caught the child unknowingly endangering himself as he faced a Shadow for the first time. I'k'Nole had always been precocious.

He hoped that Veln was being cautious. He was so close to what they thought might be the blood mage's lair.

Ba'tvian Delthanurk. He could hear the mental voice of Master Oknare as he spoke of the boy he'd been forced to exile in the mage sending that had been their first contact. Absol could see Oknare and Hamil standing with him on the deck of the *King's Folly*, the nightmarish signs of a massacre at sea all around them. He'd been glad that he'd refused I'k'Nole's request to come with him that trip.

I'k'Nole had a lot to learn yet. Veln would take him through another set of trials soon. The next set after that were the Mastery Trials.

He wasn't getting any sleep. Exasperated with himself, he threw off the covers and rose to dress. If he couldn't at least doze, then he would take a walk. The Wood was a good place for that, its song able to lull his restlessness into something more peaceful, more serene. Once garbed, he left the cell he occupied, walking through the dark halls of the shrine complex until he exited to the rear of the main building. Following a dirt track through the moorland grass, he ventured toward the Wood of Destiny.

He heard the singing before he was halfway down the trail. The song was welcoming, joyful and somehow sad. The whispery harpsong of the Wood held notes of what had been, what was, and what would be. If he listened closely enough, he could catch hints of his future. He wandered too deeply into the forest, he'd see events held in Time's fist play out before his eyes.

He had never gone deep into the Wood, nor would he do so tonight. As he entered the treeline, he conjured a mage light and sent it sailing through the air ahead of him. The smooth silver bark of the trees gleamed in the light, their boughs seeming to lean down in a kind of greeting as he passed them.

His destination was a small glen with a couple of mossy boulders scattered throughout. The large rocks were the perfect sixe for sitting, the breaks in the canopy above suitable for star-gazing. Yet as he approached the glen, he could see the violet of I'k'Nole's mage light filtering through the trees.

"Good evening, Absol." The youth's voice was quiet, serene, as the Mancer walked into the glen. I'k'Nole was seated on a boulder near the center, his face turned up to the sky above. "You couldn't sleep either?"

"No." The older man found another rock close to I'k'Nole's and joined him. "How long have you been here?"

"Not long."

The two sat in silence for a long moment. The Wood's song wove around them, the melody taking on a more melancholy tone.

"When's Veln coming back?"

"Uncertain." Absol rubbed at the back of his neck. "He's in Rathburn right now, following up on something. There's no way to know how long that will take."

I'k'Nole sighed, pulling up one leg to wrap his arms around it and rest his chin on his knee.

"He'll be back soon enough, lad."

"I tried to recreate that blast of power from last night and wasn't able to. I wanted to talk to him about it."

"It'll keep until he returns," Absol assured him.

"The blacksmith is almost finished the iron plating on the gate doors. They should be done in a few days."

"It'll take a full day to mount them on the hinges." He wasn't looking forward to it. "That'll be a hard day's work, lad."

"We'll get it done, Absol. We usually do." They lapsed unto companionable silence once again.

The song drifting around them changed. The tempo sped up, the notes became skewed, disharmonic – as if the song was just a bit out of sync with time itself. A gust of wind blew through the glen. The trees rustled, the grass rippled, the sky darkened. The breeze came again, and this time brought motes of light with it.

The motes were as bright as flame, the color of fire, and swirled into the shape of a building that burned. As soon as the image coalesced, it began to break apart, giving Absol no time to identify the structure before the wind tore the motes apart again. The glen stilled, the song slipping back into its normal rhythm.

Absol sat for a long moment, wondering if I'k'Nole had seen what he had. But when his apprentice wished him goodnight sometime later then left for the shrine, he made no mention of it. Unsettled, the Mancer let his mage light die. He sat in the dark, questioning what he had witnessed.

70

THE MANOR OF THE CARTHIER ESTATE, EAST OF RATHBURN

BA'TVIAN was getting weary of the stench of fear.

It wasn't the sour-sweet smell of it. Fear, was the kind of savory sauce one liked to have at a fine meal. Mixed with awe it took on richer, sweeter overtones. Blind terror, the whispered hints of panic, were meatier. That, he thought, was filling, empowering.

No, what he tired of was the stink of urine and bowel, the reactions of the body to knowing that the pain-ridden end was both close at hand, yet so far away. As the blood mage dragged a naked former butler behind him, the man left a filmy streak of filth on the floor, while that vile smell lingered in the air.

The nakedness didn't help. It was another tool he'd learned to use in last few years. On one hand, it was practical; things that could be made into would not be hidden in clothing. On the other hand, it had a psychological effect that tended to heighten the results of the rites, though not by much. Still, the vulnerability, helplessness, despair, and humiliation gave the power they harvested a little boost.

Ba'tvian would make of use every iota of magic.

The man didn't fight. As Shadows slithered on either side, a few darting in for a quick lick of an ethereal tongue on flesh, Ba'tvian hauled him through the rear entrance of Carthier manor to the covered wagon they used to transport victims. With no windows, it resembled a large box on wheels. Ibestor leapt down from the driver's seat to undo the bolts holding the door shut. The barbarian took the one-time-servant from his lord, flinging him into the depths of the mobile prison. As he secured the door, Ba'tvian stepped alongside the converted wagon to take a closer look at what pulled it.

It looked almost like a horse. The bones of the thing looked bigger than an equine's graceful limbs. The hide was patchy, alternating between a rich chestnut and a coarser tawny color. It was the size of a small draft horse, yet sported the curling horns of a plow -ox. It did not resemble any of the moorland bulls the barbarian had requisitioned from the Tretoan Estate. He looked back at Ibestor.

"One of your projects with Raptu?"

The barbarian glanced at the beast, then nodded. There was no pride, happiness, unease, or need of any kind in his expression. There never was. Ibestor's face held just a hint of curiosity, nothing more.

"Useful, I suppose."

He studied it again, noting out of the corner of his eye that the barbarian seemed satisfied with the pronouncement. As for the amalgamous beast, it stood in its traces like stone. When Raptu came out of the manor hauling another – this time, a chambermaid – who wasn't as paralyzed by fear as the butler had been, it slowly swung its head around to look.

Ba'tvian followed its gaze. The woman – not a young girl, as most in the manor were – had been stripped. The lack of clothing didn't diminish her fighting spirit, however. She swiped at Raptu's face with fingers hooked like claws, letting out a screech of desperate fury. She missed. With a laugh, Raptu swung her around, kicked her legs out from under her, and grabbed a fistful of her hair. Yanking her head back, he slapped her.

"Now, now, none of that," he chided, grinning. He jerked head to the side so that could their audience. Leaning in close, he posed a jovial question. "So you want their attention so much? You have it. Want more?" He hauled her to her feet. "I'll make sure you get it. Ibestor, un-hitch that thing of yours. The little maid wants a wild ride, lusty bitch that she is."

The woman – not a girl – stopped struggling, shaking her head in silent protest. Ba'tvian let the moment hang, as the barbairian moved to free the beast. As he did so, the creature stepped out from the traces. Ibestor worked to remove the breast straps but it shoved against him, stretching out its neck towards the cowering female. Then it opened its mouth.

It was lined with very sharp teeth.

The maid screamed herself into a faint. Raptu erupted in laughter. With a wave of his hand, Ba'tvian countered the lord's prior command with one of his own.

"Hitch it back up. It can have what's left of her later."

Ibestor wrestled the beast back in place while Ba'tvian opened the back door. Raptu threw the unconscious woman inside, then secured the prison shut once more, before turning back to his leader.

"Halvark has just come in."

About time. The man had taken longer than Ba'tvian was comfortable with. "Where is he?"

"The den. Haven't received any word on the twins as yet."

"They are en route from Foghill," Ba'tvian replied, referring to a cattle farm on the other side of Rathburn. "They won't be back for another hour or so. Continue helping Nerisse while I speak with Tretoan." With that, he left the two for the den inside the house.

He found Halvark at Raptu's desk, a goblet of wine in one hand. Weariness lined his face, and the grim set of his jaw told the blood mage that he would not care for the report he was about to get.

"Halvark." It was both a greeting and a command.

"Ba'tvian." He sipped the wine. "I'm in the investigation working with Captain Morrin. There's a potential complication: a 'special constable' from Chalbrooke. I doubt that he's really a watchman as he has mental shields, but that is how he was introduced. The Watch also got the letter today."

Ba'tvian hissed. "Do they believe it?"

"Whether they do or not, they have to verify it. They'll be coming in the morning to search the Carthier Estate."

He could feel the click of something fall into place. Rather than curse the search, he paced to the window – the same window through which Nerisse had spied their unwanted visitor earlier. A plan began to take shape in his mind as he spoke.

"The 'special constable' – what does he look like? Do you have a name?"

"Greenmeadow. Blonde, some gray at the temples, brown eyes. Slimly built, stands about six feet or so tall – he's slightly shorter than I am." There was a pause. "He wasn't wearing a watch's uniform."

"Is that so?" Ba'tvian turned to face Halvark.

"A brown tunic, broad belt, black trews, heavy boots." The lord's lips thinned. "He had a black cape, though he wasn't wearing it when we met. I didn't see a brooch or clasp. He does, however, have the psychic protections of a skilled Mancer."

"There was a man matching that description here this afternoon. He didn't stay long." He held up a hand to forestall Tretoan's outburst; he'd the seen the flash of outrage at the news. "He wasn't here to chat. He came over the wall, began snooping in the courtyard while it rained. He became...spooked. The man must be sensitive; most Mancers are. He went near the spot where we executed the traitor, saw something, and ran back the way he'd come."

The oath his Halvark spat was vile.

"He'll be with the Captain for the search. Can a Mancer uncover what we've done?"

"He should have the ability to, yes." Ba'tvian gave him a chill smile. "He won't find anything. We'll make certain he doesn't. Finish your wine. Eat. When Lakit and Tavor return, we will do what needs to be done."

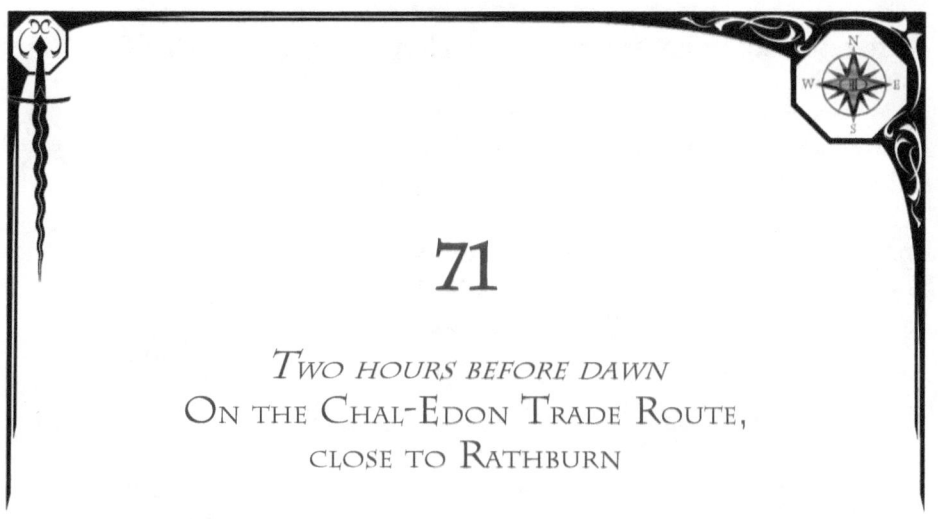

71

Two hours before dawn
On the Chal-Edon Trade Route,
close to Rathburn

IT was raining. Again. There were dramatic cracks of thunder and showy flashes of lightning. Prialla decided that Ba'tvian must love the dreary weather because every time they had something to do in town, he made Lakit call in a storm. When they got to their destination, she was sure to get wet. The conclusion fouled her already cross mood.

She scowled out the window a moment longer, then turned her attention to her three companions. Raptu was dozing beside her on the seat – something she would have loved to do. Last night's activities coupled with the pre-dawn trip this morning meant that none of them had slept much.

Halvark looked to be Raptu's blond twin, as they wore identical gray, non-descript clothing, something any average middle-class workman might wear. They used heavy cloth caps to cover their hair, smeared traces of dirt on their cheeks. Prialla, in her guise as a young man, was dressed in similar clothing that was a bit over-large. Though she didn't like the drab color, it would help conceal them in the rain.

The fourth occupant was the witch's watchman.

Leather brown and dusky blue were the colors of Rathburn's Watch, their uniforms possessing a somewhat military cut. He was clean, his clothes slightly rumpled, and his body unmarked by whatever it was that Ba'tvian's elven witch had done. The only thing different about him was his eyes. They were vacant. She found the stare a bit unnerving.

"I don't think he's blinked once," Halvark commented when he noticed his sister staring back at their spy. "I hope he doesn't stay like this when we set him loose in the city."

"Nerisse said he wouldn't. He'll act normally when I say the phrase." The witch had written the words down for her. As if she needed a reminder; it was a simple phrase, after all. "If he doesn't we'll brain him in an alley, make it look like a bad mugging."

They fell silent. Raptu began to snore. Prialla gave him an irritable nudge in the ribs. He shifted in the seat, mumbled something, and resumed. With a huff of displeasure, she stared out the window as they finished the journey into Rathburn.

The carriage passed through the city gate without incident. It was quickly drawn into the bustling traffic of the merchant's quarter. Even at this hour, its streets filled with the day-to-day of wagons, other carriages, and the odd mounted traveler. Weather didn't seem to impact business here very much.

They drove from the merchants' quarter into the main market, heading for the docks on the far-side of the city. Taverns, brothels, and other places of ill-repute abounded on the wharves. The populace tended to be transient, moving on with the ships or wandering the streets. No one was expected to stay. Considering that there was also more crime in this district, it was little wonder that it was the trio's preferred hunting grounds.

Their vehicle looked as plain, utilitarian as any of the hackneys for hire; a deliberate choice. No one took it askance when it turned down a side road that cut through the warren of back alleys. It lead to an off-loading area between two dilapidated buildings, with an opening that continued out to the docks. There, they pulled to a halt.

Halvark reached over to give Raptu's hair a good yank.

"Eyah." Raptu blinked his eyes open, yawning. He stretched as he rose from the seat. "I'm awake."

"You snored," Prialla accused as they clambered out onto the cobbles. "Loudly."

"Sorry, my sweet. I didn't sleep much last night." He gave her a lopsided smile, charm and what might have been true affection warming his eyes.

"None of us did." The tart reply held the sharpness that came with fatigue. "If it wasn't going through the servants, it was moving them or cleaning up the mess the rest of you left behind."

"You couldn't sleep during the ride?"

Prialla gave him a fulminating look.

"Ah. Well, maybe on the way back then."

"We need to finish what we're here to do," her half-brother cut in. "Prialla?"

"Right." She looked at the watchman. He'd stood quiet, unmoving, through their conversation. "It's time to go to work."

The spy blinked at her, his eyes focusing. After a moment or two, he seemed quite normal, if a bit confused. He gazed around him, taking in the broken or empty crates along the backs of the buildings, the rain, the cobbles, and the wharves beyond them. Finally, he returned his gaze to her.

"Do I know you?" He sounded dazed.

"No, messire," she responded, slipping into the cheeky male persona she used when dressed as she was. "You been wandering 'round here, though, looking a bit lost. Is something amiss?"

"Oh, I – " Something seemed to snap into place in his mind. He lost the confused air as he shook his head. "No, lad. I just seem to have lost track of time. I'd better head in." With that, he turned to walk down the side street they'd just come through.

"Well. That's that." Raptu made a show of dusting off his hands, an act that lost its impact in the rain. "We'd best finish out our errand list. How many does Ba'tvian want?"

"Two." At their nods, Prialla cast around, then pointed down another alley. "Let's try there."

Together, the trio set off to hunt.

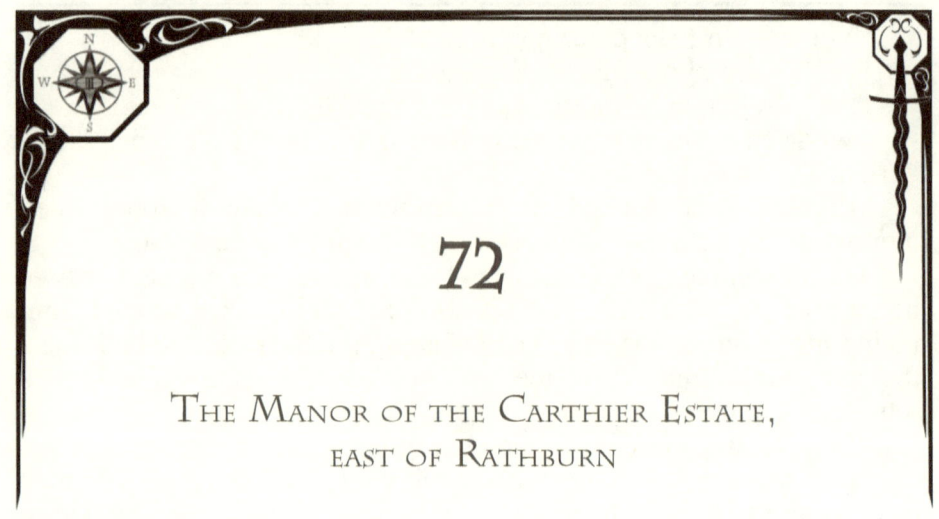

72

The Manor of the Carthier Estate, east of Rathburn

NERISSE woke with a scream in her throat. Gasping, as she bolted upright, throwing off the blankets as she fought for air, her mind careened with memory and terror. She didn't recognize her surroundings – all she saw was the darkness, the close earth, *them* – the mouths – gaping maws of the dead that shrieked without end –

She scrambled over the softness beneath her, fumbled at the sudden edge, and fell to the floor. The physical shock of the impact gave her the jolt she needed. Heart beating against her breast bone, mind reeling, she lay staring up as her eyes adjusted to the gloom.

There was an ornate plastered ceiling above her, a thick woven rug beneath her. Trembling, she struggled to her knees. She couldn't quell the shaking.

"Light." The word was a hoarse prayer as she called up a ball of mage power to illuminate the room. "I need light."

Cupped in her palm, the little ball manifested in a bright flare that blinded. She dimmed it just enough to allow her to see, then gazed around. She was in a familiar bedroom, not somewhere within buried ruins. Limp with relief, she leaned back against the bed she'd been sleeping in, letting the ball go. The light floated above her, bathing everything in a brilliant white.

A nightmare, just another nightmare...

Had she screamed? Or had that been part of the dream as well? She cocked her head toward the door, listening for sounds in the hall.

Minutes ticked by. Nothing happened; no one came. She sighed. *Good.*

She didn't want them to know. Ibestor was aware of her dreams, yet the barbarian spoke to no one. Whenever she had woken in terror during their travels, he had searched for the threat, then settled back down with his animals once he'd found was nothing amiss. Ba'tvian knew, but he was often not with her when she had them. Like tonight.

He'd been involved in some experiment or other. Magic was meant to be used, he'd once told her. It was up to the user to make the most of the power he had. So he often worked late into the night, devising new methods or spells. Nerisse had seen no reason to stay with him as he worked on…whatever it was. So she had gone to bed alone.

Sleep held no appeal now. Her heart still raced, though it no longer beat like a mad thing. She lifted a hand, saw lingering tremors. She fisted that hand, deciding that sleep, no matter how much she might need the rest, would be a futile effort.

Nerisse stood, exchanged her chemise for a simple linen frock, then left the bedroom for the corridors of the manse. Pausing just outside the door, she turned back to the room to hold out a hand to the mage light she'd conjured. The intensity dampening as it sailed through the air, it was half its original size by the time it stopped to hover over her head.

She ventured away from the wing where they were quartered, not wanting to disturb anyone else. The halls were quiet as she walked. Silent, and dark. Hers was the only light to be found anywhere. The gloom was thick, like a dense fog that crowded around her mage light, making it shrink around her. It made her feel claustrophobic.

She thought of the library, one of the few places on the estate she found comforting. A small fire in the hearth there would chase away the remnants of her nightmare while keeping the darkness at bay. The problem was that the corridors all looked the same in the gloom. She couldn't be certain where she was now that there were no lit lanterns or sconces to guide her.

Eventually, she came upon a set of stairs, the wooden newel posts at its head carved with an ornate design. She lifted her skirts as she descended, hoping that the ground floor would be easier to navigate in the night than the second story. It lead to an open room where three corridors converged. Picking one at random, she continued to wander.

The darkness was dense here. Feeling uneasy, the memory of her dream still fresh in her mind, she sought for anything familiar – rug patterns, paintings on the wall, decorative fixtures, anything.

A noise sounded behind her. She jerked around, tried to figure out what it was. A mouse? A servant? Perhaps Halvark or one of his companions? The gloom gave up no secrets as she stood there, heart picking up speed in her chest.

"Hello?" Her voice was tremulous. She took a deep breath to steady it. "Is anyone there?"

Silence was her only answer. Perhaps the sound had been imagined.

The nightmare has made me skittish. That's all. She took a few more calming breaths, then turned to resume her walk down the hall.

The corridor she traveled through gave way to the main hall of the mansion. She paused, getting her bearings. She recognized a few of the family portraits on the walls, even the design of the candle chandeliers above. Assured, she began to go deeper into the house, heading for the library now that she knew where she was.

A faint gasp reached her as she neared the grand stairs that bracketed the entrance to the library. She stopped, listening. Her light intensified, illuminating much of the room. In the distance, someone sobbed.

Frowning, she began to follow the weeping. It led her through a maze of hallways to a plain looking door. She frowned. It was the door leading down the cellar she used. She placed a hand on the latch. The crying grew louder in her ears.

"Nerisse?"

Ba'tvian's harsh voice cut off the weeping, startling her. She jumped back a little from the door to look over at him. Garbed in black from head to foot, her lord stared at her with narrowed eyes, his face otherwise impassive.

"You startled me." She dimmed her light, glad that she was no longer. "I thought I heard something. I'm sorry if I disturbed you."

He came forward to study her more closely. His mouth thinned with displeasure. "Dreams again?"

She ducked her head with a hesitant nod.

"Did I not tell you to inform me if they plagued you?" His voice had gone soft.

She flushed.

"I-I'm sorry, my lord. None of us had much time for sleep. I didn't want to wake you."

"Nerisse." She looked up at the command in his tone. His black eyes glittered with crimson. "Your well-being is too important to my plans for you to hide this. Do you understand?"

"Yes." Her eyes stung. She clasped her hands together tightly as she fought off the tears. Ba'tvian hated it when she cried. He watched her a moment, his gaze dropping to her hands before he held out one of his own.

"Come. You will spend the remainder of the night with me."

She took his hand, grateful that he wasn't angry so much as concerned. As they walked away, the conjured light went with them. Behind the door she hadn't opened, the weeping resumed.

73

JUST AFTER DAWN
THE WATCH HOUSE OF RATHBURN

H E couldn't remember his name.
It didn't alarm him. Someone would tell him what it was. In the meantime, he moved through the corridors of the Watch House despite a mental fog that skewed his perception of the world. Color seemed to have drained away from his vision, yet certain things retained their hue in his sight. Uniforms remained blue. Red – anything colored red showed as well.

It made him think of blood. Thinking of blood made him hungry. Perhaps after shift he would find something to fill his belly.

Thoughts of food slipped from his mind as he walked into a room that was familiar. He shared it with five others, all watchmen handling murder investigations. The desk he customarily used sat in the back corner. Of the remaining desks in the room, two others were occupied. He nodded to the watchmen as he passed them, noting that they were filling out reports. He wondered if he needed to do the same.

Yes…write…it…down.

This time, the mental voice was his own. He pulled out fresh paper, one of those pens with the metal nibs that the Watch had recently begun using, and an ink well. Dipping the pen in the ink, he began to write his report on what the apothecary had told him the day before. It wasn't much. He was having trouble recalling the exact words so just summarized instead. Moments stretched into minutes,

minutes into an hour. After an eternity later, he set the pen down and looked over his report.

> *...help me help me help me help me help me*
> *help me help me help me...*

Something clicked off in his mind, like a heavy door slamming shut. Every trace of expression vanished from his face. He flipped through the pages he had written. Each line, each paragraph, said the same thing.

He gathered up the papers, folding them into a small packet that he slipped inside his coat. The instant the writing was hidden from view, his features relaxed. That subconscious door creaked open, and personality bled back into his face. He decided against attempting another report. Instead, he pulled out the larger desk drawer, found older papers, drafts he'd done when he was still – before he – prior to yesterday. He dug them out, then began to sort through them, reading each one with all the attentiveness of someone new to the case.

They did this to me...so lost...their fault...

They. Who were they? That was why he was investigating. The murdered female – murdered girl – the name slipped away. He felt a faint surge of panic. He knew the name; why couldn't he recall it?

A woman's voice whispered in his thoughts. *It's fine. It's there. You will remember it later.* Tension leeched out of him. Something deep inside cringed inward. He ignored it, resuming his review.

The girl...she'd gone to – to work. She'd gone to work before disappearing, and being found two days later as a corpse. Had he spoken with her employer? He mulled over his notes for a moment. No, he hadn't. She'd gone for an interview yet never arrived. He tapped the scrawl on the paper that named the person – a woman – she was supposed to see that day.

He would have to question that woman. Not yet, though. There was another thing he needed to do first.

"Olef?"

Yes. That was his name. Olef Altheson.

Happy to finally have that small matter resolved, he looked up to see one of his fellow watchmen getting up from his desk. He was familiar but Olef found that he couldn't describe the man. It was like looking at a paper doll, the kind that young girls made – non-descript, vague in detail, with just enough features to tell it apart from another.

...what is...happening...to me...?

He didn't find this perception disturbing. It felt right that people around him be anonymous. They were all paper dolls.

"I thought you wouldn't be back for another few days." Sympathy played over the watchman doll's face. "It must be hard, losing your sister that way."

"Yes." His mind shifted gears seamlessly. He sighed, let his shoulders sag a bit. "I need to keep busy. I'll rest easier – and so will she – when the killer is caught." He looked down at the reports in his hands. "I keep thinking that I might find something if I just look at everything again."

"We all do." The doll stepped towards Olef's desk, glanced down at the reports. "The Captain pulled your most recent case notes. He's been going over everything with a special constable from Chalbrooke. It's all in the file room." He nodded at the papers. "He already had copies of the odler stuff on file."

"Ah, well." Olef gave his fellow watchman a sad smile. "I'll go see if they're done with them. They might have questions in any case."

His friend nodded, squeezed his shoulder in gesture of comfort. He left the room as Olef dropped the reports back into the drawer. He got up, one hand patting his coat pocket in an absent motion as he ventured out into the hall.

He heard the Captain before he saw him. The man was talking to someone near the entrance. He inched forward, glimpsed the blue uniform of Reg Morrin as well as the cloaked back of a man he didn't recognize. They moved from the spot inside the door to the base of the stairs. He hung back in the hall, straining his ears to catch what he could of the conversation.

"...there's something at the estate then. You're certain?" The Captain's voice was grim.

"A blood ritual is hard for me to miss."

"Any sign of the seneschal?"

"No." The other man's reply was subdued. "I only saw the burned area and ghosts, Captain. No one alive."

"Ghosts?"

"Yes. It's an ability I acquired after leaving the Watch."

"Always knew Mancers were a bit odd. We'd better take this upstairs. Lord Tretoan will be here soon." The voices faded as their booted feet thumped up the stairs.

Letter. Estate. Tretoan. Mancer. There was a click in his mind, a flash of pain, that left him reeling inside. He needed to do something. He turned on his heel, found the old servants' entrance in the back. When he stepped out into the alley, he glanced around. Seeing just small bits of trash, a few rubbish bins, he peered into a dark corner by the stoop. He waited.

After a moment, a lithe ethereal body uncoiled in the gloom, sliding out to blink leprous white eyes at him. He told it what he'd heard. He gave it the packet in his pocket. It took the packet into its mouth, then slipped away without a sound.

He blinked.

Olef stood in the alley behind the Watch House, confused. How had he gotten there? Why? Perhaps he really did need some rest. He couldn't, though. He had to help. He had to go back over his notes, find the clues he knew were there.

Something in his mind shifted, like fingers rearranging pieces on the mental landscape. A noise – that was why he was in the alley. Since no one was here, he was free to go about his business. Without another thought, he went back inside.

Somewhere deep in his soul, the real Olef Altheson wept.

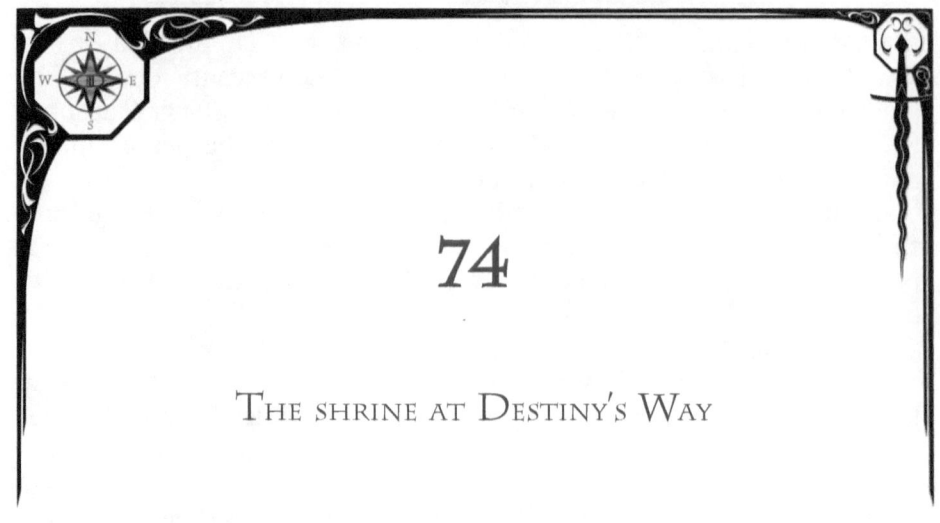

74

The shrine at Destiny's Way

ABSOL stood atop the wall surrounding the shrine's courtyard, watching the carts roll in through the new, iron plated wooden doors that stood open to receive them. Three mounted Mancers came with them, vigilante and grim. The wagons did not bear local produce or weaponry. They bore children.

Celina Behr and two of the newer recruits had stumbled upon the wreckage of a family caravan just before dawn. They'd been on patrol, with Celina teaching her apprentices about the hazards and weaknesses of Shadows. The forsaken things were taking over the moors to the east, ranging from the plains to the south up to the frozen northlands. Their numbers had increased in last few days, forcing the Mancers to respond with more frequent patrols.

They couldn't venture too far from the safety of the Wood, however. There simply were not enough of them. Farther out into the desolation of the moors, the Shadows slithered through the grass in huge packs; they would overwhelm any who ventured there. Those packs were forming closer to home now. Celina had reported that one such pack was responsible for decimating the caravan.

Yet not everyone had fallen to their initial attack. One of the covered wagons had run full tilt for the eastern side of the Wood. It might have made it if the axel hadn't broken on the uneven terrain. The busted axel had dug into the ground, stopping the vehicle only yards from sanctuary. The nine children – most of them no older than six years – had fled the wagon for the trees.

There had been one adult with them. What remained of him was lying just outside the Wood.

Absol had dispatched Mancers with borrowed carts out to fetch the survivors the moment he'd received Celina's mage sending. The village elders would to take the children in until home were found for all of them.

He abandoned the wall for the courtyard. A small crowd was gathering around the wagons. Monks and several of the younger Mancers comforted the children as best they could as they took them into the dining hall. As they left, Celina directed that the carts be returned to the farmers who owned them. Then she spied Absol. She gave a few final words to those who were left, handing off her mount to one of them, before striding toward him.

"It was a bad scene," she told him without preamble. "We found the rest of caravan. It looked as if they were crossing the moors on the Wanderer's Trail."

The Wanderer's Trail was an unpaved path that cut through the moorlands south of Rathburn. It connected the wandering trading families of the plains to the Chal-Edon road. It was seldom traveled nowadays.

"We'll see if anyone has a contact on the plains. We should pass on the fate of this family if we can." Absol sighed as she nodded in agreement. Before he could continue, she spoke again.

"The Shadows watched us. They didn't come near, didn't get anywhere within range, but they watched." Her unease showed in her eyes. "They trailed us as we came back then vanished when we within sight of the outlying fields. It's not the first time they've done so, Absol, but I've never seen so many of them at once."

"I know." Not for the first time, he wondered just how many of the 'wild' Shadows looked to Ba'tvian Delthanurk. "I've had similar reports from the others. I'k'Nole thinks they're waiting for something."

"And you?"

"Coincidence is a fantasy we cannot afford to entertain." He kept his tone low, not letting the words carry to anyone else. "They know we're here. There is no way for us to verify if Ba'tvian does as well."

"You believe that he will come after us here." Celina kept her voice low. "Soon."

"Yes." It was nothing new. They were all aware of it. "Not today; perhaps not tomorrow. It appears that he is busy elsewhere at the moment. I received a troubling message from Veln about mid-morning. We need to talk about the Elvanarae."

"Let's grab a meal then." She gave him a small smile. "Breakfast was ages ago."

They built sandwiches of onion and cheese, grabbed mugs along with a pot of hot tea. Absol led his comrade into the shrine's library where Dannon sat at the table, poring over accounts. Seated across from him, I'k'Nole studied a moldering tome on magic. Beside each of them was a plated midday meal and mug. The Mancers joined them.

"Set that aside for the moment, I'k'Nole," Absol ordered. "If you can as well, Dannon? I want your insight on this." He relayed Veln's ghostly encounter. "Why would an Elvanaran spirit haunt a place she is not bound to?"

"The Elvanarae revered the earth. They were all tied to it in some way." Celina frowned, brow furrowing. "Perhaps that has given them the means to roam?"

"Souls are bound by emotion, blood, or intense spiritual belief." This came from I'k'Nole. His violet eyes were distant as he thought it through. "It's in one the Mancer chronicles, I think. Reverence to the earth as a whole is too broad to be a factor. If they are bound to the earth through belief, it will be the place or region that represented that belief most strongly."

"Like the Temple of Earth in Jevanel." Celina nodded. "That might explain the presence of so many of their dead lingering around the Elvanaeran surface lands."

"Traumatic death evokes intense emotions; those emotions can attach to either a place, object, or person, but there's a catch." I'k'Nole began flipping through his book to find the reference. Absol paraphrased it from memory before he found it.

"Ties made of strong emotion don't let the spirit wander too far from it, and emotional ties weaken eventually. As they do, the spirit fades back into the realm of the dead." He took a sip from his mug. "The connection won't last for more than a few years at best, unless someone renews that connection. That said, it is rare for such ties to be renewed as it requires the participation of the spirit in question."

"Right." I'k'Nole set the tome aside again. "It's been five years since Jevanel. Those ties should have begun to weaken, if not failed completely."

"That's assuming she died in Jevanel. If there was no indication of a person or item that the ghost might be bound..." Dannon tapped the nib of quill pen on the inkwell's rim. "We're sure that the land or building can be ruled out?"

"According to Veln, the Elvanaraen ghost had no reason to be there," Absol replied.

"That's not the case for the male spirit, though." Celina played her fingers over the ceramic girth of her mug as she thought. "He was tied to the spot in the courtyard."

"Yes. There were lines of blood and power there."

I'k'Nole's eyes took on a far-away look. "Blood ties do not have to be visible, nor does the blood have to be spilled in order to form them. If the spirit refuses to let of a living blood tie, then it may explain why the woman was there."

All three of them looked at their junior companion. There was a quick intake of breath from Celina.

"Family ties."

"There's only one Elvanarae left. That would mean that Nerisse se li Astorae is at the estate, wouldn't it?" Absol felt his stomach pitch. "Ba'tvian Delthanurk will not be far off."

And Veln Greenmeadow was in Rathburn. Alone.

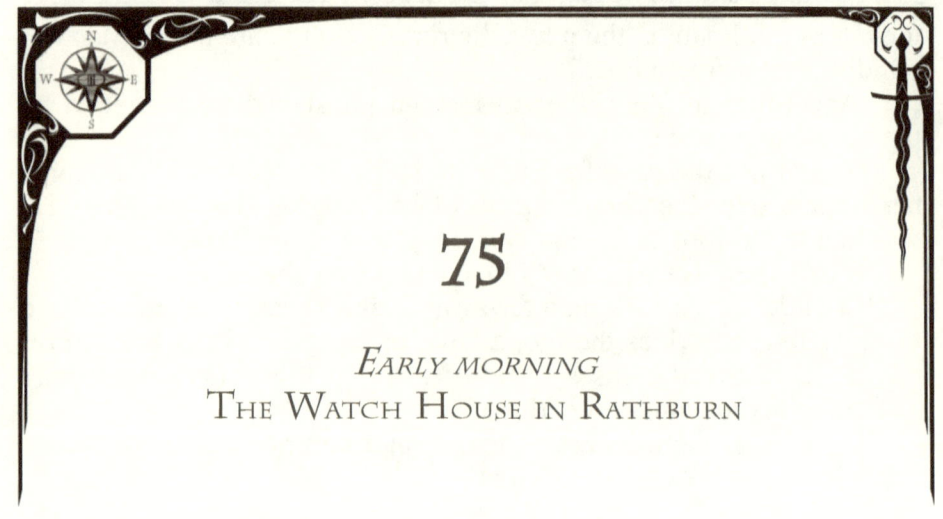

75

EARLY MORNING
THE WATCH HOUSE IN RATHBURN

THE place was full of animated paper dolls. That was how Olef viewed all mankind now. One was much like another, their features ill-defined in his changed sight, the colors of their lives leeched away. He sat among them, taking a seat on one of the benches in the rear of the meeting hall. Next to him was the young doll with whom he'd spoken to earlier that morning.

He still didn't know the man's name. At this point, he no longer cared to.

"Here comes the Captain," the doll whispered. He leaned forward a bit, as if the action would enable him to hear with more clarity.

The Captain came to stand at the front of the assemblage, his back ramrod straight, a silver-haired man in a neat uniform. As the murmurs of the crowd died down, he gave a curt nod, then began to speak. His words rolled out with authority, yet Olef found himself drifting. His mind kept circling back to blood. Visions of dripping crimson flickered in his mind and he felt his hunger grow. He needed to eat soon.

"...discovered more evidence this morning that indicates someone was killed on the estate."

Olef's mind snapped back into focus. At the front of the room, the Captain introduced a man standing off to the side, just inside the room's entrance. It was someone he had not noticed before this.

"We have come into possession of the written testimony of one of the Carthier servants. This testimony, in addition to various other evidentiary pieces we've gathered, has given us just cause to search the Carthier Estate. We have the support of the mayor and Lord Tretoan – " The Captain gestured to the smartly dressed man to his right. " – to take this course of action, and Lord Carthier has been gracious enough to agree to the search. Our express goal is to search for any sign of the perpetrator, perpetrators, believed to be responsible for the deaths of multiple Rathburn citizens. Your sergeants will be briefing each of you on the role you are to play in the raid later this evening."

The speaker indicated the man standing on his left.

"This is Veln Greenmeadow. Quite a few of you may know him; he is a former member of the Rathburn Watch." There were nods of recognition as their leader continued. "He's back with us as a special constable for his...expertise with esoteric crimes. He will be assisting with the search."

The Captain droned on but Olef didn't need to hear more. He stared at the man called Greenmeadow This was the important one. He was not a paper doll like the others. Something about him that spoke of knowledge, of power...

...help. He can help...help me...

He felt the door in the mind slam shut again. That tiny, desperate whisper ceased, then was forgotten. He studied the enemy – for that's what he had to be – memorizing every detail, until the meeting's dismissal. They were to gather in their respective areas under their sergeants for further instructions.

He had his own orders to carry out. They replayed in his mind, a whispery voice that slithered through thought.

Destroy what evidence you can.

Everyone rose. He calculated how much time he had, decided that there was enough. Muttering something about needing to relieve himself, he slipped through the crowd toward to front of the Watch House. There, he stole up the steps, hurrying down to the room holding the evidence on the case.

Every investigative watchman had a key to the cabinets. Fishing his out of his pocket, he cast around the room until he found a still-warm bier in the corner. A pail of charcoal sat next to it. Satisfied, he unlocked one of the cabinets to begin to going through the files.

INTERLUDE 7

LABIYAL Biyalban waited.

The room in which he sat was lavishly appointed: alabaster walls, gilt plaster-work on the ceiling, large mirrors on the walls, a few bronze statues, velvet chairs, an ornate rug lining the hardwood floor. One heavy oaken door led to the rest of the house, another to a private office. All of it spoke of wealth. All of it screamed of vanity.

The mirror opposite Labiyal's seat showed not the half-daemon he was but the enigmatic, rich human patron he portrayed himself to be. His hair, naturally a blood red, had been darkened to brown; the rest of his features he'd left to a glamour. He was careful about the parameters of the spell-work. It was subtle, suggesting a different appearance, one that the observer expected.

He glanced down at the tiny piece of silvered glass cupped in his hand. It showed him a small fire burning in the corner of a room. The flaky, papery ash surrounding the base of the bier gave testament to what transpired there. It would not be enough to dissuade the hunt. He wondered if Ba'tvian realized that.

Nerisse had done excellent work with the watchman. Her tinkering left the human mind open to subversion, presenting an opportunity of which Ba'vian had taken full advantage. There were those among daemon-kind that could slip in through such an opening, take control. Doing so made them subject to the compulsions planted within the host, yet their possession of the body would also enhance some of the alterations. The Dark Adept's choice of a whyte – a simplistic low-caste daemon – aligned with Labiyal's own.

He put the small mirror away as the office door opened.

"Sire, it is good to see you." Mayor Yilsed, garbed in a doublet of pink and yellow, smiled as he urged him inside with an anxious wave. "I'm sorry to keep you waiting."

Labiyal – or rather, Jored Ult, aristocrat in political exile from Genoria – obliged, ignoring the eye-sore that was the man's clothing. Once the door was shut, he took a moment to cast an unobtrusive ward on the room. A mage would have to be very sensitive to the ebb and flows of power to sense it. It served only one purpose: to tell him if anyone else listened. The the feedback intrigued him. One of Ba'tvian's Shadows lurked unseen somewhere in the room.

He has certainly learned well, hasn't he?

He took the seat opposite the mayor's desk, giving him time to take his chair behind it.

"The investigation…disturbs me, Yilsed. I do not like the rumors being bandied about."

"Ah?" The fop picked up a quill pen, played the feathery end through his fingers.

"The city's lords are being tarnished by this situation. This could damage my financial interests in Rathburn. Too much damage," he warned in a polite tone of voice, "and I may have to pull my support. You understand."

Because Tretoan's money isn't the only coin pouring into your coffers.

The mayor paused, then gave a slow nod.

"Yes, sire. I do." He made a show of shuffling papers while he thought. Labiyal could almost see the frenetic wheels spinning in his mind. "As it happens, the investigation is now aided by Lord Tretoan. Lord Carthier's estate is being searched this morning as some sort of letter needs to be discredited." The man waved a hand, flicking the fingers to indicate that the matter was a trivial one. "Both nobles have acceded to the process as a demonstration of their innocence in the matter. I will follow up with Watch Captain Morrin to ensure that this is concluded as anticipated."

"Ah." It was an interesting move on Ba'tvian's part. "If it has not?"

"I – then I will take further steps in the matter, sire." He pursed his lips, hesitated. "I will need to re-evaluate the situation to determine which steps to take. I may need some advice at that time."

"Of course. You will keep me apprised, either way."

"Yes, sire."

"Now, on to other matters. I am given to understand that the cattle and grain markets are being driven to high prices." Labiyal leaned back in his chair. "This is not affecting my own profits, as I've invested in the Tretoan stock. Still, I have some concerns."

"There's been a plague. Tretoan's breeding regime is much more regulated than the regimes of others. He seems to have succeeded in creating a breed that has a far greater immunity to such things. The same can be said for their crops. Carthier has had similar results with his horses." He gave a rueful smile. "I don't pretend to understand the husbandry or hybridization; it is quite beyond me. However, I do know that many of the other farmsteads running cattle or growing grain have made overtures to Tretoan and Carthier both. There may be some negotiating for stock and seed in the near future."

"It will certainly help to stabilize the market." He made a mental note to find out more about what Ba'tvian had the Jeste twins doing; this sounded like their work. There was an opportunity for long-term financial gain if played right.

The conversation turned to other businesses he had a stake in, pies that the mayor also had his fingers in. Gertur Yilsed was a silly fop when it came to his wardrobe, possessing a predilection for currying favor. Despite that, he was a good businessman. Labiyal had needed to guide him just a little to improve his profits. All the while, he'd lined his own pockets, accumulated information, and covertly nudged the city's politics in the direction he desired.

As the meeting concluded, he decided to delay returning to his 'home'. He would see how Ba'tvian's game played out for himself.

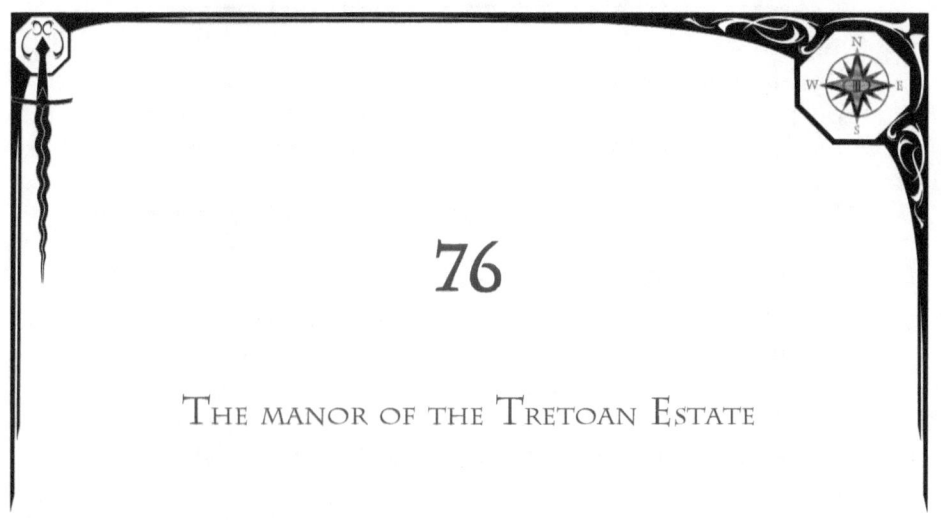

76

THE MANOR OF THE TRETOAN ESTATE

THE carriage was crowded. The whimpering of the morning's catch was enough to get on her nerves. The smell – she didn't want to dwell on the stench wafting up from the floor.

When the vehicle rolled to a stop on the lawn behind the Tretoan manse, Prialla could not have been more grateful. Within moments, the door was open. The two vagrants trussed on the floor caught a careless kick as she made a hasty exit. Halvark and Raptu weren't far behind.

The Jeste twins stood on the grass with two mounts. They led the horses closer as she doffed her cap to shake out her blond hair. The Dithume gave the reins to Raptu and Halvark without a word then went to collect the prisoners. Both men took the horses off a ways before mounting. Wanting away from the stink, Prialla followed.

"You're not going to change?" She narrowed her eyes at her half -brother's attire.

"No." Halvark took off his own hat, reached into his jacket for a rag to clean the dirt smears from his face. Raptu handed him a comb for his hair. "I would prefer to let them see a laboring noble. If we are to take over Rathburn, being seen as someone willing to work would serve us better – in short-run, at least."

"By the time the shine starts to wear off, we'll be entrenched too deep to be uprooted." She nodded, an approving smile on her lips. "That should do it, Halvark. Not so clean as to be freshly bathed, but not filthy, either."

"I'll ride the back way home." Raptu took back the comb, tucked it into a pocket. He glanced at the twins who were now dragging their captives across the lawn to the manor's rear door. "What do you think they'll be used for?"

"Ba'tvian set the witch on a task." Prialla didn't hide her disdain for Nerisse. "We're to deliver them to her. You need to get going." Her eyes flicked to Halvark. "Both of you."

"See you tonight, my sweet." Raptu flashed her a grin. He wheeled his horse, taking off to disappear into the treeline in the distance.

Halvark nodded at her, then trotted his horse around the manor, heading for the road. For her part, Prialla hurried to the door, holding it open for the twins as they half-carried, half-dragged their burdens into the house. Once inside, she led the way toward the cellar stairs to do the same there.

Making sure to latch the basement door securely behind her, she followed the Jeste brothers down the stone steps, bracing one hand on the stone wall to her right. The passage was dark, yet there was a warm glow of light creeping up from the doorway to the left of the bottom steps. She narrowed her eyes. It seemed that the elf witch had decided to use candles to keep her company while she worked.

Walking into the basement proper, she saw the Dithume deposit their live loads into the cages situated in a row along the back wall. Lakit frown at the candles as he held cage door open. Was he aware of the money being burned away? The thin waxen pillars were everywhere, lining the walls, set on the worktable, stood upon two barrels that bracketed the second table. The room was as bright as a summer day with clear skies.

What is she thinking?

Even as the question sped through her mind, she took note of the scent in the air. The fatty scent of grease permeated the room. She held her tongue, taking a tour to inspect the candles in use. All of them were made of high-grade tallow, not wax.

"Most of them are from the stores here." The serene, female voice had her turning to face the witch. She looked as she sounded: elegant, young, infused with a quiet surety that Prialla envied. Even that dratted white hair and slate blue skin spoke of exotic grace.

"I bought a few cases of tallow candles when I was in town last." Nerisse hesitated, then asked, "Would oil lamps be more cost efficient?"

Prialla pursed her lips as she considered it. Running the market values and projected costs in her head, she gave a slow nod.

"Yes. Fish oil is cheapest." It would also leave the elf smelling like marine offal, especially if she used it in abundance as she did the candles. The notion gave her a spark of pleasure.

"Do we have any here or do they and the oil need to be acquired?"

"We have a few lamps in storage. The oil will have to be acquired. I'll see to it." She let her gaze fall on the table beside the elf. Strapped flat to it was one of the traitors from the Carthier Estate. He lay still, as if asleep. "What are you doing with this one?"

"Altering his mind. When I am done, he will be like the watchman. He will be loyal, obedient, and discreet." She turned back to him on the table, placing one lady-like hand on the man's brow. "To attain the level of discretion we need, however, will sacrifice his personality. We will not be able to send him into town on errands, but he can assist here with the captives."

"Which would mean no more manual labor for us?"

"Yes."

The prospect made Prialla smile. Lakit, who had been watching the exchange while Tavor entertained himself by sharpening his knife in front of the cages, spoke up.

"Why so many candles?" He waved a hand at the candles displayed around the room.

It was an answer that Prialla would like to know as well.

"It is a technique. Light and darkness can affect the mind and thought patterns of an individual. I find it useful to use both when altering those patterns." The explanation seemed to satisfy Lakit.

A clang drew their attention to Tavor. He picked up his knife from the stone floor where it had fallen.

"Play time is over, Tavor. We need to go and let Nerisse continue her work." She nodded to the witch, then led the way back to the stairwell leading up to manor. She would have to keep an eye on the elf. If the candles were not useful in the mind tricks she played, then it meant something else. For Prialla, that may prove useful.

77

NERISSE watched them leave, waiting for the sound of the heavy door closing at the top of the steps. She heard the creak of hinges, the thunk of wood on stone. Closing her eyes, she let herself relax. Just a little. With the captives watching, she didn't feel free enough to let her guard down completely.

A low moan from the cages reminded her of what she needed to do next. She schooled her features into a serene mask as she approached the newest additions. They'd been thrown into the same cage. Dressed in ragged clothing, smeared with filth, the pair were a tangle of limbs. One of them was beginning to rouse.

She called up power without speaking a word, weaving a spell that would keep the prisoners silent. With a flick of her fingers, she cast it on the two men. After making sure that the arcane weaving was correct, she picked up a large piece of canvas cloth from the floor beside the cage to cover the prison. She would break the spells and uncover the prisoners once she was done, or if someone else came into the cellars.

Returning to the worktable, she sipped from the mug of tea she had waiting for her. The tea was a new draught, one that she and the apothecary had worked out during her last trip into town. It tasted vile, but seemed to do the job. Unlike the previous medicinal concoction, this one did not fully disengage her empathy. Instead, it muted it, allowing for her to distance her mind from the emotional feedback. She had to be careful with the dosage. An entire mug would affect more than just her empathy; she'd lose most of her psychic and arcane abilities for a time. One sip lasted about an hour with no impact on her other senses. It was the best dosage for, though it meant keeping the concoction on hand throughout her work sessions.

She set the mug aside, took up another one filled with water to clear the taste of the tea from her tongue. Then she turned back to the man on the table and resumed the work.

She had already restructured most of his mind. The vaults of memory were locked, the keys and locks destroyed so that they'd never be opened again. The pathways of thought had been re-aligned, the pillars representing components of personality had been replaced. She was unable alter instinctive behavior; changing the lines of experience that linked memory to knowledge, knowledge to action, was another matter.

She was on the right track. The end-goal was to re-create a patient as a tool to be used for weeks, months, or years to come. As Ba'tvian had stated, she would break people along the way, but would one day succeed.

It would be hours yet before this one was finished. She needed to double-check her work, then let the man's mind awaken slowly to adjust to the changes. If successful, he would be discreet, reliable, and loyal to the bone for the rest of his existence. If she'd failed, then he would die screaming as the first one had.

Engrossed, she didn't hear the first susurration from the darkened stairwell. Nor did she hear the weeping. It was the restless movement of the people in the cages, the rattling of the heavy wire walls being yanked at, that broke through her concentration. She looked up, about to speak, when the crying reached her.

Her heart began to pound.

Nerisse forced herself to straighten, to face the doorway to the stairs. No one stood there that she could see. She picked up a candlestick, cradling the holder in her hands as she ventured toward the steps. She stood in the doorway, peered into the gloom.

A transparent figure crouched in the farthest corner, back to the walls. Her alabaster hair was stringy, filthy, her clothes of rough-spun gray wool streaked with darker stains. Her face was buried in her hands as she sobbed. Then the woman raised her head. Vacant eyes stared, glazed over in death. Tears of crimson seeped from them. Her mouth opened to vomit bloodied dirt onto the floor.

Nerisse threw herself back with such violence that she dropped the candlestick. It fell with a clatter to the floor, the wick snuffing out. Stumbling, she ran for the worktable, putting it between her and the apparition by the stairs. Her mind was icy with fear. For what seemed like an eternity, the only sound was her own labored breathing.

Stay in the light. She can't follow you into the light…

The dead belonged to the darkness. They were buried there.

Eyes squeezed shut, she waited. Nothing happened. No nightmare came after her, no weeping or screams pursued her. Her heart rate slowed, her mind thawed, her eyes opened. Still shaking, she gathered herself, calmed her mind, then looked around. She had work to do still. Much as she wanted to, she couldn't just leave.

She reached out telepathically to Ba'tvian, using the earth to augment her range as he was at the Carthier Estate some distance away. He was the only one she was able to this with. It was because of the blood, the rites, the things she'd done to bind this piece of Einlienn to her lord.

What is it? He didn't sound happy over the interruption.

Are you using Ibestor for anything? Asking for the beast-like man seemed the better move. She didn't want Ba'tvian to know about what she'd seen, let alone her reaction to it. He expected more from her.

Why?

I could use his presence. Her answer elicited a brooding pause. She felt her anxiety spike.

What happened, Nerisse? And don't lie to me.

Tears pricked the backs of her eyes. She hadn't wanted to tell him.

I saw something – in the dark. I can continue my work, I swear. I – I would be more comfortable with someone else here.

What did you see?

Instead of describing it, she sent him the memory. She sensed him weigh the image's import.

I will send Ibestor to you. We are almost ready at the Carthier Estate so I have no immediate need of him.

Thank you, my lord. Relief flooded through her.

The next time you see this spirit, you will call me.

Yes, lord.

Grateful, she leaned on the table as he broke the connection, let the tears leak through. She had a few minutes yet before Ibestor arrived. Then she would finish what she had begun.

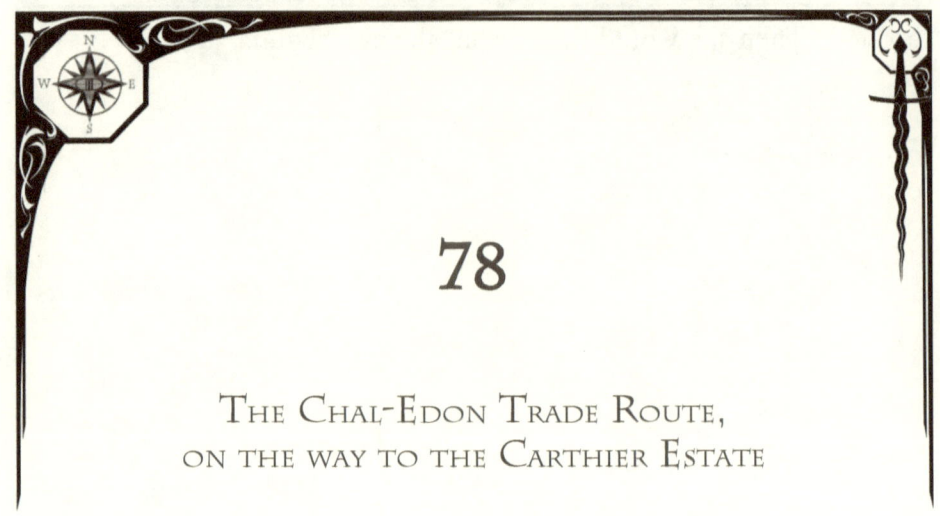

78

VELN rode at the front of the small column heading out to pay visit Lord Carthier an unwelcome visit. Beside him, Captain Morrin scowled at his bay horse whenever it tried to rub its head against Veln's mount.

"The cheek strap on the bridle may be irritating to him," Veln opined as the bay tried, again, to lag a little so it could scratch its cheek on his leg. "Get some fleece to line the underside of it."

"Think that would work?" Reg frowned at the twitching ears in front of him. "I'll try it. We're getting close to the rendezvous point." He nodded at a roadside marker, a short column of stone and mortar. Mounted near the top on the side facing the road was a bronze casting of the Tretoan family seal. "That marks the edge of Halvark's lands."

"That will be him up ahead, then."

The silhouette of a rider waited atop a crest in the road.

"Do you trust him?" He had wanted to ask before this.

"You can never trust a noble. Not in Rathburn." Morrin gave him a grim smile. "Of course, I'm biased. Do I trust him insofar as the investigation is concerned? Not really. His stake in the outcome is tenuous at best. Something else is motivating him."

"It could be as simple as him wanting to help clear his friend's name."

"Possible." The tone was doubtful, however. "I can't help but think that it's very convenient for him to be squeezing his way into the case the same day that you arrive."

"'Coincidence isn't'," Veln quoted. Reg gave him an appraising look.

"Remember that, do you?"

"It's a good maxim for anyone in our lines of work. It's something I pass on to my students, when I have them."

"Do *you* trust him?"

"No." The Mancer sighed. "And for much the same reasons."

The two lapsed into silence as they approached Halvark. He wasn't dressed in the finery of his station, opting for drab, practical garb. The man looked weary, as if he'd been out all night. They exchanged nods in lieu of greetings. When they reached him, he guided his mount – a pleasure palfrey, if Veln was any judge – to walk on the other side of the Captain.

"I have spoken to Raptu; he has agreed to the search. He will meet us at the gates," Halvark told them.

"Stayed up late, my lord?" The Mancer gave his question a casual tone.

"Yes. My favorite mare foaled last night. As she'd had some trouble during the pregnancy I wanted to make sure that the birthing went smoothly." The noble sighed. "Which it did not. We had to turn the foal. We didn't lose either one, though."

"A night well spent then," Veln murmured. His thoughts were very different. *Raptu is the horse enthusiast. Halvark has never given the impression of being very partial to anything except his friend and the girl Prialla.* He filed the story away for verification later as Halvark posed a query of his own.

"What are we looking for at the estate?"

"Evidence of murder: blood, human bones, bodies, to start. Greenmeadow is our expert on the more ritualistic style of killers." The Captain inclined his head toward Veln who took up the thread of conversation again.

"Ritualistic killers often leave little indications of their interests in the spaces they occupy. Texts, drawings, even souvenirs of their victims. Some will keep the blood of a victim, to either drink or write with it. Others will sketch out the fantasies that they then make reality at a later point." As he spoke, he saw that Halvark was paying avid attention to his words. "Then there are the cleaning efforts. Unusual cleaning activity, burn piles, fresh turned soil can all point to efforts of a killer cleaning up the mess of his crime."

He expounded on that for bit, describing how blood could hide in places not often looked at, how the scent of butcher lingered, even how certain molds would grow only on the patches of blood and flesh. Morrin added his own experiences from time-to-time, leaving the majority of the lecture to his former corporal. The educational oration would have done his Mancer teachers proud had they still lived. It lasted until they arrived at Cather Estate.

Raptu Carthier, his roguish face solemn, stood beside the gate leading into the courtyard. Unlike his fellow noble, he was freshly scrubbed, his hair still wet. The riding habit he sported implied the the belief that this affair would be a brief one. He stepped forward to welcome them, then led the column within the walls of his home. The first thing Veln noticed was the dark spot staining the ground. They'd chosen not to hide it. He dwelled on that as they dismounted.

"Captain Morrin. You've a fine turnout this morning. Very militant-looking." Lord Carthier glanced over the column as the men waited for their orders, before turning back to Reg. "I hope this business won't take long."

"I'm afraid to say that, given the size of your estate, this will likely take all morning, perhaps part of the afternoon. We will do our best to expedite this as quickly as possible." Morrin stood ramrod straight, more like the militia soldier he'd been than a watchman. "Our apologies for the necessity, my lord. May we begin?"

"Yes, of course." Raptu stepped aside, waved a hand. "If you don't mind, I'd like to start with this. You can hardly miss it so I'm certain that you have questions."

"We do." The Captain's eyes flicked to the dark spot on the ground a moment. "Greenmeadow will take your statement. I'll join you after I've given instructions to my men."

Veln walked with both lords to where he'd encountered the ghosts. Already, he saw some of what they'd done. To the naked eye, it was the same. To a mage's sight, it lacked the crimson lines of power. The atmosphere there felt no different than it had out on the road.

"What caused this?" Kneeling down, he touched the stain, rubbed the greasy soot between his fingers. As he did so, Raptu spoke.

"We found it about two days ago. We'd laid poison down for rats in the stables the previous day. One of the stablehands – a slow, thick-witted lad – had tried to dispose of the rats by burning them in the courtyard. We've a designated area for burning rubbish. This?

It's too close to the stables, and it's right in the yard." He sounded indignant and disgusted. "Foolish boy knew better."

"Is the foolish boy still around?" Veln asked it almost absently. He felt a little strange, light-headed. He checked his shields, bolstered them when he found them pristine. Rising, he tried to see if he could find traces of the ghosts. The male ghost should have been there; he'd been bound to the spot. Yet there was no sign of him.

"No. I turned him out. Can't have a man like that endangering my horses. They're the life's blood of my courier service." Carthier gave him a slightly condescending smile. "Business is business, after all."

"We'll need his name – his place of residence, if you have it."

"The stablemaster will. I'll make sure he speaks with you."

The Captain joined them a moment later. As the others spoke, going back over the story Raptu had given him, Veln looked down at the char smeared on his fingers. They'd cleansed the burn spot. If not the two men in front of him, then at least one other who'd known of it. To do so this soon after he'd seen it in its original state meant that someone had tipped the Watch's hand. Odds were good that it was Halvark. Still, they needed proof.

Considering the men, the letter, the likelihood of Ba'tvian's proximity to the area, he had to wonder what else they had done.

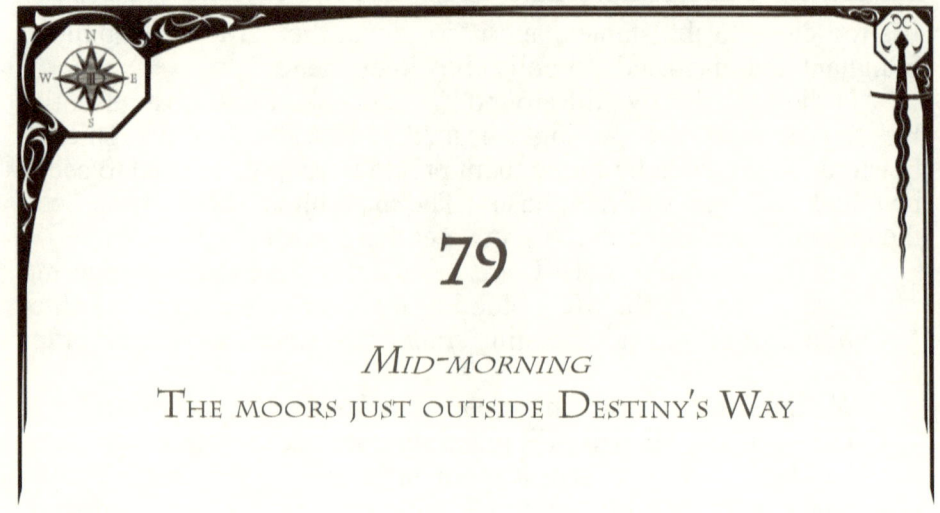

79

ABSOL Omine's mind was crowded as he took his protégé out on patrol. Two cartloads of quarried stone had come in from Goose-Bree; it was now being added to the walls of the shrine. Master Abbot Dannon was meeting with the village elders to discuss emergency plans for the people of Destiny's Way. The night patrol had reported – again – that the Shadows had tailed them just out of reach. Veln had sent a message that he was accompanying the Rathburn Watch on a search of the haunted estate.

He was certain that Ba'tvian was out there somewhere, sitting in a hidden of the web he'd woven like a spider ready to strike.

"They're doing it again."

I'k'Nole's whisper reached Absol as the two rode their mounts past the crops nurtured by the village. He gazed around, caught sight of a dark shape drifting through the grain field on their left. Twisting in the saddle, he saw them slithering on either side of the road. None of them seemed solid in form.

"The texts say that they shift their state from 'spirit' to solid if they consume enough death." Absol's apprentice fingered the hilt of his own weapon as he spoke. "If they consume enough of the living, they can become something else entirely."

"Legend says that they are cursed, and the way back to what they once were is through their gullets." Absol loosened his own sword from its scabbard. "I don't like this, lad. They're not making an effort to hide from us."

"Here?"

"Farther out."

As one, the pair dug in their heels. Their horses launched into a full gallop, shooting down the road quick as arrows, kicking up dust that obscured their view of what lay behind them. Equine flanks were lathered when they pulled up short yards away for the last cropland off the road. They wheeled around and waited for the dust to settle. Each had their swords drawn.

"Can you see them, I'k'Nole?" Absol asked, giving the long grass a suspicious stare.

"They're here. I can feel them."

Something moved in the grass, like a sharks circling in the sea. Omine counted the glimpses, trying to gauge how many of the things surrounded them. The number he came up with made his heart sink.

"More than forty." The last time he'd encountered that many had been at the dying Spirlan Forest after the Great Earthquake had rocked the world of Einlienn. Hundreds had died there, attracting Shadows from all over.

"Sixty-seven." I'k'Nole made the correction, a far-away tone in his voice. The lad was focusing more than his eyes by the sound of it. "More are coming in from the moors."

"Why? They normally avoid this area –" He cut himself off with a vile curse. "Ba'tvian."

The word fell into a sudden silence. The air went still. A whisper at the edge of consciousness repeated the name, slowly at first, gaining momentum as other whispers joined the first. They could just make out the blood mage's name.

It's as I thought. They are his.

"This isn't his Place."

The determination in his protégé's voice, the barest echo of power evident in his speech, drew Absol's attention away from the circling Shadows. I'k'Nole raised his blade, a violet flame flickering to life along its length. He swung it in a horizontal arc, spinning the horse around on its haunches in a full circle to increase the range. The fire leaped off the sword in a wave, shooting through the grass – and Absol.

He felt the impact, jerked back in reflex, over-balanced in the saddle, and fell to the ground. The flames surged through him like an arctic current. His horse danced in place, rolling its eyes, but didn't bolt. The Mancer had enough presence of mind to roll away from the horse to avoid being kicked. That's when he saw the flame pass into the grass.

The whispering turned into shrieks.

Absol clamped his hands on his ears. It did nothing to muffle the psychic sound. After a moment or two, the piercing screams of the Shadows began to die off.

"They're leaving. Are you hurt? Absol?"

He heard I'k'Nole dismount as he rose, shaking, to his feet. He checked himself, running his hands over his torso. He felt unsteady, yet couldn't find any sign of injury.

"I'm not wounded." He looked over at I'k'Nole, caught the worry in his violet eyes. Eyes the same color as the flame. "What *is* that – " The Mancer groped for the right term.

"It wasn't meant to hurt you. I didn't mean for it to." Now the younger began to pat his shoulders and chest, checking for himself that his mentor was fine. "Are you in pain?"

"No." He took a breath, forced himself to steady. "There's no pain, no injury. I'll see the healer at the shrine but I appear to be in good health." He clamped a hand on I'k'Nole's shoulder. "Just… lad, give me some warning next time. The last thing we want to happen is for someone to fall out of the saddle in the middle of a fight."

"I'm sorry." I'k'Nole winced. "I – they don't belong here, Absol."

"No, they don't." He scanned the surrounding moors, found them devoid of any sign of life. "We need to go back. If Ba'tvian Delthanurk didn't know we were here before this, he does now." He looked at his protégé. "And he'll know about you, what you can do. That makes you a target, lad."

"He'll try to kill me." A battle light shone in the young man's eyes. "If I die, I'll take him – and whatever is with him – with me."

Absol hoped it wouldn't come to that.

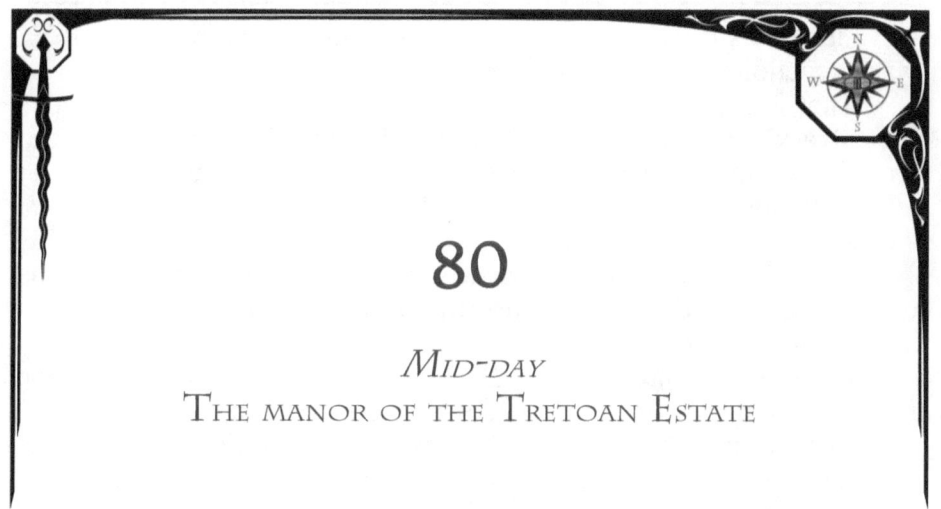

80

BA'TVIAN watched the search as it came to an end.

The images in the scrying bowl showed him how the Rathburn Watch crawled through the manor, stables, and yard like maggots in a corpse. They wriggled into every niche they found, inspected each crack, every cranny. The only things they discovered were the items Ba'tvian and his people had planted: a few scraps of diagrams, some ritualistic jargon, one or two of the more common implements. The quality of the items was poor, the details vague – and nothing of enough value to a blood mage to be taken with him. It lent weight to Raptu's story of the stable-hand.

Ba'tvian had vacated Raptu's home just as the Watch had arrived there. Now he sat with Nerisse in the study at the Tretoan manor, waiting for the right time. The elf ran a finger along the rim of the bowl. The scene changed. This time, it focused on the man he suspected to be a Mancer.

"Did it work?"

"I think so." Nerisse studied the image. "Halvark said his name was Veln Greendmeadow, correct?"

"Yes." Ba'tvian narrowed his eyes at her. "Does he normally impart information to you?"

"Sometimes. They all know with whom my loyalty lies." Unconcerned, she leaned a little closer to observe Veln as he examined the room in which they'd 'interrogated' the Carthier servants. "It's difficult to tell just by looking if it worked, but there was a reaction to it."

"That I saw." Ba'tvian made a mental note to keep a closer eye on Halvark's interactions with Nerisse. The lordling tended to regard Nerisse as a lady worthy of a noble's courtesy. Ba'tvian could never tell if the attention was simple respect on his part or true attraction. "We – "

He broke off as a Shadow snaked into the room from beneath the closed door. It didn't glide or drift; it raced across the floor to skid to a halt at its master's feet.

Something has happened at Destiny's Way, lord. It began to send pictures, memories from the Shadows he had ordered to the area.

There were the two men; one was Absol Omine. Beside the Mancer was a much younger man, the same man reported on earlier. The Shadows had stayed out of range, as ordered. They hadn't engaged, though they'd made their presence known.

After the fire of the mental sending faded away, the chill of his ire was in his voice. "How far into the village did they go?"

They did not. The closest they ventured inward were croplands just outside the village, and only in the section farthest away from the Wood.

"How many were lost?"

Forty-three.

"That's too many." The anger began to well up, a cold, thick lava that seared. They would pay. *Omine, you have so much to answer for.* "No Shadows are to go near the outlying fields. Stay away from the Mancers. I want a few of your brethren in the area; all others are to withdraw."

Retreating, lord?

"No." To retreat was to admit some degree of defeat. Temper seething, he began to stalk about the room, halting when Nerisse spoke. "Re-positioning. Those that remain in the area are to remain unseen. I want patrol patterns, the number of able-bodied. If they have traders or supplies rolling in, I want know to what, how much, and where it came from." As soon as this was over, the twins were being sent out. The sooner they hired the mercenaries, the sooner they would be rid of the Mancer plague.

"Can the Shadows verify if Greenmeadow is a Mancer, as you believe?" Nerisse moved the scrying bowl to the floor, gestured for the creature to take a look. It turned to Ba'tvian, then slithered to the bowl at his nod.

He has been to Destiny's Way. We have seen him, though not in the last few weeks.

"I want him, Nerisse." The words came out in a harsh demand. She looked up to his eyes.

"Then you will have him, my lord."

He glanced down at Veln's image, saw him shake his head as if trying to clear his thoughts.

"He's ready. So are we." Ba'tvian gave his elf a chill smile, felt his power spark in his eyes. "Let us go."

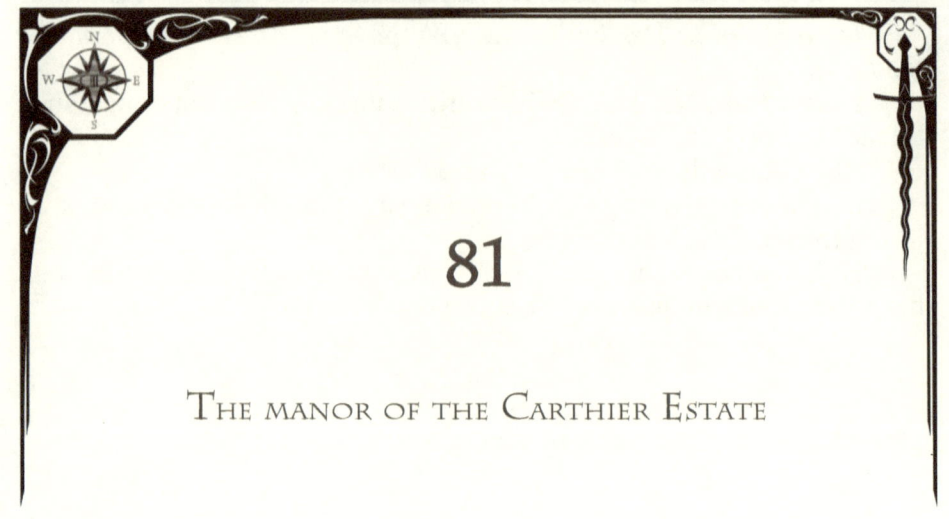

81

THE MANOR OF THE CARTHIER ESTATE

IT was over.

As the call to leave sounded in the corridor outside, Veln gave one last cursory glance at the room he'd searched. It was a small study, one of several in the house, outfitted for a man of both business and leisure. They'd found nothing here. He turned to the watchman who'd partnered with him for most of the day.

"We must be missing something." The words came out as a mutter.

Olef Altheson gave him an uncertain smile. "We've looked everywhere. What could we have missed?"

"I'm not sure." His mind felt stuffed with wool. The more time he spent on the estate, the worse the sensation became. There were periods of light-headedness as well. It made him worry.

At first, he'd thought it might be an insidious working, some spell laid out by the blood mage. Yet he'd detected no signs of magic, no traces of the darker practices. The only real evidence had been the burn spot in the courtyard, and that had been thoroughly cleansed. There was nothing unnatural to account for the malady.

Maybe Altheson is right and all I need is a good meal. None of them had eaten since dawn. Those who'd had the foresight to bring food with them would be eating on the march back to town – if they hadn't snuck bites of it during the search.

"Well, it wasn't all for naught." Olef slapped him on the

shoulder, one comrade to another. There was satisfaction in his expression. "Old Morrin found that stuff in the stable, so we've got another lead to follow."

"Yes." Veln didn't voice his concerns about what they'd found. He didn't want to rob the man of hope. If following the lead kept the Olef's spirits high, kept him keen on the hunt for his sister's killer, then he wouldn't deter him. "Come on. The others will be gathering out front."

They left the study for the stairs, encountered a few of their fellows going in the same direction. Their results had been the same as Veln's.

Perhaps that's because there is nothing here to find.

Still, he wasn't convinced. Little things niggled at his mind. The burn spot, Halvark's "help", the way Raptu hovered over the men, even the quiet tension in the Carthier staff – they hinted at something not quite right.

He wished Absol were here. The man the other Mancers looked to for leadership had a penchant for cutting through the detritus that clouded truth. He'd talk with Morrin once they got back. His former Captain shared Omine's straight-forward knack.

"Excuse me, Constable Greenmeadow, isn't it?"

Veln paused in the hallway, turning to see who had hailed him. Beside him Olef also stopped. A butler garbed in the Carthier House livery gave them a stiff half-bow.

"If you would be so good, Lord Carthier requests you to stop by his private den. A guest of the household wishes to meet you."

"A guest?" Veln frowned. "No one mentioned a guest in residence. Has this person been interviewed?"

"I cannot say." The servant was stiffly proper. "If you will follow me?"

"Do you want me to explain to the Captain?" Olef offered.

Veln gave a weary nod.

"Yes. Tell him I'll only be a few minutes."

There didn't seem to be much in the way of choice. Someone had to ensure that this 'guest' was questioned. As the watchman headed for the courtyard, Veln followed the butler down a series of corridors to the den. The man opened the heavy door, indicated that he should enter. The door shut behind him as he did so.

The lock clicked and he knew he'd made a huge mistake.

Even as dread began to build inside him, he took in the seating area, the bay window, the bookcases arrayed along the walls. Two people – he didn't know who they were – watched him from opposite corners. Halvark and Raptu stood on either side of a desk farther back in the room. Rising from the chair behind it, was a man clad in ebony, his features speaking of peasant blood-stock from the eastern coast. Crimson sparked in his dark eyes.

Ba'tvian Delthanurk.

"The Mancers owe me a debt." The blood mage signaled with one hand. The two unnamed men moved forward. "With interest."

Veln did the only thing he could: he summoned light. It flared in a blinding burst in front of him as he lunged towards the window. Raptu tackled him halfway there. He punched, grappled, bit – used every bit of dirty fighting he'd ever learned. When three more sets of hands grabbed him, the struggle was lost.

Realizing he couldn't escape, he allowed himself to be subdued. As they manhandled him, he reached for the power that lived within him. He readied a crude salvo of pure power, one strong enough to do serious damage. Then he lobbed it at Ba'tvian.

It hit the inside of Veln's shields, the impact making them visible to the naked eye. The backlash crashed through his mind and pain consumed him.

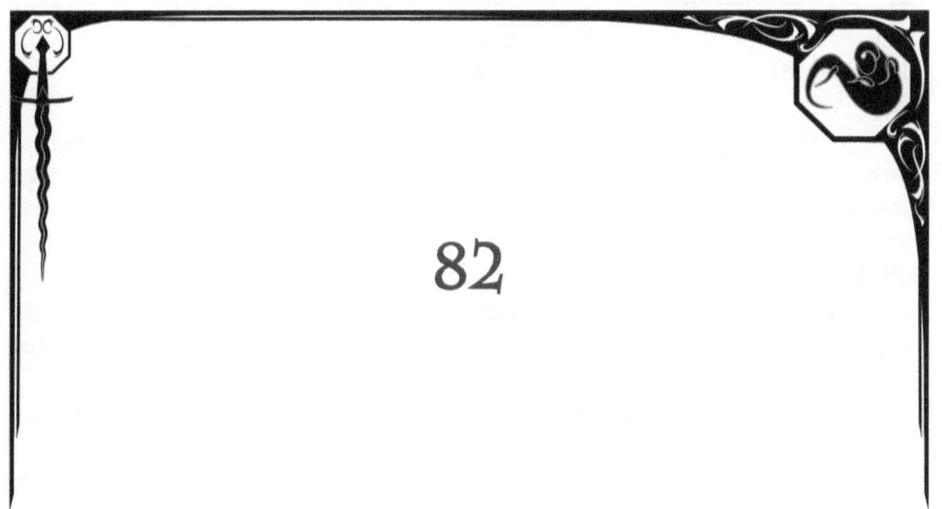

82

BA'TVIAN watched Veln's shields burst into brilliant light as the Mancer's body crumpled to the floor. Raptu rubbed at his eyes, stumbling away. The twins merely blinked. Ba'tvian refused to react in any way, despite the dark spots that danced in front of his eyes.

"Was that supposed to happen?" Halvark asked.

"Yes." He studied the Mancer's mind, now exposed, ripe for the taking. His working had done quite well, augmenting the Mancer's defenses while giving it the slightest of twists to achieve the desired result. Any offensive magic would have ended the same way. "The spell turned his shields against him. What he attempted has taken them down."

"Convenient." Raptu grimaced. "One less thing for us to do."

"Take him to Nerisse," Ba'tvian inclined his head to the twins. "Meet with me afterwards. It's time to put the next move in play." The brothers nodded, then hauled their captive off without a word. "If she is able to do as promised, the Mancer will be very useful indeed."

"What about the Watch? I doubt that they're satisfied with the results from the search of my home." The Lord Carthier scowled. "They'll be back, sniffing at our heels."

"Nerisse has taken care of it – or rather, her pet watchman will." Their leader made a dismissive gesture. "Her pawn has already explained his absence to the Captain and has further instructions.

Reg Morrin will not be in any position to question Greenmeadow's disappearance. We will, of course, monitor the situation."

"We can trust her puppet?" Raptu was doubtful.

"Yes. He is wholly ours." The dark look in his eyes spoke of forbidden knowledge. "He is also no longer human. Like the Shadows, what lives in him now serves me."

"That kind of thing makes my skin crawl." Raptu suppressed a shudder.

"The Mancer." Halvark changed the subject. "What will you do with him after? Provided he survives long enough for that to be an issue."

The Monster of Menie graced his companions with a chill smile.

"Tools are meant to be used."

83

OLEF Altheson surveyed the evidence room from the doorway before entering. The cabinets were locked, the table tidy. The brazier was loaded with fresh coals, the floor around its base swept clean of ash. Satisfied that he'd missed nothing on his previous excursion there, he shuffled forward to allow the Captain to follow him. Morrin held the evidence found during the search in his hands.

They were set on the table as Olef closed the door. The Captain unlocked the cabinet; at the same time, Olef slid the lock on the evidence door home. The first masked the sound of the second.

As the lock clicked into place, the world tilted in a surreal shift of perspective. As it did, the personality of the watchman began to fade. In its place emerged the daemonic mind of the whyte Ba'tvian had summoned into the body. Deep inside him, the real Olef began to claw at the bars of his mental cage.

The room was drenched with blacks, whites, and grays. The only color to be seen was on the paper doll shuffling through the file cases. The blue of his uniform was a bright beacon.

He didn't like blue. Red was the better hue.

No! Please, no!

Yes. He smiled to himself, waiting as the Captain muttered a curse, pulled out case files to double-check their labels. *He's just a paper doll. You are all paper dolls, dressed up, played with, discarded. Do you know what happens to paper dolls?*

Morrin looked up, saying something. He gestured, agitated. The paper doll wanted him to look in the drawer, to verify that the case file was missing. Olef came forward as the psychic leash the elven woman had put him on came free.

Strength surged in his blood as he shot out one hand to grip the doll's throat, flicked his wrist. The neck snapped as shocked surprise bloomed on the doll's dace. He grinned as Olef screamed within him.

"Paper dolls die." He reached for the knife he kept in his boot. "Some are torn, others broken. This one will be cut to bits."

His mistress had told him he could do this. She had promised him that he could have this freedom. It was his reward, she'd said, for obedience. So he sliced the uniform off the paper doll, and began to carve.

Not too much, the lady's voice warned. *Indulge a little, then trace the runes on what's left.*

He raised the first morsel to his lips, sucked the blood from the human tissue. So good, so sweet.

After, you may hunt for more.

Happily, he chewed the small piece of flesh as he cut off the next treat.

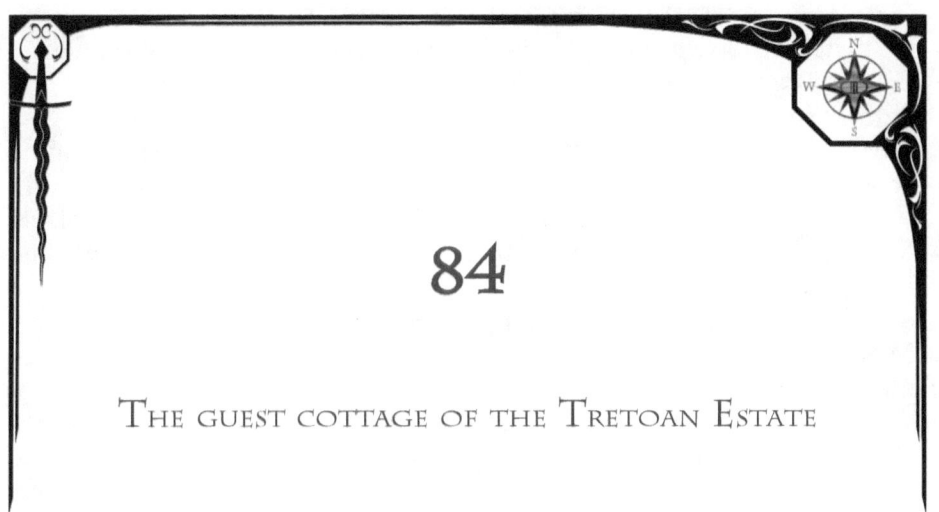

84

THE GUEST COTTAGE OF THE TRETOAN ESTATE

PRIALLA stood in the basement, the implements of her practice laid out on a small table beside her. Tied to a chair in front of her was the youngest of the ill-fated servants from the Carthier home. She was nude, still wet from the bath she'd been forced to take, her face red from the tears drying on her cheeks. The girl was perhaps fourteen. She wouldn't live long enough to see her fifteenth year.

Prialla had asked for this one. She'd earned this little bonus, had been ready to argue with him to get it. There'd been no need. Ba'tvian's agreement had been a deliberate decision to reward. Aware of that, she'd invited him to participate in her little experiment.

She wanted this to work. If it didn't, well, there was no real loss. There were other little girls to prey on, and this would be a few moments' entertainment for them both.

With Ba'tvian due to arrive in a few hours, she had time to finish the preparations. She studied the girl, tested the gag binding her face. Taut, not too tight. Satisfied, she examined the arms, chose the one that looked the cleanest. She repositioned the girl's chair so that the chosen arm was closest to the table, then turned to select her implements.

"Do you remember the others? The ones who rode with you in the barbarian's prison cart?" She carefully selected a tiny brush, a fresh quill pen. "They'll meet their ends soon. One already has. We brought him down here to play." She glanced over her shoulder at the girl, caught the sheen of fear in her eyes. It pleased her. "We didn't play with him as long as we would have liked. No time, you see." She gave her a brilliant smile. "Still, we did our best by him, splaid him out like a feast. Do you know what we did with his innards?" She picked up a glass inkbottle, swirled the red-black liquid inside. "Such fine ink this is. It would have been shameful to let it go to waste."

She uncapped the bottle, dipped the quill nib into the dark liquid. Moving closer, she drew a rune on the girl's shoulder. It began to pulse a hot red.

Runes were not common in magic anymore. According to what she'd learned with Ba'tvian, they'd fallen into disuse over the past few centuries. Once, though, there had been mages who had used runes for every arcane project they undertook. Now, it seemed that only the blood mages remembered their value, though even they seldom used them to full capacity. As Prialla drew another beside the first, she wondered if Ba'tvian were as well-versed in runic magery as she was becoming.

Her captive moaned, tried to lean away.

"Don't." Prialla gripped the girl's face in one hand, the smile giving way to cruelty. "Or do you want to drink this instead of wearing it? Perhaps you'd rather let the men rut on you? Keep moving, keep crying. See what it gets you."

The girl's eyes wheeled, flashing the whites. She quieted, trembling only a little as Prialla drew the runes, painted the designs. She made certain each was precise, neat, clean. When she was done, she surveyed her work again and smiled.

No mistakes.

On the living skin, the ink pulsed, glowed.

"And the purpose of this is what?"

Ba'tvian's voice was cool, analytical. She looked up as he came off the steps to stand beside her.

"You told me once that the key to youth could be found in blood." She touched a finger to the decorated shoulder, making sure not to smear anything. "We've accomplished much there, you and I. I've also studied on my own, worked out a few things you haven't touched on in our sessions. Now I have a hypothesis I'd like to try."

"You will need to explain it first."

Careful. His tone held no censure or approval. She wondered if he thought she was stepping outside of some boundary in attempting something like this. Yet as she outlined the arcane aspects of her theory, she saw the calculation, the *thinking* behind the eyes. That was one of the main reasons she was willing to be led by him. He didn't dicker over the details as Halvark would, or disregard them as with Raptu.

"...the runes would act as the focal point, a funnel for the energy. With the blood flowing through them as well, the magic will be infused into it directly."

"Thus enhancing any spell it's used for thereafter." He mulled over it a moment, then gestured to the ink work. "You may not get the full benefit with this alone. Let us see what we can do."

He tugged the gag away from the girl's face, made her look into his eyes.

"If you cooperate, you will not die tonight. Yield to us your blood and you will live." As Ba'tvian outlined what was required of the girl, Prialla's brows rose in surprise. Their leader wasn't known for leniency. He took, as they all did. He didn't persuade as a rule. Nonetheless, he seemed to be skilled in persuasion, in 'gentling' a scared female.

Nerisse. He had to have learned it dealing with the elven witch.

It seemed to be working with the girl. Shaking, reluctant, with a voice hoarse from fear, the captive repeated the phrases he told her to say. Prialla narrowed her eyes, committing them to memory for future research and use. The glow of the ink intensified, visible now to the naked eye. By the end, the girl was whimpering.

"It hurts," she gasped.

"The pain will end soon." He made a come-ahead motion to Prialla, stepping aside as she took up a knife. As she approached, he spoke again to the girl. "Blood is all we need. She will take it from you now. Do not move. Do not scream. Remember that cooperation is the price of life in this room."

It was clever, getting the chit to 'donate' of her own free will. Already, Prialla could the heightened intensity of the runes. She made shallow cuts around the ink, tracing the outline of each penned or brushed curve. The blood welled.

She could taste the coppery youthfulness of it on her tongue.

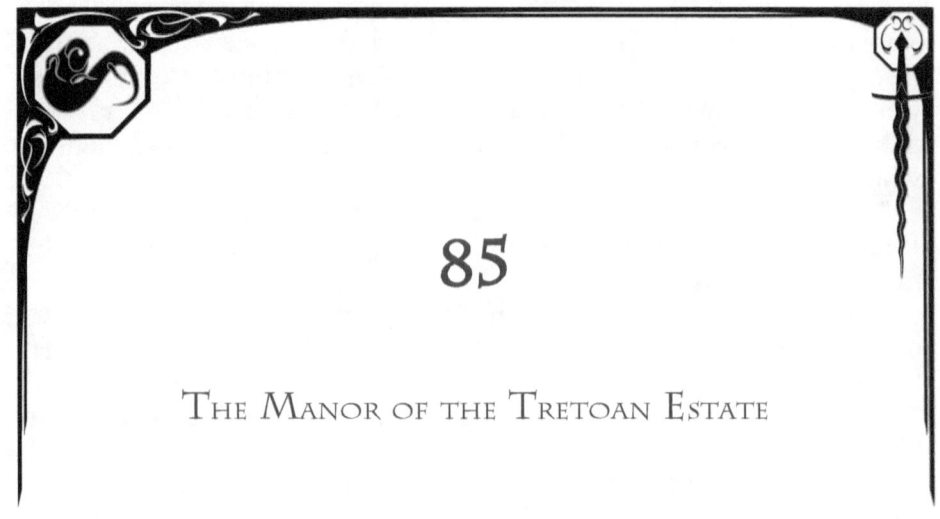

85

THE MANOR OF THE TRETOAN ESTATE

THE man's mind was a maze.

It fascinated Nerisse. She hadn't seen anything quite like it before this, a labyrinth of memory, purpose, magic, and thought woven into puzzling patterns layered one atop another. If she wasn't careful, she would become lost in it.

She backtracked to her entry point before she got too far in and spun a psychic thread to guide her back. She anchored one end to her body, spooling out more as she moved into the maze depths. She checked it often as she wound her way through the patterns, took comfort in the silvery sheen of her lifeline. She needed comfort in the Mancer's mind. The deeper she went, the more she was reminded.

The structure of Veln Greenmeadow's thoughts was so like Saerlan si le Theian. The High Priest has been like a father to her once, always ready to advise or encourage. He had seen things in the dark of the earth, heard Einlienn's voice. While she didn't think that this man could speak with the earth as the Elvanaran had, he had borne witness to some its secrets. Some its nightmares.

A flicker of memory carried the sound of sobbing. Tied to that was the screaming of a hundred throats – screaming, shrieking as the earth crumbled down around them –

She shied away from it, retreating until the cries faded. Heart thudding in her chest, she wondered where he'd gotten the memory.

The sound haunted his mind, casting weird echoes through its corridors. It flitted through the patterns like a living thing. Was it guarding of its own accord or just being used that way? She didn't have the answer, but knew that if it was being used as a sentry in the labyrinth that the Mancer was well-versed in her abilities.

If it was there of its choice…she refused to dwell on what that meant.

Perhaps it was time to surface. She clipped the psychic thread, secured it in the pattern. Tracing her way back, she sealed the thread to the maze pathway itself, determined not to lose the progress she had made. Once out, she opened her eyes then straightened.

Her back ached, her legs trembled, her head swam. She clutched the edge of the table on which the Veln lay, waiting for the room to cease wobbling. That she shivered didn't help. It was freezing in the cellar, the temperature low enough she could see her breath as fog in the air.

How much time has passed? And why is it so cold?

As her vision steadied, she glanced around her. Half of the lanterns had guttered out. The oil in them should have lasted five hours at least. When she checked the nearest, the lantern was chill to the touch. The oil reservoir was only half empty.

Out of the corner of her eye, she saw something move.

She whirled to face the entryway leading to the stairs, the place where she had thought it – she – had been. There was nothing there. As she stared at the empty spot, the lantern hanging next to it went out.

No. No, no, no, no, no –

Nerisse grabbed the lantern next to her, used a spark of magic to light the wick. The shadows in the cellar loomed, twisted at the edge of vision. She glimpsed hints of faces in the dark. Frantic, she relit the lanterns. The flames flickered, most going out. only the ones closest to her remained alight.

Fumbling, she reached for her ritual knife, slicing the blade over her palm. She sunk the flagstone floor, smearing the blood in a circle around her. She muttered prayers, broke into arcane chants. One by one, the wicks went out.

She cowered within the circle as the darkness approached. From the unseen depths flowed the whispers.

…Nerisse…murderess…filth…monster…

"No. No!" *Ba'tvian!*

Her lord answered her call immediately. *What is it?*

They're here. Tears spilled down her cheeks. *In the dark. They're here.*

Who are here?

She sent him what she saw, what she felt, what she heard. She waited, pensive, as he took it in. Even as he considered her situation, the creeping gloom retreated. The things in the cellar, whatever they were, faded away.

Ibestor is on his way to you. A few of my Shadows will be there soon.

Thank you. Gradually, the lanterns flickered to life again. As the tiny flames warmed the air, she buried her face her arms.

Go to your rooms, Nerisse. We will discuss this at length later.

I'm not done. The Mancer –

Can wait. We have time. Once Ibestor is there, go to your rooms.

Yes, lord.

He broke the telepathic connection. Amid the lights, with just an unconscious prisoner for company, she huddled where she was and waited for the barbarian.

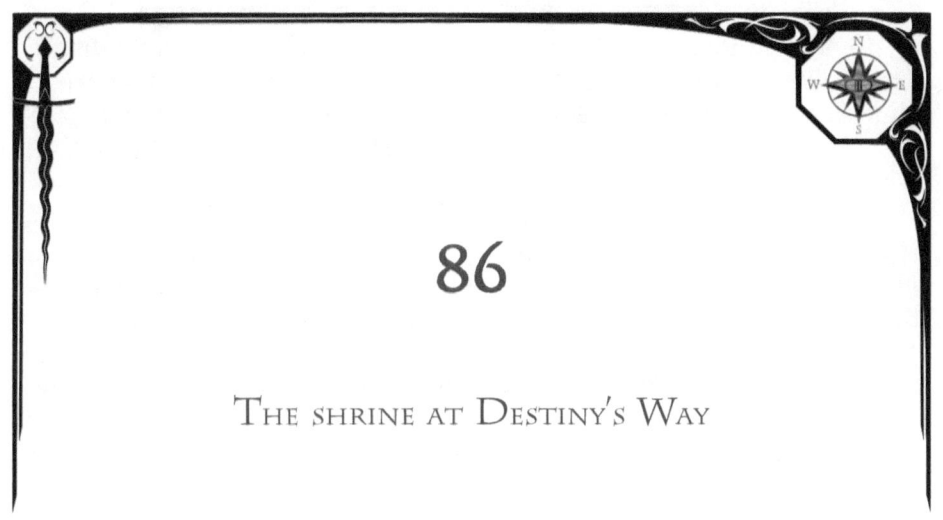

86

THE SHRINE AT DESTINY'S WAY

ABSOL Omine stood just off the kitchens, surveying the dining hall. Every table was filled with people. Some were On'Desae monks. Others were villagers. Most were Mancers.

And still there are not enough. It was a feeling he couldn't shake, that the numbers they'd carefully rebuilt were not what they needed to win. It was the same gut-reaction he'd had in at that meeting in Sundown some years before. He was careful not to let it show.

"You know about what happened this morning?" he queried the room at large. There were nods all around. "We can take it as read that Ba'tvian Delthanurk knows that we're here. We believe him to be in or around Rathburn. Veln Greenmeadow is trying to confirm this. He believes Delthanurk to be involved in a series ritual murders discovered in the city."

Murmurs greeted that statement. For most of them, this was new information. Absol waited for the noise to die down.

"We anticipate Delthanurk and his followers launching some kind of attack here. What kind, or when, we don't know. From this point forward, we're changing the patrol patterns. Those patterns will shift from day-to-day, night-to-night. Celina has charge of the day-time roster; I have the night. I'k'Nole," he nodded at his protégé, "will run night-time patrols. He's the strongest mage among us, and the most effective when it comes to killing Shadows."

It was a good choice. The Shadows were more active in the dark.

"I think the word you're looking for, Omine, is 'incinerating'." The voice at the back of the room was met with a few nervous chuckles. Word of I'k'Nole's ability had spread. The older order members had seen a demonstration earlier when they'd discussed what had happened, gone over possible strategies.

"The rest of you will be assigned randomly." He ran through the starting shift assignments. "There will be a scouting rotation for each group. Scouts go in pairs. If you catch any hint of Ba'tvian or a blood mage, do not take any chances. Cut through the Wood and return here. Master Dannon has charge of the home defense. Anyone not assigned to a shift will have duties here so report to him. All incidents, no matter how trivial, get reported to Celina, Dannon, or me. Understood?"

There was a chorus of agreement. Dannon stood.

"The people of Destiny's Way will retreat into the Wood should there be need. The Wood offers the best protection for anyone caught out in the open. Our monastery is being fortified but the structure here isn't the best for a siege, nor does it have the room to accommodate everyone."

"The Wood will harbor anyone fleeing evil. It won't tolerate a blood mage within its bounds." This came from I'k'Nole, the one Mancer who spent more time in the Wood than most sane people could stand. "You will have nothing to fear from it."

As Absol opened the floor for questions, he wondered if they were ready. More, he wondered what kind of hell the Monster of Menie would bring with him when he came to the village of Destiny's Way.

87

EVENING

THE RATHBURN WATCH HOUSE

THE thing that was once Olef licked the blood from his fingers. He was so content with the world. His hunger was sated, the screaming paper doll inside him had gone quiet, and his mistress' voice soothed. He listened to her assurances, the instructions she gave, the promises she made.

She'd told him that there would be more to come.

He looked around the room, marveled at its tidiness. The filing cabinets were in order, the table clean, the chairs tucked in close around it. The only mess was the one he squatted in, the mutilated remains of the Captain spread out before him. It was his version of the dinner table. The idea of it made him chuckle. The floor was his table, the blood pooled over it the cloth, and the carcass the leftovers from his feast.

The meal was a tasty memory.

He rose, looked down himself. Crimson had spattered and dripped all over his clothing, the deep red color showing brightly in his altered sight. *Pretty*. He touched the drying wetness, smiled. He was all dressed up, in a uniform that looked so nice with this new adornment. Festive, he thought. Celebratory.

Take another, whispered the mistress' voice in his mind. *It is time to let go.*

Something roused deep within. It whimpered. Olef ignored it. It was just the paper doll. Not him. He was so much more.

He picked his way across the room, rounding the table to the door. Unlocking it, he peeked in the hall, saw no one. Instead he heard voices, recognized one as the paper doll who had spoken to him earlier that morning. A manic smile spread his lips.

"Someone lend me a hand, will you? The Captain's made a mess in here." He suppressed a giggle.

"What?" The doll began to come up the stairs, booted feet clomping like a clumsy draft horse. "Olef? Is that you?"

"He dropped the case file, papers everywhere." Olef eased back from the door, careful to keep out of sight, and left it open a crack. "He's a headache, he has. I sent him off, which leaves the mess to me. I could really use some help with it."

"What's that smell?" The doll made a disgusted sound as he shoved the door open and came inside. "It's rank in here." He frowned. Sniffed. His face blanched. "Olef?"

As the man turned, Olef hit the door, slammed it shut – on a second paper doll that was through. The door bounced back as the man yelped and pushed. The first doll just gaped at him.

"What did you?" It came out as a whisper, then again as shout. "*Olef, what did you do?* Go – get help –"

The second doll ran down the hall, shouting for others. The noise he made was muffled as Olef slammed the door. He never took his eyes off his newest prey. His smile never faltered.

...help...me...

The words slunk through his mind, slipping into the forefront.

"You have to tell me, Olef. Talk to me. I can't help if you don't talk to me." The doll tried to reason with him.

The speech rankled. He hadn't asked for help, had he? The stupid paper doll had – the one inside that kept whining, kept crying. The damn thing wouldn't *go away*.

Then the vault within him closed, sealing off the weakest part of what he was. He grinned, let the humanity he aped slip. He was other – he was whyte.

Baring his teeth, he lunged at the watchman as the more of the paper doll's ilk burst into the room.

INTERLUDE 8

ELSEWHERE...

LABIYAL Biyalban watched the officers restrain the creature that the elven girl had forged for the mage she loved. It was a flawed monstrosity, the amalgam of man and daemon. Now the thing fought, hitting, scratching, biting – taking off pieces of its attackers. It chewed, then swallowed the tidbits, laughing at the cries of pain, the angry shouts, the horror as others discovered what had befallen Captain Reg Morrin.

No sound came with the image in the mirror standing on the desk. The pantomime was easy to interpret for someone who watched others as often as he did. His lips curved as he 'read' the puppet's mad confession to murder. Ba'tvian's touch, he was sure. The boy he'd witnessed become a man was one who planned for such things.

Still, the ploy was an obvious one. He would do better with more experience. Delthanurk would acquire that in time. Labiyal would ensure that he did.

This move would resolve the most immediate problem the so-called Dark Adepts faced. It did not address the long-term issue of Rathburn.

Still, it did open doors and Labiyal intended to walk through one in particular. He opened a drawer, removed several sheets of parchment, a quill pen, a bottle of ink – real ink, not like the bloody concoction that Prialla Filoche had brewed. The half-daemon set the items on the desk, unstoppered the bottle, already composing what he wanted to say.

He wrote letters to the mayor, to the Lords Carthier and Tretoan. The mayor was his man; it was time to make him also nobles' – then, by extension, Ba'tvian's.

There was a mortal saying: parents should provide for their children. It was not entirely apt in this case, yet it held a certain applicability. He had, in his way, nurtured Ba'tvian, helped him unseen. Humans may consider him an adult but daemons would view him as little more than a spawnling, too young to play the games of power with his elders.

Labiyal stood somewhere in the middle, his parentage split between each. He preferred to think that it gave him a greater comprehension of both races. That understanding was why he'd let the boy develop so much on his own. Ba'tvian had passed several tests before this. Now there was just one left.

While he undertook that final trial, Labiyal would see to it that the foundation of his control of Rathburn was laid firm.

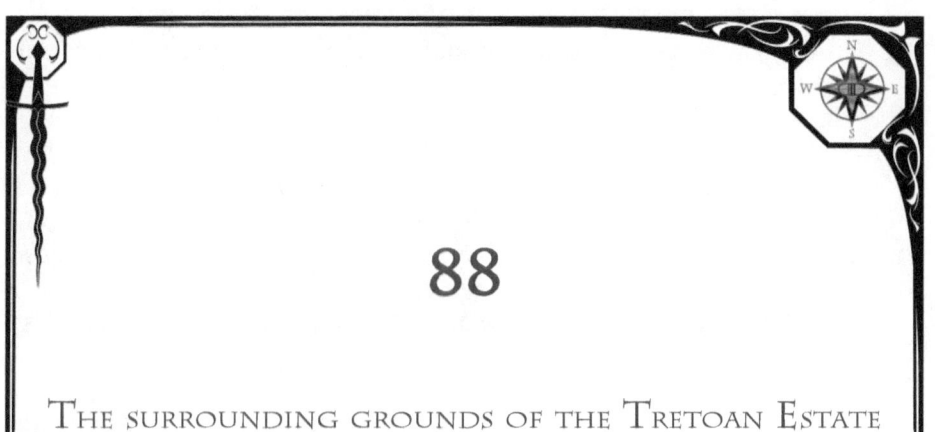

88

P RIALLA was showing her intelligence.

Ba'tvian walked along the grass, deep in thought in the aftermath of her little demonstration. It hadn't succeeded the way she'd hoped it would – a deliberate sabotage at a critical point had ensured that. Still, the experiment would have close to achieving part of her goal. It would not have lasted, would have required regular infusions of blood and life-force within a day or two.

As he went over the results, he didn't see how she could not become some sort of parasite. It was a fate he didn't want for himself. It may, however, prove useful to him if it was hers.

The wind picked up, rustling the grass, the foliage behind him. They were only sounds on the stretch of land between the guest cottage and the manor. He paused, looked up at the moon. It shone as a silvery sliver in the night sky.

Lord.

He glanced down at a Shadow as it slithered up to him. "Yes?"

We have more information on the young man sighted with Absol Omine.

"Tell me."

The Shadow sent pictures, a cascade of images showing the last encounter with him. The Mancer was called I'k'Nole. He was young, still in training, yet was the most powerful mage seen by his minions. Conversations between him and his mentor indicated that he had been with Omine from a young age, that his arcane education was not formal.

"Self-taught?"

Perhaps. The Shadow blinked its leprous white eyes slowly. *We've gleaned that his methods are unconventional. Surprise leaves his mind vulnerable.* Supporting memories slipped into the blood mage's mind. *His response to sudden attacks tends to negate the opportunities that vulnerability presents.*

"They are close, this I'k'Nole and Omine?" His eyes narrowed as he mulled it over.

Yes.

"Good." He could use that. "All of you are to keep your distance from them both. Remain on watch." After a moment, he added, "I want Prialla surveilled as well. Tell me what she studies, what she attempts. Her progress, or lack thereof, is of interest to me."

The Shadow glided away over the grass, fading into the night-time gloom.

He'd told Prialla that he would review her improvised ritual, find the cracks that had caused it to fail. He had a few 'answers' in mind already, though discussing them would wait until tomorrow. Tonight, he needed to deal with Nerisse.

He wasn't quite ready to handle her hysteria just yet. His pets kept an eye on her, relayed her calming demeanor. He would give her a few moments more before requiring her to explain her panic earlier.

She saw things.

Another of Shadows, the largest of his usual escort drifted into view beside him as he resumed his walk.

"Madness or a true seeing?" If it were the former, he would have a very difficult line to walk where she was concerned. He needed her mind, what she could do.

We cannot say. What she sees is for her alone, tied to the earth, to the dark. It haunts her dreams.

"Jevanel." He would use the memory of the event to strengthen their bond. "Can you determine if it is only in her mind?"

Yes. It is not, though we cannot see it. We feel it, as we feel all that is dead and dying.

That was interesting. He tucked the information away.

"These incidents occur whenever I am not there. Do they wait until she is alone to prey on her, or do they fear me?"

The Shadowed One took its time answering.

The earth is bound to you, it stated at last. *They are bound to the earth.*

He mulled over the words as he entered the manor, seeking Nerisse's suite. Bonds were tricky things, affecting magic in strange ways. This implied that the link his elf had forged between him and the earth also bound the haunting to him, yet...

Of course. Nerisse, as Elvanarae and a blood-relation, was more vulnerable due to the direct relationship she possessed with the deceased, as well as their view of the betrayal. He might have instigated it but she was the one who had committed the act. The binding shielded him as his connections to the haunts were indirect.

It meant that he needed to take greater care of her mental state moving forward. For now, he'd take part in all her remaining sessions with the Mancer, not just the one that required him. Perhaps his presence would prevent more occurrences. He needed her stable enough to work, on this project as well as others.

Rathburn was only the start. He would let Halvark and Prialla rule there with Raptu, while he remained the unseen power behind the proverbial throne. He had a bigger target in mind, one that he would aim at as soon as he dealt a deathblow to the Mancers at Destiny's Way.

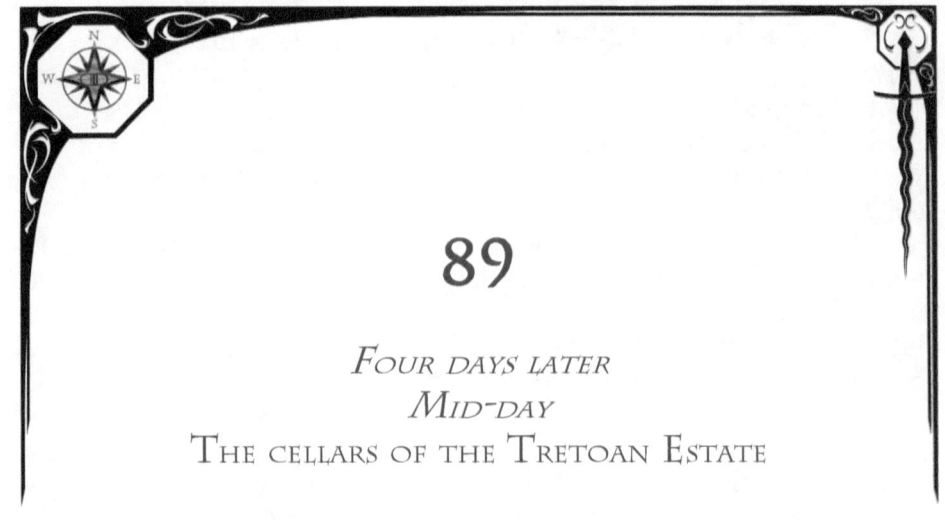

89

H E was alone at last.

Veln crouched in his cage, tiny tremors shaking his body every few moments. There wasn't room to stand or lie down in the cramped space. Empty cages sat next to his prison; he remembered rousing a few times to the sound of their occupants being dragged away. They'd died badly. They haunted the cellars, spirits trapped in catatonia glimpsed at the edge of vision.

His head throbbed. When he looked within his mind, he found the defenses he'd used to protect his thoughts cracked. He traced the fissures along his shields to a single point. It echoed with memory, told him what had caused it.

Him. He'd done it to himself.

Somehow, he'd strengthened his shields so much that nothing could breach them. The nature of mental protections kept things from getting in, yet still allowed things out if the mage so desired. Spells, magic, telepathy, empathy – it all originated within the mind and would pass through the shields when used. There was a point where 'not letting anything in' also meant 'not letting anything out'. He didn't know how he had reached it.

Yet the cracking couldn't be disputed. It was what they'd use to try to break into his mind.

They hadn't gotten far, stopped by an elaborate psychic construction. After the Mancers learned that Nerisse se li Astorae stayed with Ba'tvian Delthanurk of her own free will, he'd invested a great deal of time cultivating the maze. The Elvanaeran woman was an Empath, possessing an ability needed to heal a person's consciousness. A mental labyrinth seemed a good defense should his shields fail.

Along the pathways, he glimpsed a silvery line hazed with red running to the outer regions of his mindscape. Faded, unfueled by magic, the thread came to a stop at one of the many dead-end twists, about a third of the way through. He discovered no evidence of trespass farther in.

Thank the One.

Still, he couldn't trust himself. He wanted someone – Absol or Celina – to examine his mind and make certain that he was clean of tampering. That meant getting out of his cage.

He took stock of himself. Unlike the other prisoners they'd kept, he'd remained clothed. Veln also didn't appear to be suffering anything more debilitating than the backlash headache. His body ached from sitting too long. He didn't recall, wasn't even certain how long he'd been held. His hands seemed steady, though. It took effort to shift his body, the cage seeming to shrink around him as he moved. Once crouched forward, he slipped his fingers through the weave of the wire comprising his prison. As he fumbled with the knotted rope they'd used to keep it secured, he was grateful for the lanterns left burning in the room. Doing this blind would not have been easy.

Something pricked his fingertips, the first layer of knots came free. Spiky bits of metal were at the center of each knot, piercing the rope to cut into the fingers of anyone trying to unfasten it from inside the cage. He managed to get them undone with only shallow injuries, not deep gashes. By the end, his fingers *hurt*.

He slipped the last of the rope off the barbs, then wiped the blood from his cuts on his breeches while he studied the cage door. Two brackets, one on either side of the door, held a small wooden bar. He'd have to slide it loose. More rope embedded with barbs wound around either end of the bar, tying it to the cage.

It had taken him a long time to do the first part. No one had come. He didn't know how much time he had left to try this, had to take it slow to save his fingers. Halfway through undoing the fastening around one end of the bar, he realized that the rope and barbs weren't holding the wood. The bar moved independently of the rest.

He thrust his fingers against the end of the bar, sent it sliding out of the bracket. He pushed at it through the wires of his cage, managing to shove it out of the bracket a few minutes later. It fell to the floor with a loud clatter.

He held his breath as he waited. When no one came, he opened the door, cringing at the high-pitched creak of the hinges, and crawled out. As he did so his body screamed at him, cramping up. He suppressed a groan, taking a moment to stretch his limbs, loosen the muscles. Then he looked back at his prison.

They should have done a better job of securing it.

Why hadn't they? A glance at the neighboring cages showed him similar contrivances holding them shut. Someone must have tried them before this – unless they'd been unconscious or drugged. He'd been unconscious for most of the time he'd been in the cage. If that was all they'd relied on, it shoddy thinking.

Over-confidence. They'd succeed here so long that they'd grown lax.

A quick search of the room turned up nothing usable as a weapon. The wooden bar wasn't heavy or long enough. The rope so enmeshed with barbs that he wouldn't be able to hold it firm in the hand. His arcane reserves were low, and the trial test of summoning a mage light caused so much pain that black spots swam into his eyes. Anything more would have him blacking out.

So don't use it. If I'm careful, I won't have to.

He moved toward the stairs, finding to his relief that his muscles allowed it without anything more than a constant ache. Aches he could be ignored.

The steps leading up were well lit with lanterns, as the cellar itself had been. When he reached the top, he checked the door. The latch moved with the barest squeak. The hinges made even less noise as the door eased free of the frame.

Very over-confident – or a trap.

More cautious than ever, he cracked it open enough to peer down the hall. Seeing no one, hearing nothing, he widened the opening just enough to slip through. He was in a long corridor, oil lamp sconces lining its plastered walls, a narrow rug running down its length. Where was he? The Carthier manor? His last detailed memory was of the estate search, but that didn't mean that was where he was. Halvark had been in that study, had stood with –

Ba'tvian. I have to tell Absol and the Captain about Ba'tvian.

If this was a trap, he would have to chance it. It was either that or go back to the cage. Veln chose one direction; it didn't matter which if he didn't know the layout of the place. The hall terminated at another corridor. He looked around the corner to the right, saw an empty stretch of hallway. He looked to the left, noted another door at the end, inset with a square of pressed glass at eye level. Three iron bars showed clearly on the other side of it. Beyond them lay an open lawn and a cottage farther away.

Not the Carthier Estate. Tretoan, then.

This door, too, was unlocked when he tested it. He slipped out into the open air, cast his gaze around. There was no cover around the back of the manor, just a broad expanse of featureless lawn. There were bushes and trees around the cottage, as well as what looked like might be a small stable. He looked up at the manor windows, didn't see anyone in them, the curtains drawn shut at each.

Nerves rattling in his gut, he set off at a casual walk and prayed that no one paid attention.

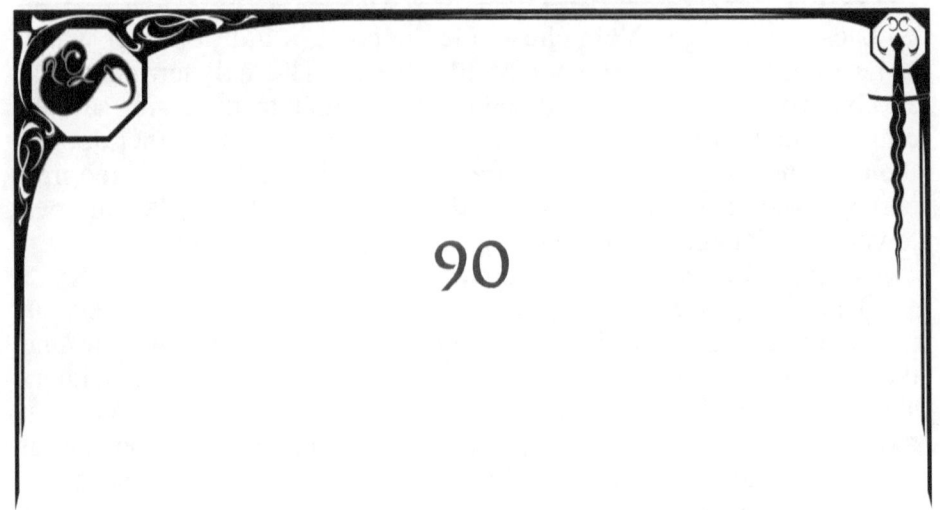

90

IN the privacy of her bedroom, Nerisse held her mug of hot tea close to her breast as she watched the Mancer in the water bowl sitting on her bedstand. She sipped at the liquid as he crossed the turf, moved behind the foliage once he reached the treeline. Eventually, he entered the stable.

His movements were stiff, his skin far too pale, his demeanor tired. She could relate. The past few days had been exhausting, even with Ba'tvian's help. There had been the sessions in the cellar, the strategy meetings, the dreams. Nightmares. They plagued her nights, were worse than before.

She wanted to sleep. Craved it. Yet she was afraid of what she'd find in slumber. Sobs, despair, blood. Cascading dirt, tumbling rock. The whispers in the dark, the mouths that screamed, and screamed, and screamed...

It was worse after the sun went down.

Ba'tvian didn't hear them. Still, he believed her when she'd described them to him, didn't think she was losing her senses. He spent the nights with her now, his presence a deterrent for the dreams, but he had so much to do. He couldn't be there always. He needed so little sleep, her lord. It gave him more time to strategize, study, plan...

She caught herself as her thoughts drifted farther away from where they should be. She shook her head, re-focused on the Mancer in the stable. He'd found a bridle on a post between two empty stalls. Farther down the aisle, Ibestor's creations watched him, craning their necks out to stare. He stayed out of their way, quitting the stable with his prize in hand.

Good. The creatures that Ibestor made would have likely eaten him.

Behind the cottage was one of several pastures close to the manor. He headed there, climbing over the fence to walk up to one of the horses. Halvark's mounts were pleasure animals, or work horses, not the fast-paced courier equines that Raptu bred. Nerisse recognized this one, knew it to be gentle and agile. It didn't give Greenmeadow much trouble as he approached it, patted its arched neck, then slipped on the bridle. He walked the horse over to the fence, using the wooden to climb onto its back. Once settled, he trotted out of scrying range.

His escape had been almost too easy. Nerisse hoped that what she'd done wouldn't arouse too much suspicion.

Mentally wishing him a safe journey, Nerisse finished her tea. She set the mug aside, rising from where she'd sat on the bed to dispel the scrying magic and empty the water bowl into the wash basin. She checked the lanterns around the room, made sure they had plenty of oil before she laid down on the bed, trying to sleep.

91

VELN approached the eastern city gate with trepidation. Returning had been a risk. If he was recognized, if he was re-captured... He shook his head, not wanting to finish the thought. They didn't know he was missing. Even if they did, they had to get word to people they trusted here. He didn't believe they had many people in the city, if any at all.

Nerves danced in his belly as he rode entered Rathburn unchallenged. No one manned the guard house. The portcullis stood open for all comers. The gate was not only thing deserted.

To all appearances, the city was void of people, a raven perched atop the roof of the guardhouse the lone sign of life. It glared with beady eyes as he nudged his mount forward, casting cautious glances down the alleys. No one stood in the shadows. As much as he wanted to avoid detection by the enemy, seeing someone about would be reassuring. Unsettled, the Mancer shuddered in the saddle.

Where is everyone?

A raucous cawing had his head jerking up. The raven launched into the air, flying towards the city center. He followed after it, still wary.

Captain Morrin was at the Watch House. He had to warn him before he left for Destiny's Way.

Halfway to his destination, it reached him: the muted roar of an angry mob. Heart kicking into high-gear, he guided his horse down a lane between the buildings that lined the street. The back way wound into the center, depositing him on another road just shy of the square where the Watch House stood.

Veln hung back, eyes scanning the area. The crowd amassed in front, hurling bitter imprecations at the building. People were still streaming in other parts of the city, the mob growing beyond the capacity of the square. They soon surrounded the Mancer, all of them riveting their attention on the Watch's door. Sentries stood around the building. They didn't wear the blue uniform of the law. Instead, they sported the leather and chainmail of mercenaries from Edon, an indistinct insignia emblazoned in red on their black jerkins.

"Greenmeadow? Veln?"

Startled, he whipped around in the saddle, the motion so sudden that he almost fell from his horse. He clutched at the saddlehorn for balance, managed to keep his seat as Jimnel Elfren stepped out from behind his mount. The expression on the old sergeant's face was a mixture of relief and concern.

"Easy, lad." Jimnel kept his voice low. "Glad to see you in one piece. We worried when you disappeared after the search."

"What's happening, Jimnel? Where's the Captain?" Veln's thoughts had scattered. Now he scrambled to put them back in order. "I need to report."

"You didn't hear?" The sergeant shook his head, sorrow in every line. "Morrin's dead, lad. He was killed after we got back into Rathburn."

"What?" *No. No, no, no, no.* He felt sick, shocked. "How? Who?"

"Olef." Anger mixed with the grief in his aged eyes. "Olef Altheson, one of our own. We caught him the same day, found evidence that he'd behind some of the murders – including his sister's." Jimnel nodded at the Watch House. "The mayor stood us down after that. Said he needed to find a replacement for the Captain before we could go back on duty. Then he asked Lord Tretoan and Lord Carthier to step in with their militia."

"No." Stricken, Veln leaned down to grab his old friend's hand. "Listen to me. Listen carefully, Jimnel. *Halvark Tretoan and Raptu Carthier are in league with Ba'tvian Delthanurk.* They're behind the murders – "

The mob exploded with sound, drowning out the Mancer's words. The door had opened. Mayor Yilsed came out with an armed escort to the cheering of the people. Behind him, bound in chains and surrounded by guards, was Olef. Even from this distance, Veln saw the glee, the elation writ on his face. At the sight of him, the crowd turned from cheers to vile screaming.

The armed escort broke a path through the mob, the mayor giving solemn nods to those who called out to him. Olef was taken along the same route. As they passed, the crowd fell in behind, trailing them as they made their way to wharves.

Jimnel was swept away as those around them surged forward to follow. Veln lost sight of him in the masses, the press of people forcing him onward as well. Unwilling to trample anyone, he let the mob push his horse. He kept an eye out for any break in the crowd, easing his mount to one side as much as possible. He'd take the first opportunity to leave.

92

*L*OOK *at all the paper dolls.* The whyte that had once been Olef Altheson grinned at them.

Black, white, and gray, they lined the streets and stared at him as he marched toward the gallows near the wharves. In their eyes he could see disgust, horror, curiosity, anger, and hate. The emotions lit up the dolls' faces, like the stars in the night sky. Many called out, their voices raucous, their speech a rage-filled litany. It was music to his ears.

Paper dolls are such interesting things.

They were delicious, for one. Dolls like the Captain made a fine repast for being such as him. *Being.* Yes, he liked the sound of that. He wasn't human anymore, though a tiny part of him still clung to that myth. The little doll that lived deep inside was the merest remnant of what he had been. Weakened, strangled, it lay in its prison, locked away from thought, sight, and sound. Its whimpers were a sweet lullaby...

Something wet and smelly hit him in the face. He blinked, shaking his head, juice running off his cheeks as the pulp fell away. More rotting vegetables flew from the back of the crowd to land on him. Two of the guards escorting him stepped forward, calling for order in the streets. Another stayed with him, holding his leash.

The leash was a thick chain, one that ran from the iron collar around his neck to the manacles around his wrists. More chain hobbled his feet. They'd given him enough slack to walk with small steps. It made for a slow procession through the city.

Olef enjoyed it. Even being pelted with rubbish by the citizenry didn't dampen his spirits. He had served his mistress, had earned his reward. He savored the memory of his bloody feast. Yet perhaps the best of all was still to come.

Once, he'd been ensnared, made a shade of what he'd been. Einlienn was no home for a daemon. The world itself sought suppress what he was. The blood mages used that to make slaves of his kind. Soon, he'd be free of Einlienn, of blood mages. Soon, he would go home.

It's almost time.

His mistress, her soothing tones whispering through his mind, making promises. He smiled. One last thing – just the one. She'd told him that it might hurt. Pain was nothing. His stomach cramped a little from hunger, the kind of deep-seated need that only fresh blood and meat could sate. Yet as he walked from the street to the pier-side gallows the cramps diminished. Anticipation began to build.

Once, he'd been ensnared, made a shade of what he'd been. Einlienn was no home for a daemon. The world itself sought suppress what he was. The blood mages used that to make slaves of his kind. Soon, he'd be free of Einlienn, of blood mages. Soon, he would go home.

It's almost time.

He ascended the scaffold, turned his back to the hangman as directed. Eager, happy, he looked over the crowd gathered in front of him as the executioner offered a hood. He shook his head.

"I want to see. I want to watch all the paper dolls as they watch me." Olef smiled at his executioner. "Dolls break, you know. Break, tear, cut into pieces. Soon enough, all of them will lie on the ground, delicious little treats for my king to eat."

There was no reply to his comment, nor did he wait for one. He rambled on about the fates of paper dolls as the hangman lowered the noose around his head, snugged it against his neck. The crowd pushed forward, everyone wanting to see. Some may have wanted to hear. As Olef repeated his rambling speech, he caught sight of a familiar figure. Pale and hollow-eyed, he sat on a barebacked horse at the back of mob, a beacon of bright color in the wash of gray.

Across the distance, their eyes met. Olef began to laugh. He continued laughing as the trap door dropped. The noose caught him, tightened. Something snapped. His vision turned a luscious red before the black crept in. Olef Altheson had one last gleeful thought as he died.

The Mancer was no paper doll.

93

V ELN shivered in reaction as Olef burst out laughing on the scaffold. It was not the laughter of a sane person. When the trap door opened, he saw the drop, the jerk, the strange loll of the head. The hangman was an expert. The condemned died a quick death, the neck broken.

He recognized me. He knew what they'd done to me. There was no question that the former watchman found it amusing. Had he participated somehow? It made him nauseous to consider it.

As the people cheered the death, Veln nudged his horse to the outer edge of the mob, trotting into a back alley that led to the wharves. Another tremor racked his body. He was so tired, yet he couldn't stay. He'd escaped notice so far. That luck wouldn't hold for long.

Destiny's Way. He needed to get to Absol, make a report. The journey would not be easy. He possessed no weapons, no supplies, just the clothes on his back. Returning to the Guardarm Inn for his things was too risky.

It will be first place they look once they realize I'm gone.

He'd traveled like this before, had done it while wounded. Berries and grass grew on the moors so he and the horse would be able to eat. With his mount carrying him, he'd be able to doze in the saddle.

I have to try.

He came of the alley onto the road that ran along the docks. In the distance, he spotted the gallows. The mass of people was thinning out. Ducking his head, he rode along the wharves, seeking an out-of-the-way route to the west gate. There used to be a path that led through the slums behind the docks. The dim memory led him through without incident. An eternity seemed to pass before he found himself on the road leading out of the city, just yards from the gate.

The portcullis was open. As with the eastern gate, no one appeared to be manning the guardhouse here. The entire city had turned out for hanging; perhaps the execution had required all hands...or the lords' militia were neglecting the duty. Either could be true.

Veln guided his horse through the gate, kept the pace to a sedate walk. No one came to accost him as he went. He held to the slower gate until the road crested a rise. Once out of sight of Rathburn's walls, he kicked into a gallop across the moors.

94

BA'TVIAN halted his horse – one of the Carthier courier steeds – on the crest. Beside him, the Jeste twins pulled up. Together, they watched the Mancer run for home. Greenmeadow was a dwindling dot in the landscape, clinging to the back of his mount as tenaciously as a burr.

"He won't make it on his own." Lakit flicked a glance at his leader. "Lady Nerisse didn't leave him in that good a condition."

"Then see that he does." Ba'tvian didn't take his eyes off the distant figure. "You know what needs to be done."

Tavor nodded, his twin speaking for both of them.

"If you're sure you don't need us here?" Lakit looked back at the city. "It isn't secure as yet."

"Halvark, Prialla, and Raptu have it in hand. We also have the troops you hired should we need more brawn. I need your special skills there." The blood mage took up his reins again. "Go. Get it done. We will join you come the finish."

As the Dithume rode off after the Mancer, their leader turned back into the city. He didn't hide his face. Nor did he proclaim what he was. Halvark met him at the gate, his acceptance of Ba'tvian's presence enough to reassure – for now.

"Are the tents sufficient for the mercenaries?"

Halvark gave a curt nod. "I'm concerned that the fifty Lakit came back with will be adequate."

"It will be." Ba'tvian continued as they rode along the street. "Ibestor will augment them."

"Is that why he took my bulls?" The noble's stiff reply was amusing.

"My spies tell me that they've fortified the shrine. We need something to show them that, whatever they build, we will tear it down." He looked into Halvark's eyes. "We are Dark Adepts, after all."

They would leave destruction in their wake.

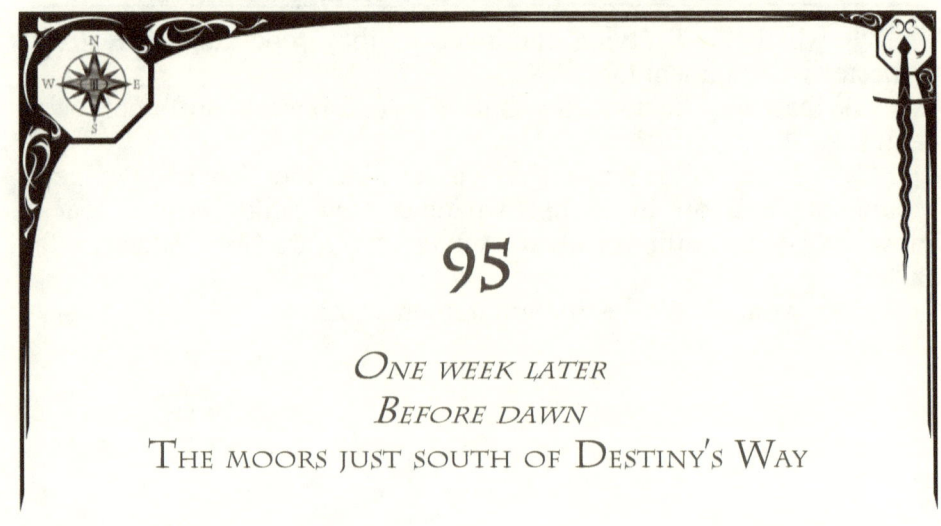

95

ONE WEEK LATER
BEFORE DAWN
THE MOORS JUST SOUTH OF DESTINY'S WAY

"IT'S been a quiet night. There's been no sign of any Shadows, but my gut tells me that they're not that far away." Absol shifted in his saddle, his cloak still damp from the light shower of rain they'd had earlier. "Be careful."

"Yes, sir."

The pair of Mancers relieving Absol and I'k'Nole on patrol didn't linger to chat after the short report they'd been given. They moved off into the gloom on the moors, their horses prancing a little in the unseasonal chill. Soon Omine and his one-time ward rode alone on the desolate moors.

The air was chilled. The drop in temperature came with the storms that had started up a week ago. It rained every day, saturating the soil to the point where the crops were beginning to fail. Early harvests salvaged some of them. A few fields were saved by digging ditches to carry off the excess water. The rest of crops rotted from the roots on up.

Not even the food stores were unscathed. Mold invaded anything not sealed in a clay jug or glass jar. They'd lost as much to spoiling as they had to the weather.

If the prospect of famine wasn't bad enough, pestilence had become a dire issue. The storms drove the rats out of the moors, the mice from the fields. They came into the village, infesting the storage areas, stables, barns, even homes. At least two of the children in the village had been bitten by rodents in their sleep.

The vermin brought with them the danger of illness: the Gastaean Plague, a disease that erupted occasionally on the plains and moors. When the rodent population swelled, as it tended to once every decade or so, the plague spread. Absol wasn't sure when the last outbreak had been. In the village, people were beginning to cough. One had lesions starting to form on his skin. As the only practitioners of medicine in the area, the On'Desae monks they checked everyone's health, quarantining the sick, passing out what remedies they could.

The timing could not be worse.

"It's starting to get lighter." I'k'Nole's idle observation brought Absol out of his reverie as they rode for home.

"So it is."

"I can take the horses once we get there," the younger man offered. "The sooner you get the week's roster done, the sooner you can sleep."

Amused, Absol glanced over at his protégé. "Are you implying that I'm getting old, lad?"

"No, sir." I'k'Nole gave him a small smile. "Only that you are tired."

"Ha. Well, I'll take your offer."

They continued in silence until they reached the road leading into Destiny's Way. Muted lights gave the windows of the farmhouses they passed a soft glow. The farmers were beginning their day. It promised to be a dismal one.

"Have you heard from Veln?"

"No, lad, not for a fortnight." It bothered him. Still, he didn't dare send a mage message to his comrade. Veln wasn't presenting himself as a Mancer in Rathburn. Absol didn't want to inadvertently raise suspicion by sending him something so visible as a sending. "I'm sure he's well. He'd alert us if something happened."

I hope.

He didn't voice the words. I'k'Nole heard them anyway. He seemed to always know what his mentor was thinking.

"Come whatever may, Absol, there will be a reckoning." I'k'Nole spoke as if giving a promise. "Even if none of us are there to see it."

It was an echo of Absol's daily prayer.

INTERLUDE 9

ELSEWHERE...

LABIYAL Biyalban strode into his study on cat-like feet to find everything in order. Nagun had, as usual, been accurate in his anticipation of his master's needs. Mirrors stood covered on their stand around his desk, each positioned well for viewing. The desk was clear save for a covered platter and a decanter of wine. A second chair sat to one side.

He took his seat. Now that he'd returned to his current residence, he had discarded the guise he'd worn in Rathburn. Nagun entered carrying a tray with small plates and crystal goblet for two. He placed them on the desk. Labiyal waited until he was finished before speaking.

"Were there any issues in my absence?"

"None, my lord." He tucked the tray under one arm. "Do you require anything else?"

"No, Nagun. Just see that we aren't disturbed. The servers can replenish the refreshments as necessary."

"Of course."

His man bowed, leaving without another word. Labiyal waited, thinking of the city he had just left. More, he thought of how much his chosen mage had become like him.

Ba'tvian had not taken center-stage in Rathburn, letting his influence crept in like a thief in the night. The policies being set in place were dictated by the young blood mage, or merely tweaked at his direction. Mayor Yilsed was a good mouth-piece for spouting those changes to the populace. The man had earned a boon for the way he'd transferred the duties of the Watch to Ba'tvian's nobles.

Though Rathburn was not yet under Ba'tvian Delthanurk's total control, it soon would be.

The door to his study opened again. He rose to meet Lord Biyal, gave a slight bow. He received a mocking bow in return.

"Sire."

"Spawnling."

He gestured the Daemon Lord to the second chair, then began to uncover the mirrors. After the cloths were set aside, he poured the wine and uncovered the platter. Fruits, meats, and cheeses sat in an appealing arrangement. His sire picked up a tiny wedge of cheese, bit in. Taking his seat, Labiyal nibbled on a piece of roasted fowl, more out of politeness than hunger. All around them, the mirrors began to light up one by one.

"It's time."

A great deal was on the line now. Come success or failure, people would die tonight. Labiyal did not want to be one of them.

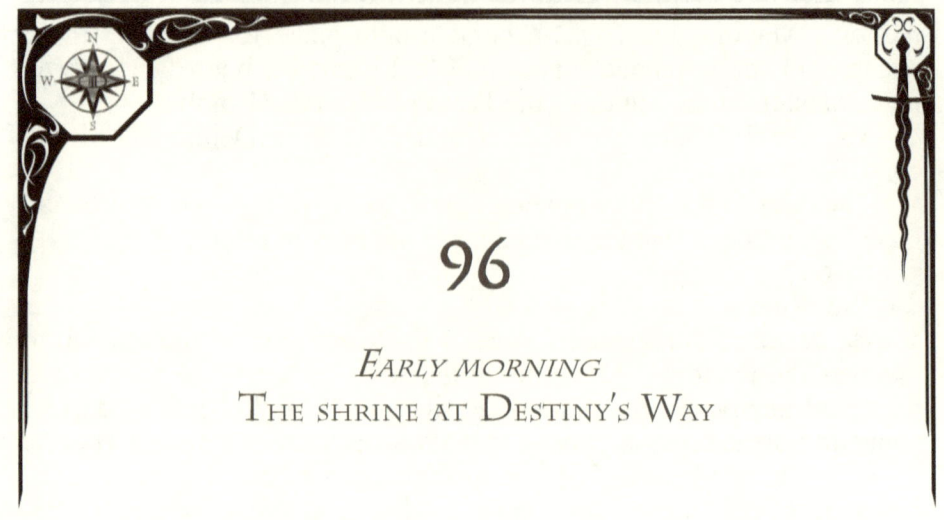

96

ABSOL was reviewing the duty roster with Celina in the shrine's library when the news came in. I'k'Nole rushed into the room, the door banging on the wall.

"Veln's been sighted on the moors just outside the fields."

Absol looked up from the papers they had spread out over the table, relieved to hear the words. Then he caught the worry in his protégé's face.

"What is it?"

"His horse has no saddle. He looks as if he's about to fall off at any moment. A few of the others rode out to meet him." Expression troubled, I'k'Nole's gaze went from Absol to Celina then back again. "This is bad."

"Don't jump to conclusions, lad. We'll get him in, find out what's happened. You need to get your head down for a bit. It was a long night patrol." Absol began to tidy the loose pages as Celina started out of the room. "We'll see to Veln."

"The Wood's gone quiet."

Omine paused, his head coming back up. Even Celina stepped back into the doorway to hear more.

"The song stopped after we got in," I'k'Nole went on. "It still whispered to anyone who would listen. That ceased about the same time that Veln passed into the fields."

"Has it ever gone silent?" Celina wondered. "You've been in this region the longest, Absol."

"Not insofar as I'm aware. Dannon might know of past instances." He frowned. "I'll ask him. Celina, go down and meet Veln. I'k'Nole, get some sleep. If we need you, lad, we'll find you."

The young man obeyed without protest, though his reluctance was written on his. Absol sympathized. Yet he was well aware that the two best mages they had – one the most skilled, the other the most powerful – may have just been reduced to one. If that were the case, I'k'Nole would need to handle that end on his own.

"He's really worried. Should we be?" His old friend cocked her head at him, her eyes questioning. "He may be young, but his intuition hasn't been wrong in my experience."

"You will have to tell me. After Veln, you've most mage-skill and knowledge." He sighed. "I'll join you once I've spoken to Dannon."

Speaking to the Master Abbott turned out to be more difficult than anticipated. He wasn't inside the shrine. When Absol asked one of the monks he was told that Dannon had gone into the Wood.

"He's trying to learn the reason it's stopped singing. He was very concerned about it," Brother Filtan informed him as he oiled some of the newer pieces of tack. The two were in the stables, the last place Absol checked for his old friend. "He said he should be back before mid-morning prayers."

"When you see him, please tell him I need to speak with him." Absol frowned a moment, thinking. "Has the Wood done this before?"

"No, I don't think so. That's why Dannon was so worried."

Now so am I.

He thanked the monk, leaving the stables to search out Celina. He found her in the infirmary. Occupying a cot beside her was Veln. He sat, shivering, as one of the monks training in medicine examined him. Celina caught his eye, nodded to the hallway. Without a word, the two stepped out, keeping their voices low.

"He says that Ba'tvian owns Rathburn now. The Watch was disbanded, the old captain dead, and the local lords are in Ba'tvian's pocket."

"How in the name of the One did he manage to fall in with the aristocracy?" Absol could scarcely credit it. "He was born a serf, is a blood mage. He's arrogant – too arrogant to take orders from someone of a higher rank. It boggles my mind, Celina."

"People of any social standing can be bought and sold." She

shook her head. "It's only a matter of finding the right kind of currency."

"Veln confirmed this?"

"He was held captive by them." She held up a hand to forestall questions as she continued. "He's not certain how long they had him. He's verified that Lords Halvark Tretoan and Raptu Carthier are working with Ba'tvian, along with at least two others. He doesn't remember Nerisse. Delthanurk was in charge when he was caught."

"The barbarian?"

"If he's still with them, he never came around Veln. I asked."

"How bad is he?" He hadn't liked the way he'd looked – far too thin, pale, almost wasted in a way.

"Not good. The healer hasn't said much, won't until he finished, but I can tell you that he suffered tremendous arcane damage. His shields are fractured, Absol." Celina's eyes held echoes of her initial shock at seeing them. "Cracked like an egg. It doesn't look as if there's been any psychic recovery at all since it happened. He said he did it to himself. When they caught him, he tried to attack Ba'tvian. It hit cracked his shields, knocked him out."

"He over-enforced his protections?"

"I can't think of another explanation." She frowned. "I didn't know that was possible."

"Anything else?"

"He told me not to trust him." More worry, and just a little fear, came into her eyes. "He wants me to look into his mind, make sure he's still him."

Absol muttered a vile oath. "What did they do to him?"

"He doesn't know. That's what scares me."

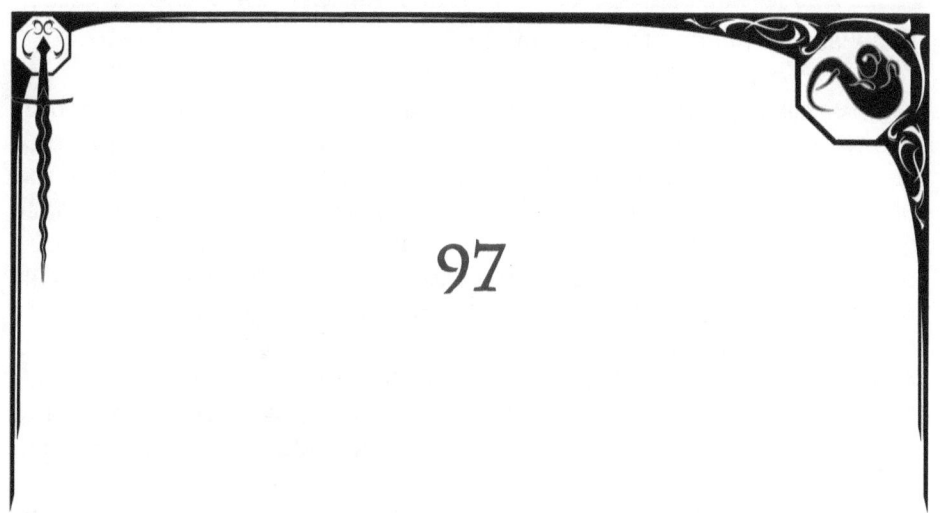

97

THE infirmary was hushed. No other patients lingered in the beds, no monks ushered through the aisles. The healer tending Veln wasn't there, called away to administer the sick in the village. With no one around, he'd though sleep would be easy.

It wasn't.

Noise crowded into Veln's head. Thoughts, emotions, wisps of conversation – they all trickled in through the fractures in his shields. Each one dripped into his mind like a hammer blow on the anvil.

It hadn't been like this in Rathburn, when his mind still vibrated with the psychic shock that left it numb. The numbness had worn off on the moors. It hadn't presented a problem then, with just the horse and a few small animals scurrying in the grass about. Now he was among people. The press of minds – humans, the livestock they kept – pushed in at him. It made his head throb.

More, it widened the jagged cracks in his shields. He could see it happening, saw one crack merge with another in slow-motion. It snapped, a sharp mental sound. Another shattered piece of his protections fell away.

Celina had tried to give him new shields, something temporary to spare him torment until his own regenerated. They'd been stood strong, a vibrant wall in the azure colors of her magic. They'd crumpled not long after she'd left.

There wasn't any choice. He needed to get out. He'd never find the peace he needed to heal in the shrine.

The Wood...no one goes to the Wood.

Veln sat up in the cot, shivering despite the blanket or the warmth of the woolen tunic and breeches he'd been given. He wasn't cold. Not physically. Yet the shivers wouldn't stop. He wrapped the blanket around him as he searched for his boots. Finding them under the cot, he put them on. When Veln emerged in the hall he wasn't far from the tiny rooms in which the monks and those who stayed with them slept. He turned away from them, heading toward the back.

He exited the building. Sunlight spilled over the walls into the courtyard; dawn had broken. Mancers and monks bustled about, tending to horses, patrolling the walls, speaking with people from the village. He slipped into the shadows. He didn't want to talk. He didn't want to interact with anyone.

Head pounding, he shuffled around the monastery, then the smaller shrine at its rear. Behind the shrine was the heavy door that led out to the Wood. He stopped in his tracks when he saw it was guarded. He almost turned back. The horrendous pressure on his mind forced him to walk forward.

He recognized the pair standing duty at the door – not the names, the faces. They were young, still in training. Inside, in a part of him left untouched by the pain of his head, he relaxed.

"Veln? Sir, are you well?" one of them asked as he approached.

"Not really." He grimaced at the sound of his voice. It seemed far too loud in his ears. "My shields are damaged. I need to be away from people while they recover. I thought a brief walk in the Wood would help."

"Perhaps we should get the healer." The other Mancer eyed him with a frowned. "No disrespect, Mancer Greenmeadow, but you don't look as if you should be standing up."

"The healer's seen to me. A bit of time outside the shrine ground, away from people is all I need." He did his best to sound firm. "Absol understands what I'm doing."

The last slipped out without conscious thought. He wasn't sure why he'd said it; it wasn't true. The guards, however, relented.

"If he knows..." The first one looked at his partner and shrugged. "We'll report to him if you're not back soon. You have until the sun tops the wall there." He nodded to the eastern one.

"Good."

They opened the door for him, let him through.

He wandered for a bit, just walked in the direction he was facing.

The press of minds receded as he went farther out. The headache eased enough that he began to take more note of his surroundings.

He had not gone into the Wood, having turned off the path at some point. The huge expanse of forest stood to his left and the pasture used by the monastery lay on his right. The shrine lay behind him. In the distance ahead were the open moors.

Frowning, head still throbbing, he stood there. Something was amiss. The damn pain made it so hard to think clearly. He rubbed his temples. He took a few deep breaths, turned to go back to the path – then realized what it was wrong.

There was no harpsong.

Again, he paused, straining to hear. The Wood had gone quiet. Eerie silence it left made the hairs stand on the back of his neck. A tremor passed through him. Whatever that meant, it couldn't be good.

...buried...

The single word whispered in the air. Veln spun around, his blanket tangling his legs. He stumbled, fell to the ground. He struggled to a sitting position, wrestled with the blanket. As he free it, he noticed that he wasn't alone.

A woman stood in the pasture a few yeards away, her clothes stained with dirt. There was a gaping hole in her skull. The sunlight shone through her form even as blood dribbled from her tangled white hair. The dark red streaked the back of her dress. He had seen her once before. She'd wept then, wandering in the rain to scream at a manor house. Now she faced the shrine, tears gone, swaying in place.

She comes...she comes...

She lifted a hand toward the walled monastery, stumbled forward a few steps. Her shoulders shook as she began to sob.

...buried us in the earth...all of us in the earth...

Jevanel. Elvanarae. Nerisse. If the ghost was here, she had to be. That meant Ba'tvian couldn't be far.

They'd broken in – traversed the labyrinth. They'd dug psychic fingers into his brain, tearing, ripping –

Agony speared through his mind, tearing at his brain. Gasping, he clutched at his head, the ghost looking on with pity in her dead eyes. As he collapsed on his side, crimson stained silver threading around his awareness and pulling it deep within his mental maze, she threw back her head. Her despair screamed into the sky.

The world screamed with her.

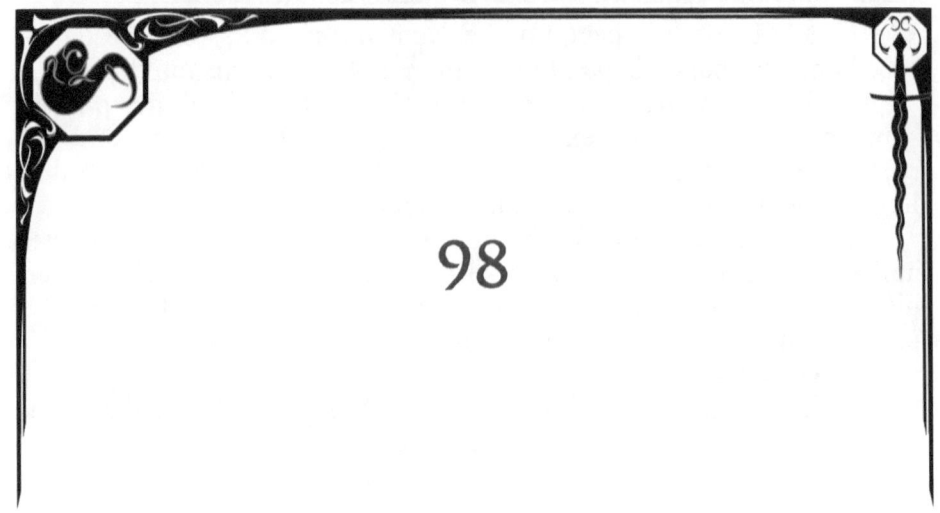

98

A loud banging on the door roused Absol from slumber. Groaning, he rose, grabbed the tunic he'd discarded earlier and hauled it over his torso before answering the knock. Celina wasted no time with greetings.

"Veln is missing."

Absol turned back into the room with a curse to get the rest of his attire. With no regard for modesty or convention, he dressed in haste. "How long?"

"Not quite an hour. He left the infirmary while the healer was out – the sickness in the village is getting worse." She paced in the hall as she spoke, the door still open between them. "I should have had someone watching him."

"Neither you nor the healer could see any tampering with his mind, Celina." Despite that, he, too, damned his lack of foresight. "His shields are ruined; that's probably why he left."

"I shielded him, gave him control of the new protections. He shouldn't have needed to leave." She shook her head as he joined her outside his dorm. "He left through the back, along the Wood path. The guards reported it at the change in shift, then came to see me because he didn't come back when he said he would. Veln had told them you knew he was heading out."

"I bloody well did not." The lie, so unlike the Veln, twisted his stomach. They hurried down the corridor to the courtyard, Absol hoping that they hadn't made a monumental mistake. "How possible is it that we were wrong about him? His mental condition?"

"None of us are Empaths, Absol."

Nerisse is. The thought made him sick.

He ran up to the crude, concave circle of metal they'd hung in the courtyard for occasions such as this. He picked up the wooden mallet next to it, struck the gong hard. The resounding noise brought people out of every building. The sound hadn't quite faded when Omine started to speak.

"Veln Greenmeadow is missing. All of you are aware he came back to us in a bad state; it may be worse than we'd initially assessed. We cannot disregard the possibility that Veln has somehow been – compromised." A moment of disturbed silence bloomed in the audience. They looked at each other, uneasy. A few of the younger Mancers looked stricken. "We need to search the monastery grounds and make ready for an attack. We can't take chances."

He outlined the duties, ordering anyone still asleep to be woken and put to work. Master Dannon took over the defensive preparations. Celina organized the search parties. Absol took off in the direction Veln was supposed to have taken. He prayed that he was over -reacting, that his fears were unfounded.

Above them, dark clouds gathered in the morning sky.

99

I'K'NOLE hurried to the stables, directed there by the Master Abbot when he'd reported in. Dread was a thick ball in his belly as he entered. The sky was darkening fast. Too fast. He wasn't a weather-mage, couldn't sense the tampering in the air currents, but he recognized a natural storm when he saw one. This wasn't it.

Brother Filtan met him between the rows of stalls. Around them, the horses were agitated, uneasy whinnies issued at every movement. The eyes of the animals rolled white. Many of them were kicking the walls of their boxes.

"They're all spooked, boy. We've got to get them settled. You've a way with animals; it's why I asked for you." The monk stopped as light flashed in the courtyard, thunder booming. Startled, horses began to buck. Even as the two men rushed to soothe the beasts, shouts sounded outside.

"Lightning sturck one of the wagons; it caught fire." I'k'Nole's eyes took on a faraway look as he pulled down the head of a startled gelding. The telepathic exchange with another Mancer in the courtyard was brief. "They're handling it."

"We can be thankful that it didn't strike the thatching on the stables." Filtan began to murmur to his charges. They worked to calm them, yet when they moved more than a stall or two away, their work came undone. The storm, noisome and directly overhead, didn't help any. The stables shuddered with each peal of thunder, sending the lanterns hanging above the aisle swinging. Light and shadows danced eerily.

"Do you think Ba'tvian can cause a storm?" I'k'Nole asked the monk, dragging down a gelding's head to attach a lead to its halter. He tied the rope to one of the stall posts, leaving no slack for the horse to rear up.

"You're the mage, boy. You know more about that sort of thing than I." He grimaced as a temperamental mount snapped its teeth at him. He administered an admonishing slap on the muzzle. "Stop that. We don't have time to deal with your games today."

I'k'Nole thought of Absol. The older Mancer would be the better judge, but he might not hear him should he reach out mind-to-mind. More, his mentor was searching for Veln. If he'd found him – if Veln had been corrupted somehow –

Best not distract him.

Everyone had their hands full, and the situation was getting worse. The sound of wood cracking accompanied the bucking of a stallion down the row. He hurried to the stall, grabbed hold of the halter –

The air filled with the piercing scream of a woman's agony.

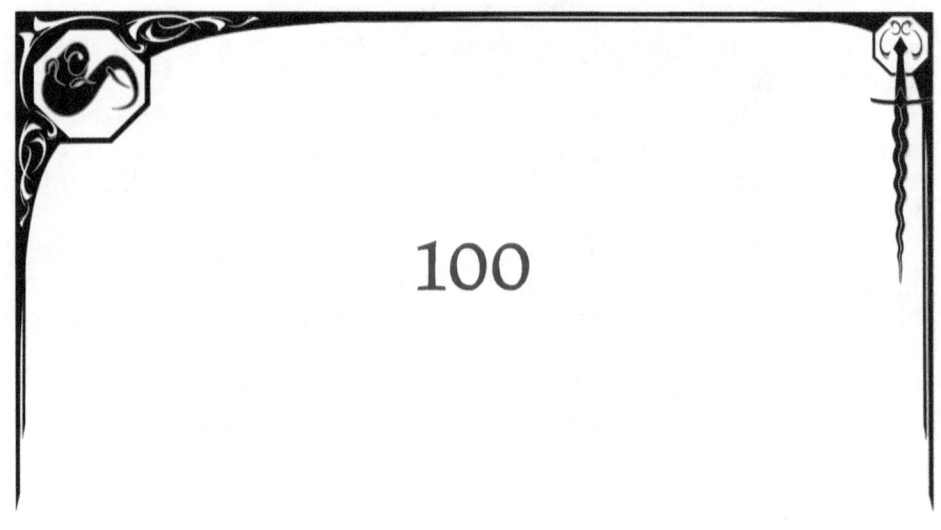

100

"VELN!"

Absol called out, then heard the scream as it tore through the air. He ran toward it, lightning stabbing at the pasture not far from him. Blinded by the flash, he stopped, stumbled, fell to one knee. Blinking to clear the after-image of the bolt from his vision, he spotted Veln just ahead. Like him, the man was kneeling, hands braced in the grass, head drooping. Fat drops of rain began to fall as Absol shoved onto his feet.

"Veln!" He called the name again, approaching with caution. "Answer me!"

The other Mancer staggered upright, staring off into the moors. Absol followed his gaze, saw nothing. He refocusing on Veln, coming closer to halt only a few feet away.

"Veln, it's dangerous out here in the storm. We have to go inside." On cue, the sky rumbled again, then opened up. Rain poured down in heavy sheets on top of them. More lightning streaked to earth. Absol reach out to touch Veln's shoulder.

The man's head whipped toward him, his eyes dark pools of agony set in a face so pale it looked like parchment. Startled, Absol stepped back. His gut clenched as he stared.

"You'll die tonight." The voice was almost conversational. The eyes pleaded. "All chances have run out."

"Veln?" The Mancer wasn't sure if the man he knew was the one speaking.

"I'm not him anymore." His face smiled, sharp and surreal. "He's locked away inside. A paper doll shut up in the vault."

Possessed. Fear for his friend had to be quelled. Veln Greenmeadow might be inside somewhere but if Ba'tvian had managed to lodge a daemon inside the Mancer's body it was doubtful that he could be freed. Absol buried the grief as he moved farther back, putting ground between him and the other as he pulled his sword free of its scabbard. That was when he saw them. The Shadows slithered along the grass; one coiled around Veln's feet. He glanced around him. The pasture crawling with them – more than he'd ever seen before.

I'll never make it. The creatures would catch him before he got halfway back to the shrine.

"You shouldn't have come, Absol."

Even as the one-time Mancer spoke, Absol desperately flung thoughts into the wind. I'k'Nole had the telepathic reach that he lacked – he would hear him. He would alert the others. With the Shadows closing in, and whatever was in Veln advancing, he took the only route he had left.

Absol Omine ran into the silent Wood, slashing at anything that moved in his path.

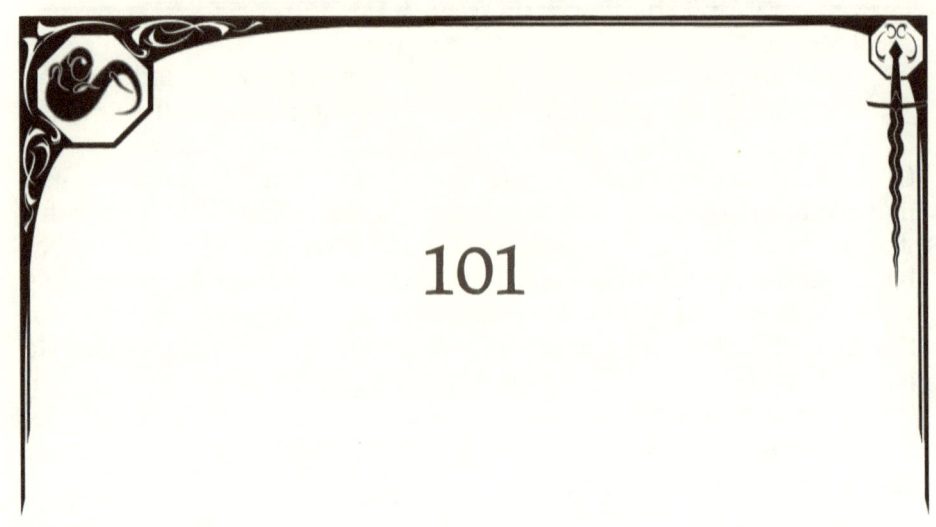

101

BA'TVIAN stood amid the downpour in the middle of monastery's pasture with several of his Dark Adepts. The twins and Nerisse waited at the ready, each astride one of Ibestor's creations as their leader watched through the eyes of a Shadow. Ba'tvian saw his nemesis fleeing into the Wood, his oldest followers stopping at the forest's edge. Returning to himself, he severed the connection with his pet, then he nodded curtly in Absol's direction.

"Tavor. After him." He didn't want his enemy hiding while they ruined his haven.

Tavor Jeste dug his heels into the sides of his own unnatural steed to take off through the rain. Ba'tvian looked at Nerisse, who remained quiet at his side.

"The whyte is in full control. Send Greenmeadow ahead of us. Raptu and Ibestor need to move. Lakit, give the Mancers something to worry about."

The weather-mage raised a hand, concentrated. Lightning flashed above the shrine and village. Bolts struck down in a random pattern, hitting anything out in the open. Nerisse spoke.

"Omine sent a warning. Not a formal sending, just thoughts in the ether."

"It won't matter." Ba'tvian sent a mental call out to his pets. "Nothing he does will matter."

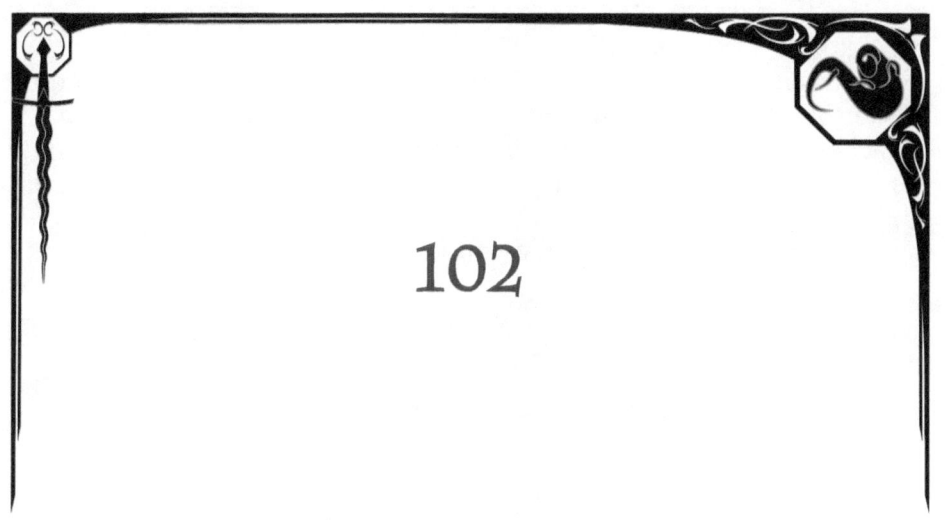

102

I'K'NOLE flung open the last stall door, allowing the spooked equine to charge out. It took off for the open double-doors that led out into the pasture. He hoped it wouldn't be killed out there; the storm was vicious. Yet if the horses hadn't been set free, they'd have hurt themselves trying to get out of their stalls. That scream had made them all frantic, crazed.

– Veln – possessed – turned – enemy here –

I'k'Nole caught the fragments of the loose thought, knew who'd sent them out. With them came a momentary image depicting Veln Greenmeadow standing with Shadows; it looked like hundreds of them. Grief stabbed at his heart. The mage who'd tutored him was lost. He hoped the same would not be said of Omine.

"Brother Filtan! Absol's in trouble. Veln's been corrupted and we're under attack. Tell Master Dannon!" He shouted over his shoulder as he ran, thunder crashing overhead, into the courtyard. He yelled the warning to everyone in hearing range, at the same time broadcasting telepathically to anyone who could receive his sending.

"Where are they coming from?" A Mancer demanded from the catwalk at the walls. "I can't see anything in this infernal rain!"

"I – " I'k'Nole flinched as white-hot bolt of lightning slammed into the stable roof. Flames erupted in the thatch. Despite the rain, the fire took hold and grew. In its light, on the catwalk nearest the stables, a black, lizard-like creature slide over the top of the wall.

"Lookout! Next to you!"

The sounded an alarm as the Mancer whirled, pulling his sword to strike out. The blade bit into the Shadow. It thrashed toward its attacker as I'k'Nole prepared an arcane blast. He let it loose to hit a second Shadow climbing onto the catwalk as his comrade finished off the first.

They were followed by many more.

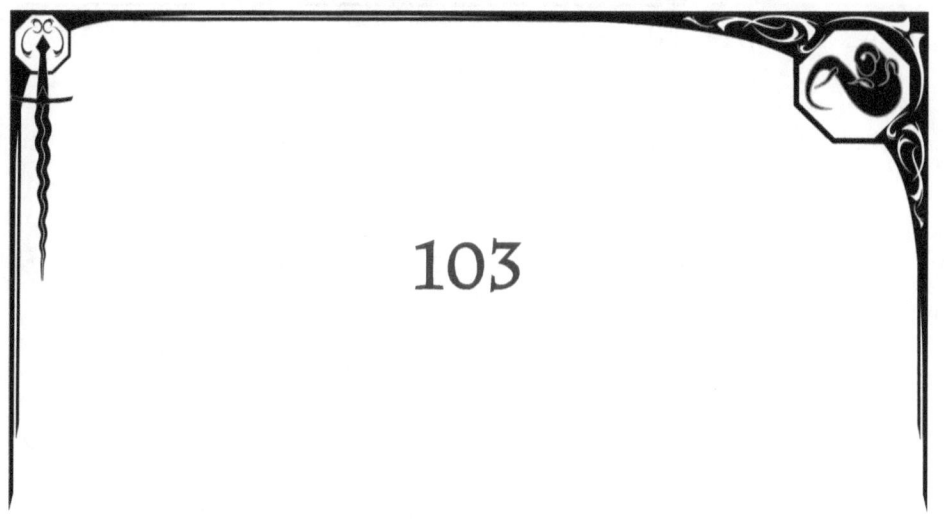

103

ABSOL Omine heard the thing his pursuer rode before he saw it. It didn't sound like a horse. It prodded his memory as he ran. The mage-sending from Timbrel Jodrek prior to his death had had mentioned a cobbled-together beast. He wondered if it was a drake, or makeshift animal. Whatever it was, it moved fast.

"If you're inclined to help a man in need," Absol muttered to the Wood as he dodged around the trees, "now is the time to do so. Please."

The harsh roll of thunder became muted. Strange lights winked at the edge of sight. The harpsong – absent through the moment – echoed in his mind, the notes soft, discordant. A shriek sounded behind him, followed by thrashing in the bushes.

Thank you.

He fled on through the undergrowth, praying that I'k'Nole had caught his message. Absol hoped, too, that he wouldn't get lost. He'd veered away from his intended direction to avoid what chased earlier, wasn't sure if he was heading the right way anymore. Those fears dissipated when he broke out of the trees onto the path that led up to the shrine.

The rain was still torrential. Through the wet haze, he could just make out the dark, distant shape of the walled-in structure. Even as he turned onto the path motes of orange and red light swirled into the air in front of him. They overlaid the monastery and its buildings, painting them with flames.

No. That's not going to happen.

He wouldn't let it.

The motes scattered as Absol ran through them and out of the Wood.

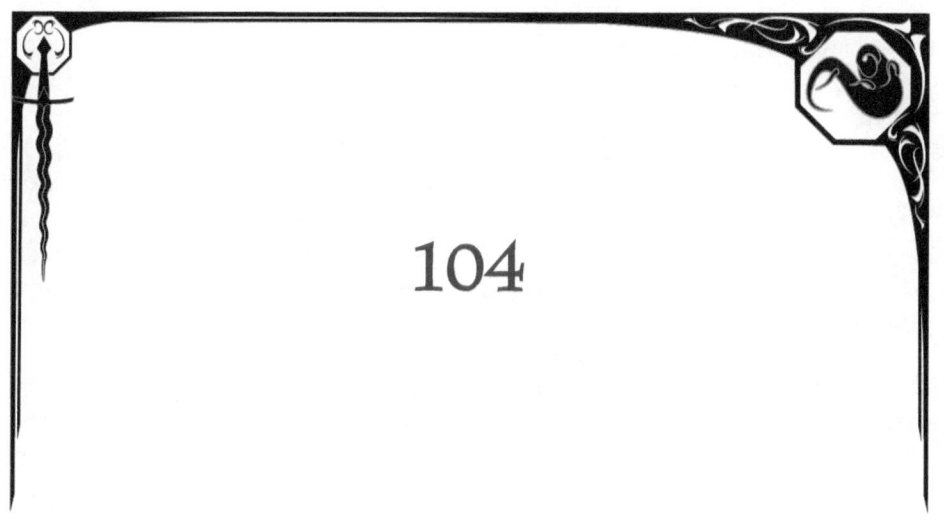

104

B A'TVIAN dismounted outside the rear entrance to the shrine. Greenmeadow had been admitted just moments before their arrival. Handing his reins to Nerisse, he unsheathed his sword and placed a palm on the heavy door, channeled power into it. The dense wood burned, turning to ash in the wake of the magic as it pushed outward from his hand. There was a cry of alarm from the guards on the other side. A blade thrust through at chest-height, collapsing it ash around it.

The blood mage deflected the attack, kicking through what remained of the incinerating door to knock his opponent back. His Shadows darted through the opening as a levin bolt hit his shields, flaring them into view. It was a weak attempt. He responded with one of his own, stepping inside the walls to see the blood red of power smash into the second sentry. The Mancer hit the ground hard, dropping his weapon. His pets swarmed him, one wriggling ontop of the stunned man to plunge into his mouth.

The first sentry fared better. He was still on his feet, hacking at the Shadows that menaced him. One lunged forward, sinking teeth into his calf. As he turned to slash at it, Ba'tvian plunged his sword into his side, angling the blade to pierce the heart. The Mancer staggered as he pulled it free. His followers had him on the ground a moment later. He turned back as the others joined him inside the walls. Their mounts barely passed through the doorway.

"Tavor has lost Omine."

Ba'tvian wasn't surprised at Lakit's news. The Wood had a mind of its own. "He's to rejoin us, then. Omine won't have gone far."

He wiped his sword clean on the cloak of the fallen guard. Straightening, he glanced at dead man's partner. His pets were feeding. *Don't glut yourselves just yet,* he cautioned. *There will be plenty for you here.* He took back his reins, remounted. The others did the same, as he skirted the shrine to move alongside the monastery's main building.

"Greenmeadow isn't stable." Nerisse caught up with him, Lakit behind her. A few yards in front of them, the subject of her concern stumbled on. He hadn't assisted with the assault on the sentries. "He will break himself fighting it."

"His well-being isn't my concern, Nerisse. Will he obey the command?"

"Yes." She met his eyes, let him see that she wasn't prevaricating. "He will find the one called I'k'Nole."

"Good." He dismissed the man, looking around. They had chosen an abysmal structure for their stronghold. Their rear was the weakest point of defensibility. There were no catwalks on the walls, no one else keeping a post nearby.

Of course, that may have been due to the noise emanating from the front. Amid the shouts and cries of pain, he heard the crash of something enormous striking wood. He felt his lips curve, motioned for his companions to wait in the gloom, out of the way.

A little ahead of him, the pale figure of Veln staggered around the corner and out of sight.

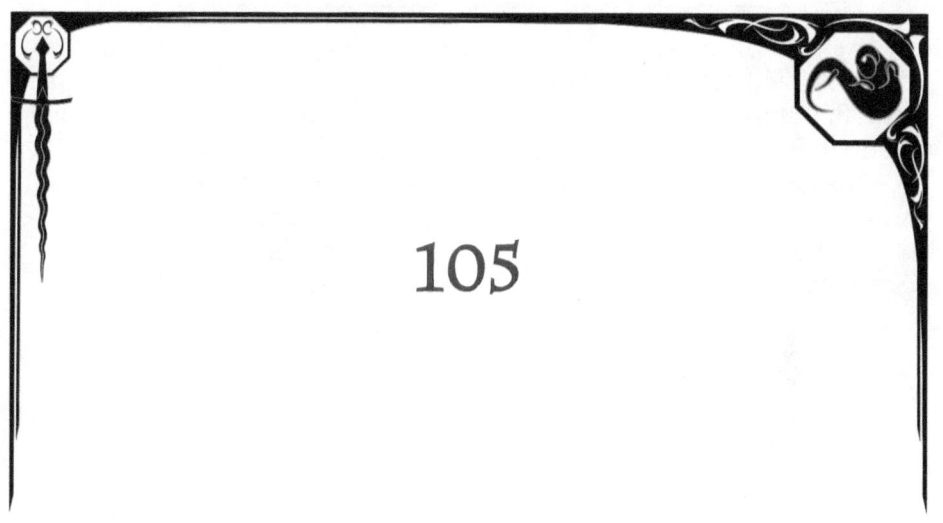

105

*F*IND *I'k'Nole.*
  The incessant demand whispered through his mind in a
  woman's soothing voice, yet Veln knew who'd given the order.
In the depths of the labyrinth he'd made, he flung himself at the
silvery bars of his cage. They flexed like a spider's web and held.

Whatever they had done to him – whatever they'd planted *inside*
him – held him prisoner here. He able to see the outside, hear the
battle, the beating of some sort of ram on the shrine doors. He just
couldn't get out. His maze shifted around him, in the control of the
thing that ruled his body.

It was, gleeful, eager, inhuman.

It had to be a low-level daemon, the opportunistic, ethereal kind
that was the lowest of the low in the daemon caste-system. The
Mancers had documented their existence well over the years. They
animated the newly dead, were sometimes summoned by blood
mages. His experience was limited to just one encounter in his early
years.

Whytes, he recalled. They were whytes.

There were ways to deal with them, spells and rites passed from
Mancer to Mancer. He dug into memory, found what he needed. He
tried to dredge up power. It slipped out of his arcane grasp before he
could touch it. The thing inside him laughed.

You will die here, it said. *I will consume you.*

Veln didn't reply. He made another attempt, sending out thoughts without structure or target. They passed through the bars into the maze where the shifting patterns caught them, shredded them. His isolation was complete.

His people – I'k'Nole – would face him without warning. It left him with only one option. He hoped it wouldn't be in vain.

In the world outside, there was the horrible crack of dense wood giving way.

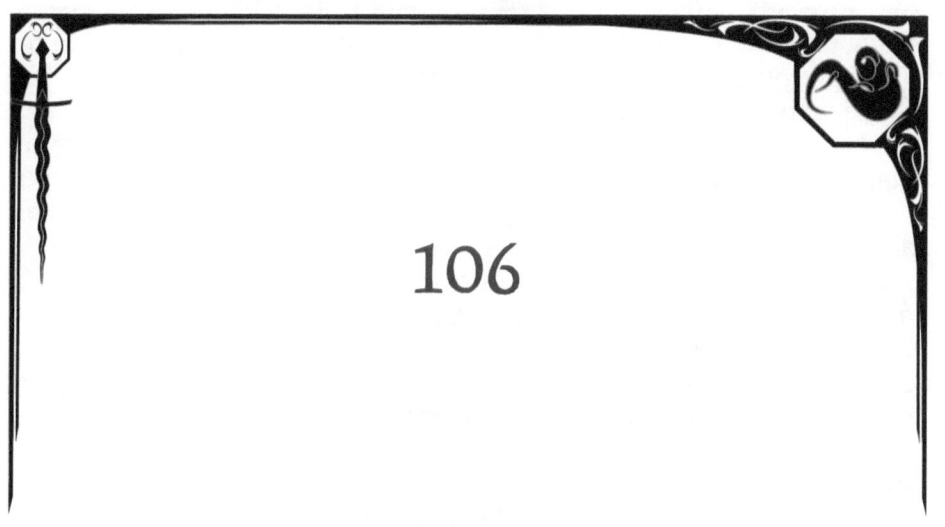

106

THEY are everywhere.

Blade in hand, I'k'Nole found himself surrounded in the middle of the courtyard. The dark creatures covered the ground, leaping up to bite and claw as the rain continued to fall. He swung his sword in a hasty arc, let loose a wave of power. The amethyst flame spilled out. Shadows scattered, shrieking as the wave caught up with the stragglers.

Behind him, the steady assault on the gate continued, the wood cracking. The iron held it together, but that wouldn't last for much longer.

The mage fire didn't help those on the catwalks. Mancers dodged, hacked, and slashed as more Shadowed Ones cascaded over the walls. There was no end to them. At his back, they slipped in through the cracks around the large doors. More slithered in from behind the monastery.

Mancers, monks, a handful of villagers caught inside the shrine walls when the attack began faced off with them. Instead of meeting their opponents, the creatures slid along the edges, just out of range, circling around to feint and taunt. They're first volley had been frenzied. Now they moved with caution. A sinking feeling in his gut, I'k'Nole scanned the yard, then walks above.

By the burning stable, a soldier with black armor sporting a red sigil, hauled himself over the wall onto the catwalk. He plunged his blade into the back of the nearest Mancer. As the dead man fell to be swarmed over by Shadows, more soldiers began to appear at the top of the walls.

He reacted instinctively, sending out another explosive wave of magic. This one he made more powerful than the last, increasing its reach. It surged in all directions, crashing through friends and foes alike. Shadowed Ones fled back over the walls, through the cracks, seeking any escape. Enemy human soldiers were knocked back, many thrown off the catwalks to land outside.

The Mancers began to move, intent on regaining weapons, covering weak points, tending the wounded. The monks followed their example as the few villagers present sagged in place. Most were bloodied. I'k'Nole was no exception. Blood trickled down his arm from a Shadow's gash, made his sword-hilt slick in his hand.

The relentless battering on the iron-bound doors increased. Metal shrieked as it began to give way.

"I'k'Nole! Stand at the ready!" Celina Behr climbed down from the western wall, calling out orders. "Mancers, we need more people on the walks! Everyone else, brace the doors!"

I'k'Nole tore a strip from his cloak, had a monk tie it snug around his arm wound. He took up a position facing the monastery, cast his gaze about for the enemy. The Shadows had fled. The soldiers were gone.

Something's not right about this. Fear began to coil inside him. *What am I missing?*

As another blow sent the doors bucking beneath the combined weight of everyone else, it dawned on him. Numbers – people – more people should have responded to the attack. The monks out-numbered the Mancers in the monastery yet the opposite was true in the courtyard

One set of iron bindings snapped. I'k'Nole just missed being hit by a piece of the metal as it flew through the air. Startled, he turned to see the doors gaping at the top, glimpsed the furred, horned head of something huge on the other side. He turned back to his task as Celina shouted encouragement to her fellows.

From the barracks side of the courtyard, Veln stumbled out into the open.

He was wet, streaked with mud and grass. Face pale, he looked around as if confused.

"Veln?" I'k'Nole whispered the name, almost called out in a louder tone. Then he remembered. *Possessed.* He took a deep breath, used his arcane senses.

Crimson and tarnished silver wrapped around Veln's frame. Inside it, a daemon looked out, an blurred thing the color of pus with jagged features. It locked gazes with him and grinned.

He didn't think. Yanking a dagger from his belt, he threw it hard, concentrating on the blade as it sliced through the air. Violet power flashed bright as it hit Veln full in the chest.

With a resounding breakage of wood, the doors gave way.

107

ABSOL heard the battle, the booming at the gate. The storm still roiled overhead unnoticed as he darted through the rear entrance and into the shrine itself. The hallowed place was empty. With no care for sanctity, he hastened toward the small colonnade that led into the monastery. He'd just made it in when the commotion of the doors failing echoed.

Cursing, he ran down the main corridor, sword raised. In the gloomy corners, tails flickered, white eyes blinked. The Shadows stayed away from him as he moved through the building. Near the dining hall, he caught sight of a mass of the creatures and skidded to a halt.

They were piled on top of each other, writhing, hissing. From somewhere beneath their bulk he made out the tearing of flesh. He struck out with the sword, channeling his meager magery into the blade. As the weapon bit into the black bodies, the room filled with startled squeals. The creatures scattered to the far reaches of the dining area, leaving their dead to twitch in their wake. As one, they turned back to assess him as he recognized the remains of Brother Filtan.

"No." Anger welled within him, augmenting what little magic he had. But he didn't use it. Not here. There was no saving the dead now, and the dining hall, he could see, was full of the dead. Monks lay scattered on the floor. Few had faces left to be identified by. He didn't know if any of them were his oldest friend Dannon.

In the distance, an unknown beast roared. He was dimly aware of shouts, screams. The living needed him. So he abandoned the dead to continue on towards the courtyard. In his heart, fueled by grief, rage began to build.

Ba'tvian Delthanurk had much to answer for.

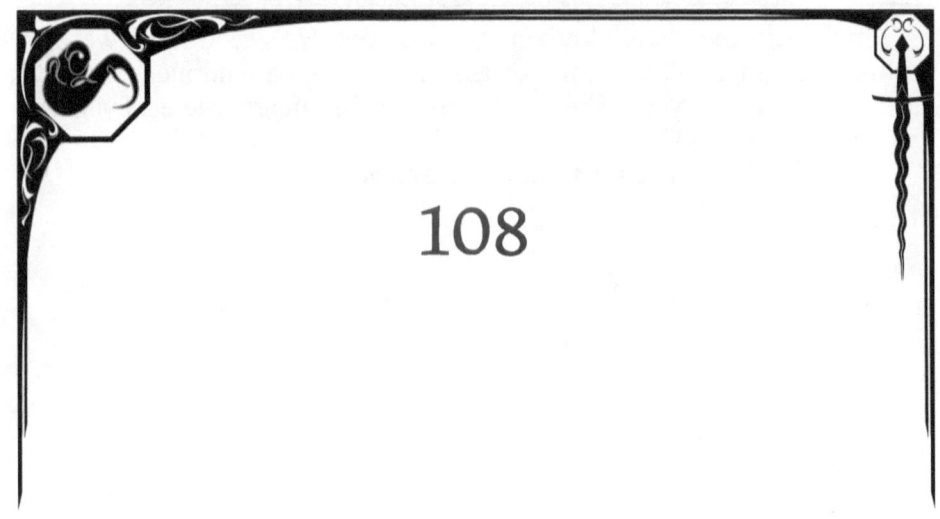

108

THE doors flung open, pieces of timber and metal joining the bodies sailing through the air. Many of those bracing the gate landed stunned on the ground. Ruined, the doors fell on either side of the gate, sagging from their hinges as the misshapen creature than had done damage stepped through with a bellow.

I'k'Nole hauled up a fellow Mancer, mouth dropping at the beast. *It's huge –*

It was also boring down on him. The young man scrambled out out of its way, dragging his dazed comrade with him. Flowing in from behind the thing came armed men. The enemy outnumbered them at least two to one.

"Rise up!" Dannon's voice rang like a clarion bell. The Master Abbott stood as a rally point in front of the monastery, sword in one hand, a small shield in the other. Divested of his robe, his ivory tunic showed spatters of blood, the color faded from the rain. He stood defiant as he called out again. "Rise up!"

Celina seconded his cry. Their people gathered around the abbott, those manning the catwalks, notching arrows aimed at the enemy as they formed up on either side of their living battering ram. Not all were on foot.

"Now we send them back to Hell!"

The enemy rushed in as Dannon shouted the words. A handful of soldiers rode things that resembled horses with fangs, trampling all in their way. One rider flashed a wicked grin as he ran over a monk still fumbling to get to his feet. The beast whipped its head down to bite into the man's neck, fangs tearing into flesh. He didn't have a chance to scream.

The Mancers and their allies met the charge. They took up Dannon's battle cry, their voices soon lost in the fray. I'k'Nole found himself standing eerily alone amid the chaos, the sounds of the fighting muted in his ears. No one came at him as he moved through the fighting.

He took advantage, thrusting his sword into the kidneys of a nearby Mancer's opponent. He collapsed. Pulling it free, he turned – to look into the face of the beast.

Empty eyes stared from the battered head, its bulk skinned in a patchwork of various hides. Arrows bounced off the thick hide. It lumbered forth, the massive head swinging from side to side to sweep its path clear with broad, curved horns large enough to skewer a horse. It snorted as it spied him, brandished its horns. He darted to the side, dodging a swipe that almost impaled him, and went for the sturdy hind limbs. Thick as tree trunks, the cloven hooves dark, they lacked any protection. Sheathing his sword, he leapt, grabbing the whip-like tail. It flung him around as the beast began to turn. He managed to climb despite the attempts to shake him off.

Just a little more... He hauled himself up a bit higher, then clung to the tail as he went for his sword. Blade in hand, he timed the swing then slashed out. The weapon bit through the hide to sever the hamstring.

It bellowed as the hind leg gave way.

I'k'Nole grasped the tail tight as it thrashed back and forth, lashing out with the sword. On the fourth attempt the blade cut into the second limb, but he lost his grip before he could see how successful he'd been. He dropped like a tossed stone onto the ground.

He rolled onto his feet, let loose a levin bolt on the broadside of the amalgamous beast. Arcane light lit up the courtyard. Lightning streaked to earth. There were screams, the smell of burnt flesh, another flash of violet as I'k'Nole launched a volley of raw magic at the beast's bovine face.

It jerked away violently, bellowing again in pain. It staggered then fell, trapping anyone near it beneath its crushing weight. He moved after it, sword ready to slit the throat.

He was hit hard in the back, a wash of power painting his world blood red.

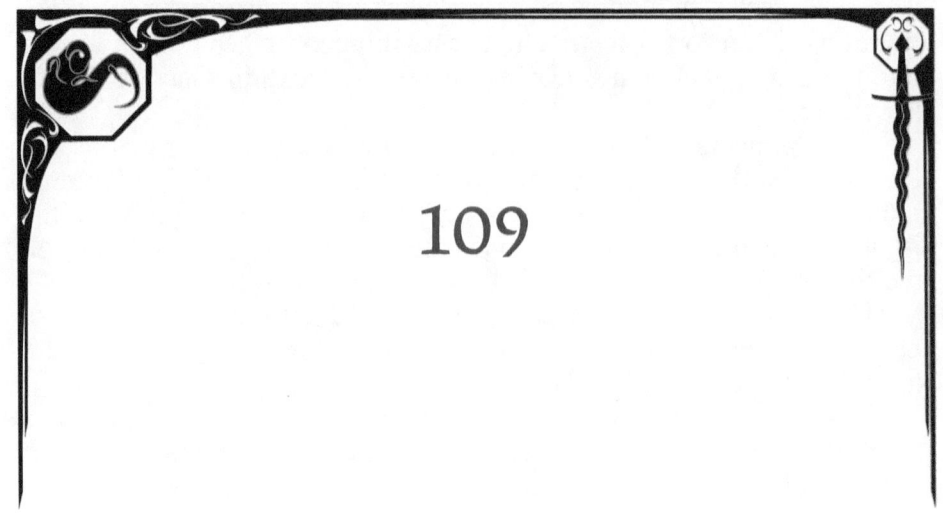

109

A dagger in the chest didn't stop what now lived inside Veln Greenmeadow.

The whyte seethed, the rage it felt overriding the pain of the injury. The Mancer had *hurt* it, and it couldn't return the favor. Yanking the knife free, the daemon used the weapon the foolish mage had given it, stabbing and slicing its way across the battleground to where I'k'Nole fought the huge creature.

The body coughed up blood. This vessel wouldn't last long. It had to finish its mission before then. If it failed...Daemon Lords were not the only ones punished by Chaining.

These thoughts were transparent to Veln, still caged deep within his mind. He grew weaker by the moment, the blood loss taking its toll. He was running out time. Through the whyte's eyes, he saw the flare of crimson as the levin bolt struck I'k'Nole. Burning bright in the power was the arcane signature of Ba'tvian Delthanurk.

Glee spread through the daemon as the young Mancer staggered under the blow. It ducked attacks, dodged dueling pairs, wove through the chaos, moving as fast as it could to reach him. The man didn't fall. He began to turn, to searching for the origin of the strike. Another bolt of crimson caught him in the side. This time, he went down on his knees.

Almost there.

With the whyte's attention diverted, Veln dug down through the cage bars, reached deep within. Unable to pull magic from anywhere else, he used the single thing at hand: his waning life-force. He shaped the essence into a lance, thrust the arcane weapon into his own heart.

Burning agony erupted. The daemon shrieked, then Veln Greenmeadow was no more.

110

ABSOL threw open the monastery's door. The fray in the courtyard was a jumbled mix of violence, humans, Shadows, and unnatural creatures. The enemy wore the arcane insignia of Ba'tvian Delthanurk emblazoned on their armor.

He plunged into the violence, fighting to get to Celina, the nearest defender. The enemy spotted him, converged on him. He slammed the pommel of his sword into the side of one soldier's helm, spun to parry the attack of another. The man's mace swung at his head. Ducking, Absol grabbed a long knife from his belt, drove the blade deep into his opponent's armpit. As the man fell back coughing up blood, the Mancer stole his mace. He wielded the spiked club with one hand as he stabbed and sliced with the sword in the other. His comrade's assailant was dispatched just as he reached them. The two Mancers didn't speak, moving into a back-to-back position to continue fighting.

Crimson streaked across the courtyard. It struck I'k'Nole, the red energy crawling over his body as his legs buckled. Then Absol caught sight of Veln, gaze locked on his prey, weaving through the melee toward his ward. Calling out a warning to his protégé, he tried to scan the battlefield for Ba'tvian. Behind him, Celina cried out. A blast of power missed him – but not her. She dropped to the ground, struggling to rise. Absol turned, glimpsed her attacker just before the mounted mage bowled him over. The steed raked one arm with its fangs as it passed.

He hit the ground, rolled to his feet, caught a blast of ruddy gold in the chest. His back hit the ground hard enough to knock the breath from him. The rider laughed as he swung back around. His path took him back to Celina, who flailed her sword as the beast's legs. It kicked at her, the blow causing her to lose her grip on the weapon. Whipping its head down, it bit into her throat, clawing at her belly with one forelimb. Its rider never took his eyes off Absol.

"So you're the one called Absol Omine. You're a bit long in the tooth, aren't you?"

He ignored the manic humor in the voice as he regained his feet, hefted his blade. The rider wore all black, the garb expensive in its cut. The runic combination that Ba'tvian had claimed for himself sat high on his shoulder. The man's dark brown hair and wicked expression helped to identify him from Veln's reports.

"Raptu Carthier." He strengthened his shields, channeled a bit of power into his weapon. The blade began to smoke, just a little. Magical combat wasn't his strength; augmenting the damage he could do would have to suffice.

The rider gave a mocking bow.

"*Lord* Carthier to you, Mancer." He made the last word sound like the filthiest excrement. "Yet I'm not the one who'll be ending you."

Ba'tvian. Before he could do more than think the name, the noble urged his steed away, barreling through the violent crowd toward I'k'Nole. The lad was now motionless on the ground, Greenmeadow's body collapsed next to him. Instinctively, Absol started after Raptu, then sensed power building behind him. He flung himself to the side as a volley of red magic tore through the spot he'd been. It hurtled through the fighters, leaving a bloody, body-strewn wake before earthing itself halfway across the courtyard.

I'k'Nole was down. His Mancers were dying around him. He would be facing the worst blood mage in all of Orthanor alone.

This must end here.

The sounds of battle dimmed, his focus narrowed. Movement to right had Omine spinning, arching his sword to block the downward blow of Ba'tvian's. The blood mage's eyes glowed crimson, his face a mask of determination and hate. The Mancer gritted his teeth, pushed hard, twisted the blade in an attempt to bind the weapons. Ba'tvian broke off, circled him. Absol mirrored him, watching for an opening.

"This is between us, Delthanurk. Why bring anyone else into it?"

"This place, these people, you mean? That's on you, Omine. You brought them into this." He feinted, darted to the side, feinted again. "They are no better than you."

Absol parried another swipe of the sword, struck a glancing blow with the mace in return.

"And yet they are so far above what you are." He saw the words hit home, the fury sparking in his opponents' eyes. Ba'tvian didn't react to them, however. "You are nothing, Ba'tvian Delthanurk. Even when I am gone, no matter how far you go, who you kill, you will still be nothing."

"I am not nothing." The words came out as a quiet whisper, defiance and rage in every syllable.

Pride. Master Oknare had said it was Ba'tvian's greatest flaw. Omine feinted, dodged around him, countered a whirling blow but took a vicious kick in the thigh. Back-pedaling, he resumed circling.

"You came from dirt, Ba'tvian. It's dirt you are, the lowest of the low, as nothing to the world."

"I am not the dirt beneath your feet." Power echoed in the words, each ringing like a bell in the air. The blood mage charged, darted to the side at the last second. He slashed his sword with one hand – and launched a bolt of pure arcane energy at Absol with the other.

There was no time to dodge. It hit Absol at close range, eating through his shields like fire consuming dry grass. *Such strength.* It confirmed what he'd suspected all along. Taking the pain, the blood he felt trickling from his nose and ears, the anger, the grief, he poured it into his magic. It flared up, burst from his outstretched hand.

It blasted into Ba'tvian's unprotected face.

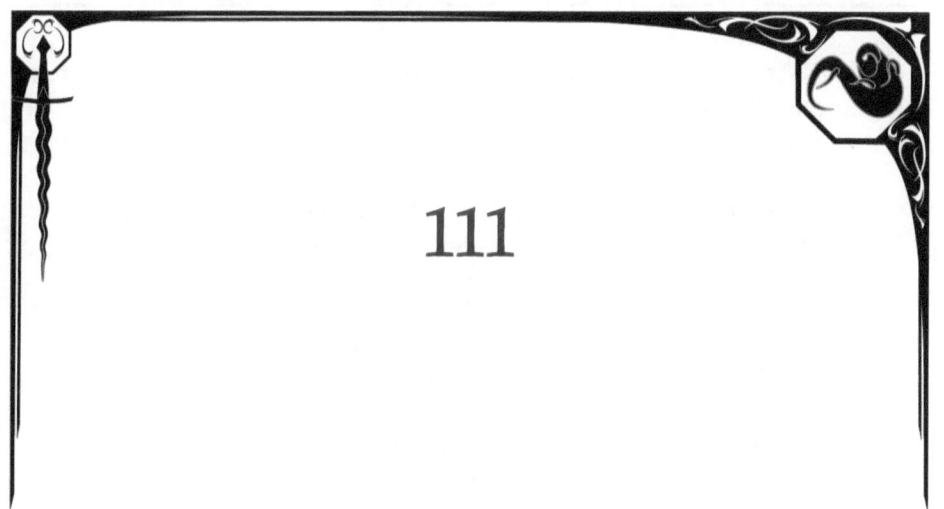

111

B A'TVIAN glimpsed the attack coming, augmented his shields. They turned a brilliant, blinding red as Absol's retaliation struck. The power arced over the surface of them, flowing around their curvature to earth itself around his feet. There was a stab of pain as a single, hair-thin crack appeared in the outer shields. He sealed it immediately.

It took a moment for his vision to clear. When it did, he could see the scorching on the ground, the tiny fires that had taken hold in the grass. Anyone caught in the arcane exchange had fallen. Charred bodies – enemy and allies both – littered the edges. Lying in the worst of the burn-damage was Absol Omine.

His clothing was scorched, his face a mess. Blood ran from his nose, eyes, and ears. Doubtless, his ribs were cracked. Yet he wasn't dead. Even now he moved, groaning, to regain his feet.

Ba'tvian didn't give him the chance to rise. He stalked forward, drove his sword deep into the Mancer's chest. He felt the blade bite into bone. Omine's spine arched in pain, hands spasming on the ground. Blood welled in his mouth.

"Absol!"

The cry echoed in the courtyard. Ba'tvian turned, yanking his sword out of the Mancer, to see a burst of violet flame speeding towards him. He ducked, rolled, came up with his free hand engulfed in pulsed red light, returned the fire. It struck the one called I'k'Nole at the same time as Raptu's levin bolt. He collapsed, his form smoking.

"Ibestor! Nerisse!" Ba'tvian gestured toward the young man. He watched Raptu dismount to check him. He looked up at his leader, his grin wide. As his Dark Adepts came running to Carthier's side, he turned back to Omine.

His nemesis was till alive, trying to crawl toward I'k'Nole. He wasn't getting far. His legs didn't seem to be working right.

"I will give you this much, old man." Ba'tvian walked over to kick him in the ribs. He slumped with a moan onto his side. "For someone who lacks the innate power of an adept level mage, you gave more than I anticipated. Still for someone who's hunted me for as long as you have, your dismal efforts are a disappointment."

He placed a booted foot on his stomach, held his sword high and point-down. Omine's blood-filled eyes looked his. Ba'tvian allowed himself a small, chill smile.

"Don't worry about I'k'Nole. We won't be killing him – yet."

The sword pierced Omine's chest, this time spearing the heart. Ba'tvian waiting for the death gurgle, watched the blood bubble at the mouth as the Mancer gave his last breath. Then he withdrew his sword, wiped the blade on the tunic of the corpse before surveying the surrounding carnage.

The battle was over. Ruined bodies lay everywhere. The mercenaries Raptu had led were finishing off the wounded and dying. Ibestor hefted the bound I'k'Nole onto his shoulder and began to trudge off for the monastery. At some point during the fight, the rain had tapered to a drizzle. Through the wet haze, Carthier, Nerisse, and the Jeste twins picked their way toward him.

"Raze the village. Sow the earth with salt. Let the destruction of Destiny's Way be a lesson to any who would harbor our enemies." He dismissed the men, crooked a finger at the elf. "Is our captive viable?"

"Yes. I've already laid some of the foundation." She paused, taking care with her next words. "When his mentor was killed something in him broke. He's not insane, not unstable. He is…what I might have been had they killed you."

"He loved Omine?" Ba'tvian let the notion churn through his mind.

"Very much. He saw him as his father, his role-model. He differs in that way from me."

"We can use that." He gave her a thoughtful look, noting that her slate blue skin was more gray than usual. "How bad was the backlash from Greenmeadow's death?"

"Bad." She let the simple statement speak for itself. "I can continue if you need me to."

"No." Nerisse had been closely linked with both their puppets. She'd freed herself of the watchman before his execution; she'd had no opportunity to release control of Veln before he died. *There is no use breaking a valued tool.* "Go with Ibestor. Make certain that I'k'Nole is secured, then send for Halvark to Gate you back to his estate."

"Thank you."

She left as his Shadows crept forth. Most of them were fat from gorging, their leprous white eyes bulging with excitement. They'd grown in size, too. A number of the wild ones had joined his usual pets.

"The dead are yours – after we have reduced the village to ash."

The rain stopped as he strode through the battlefield towards Destiny's Way. Deep inside, elation warmed him. He'd succeeded. His enemy was vanquished, leaving a new field of opportunities ripe for his plucking. What happened here, in this hopeless place, was only the beginning.

INTERLUDE 10

A raven soared on the wind.

The sky was clearing. Clouds drifted off, having disgorged their burden. The sun shone down on the desolation of the moors. The long grass was wet and trampled, as were the crops in the fields outside the village. Animals dotted the landscape. A lucky few ran off into the open expanse but many more lay unmoving on the ground. Teeming over their corpses were the Shadowed Ones. Beyond them, smoke billowed in streaming columns.

The bird angled down, kiting on the updrafts to get a better view.

The monastery burned, the heat so intense that the stones glowed an orange-red. The scent of charring meat rode the smoke, teasing the raven's nares. It was the largest fire, though not the only. Also alight were the farmsteads, the inner fields. Yet there were no flames at the center of Destiny's Way.

The raven flew closer, gliding down to perch atop the tavern – the single building left intact. It hopped along the roof until it found a good vantage point. With a flick of wings to settle its feathers, it cocked its head to watch.

A table had been dragged out into the square. The wood was stained rusty with blood and gore. Behind it stood Ba'tvian Delthanurk. He gestured to the scion of the Carthier House, who walked down the line of trussed up prisoners – villagers who hadn't managed to escape. They cringed, wept, pleaded. Raptu stopped by the bound figure of a child. He hauled the boy up, brought him to

Ba'tvian's table.

The latest in a long string of them, the blood rite was quick, dirty, precise. The runes were carved into living flesh, the chant intoned, the knife put to the chest. As the boy screamed, his heart was taken out. Power swelled, was captured, stored away somewhere. It was done too fast for the Chained One within the raven to see. Within minutes of the child being chosen from the line, his eviscerated body was being discarded on a growing pile of dead victims.

Labiyal Biyalban observed it all through the Chained One's sight, sipping wine in the comfort of his current abode. Beside him, his sire gave a slow nod.

"To serve our needs, he cannot stop there," the Daemon Lord stated, eyes still on the mirror. "Our king demands more."

"He will get it." Labiyal's voice held quiet assurance. "This is the one who set him free."

"And your repayment should he succeed?" Biyal, his appearance still resembling that of his son's, turned his golden eyes to him.

"My life is enough. It is the promised boon." Asking for more would be risking too much.

"We shall see what the king will bestow upon your success." The Daemon Lord rose from his chair, popping a bit of cheese into his mouth. He swallowed, adding, "Remember, my spawnling, that freedom isn't the only thing Hell expects to gain."

His sire left, departing as quietly as he'd come. Labiyal remained seated behind his desk, looking over the mirrors arrayed around him. Most of them showed Destiny's Way. A few followed the minions Ba'tvian had left behind in Rathburn.

Nerisse lay asleep in her bed at Halvark's home. He had done well in selecting the naïve girl for Delthanurk. She was intelligent, imaginative, the kind of tool that would build upon past successes to expand her lord's power. The whytes may have been Ba'tvian's idea, but the controls used came from her. They were simple, eager creatures, malleable to just about any course or cause – an ideal starting point for the pair.

Labiyal turned his attention to another mirror amid the glass. It depicted a ship at sea. With a thought, the half-daemon directed the image to shift. A Dithume male strode across the top deck to take the wheel from his coxswain. A handsome, weathered seaman who wore his past as a granite expression, he guided his vessel along her course. The soaring bird the half-daemon used to spy on him dipped, veering to the side. The ship's bow wore her name, *Kraken,* carved deep into the timber. Soon, her captain would be sailing her into the life of Hell's chosen child.

A promise was, after all, a promise.

THE
APPENDIX

AF – "After Flood". The calendar for Einlienn places year 0 at the point when the global flood receded.

ABSOL OMINE – (pronounced *Ahb-sohl O-meen*) A human male serving as a Mancer in Orthanor, Absol Omine was one of the foremost pursuers of the blood mage Ba'tvian Delthanurk. In his forties, he traveled a great deal and was highly proficient in his work. Though his claim to mage-craft was marginal at best, he made up for the lack with knowledge, determination, and skill. Absol was well regarded as a senior member of the Mancers' Guild, eventually becoming the de factor leader of his order after the fall of his Chalbrooke Guild House in 1306 AF. Two years prior, just before he began his hunt for Ba'tvian, Absol took in a boy orphaned by the Great Earthquake. The child, I'k'Nole Kar'k'Eige, became his ward and Absol trained him to become a Mancer, often partnering with him on patrols after the Mancers went to ground in the village of Destiny's Way. When Ba'tvian Delthanurk attacked the village in 1311 AF, Absol Omine finally faced the man he'd hunted for seven years. The fight ended tragically.

ADEPT – Adept is the third of the four classes, or levels, of magery. As the fourth class, sage, is an extremely seldom seen caliber, most people hold the mistaken belief that the mage-rank of adept is the highest. The ranking is attained through a serious of trials that test a mage's skill, knowledge, and capacity for power.

AFFINITY – see Arcane Affinity.

ANNIA – (pronounced *Ah-nee-ah*) Annia is the second largest of the three major continents of Einlienn. It is located to the west of Orthanor, and north of Genoria.

ARCANE AFFINITY – A mage's arcane affinity is a characteristic trait that sometimes develops where the mage is particularly strong in magic associated with a given 'element'. Not all mages have such an affinity and those that do are often not above the master rank. Most affinities are classified as follows: earth, air, fire, water, death, and life. Mages strong in one element are often weak in another; that weakness rarely manifests as an acute vulnerability to magic of the 'opposite' or contrasting element. Affinities occur without rhyme or reason and are not fully understood.

ARELLE DESERT – (pronounced *Ah-rehl*) A small desert along the south-western coast of Orthanor, the Arelle Desert is south of the city of Nilbre.

ASHA SE LI VEDEAAE – (pronounced *Ahsh-ah seh lih Veh-day-ah*) Asha se le Vedeaea is the alias Nerisse se li Astorae uses when she visits the healer of Piete Town in 1306 AF.

ASHBURGH – (pronounced *Ahsh-behrg*) Ashburgh is a town of the Northern Wilderness of Orthanor. It is situated to the southwest of Piete Town and to the west of Winede. Like most other settlements in the region, its residents are loggers, trappers, and small-time traders.

BA'TVIAN DELTHANURK – (pronounced *Bah-t-vee-uhn Dehl-thah-nehrk*) A young human male from a serf family living in squalor on the estates of the Lord of Menie, Ba'tvian Delthanurk is a renowned blood mage. As a youth, he was given the chance to attend the Trinity College of Magery on scholarship, where he later became interested in the darker arts of magic. At the time of his exile from the Trinity, he was sixteen years of age. While in exile, he was pursued by the Mancers as a blood mage, most notably by the Mancer Absol Omine. He stayed ahead of the pursuit for seven years, making plans that would carve his name deep into the history of Einlienn. Along the way, he recruited others: Nerisse se li Astorae in 1304 AF, Ibestor the barbarian in 1306 AF, then Raptu Carthier, Prialla Filoche, and Halvark Tretoan later that same year, and the twins Lakit and Tavor Jeste in 1307 AF. Ba'tvian was responsible for the destruction of the Mancer Guild House in 1306 AF, and finally wiped out the Mancer Order at Destiny's Way in 1311 AF.

BARBARIANS – The term 'barbarian' is used to describe any one of the rough, often volatile tribes that live on the edges of the Northern Ring and Northern Ice Fields. Barbarians are often superstitious, insular, and territorial. The closer to the northern pole they are, the less rational they tend to be. The further south the tribe resides, the more civilized it tends to be.

BIYAL, LORD – (pronounced *B-i-yahl*) A Daemon Lord of high favor, Biyal is the sire of the half-daemon Labiyal Biyalban, and is one of the very few first generation Daemons left in service to Hell.

BLACK MAGE – A black mage is a magic-user who does not resort to blood and death as power sources but will use his magic for personal, and usually wrongful, gain. Black mages will sometimes also dabble in low-level necromantic practices.

BLOOD MAGE – A blood mage is a magic-user who uses the blood and death of anything living being in order to generate magical energy. Blood mages tend to also practice daemon summoning and necromancy. They are considered anathema and are usually executed after a swift trial, if any trial is given at all.

BLOODED – It is a term used to describe someone who has experience in actual battle and has shed blood. The unspoken implication of the label is that the person being described has killed in combat.

BLUE TOWER, THE – The Trinity College of Artisanry, and the natural stone column it perches on, is often referred to as the Blue Tower. The nick-name is derived from the blue tiled roofs featured on all school and town buildings.

BROKEN FALLS, THE – The only waterfall to be found in the Plains of Gastaeia, the Broken Falls are located near the central region along the Spir-Gas River. The falls were formed during the Great Earthquake, close to the underground springs that feed into the Spir-Gas River. The earthquake had jumbled the land, changing the course of the Spir-Gas, elevating the underground springs so that the river spilling out of them poured down over a newly exposed jagged rock face.

BROTHER FILTAN – (pronounced *Bruh-thehr Fihl-tahn*) Brother Filtan was one of the monks at the shrine of Destiny's Way. He tended the stables and livestock associated with the On'Desae monastery. He died there, eaten by Ba'tvian Delthanurk's Shadows, in 1311 AF.

BROTHER MILON – (pronounced *Bruh-thehr Mihl-ohn*) Brother Milon was one of the senior monks at the shrine of Destiny's Way. He died of old age in 1305 AF. His passing is notable because it confirmed I'k'Nole Kar'k'Eige's sensitivity to death.

BROWN - The horse Absol Omine rode during I'k'Nole's childhood, Brown was 'retired' from use as a Mancer's mount in 1306 AF. A somewhat skittish horse of undetermined bloodlines, it was named by I'k'Nole soon after Absol found the child in the Spirlan Forest after the Great Earthquake. The horse remained in service at the shrine of Destiny's Way to help train new Mancers in how to handle a horse of his nature in battle. In 1311 AF, he met the fate of all livestock after Ba'tvian Delthanurk's attack on Destiny's Way: he was sacrificed for blood and power.

CAMEN DESERT – (pronounced *Cay-mehn*) The Camen Desert is a region found in the south-western portion of the Annian Continent. The desert does not have very many cities but the few it does have are known for their princely architecture, the rare spices for sale, centers of philosophy, and myriad theologians.

CAPIL OCEAN – (pronounced *Cah-peel*) The largest ocean on Einlienn, the Capil Ocean sits between the continents of Annia, Genoria, and Orthanor.

CARTER FAIRWRIGHT – One of the foremost generals of his time, Carter Fairwright was known for his many victories in the Daemon Wars preceding the Flood. Most of the details concerning his life and deeds have been lost to time. What little is known about him comes from a single damaged scroll that now resides at the Trinity College of Knowledge. He is believed to have died at Carter's Rock during a pitched battle that was almost lost to the daemons. His death and his forces' victory are carved upon the rock that bears his name.

CARTER'S ROCK – Carter's Rock is a town east of Winede in the Northern Wilderness of Orthanor. The town was built on what is believe to be the site of a legendary battle between the human forces of Carter Fairwright and a small daemon army in the last years prior to the Flood. The rock, from which the town drew its name, is a large boulder sitting atop a rocky outcropping jutting up from the crest of a hill and is where Carter made his last stand. At some point after the battle, the rock was carved with a relief depicting the battle. The town surrounds the outcropping. It is considered to be a waypoint for Mancers in the north.

CARTHIER ESTATE – The Carthier Estate is one of several wealthy estates situated along the Chal-Edon Trade Route east of Rathburn. It is owned by the Carthier family, a wealthy entrepreneurial family who bought their way into the Rathburn aristocracy about a hundred years ago. It is the center of the family's most successful business, a courier service that utilizes the fast horses the Carthiers breed themselves.

CEDANE HARVIER – (pronounced *Seh-dayn Har-vee-ehr*) Cedane Harvier is the alias that Ba'tvian Delthanurk used at Winede Village. The persona is that of a journeyman trader from Menie Port who is on his first solo trading tour of the north.

CELINA BEHR – (pronounced *She-lee-nah Bayhr*) One of the few women to reach seniority among the Mancers, Celina Behr was only a year younger than the more well-known Mancer Absol Omine. Her mage skills were mediocre at best, and her fighting skills just above average. She had good instincts, a level head, a knack for training others, and an intuitive sense about the preternatural, all of which contributed greatly to her longevity. After the the fall of the Mancers' Guild House in 1306 AF, she was considered the second best-trained mage after Veln Greenmeadow. Celina was the first Mancer to learn of the hauntings at Jevanel, a place she'd visited often in the past while on patrol in the area. Those visits have led to her familiarity with the Elvanarae and their customs. She was killed by Ba'tvian Delthanurk's forces at Destiny's Way in 1311 AF.

CHAL-EDON TRADE ROUTE – (pronounced *Chahl-Eh-dohn*) The Chal -Edon Trade Route begins in Rathburn in eastern Orthanor, runs through Chalbrooke to the east, then angles north to Edon Port. From Edon, it continues west, running across the continent just below the Northern Wilderness and ending at the Sradeein Trade Route. Originally, the route began with Chalbrooke but was extended to include Rathburn after the city's founding. This trade route was built, and is taxed and maintained, by an alliance of the Merchants' and Traders' Guild.

CHALBROOKE – (pronounced *Chahl-bruhk*) Chalbrooke is the second largest, and the oldest surviving, city-state on the eastern side of Orthanor. The city-state has the unique distinction of hosting houses from every Guild in Orthanor, including the solitary Mancer Guild House. This has enabled the city to thrive and has given it the nickname the City of Guilds. The city is surrounded by thick walls and has two main gates. The east city gate opens up to the section of the Chal-Edon Trade Route that leads to Rathburn while the west city gate opens up to the section of the Chal-Edon Trade Route that goes on to Edon Port. There are two other, much smaller gates to accommodate small groups of travelers; these are the north and south gates. The names of these entrances are a bit misleading as they are not situated in-line with the traditional cardinal directions. It is the practice of the city guard to close the city gates at sunset, and re-open them just after dawn. Trade shipments and travelers coming into the city at night are inspected thoroughly, but these regulations are relaxed a bit in the day-time in order to keep the traffic moving.

CHAINED, THE – The Chained are Daemons of high rank and power who have fallen out of favor with their king, also called Chained Ones. As punishment, they are trapped within the bodies of animals and made to serve others of their kind as the king sees fit. Though their animal bodies remain ageless as part of their ensorcellment, they are far from immortal. A Chained One who is killed, will die with the body he inhabits.

CHESRA – *Chesra* is a board game featuring two opposing sides, each with twenty pieces, five of which are important to the game as they represent a royal family. Each side has a different set of moves. The object of the game is to capture all five members of the royal family. If any one of those pieces reaches the opposite side without capture, all captured royal pieces for that side is returned to the board.

CLAIRE ALTHESON – The younger sister of Olef Altheson, Claire Altheson was murdered while on her way to the Tretoan Estate to apply for work.

CLEANSING POOLS – One of the three sacred grounds the lay behind the Temple of Earth at Jevanel, the Cleansing Pools were natural pools of mineral water that are used to ritually cleanse the body and spirit of Elvanaeran petitioners. Legend has it that the pools contained the tears of Xera, who is believed to be the father of the Elvanarae.

CLERIC'S ROOM – The Cleric's Room is a concealed room within the Trinity College of Magery that is used for judgments of student transgressions, questioning of students on serious matters, and other sensitive meetings involving school staff members.

CREATION MYTHS – Creation myths, as their name suggests, detail the creation of the universe and the world of Einlienn. The most common version includes the introduction of Death, and the beginnings of what may lead to the end of the universe. The story states that the One created the universe and began to fill it with worlds, dimensions, planes of existence, stars, etc. He did this by speaking. The universe heard the words spoken, then would help make it reality. Eventually, He became lonely in His task and created the Eldarae, a race of demi-deities, to keep Him company as He worked. His children took an interest in what He was doing so He granted them the power to create by speaking to the universe. There was only one rule to be obeyed: they could not destroy anything that had already been created. Each of them was an expert in one thing – one aspect of life – though they were able to create whole worlds, races, flora, fauna, and other cosmic things. The Eldarae known as Hell, one of the One's older children, fashioned a plane of existence known as Hell, which spanned all dimensions. It was rigid and harsh in design, possessing mostly straight lines, jagged edges, and no beauty. He was praised for his work and basked in the accolades. Then Xera, one of the younger Eldarae, created the world of Einlienn, a place of serenity, beauty, and joy. The world quickly became beloved by all. Jealous, Hell coveted Einlienn and offered to trade Xera his plane for the world. Xera refused. Twice more the offer was made. Twice more it was turned down. At the third refusal, Hell bespoke Xera's destruction. Unwilling to break the one rule, yet bound to obey the words spoken, the universe tore a hole in its heart and cried out. Furious at the failure, Hell tore Xera to pieces. It was then that Death entered the universe for the first time. Xera's remains were merged with the world he loved so much and Hell was imprisoned with his plane as punishment. He is to remain imprisoned until he allows himself to be made into the bandage that will heal the universe's wound, or the universe dies. Until then, the Eldarae use Hope to close the wound and wait.

DAEMON – A race descended from the Eldarae known as Hell, the daemon are from a plane of existence that parallels Einlienn's. That plane is also called Hell, or Hell's Plane, after the race's progenitor. It is the goal of daemon race to help Hell to break free of Hell's Plane in any way possible. Though there are lesser ilk, monsters that are labeled daemons by the rest of the world, a true daemon cannot be killed by the expedience of slaying its body. The daemon will exist in an incorporeal form until it can replace the body it has lost, either by the grace of their king (of which he has little) or through a complicated rite that is completed over a number of years, sometimes decades. As the loss of a body is also seen as a loss of status, daemon kind strive to avoid putting themselves in danger as much as possible.

DAEMON LORD – A Daemon Lord is of the purest blood, highest status, and most power. They are also the daemons whose loyalty to Hell goes unquestioned. The first group of Daemon Lords were chosen from the first generation of children sired by Hell. Most of them were lost in the Daemon Wars and the Flood that came after them.

DAEMON WARS – (pronounced *Day-mon*) The Daemon Wars were a world-wide collection of wars in which the daemons fought against all other races of Einlienn in a bid for conquest. They were led by their sire and king, the Eldarae known as Hell. The Daemon Wars ended when the Flood came, cursing the surviving daemons and drowning most of the world's population. *Also called Hell's War.*

DANNON, MASTER ABBOTT – The last Master Abbott at the shrine in Destiny's Way, Dannon was a long-time friend of the Mancer Absol Omine and sometime caretaker of the orphan, I'k'Nole. As a member of the Order of On'Desae, he had strong faith in, and a close spiritual relationship with, the One. When the Mancers decided to go to ground in 1307 AF, Dannon offered them the use of his monastery. He aided in training the new recruits the Mancers brought in, and took part in the battle when Ba'tvian Delthanurk attacked in 1311 AF. He was killed during the fighting.

DARK ADEPTS – This is the label given to Ba'tvian Delthanurk and his band of blood mages. It is not an indicator of their mage class, though several of them have adept level potential.

DESTINY'S WAY – Destiny's Way is a small farming village sitting on the boundary between the Plains of Gastaeia and the Wood of Destiny. It was a pilgrimage destination for believers in the One. Few people traveled to it after 1306 AF, however, as the moorlands around the village had become increasingly dangerous. In 1307 AF, it became the refuge of the Mancer Order. The village was razed to the ground by Ba'tvian Delthanurk and his forces in 1311 AF.

DERSTI – (pronounced *Dehrs-tee*) A member of the deer family that lives in northern climes, the *dersti* is the size of a small horse (approximately 14 hands at the withers) and sports a set of antlers whose central tines often fuse together as they grow. Females shed their antlers winter. Males keep theirs year round.

Dithume – (pronounced *D-i-thoom*) A race that is largely believed to be an off-shoot of humanity, Dithume are long-lived; their life-span averages around 200 years of age. An ancient race, they predate the Flood, and though the recorded histories of the pre-Flood era have been lost, legend says that they came into being during the first years of Hell's War. Regardless of the truth of their origins, it is accepted fact that they participated in Hell's War by fielding a large navy. When the world Flooded, the only Dithume survivors were those onboard their vessels. To this day, the race maintains a strong affinity for maritime trades and crafts, often birthing weather workers. They reside in the Isles of Narye, an archipelago located south of Orthanor and east of Exile's Peril.

Dragon's Head Tavern – The Dragon's Head is a tavern and inn at the Red Tower that is popular among the students of the College of the Magery.

Earth Bond – The earth bond is a metaphysical link with Einlienn itself. A trait of the Elvanarae race, the earth bond was vital to their well-being. It served as a psychic anchor for their minds, a spiritual link to what remains of Xera, from whom they believed their race was descended. It also provided a constant transfusion of natural energy that their bodies have become dependent on. The earth bond amplified the senses: intuition became more accurate, sight and hearing sharpened. Warnings of impending danger were often felt by those with the strongest bonds well in advance of the actual event. For farmers, they were better able to perceive issues with their crops. For priests, they were better able to help others find an inner balance and know peace. For healers, they used the bond to draw upon the earth's energy to aid them in their work. Without the earth bond, the Elvanarae felt isolated, their senses were dulled, their mental state deteriorated. They were plagued with fatigue and listlessness, and their bodies wore down more easily. Even if they managed to hold onto to sanity, they would physically waste away. Most suicided before they died naturally.

Eastern Cliffs – The simply named Eastern Cliffs are the coastal cliffs ranging along the upper eastern coast of Exile's Peril.

EDON PORT – (pronounced *Eh-dohn*) The largest city-state on the eastern side of Orthanor, Edon, also called Edon Port, is the largest port on the continent. It is a place of maritime commerce and craftsmanship, a city that makes the most of innovations that comes its way. However, as open-minded as the city is, its rulers tend to be less so. There is a long-standing history of city rulers who have guided the currents of commerce to benefit their own interests first, sometimes at the expense of the general populace. Hand-in-hand with that historic record is a tendency for many of the opposing business leaders in the city to band together when things get too bad and lynch the ruler. Though some might say that this practice is barbaric, it does maintain a tolerable balance between the ruler's greed and ambition, and the interests of the city itself.

EINLIENN – (pronounced *I-n-lee-ihn*) Einlienn is the world in which *Descent Into Darkness* is set. It is said to be the creation of the Eldarae Xera, and is supposed to house Xera's spirit deep within it.

ELDARAE – (pronounced *Ehl-dahr-ay*) The Eldarae are the children on the One, demi-deities who took part in the creation of the universe. The term comes from the Old Tongue, the language used by the Eldarae as well as the first races of Einlienn.

ELISSE SE LI ASTORAE – (pronounced *Eh-lees say lih Ahs-torh-ay*) The mother of Nerisse se li Astorae, Elissa se li Astorae was married to Nerthet si le Astorae. A gentle Elvanaeran woman whose profession was that of a weaver, she resembled her daughter. It is believed by some that after the Fall of Jevanel, her grieving spirit is the woman seen weeping as she wonders the fields her husband once worked. It is unknown if she weeps over the fate of her race, or the horrendous shame of her daughter.

ELVANARAE – (pronounced *Ehl-vahn-ayr*) The Elvanarae were a subspecies of elves that live underground and had close ties to the earth. The racial name was derived from the Old Tongue term Eldarae, in an effort to indicate their close spiritual association with Einlienn and the spirit of Xera. The Elvanarae had slate blue skin, white hair, and their eye color could vary from black, white, gray, and purple. They were a peaceful and deeply religious race, if rather insular. Their society was simple, with no social ranking other than that of the priesthood, and they were governed by the High Priest. Most of the Elvanarae dwelled in their subterranean city of Jevanel, having little contact with the outside world. Individuals did, however, venture out from their city for the purposes of tending to surface crops, trade, or education. A point of interest is the trademark characteristic of their naming system: male names incorporate "si le", meaning "son of", while females incorporate "se li", meaning "daughter of".

ELVANAERAN – (pronounced *Eh-vahn-ayr-ahn*) Of, or pertaining to, the Elvanarae. Alternatively spelled Elvanaran.

ELVANARAN – (pronounced *Eh-vahn-ayr-ahn*) see Elvanaeran.

EMP – (pronounced *Ehmp*) A shortened or slang form of the word Empath.

EMPATH – (pronounced *Ehm-pahth*) As the name suggests, an Empath is an individual who possesses empathy – the ability to experience, sense, and/or manipulate the emotions/emotional psyche of other living things.

EARTH BOND – An earth bond is a metaphysical, psychic, and spiritual link that connects the Elvanarae to Einlienn itself. As the body requires food and drink to survive, so does the mind and spirit of an Elvanaeran require the earth bond. It stabilizes them, links the people together. Without the bond, they will go mad. If they do not suicide, the psychic needs usually met by the earth will drive the Elvanaeran's mind to attempt to get the required energy from the body. The body is unable to meet this need. This leads to the psychic mind effectively cannibalizing the body, wasting it away as it drains the energy reserves. Death is inevitable.

EARTH'S WOMB, THE – The name for the cavern in which the city of Jevanel resided.

EXILE'S PERIL – Exile's Peril is a large, barren island or subcontinent that is home to only two settlements. On the eastern side, south of the Eastern Cliffs, is a fishing village founded by escaped and/or paroled prisoners from Exile's Port, which lies on the northern coast. The Port is the largest prison facility in the world, receiving inmates from major cities in Orthanor and Genoria in return for a tithe of goods. The island is called 'Peril' due to its lack of anything edible or drinkable throughout most of its terrain.

Exile's Port – The largest prison facility in the world, Exile's Port is its own city-state. Built with the labor of prisoners, it was constructed with the intention of retaining criminals whose crimes were bad enough to warrant incarceration without execution from other city-states. Over time, the city-states began to deport a certain number of convicts awaiting execution due to crowding in their own prisons. Generally, prisoners are either put to work in stone quarries used to build more prisons or repair existing ones, or hung in due time. In return for taking their convicts, a tithe of supplies is sent by all city-states who choose to deport their criminals. The Port is ruled by the Warden, who is assisted by a company of guards. The guards are enlisted from the various city-states and are placed on an annual rotation schedule. The schedule allows guards to leave their families at home while they work as it considered potentially dangerous to allow them to stay at the Port due to the prison population. The prison is funded by stone exports harvested by the inmates from quarries further inland.

Ezil Ormonson – (pronounced *Ee-zeel Ohr-mohn-sohn*) A night-time Chalbrooke city guard, Ezil Ormonson's usual post is the East City Gate. He is almost always on the same nightly rotation as his friend, Kale Hornbush.

Fall of Jevanel, The – The event in 1306 AF which the underground city of Jevanel, heart of the Elvanaraen race, was destroyed by Nerisse se li Astorae, Halvark Tretoan, and Ibestor the barbarian. The cavern in which the city was built was collapsed on top of it resulting in a sink hole basin on the surface farmland. The whole area is said to be haunted by those who perished there.

Farn Greenmeadow – The father of Veln Greenmeadow, Farn Greenmeadow served as a watchman and brought his son up to be one as well. Farn was killed in a tavern brawl in 1290 AF. His death was avenged by his son.

Fisher's Delight – The *Fisher's Delight* is the ship Absol took from Menie to the Trinity while pursuing Ba'tvian Delthurnak.

Fisherman's Point – Fisherman's Point is a small, autonomous fishing village on the eastern of Exile's Peril, just north of the Eastern Cliffs. The fishing folk there are descended from freed criminals who had served their time at Exile's Port. It is an insular, self-sustaining community, reliant on the sea for all its needs.

FLOOD, THE – The Flood was a global event that wiped out most of the races and populace of Einlienn. Only isolated groups of elves, humans, and the shape-shifting Were-Clan survived. They employed methods of survival that varied from climbing mountains to avoid the flood waters, retreating to the Northern Ice Fields where the waters were frozen, sealing themselves inside subterranean caverns, and, in one instance, petitioning the One to be transformed into beings that would not drown. The Flood lasted for three years before it receded. To commemorate the year the Flood ended, the survivors restarted their historic calendar.

FOGHILL – A cattle farm on the western side of Rathburn, Foghill is the second largest runner of cattle in the area, and the main rival of Halvark Tretoan in the business. The farmstead gets its name from an old landmark: a hill standing in a shallow pond surrounded by ancient boulders. The hill always has fog at dawn and dusk year-round. Foghill maintains the largest herd of moorland cattle in the region.

GASTAEAN PLAGUE, THE – (pronounced *Gahs-ti-ahn Playg*) A disease that is dormant in the rodents found in the moorlands and Gastaean Plains. Most species of rodent are immune, carrying it with them wherever they go. The disease is spread through biting, transferring to new hosts through the exchange of saliva and blood. Symptoms include aching joints, inflamed throat and lungs, coughing, and fever. As the disease progresses, lesions start to form on the body. Victims infected this way have a high chance of survival if the disease is caught early enough. The plague can also be spread by breathing in fecal matter. During periods when the rodent population experiences a boom, the rodent dung often mixes with dust on the plains – along the trade routes in particular – and is stirred up into the air by passersby or winds. If breathed in, the disease will start in the lungs, causing infections that scar the tissue while filling the lungs with fluid. From there, the disease will spread to the rest of the body. Victims infected in this manner will sometimes die from the initial infection in the lungs before the rest of the symptoms appear. The chances of survival for those infection by breathing in the disease are about even with medical intervention. Without medical assistance, it is almost always fatal.

GASTAEAN PLAINS, THE – (pronounced *Gahs-ti-ahn Playns*) A region comprising the southern third of Orthanor, the Gastaean Plains were once an expanse of gently rolling hills. Creeks and springs were found throughout, and several cities were founded in the eastern part of the plains. Clans of herders rove the plains, carrying their tent villages with them as they follow their herds. During the Great Earthquake of 1304 AF, the western plains buckled, becoming a jumble of cliffs, crags, and jagged hills. The land land to the east remains intact. Since the Earthquake, the nomadic herders have stayed eastward, opting to graze their animls in less hazardous terrain.

GATE – See Portal.

GENORIA – (pronounced *Jehn-orh-ee-ah*) Genoria is the smallest of the three major continents of Einlienn. It is located south of Annia and southwest of Orthanor.

GERALLE BENNIN – (pronounced *Jehr-ahl Behn-nihn*) A young female Mancer, Geralle Bennin was killed on the Moors by Ba'tvian Delthanurk and his Dark Adepts in 1307 AF. Her body was fed to the Shadows.

GERTUR YILSED – Gertur Yilsed is the mayor of Rathburn in 1311 AF. A man with an eye towards to the good life and status, he is considered foppish by most everyone who knows him. With the fashionable attire and the trappings of wealth, he has managed to maintain his office by pandering to the city's citizen's and using a lot of grease to turn the political wheels. Most of his wealth comes from business investments, and being on the payroll of both the Tretoan family and Jored Ult. In return for that additional compensation, he passes on information, conducts deals, and negotiates Rathburn's political landscape in their favor.

GLASTEN PORT – (pronounced *Glah-stehn*) Glasten Port was a once prosperous sea port south of Menie. Though lacking a natural harbor, its proximity to fishing villages made it the best choice for the exportation of seafood. It fell out of favor when the Port City of Menie lowered the fees for its natural harbor.

GOLD (OR GOLDEN) TOWER, THE – The Gold Tower is the Trinity College of Knowledge and the natural stone column it perches on. It is part of the Trinity and the nick-name is derived from the yellow tiled roofs featured on all school and town buildings.

GOOSE-BREE – Goose-Bree is a small farming community, east of Menie and northwest of Destiny's Way. The town is situated close to the Relgs and is named for the free-ranging geese raised on the poultry farms in the area.

GREAT EARTHQUAKE, THE – The worst earthquake in the historical record, the Great Earthquake occurred in the summer of 1304 AF. Originating off the eastern coast of Genoria, it affected the geography of the whole southern hemisphere, touching off tremors on a global scale. Southern Orthanor was particularly affected. The Spirlan Forest was decimated and western landscape of the Plains of Gastaeia was drastically altered by several smaller quakes that were triggered by the Great Earthquake.

GREMLINS – A low-caste daemon, gremlins are built like a man with scaly skin, a fanged, frog-like face, bulging eyes, and swollen pot-belly. They are scavengers by nature. Blood mages will occasionally summon them to clean up bodies left over from rituals, or use them for menial labor that requires no real intelligence. There are two versions of gremlin: the greater gremlin and the lesser gremlin. The lesser gremlin grows up to three feet tall, has shorter limbs, and ranges in color from off-white to brown. Greater gremlins grow up to seven feet tall, have long limbs, and range in color from dark green to dark blue.

GUARDARM TAVERN & INN – The Guardarm is a tavern in Rathburn that is favored by members of the Rathburn Watch, who frequent the place after shift. Though the food is decent, the ale tends to be a tad salty or watered down. Still, the tavern is cleaner than most, and its prices fairly low, both of which contribute to its popularity.

HALVARK TRETOAN, LORD – (pronounced *Hahl-vahrk Tray-toh-ahn*) The last surviving, legitimate member of the most prominent aristocratic family in the Rathburn area, Halvark Tretoan holds a sizable estate east of Rathburn itself. The estate is renowned for being the leading provider of cattle and sheep in the region, their breeds the most resilient to sickness. Halvark inherited the estate after his father and several retainers were found dead just off the Chal -Edon Trade Route in 1306 AF and it is believed by many that they had run afoul of bandits while returning home. The incident left him with only one other family member living: his illegitimate half-sister Prialla Filochen, whom he has known since childhood. At present, there is division amongst the citizens of Rathburn as to whether or not responsibility has reformed Halvark. Some believe that he has left the wild ways of his youth behind; others are convinced that he has just become better at hiding them. What is not common knowledge is that the arrogant and somewhat stuffy Halvark is a blood mage, one of Ba'tvian Delthanurk's Dark Adepts, and that he had participated in the murder of his parents. In recent years, his holdings have become the center for most of the group's activities, as well as a source of funding.

HAMAL, HIGH JUDGE – A human male serving as the senior court official of the Trinity's Red Tower, High Judge Hamal weighed in on the most grievous cases. He was a close friend of Master Oknare and was killed by Ba'tvian Delthanurk in 1304 AF.

HEALER-BORN – A term to describe someone who is born with the inate ability to heal another person's physical body by means of a psychic, quasi-arcane connection that allows them to manipulate natural bodily processes. That connection is often initiated via physical contact, but the more powerful healers can use a line-of-sight connection so long as it is within their range of limitation. The healer-born abilities are ranked in a fashion similar to that of mages. This is unsurprising as the most powerful healer-born also have at least some minor mage ability.

HEALING HOUSE – A healing house is a small hospital facility where healers, herbalists, and/or medical practitioners tend to the sick or injured.

HELKORIX NOXIM – (pronounced *Hehl-kohr-ihks Nahks-ihm*) The *Helkorix Noxim* is the tome of prophecies given by Hell. It serves as the blue-print of instructions for his release.

HELL – Hell is an Eldarae who turned against his brethren out of jealousy. As punishment, Hell was confined to his stark domain, Hell's Plane. There, he sired a race and strives to plot his way to freedom once again.

HELL'S WAR – see Daemon Wars.

Ibestor – (pronounced *I-behs-tohr*) A barbarian mage from the Northern Ice Fields, Ibestor's arcane skills lie mostly in the making of living amalgams of various creatures. Cast out of his own tribe as a child, he has managed to survive in the icy wastes by means of his magic, but has become feral in nature. He is mute, prone to creating obedient creatures from pieces of dead and living animals. He was driven south of the Northern Ring by the other barbarian tribes at twenty-three years of age. Shortly after that, he was recruited by Ba'tvian Delthanurk and his lover Nerisse se li Astorae.

I'K'NOLE KAR'K'EIGE – (pronounced *I'kay'Nohl Kahr'kay'Eej*) An orphaned boy found at the age of nine by Mancer Absol Omine in the Spirlan Forest after the Great Earthquake in 1304 AF. As of 1311 AF, the sixteen-year-old I'k'Nole is nearing the end of his training as an apprentice Mancer under Absol. He has proven to be an apt student, quickly picking up techniques and lore. His mage abilities have surpassed his mentor's and another Mancer, Veln Greenmeadow, has had to step in to further his arcane education. I'k'Nole's esoteric abilities are an enigma to his fellow Mancers. Though he has mastered the lore and texts of magery, his magical skills are honed sporadically as his power does not respond to conventional methods. His use of magic is more intuitive and instinctive than skilled, but he seems to be aware of the limits and dangers, often devising unconventional methods to achieve his goals. Absol has often remarked that it appears as if the lessons and texts on mage-craft merely reminded him of what he's forgotten, even though he has had no previous training. Despite his aptitude, however, I'k'Nole has not undertaken the necessary trials to elevate his mage rank above apprentice due to a lack of opportunity. In 1311 AF, I'k'Nole took part in the battle against Ba'tvian Delthanurk's forces at Destiny's Way and was captured by them.

ILLIUSS – (pronounced *Ihl-lee-uhss*) The Elvanaran name for a flowering plant that grows in caverns that are home to luminous plants or fungi. The leaves are small and feathery, the flowers tiny with white petals and brown interiors. They grow close to the ground, rarely rising more than six inches from their growing surface, and can climb up stone. If left to grow undisturbed for a century or more, colonies of *Illiuss* will cover every stone surface and all of the ground within a large cave, or cavern system, leaving only their light sources visible.

INN OF THE GOLDEN STAG – The Golden Staf is an inn and tavern that caters to well-heeled merchants, guildsmen, and nobles in Chalbrooke's Guild District. It stands on the street as the Mancers' Guild House.

ISLES OF NARYE, THE – (pronounced *I-ls uhv Nahr-yay*) The Isles of Narye are an archipelago located south of Orthanor and east of Exile's Peril. They are home to the Dithume race and are the spawning grounds for kraken.

IVERNESS – (pronounced *I-vehr-nehss*) Iverness is a town north-west of the Wood.

JEVANEL – (pronounced *Jehv-ahn-ehl*) Jevanel is the birthplace of Nerisse se li Astorae, it was the subterranean city-enclave of the Elvanarae, located on the northwestern coast of Orthanor. As the Elvanaeran religious center, it was where most of the race was concentrated, where they were ruled by the High Priest. Jevanel fell to the Dark Adepts in 1306 AF. The cavern in which the city was built, sometimes referred to as the Earth's Womb, was collapsed on top of it, resulting a sink hole on the surface farmland. No one has heard of any survivors; the whole race is believed to have been slain during the destruction. The land is now cursed, haunted by the tormented spirits of the Elvanarae who are now trapped within the earth. They can be seen roaming the abandoned fields, the ghastly manner of their deaths plainly seen on their forms. More often, they are heard crying in grief and pain or screaming in fear and agony. Few venture there.

JIMNEL ELFREN, SERGEANT – (pronounced *Jihmr-nehl Ehlf-rehn*) A veteran of the Rathburn Watch, Jimnel Elfren served with Farn Greenmeadow before his death. He stayed on at the Watch after his friend's murder, keeping an eye on Farn's widow and son, Veln. He was still in service when the Rathburn Watch was stood down in 1311 AF by Mayor Gertur Yilsed.

JORED ULT – (pronounced *Johr-ehd Uhlt*) Jored Ult is one of the personas used by Labiyal Biyalban. The alias is an aristocrat in political exile Genoria who has various business interests across Orthanor. He is also the financial backer for select politicians in several cities, including Edon, Chalbrooke, and Rathburn.

Kale Hornbush – (pronounced *Kayl Hohrn-buhsh*) A night-time Chalbrooke city guard, Kale Hornbush's usual post is the East City Gate. He is almost always on the same nightly rotation as his friend, Ezil Ormonson.

King's Folly – The *King's* Folly is a small cargo ship that took Ba'tvian Delthanurk into exile in 1304 AF. It was later found adrift at sea, with all hands dead on board.

King of Hell – The assumed title of the Eldarae known as Hell.

Kraken – Kraken are saltwater squid-like creatures boasting an array of finned spines along the main trunk of their bodies and upper portions of their fourteen tentacles. They grow continuously throughout their lives, some reaching more than two tons in weight and over three centuries in age. While they are omnivorous, they have a marked preference for meat, often preying on small whales or large fish. Males are referred to as bulls; females are called cows. Maturity is reached by the second decade for both sexes. Bulls, which grow faster than the cows, will venture out on their own after the first five years, usually by themselves and occasionally in pairs. Cows rarely go out on their own before reaching full maturity. When they go hunting in the open ocean, they do so in pairs or trios. They breed in the shallows around the Isles of Narye and have a mutually beneficially relationship with the Dithume there. The Dithume protect the spawning grounds and the kraken, in turn, protect the Isles. Though the kraken are loners when ranging the open sea, there is a permanent colony around the Isles, where most of the immature cows reside. Twice a year, all roaming mature adults return to the Isles to breed.

Labiyal Biyalban – (pronounced *Lahb-ee-yahl Bee-yahl-bahn*) The half-daemon/half-human son of Daemon Lord Biyal, Labiyal Biyalban serves the King of Hell. It is his intention to use Ba'tvian Delthanurk's rise to power as the means to free his master.c

Lakit Jeste – (pronounced *Lah-kiht Jehst*) A Dithume weather mage hailing from the Isles of Narye, Lakit Jeste is the twin brother of Tavor Jeste. Of the twins, Lakit is more expressive and vocal. As the two maintain a natural telepathic bond, he knows what Tavor is thinking and often speaks for both of them. Since they have begun using blood magic, Lakit has grown more emotionally detached, a progression that may be accelerated by Tavor's less emotional state. In 1304 AF, Lakit, Tavor, and their cousin participated in a blood rite that saved the Isles of Narye from being decimated by a tsunami triggered by the Great Earthquake. Condemned for their crimes, they were scheduled to be executed, but managed to escape shortly after their sentencing. Lakit and Tavor split off from their cousin, heading for Orthanor. In 1307 AF, the twins were recruited by the blood mage Red to join Ba'tvian Delthanurk.

MAGE – A mage is someone who possesses the ability to use magic. There are four main ranks among mages: apprentice or student, journeyman, master, and adept. Each mage starts out as an apprentice and must pass a series of tests called Mastery Trials in order to ascend to the next rank. This is done under the tutelage and supervision of a mage who is a master or higher.

MAGE AFFINITY – See Arcane Affinity.

MAGE LIGHT – A mage light is magic working the sole purpose of which is to emit light. Mage lights consist of glowing magic energy that is given shape. Some mages use a physical object on which to layer the energy, much the same way a sculptor layers clay over a wire mesh form. This method is commonly used when the mage wishes to create a permanent, re-useable mage light that any person may be able to use by saying a specific trigger word. These types of lights need to be fed more power periodically or the magic will fade away. However, most mages have little desire to create reusable mage lights unless they are being paid for them. For their own use, they gather arcane energy into a tiny ball. The ball emits light, with the light intensity being determined by the amount of power fed into it. This type of mage light is sustained by the mage until dismissed. The color of the mage light, whether reusable or not, matches the color or colors of the mage's aura.

MAGE MESSAGE – A mage message is a mode of communication that uses a mage light or similar arcane construct to carry a message to another person. The message can be presented in two forms: an arcane audio recording of someone speaking the message or a telepathic presentation of words, images, and thought conveying the message. Only mages can create and send mage messages but anyone can receive them. However, a mage must be able to identify the person the mage message is intended for, i.e. by use of a picture, a highly detailed description, an arcane signature, or by detailing the geographical place occupation title (such as the proprietor of the Dragon's Head Tavern at the Red Tower of the Trinity; it has to be a unique identifier). No mage message can be sent to anyone without some kind of identifier to include in the magic working. Once sent, the mage message uses the identifier to find its recipient. How the magic working operates is widely debated, the ancient knowledge and origins of the working having been lost to time. Also called a mage sending.

MAGE SENDING – See Mage Message.

MAGERY – Magery is the practice of manipulating natural forces commonly referred to as magic. The term is also used to refer to the magic itself, or one's ability to use it.

MALTEK BAY – (pronounced *Mahltek*) A geographical feature of Orthanor, the Maltek Bay is a great northern bay that separates the Maltek Mountains in the west from the Trelum Mountains in the east. The entrance of the bay is frozen over and is part of the Northern Ice Fields.

MALTEK MOUNTAINS – (pronounced *Mahl-tehk*) The Maltek Mountains are a mountains range that spans across northwestern Orthanor, from the Capil Ocean to Maltek Bay, and makes up part of the Northern Ring. It is home to several barbarian tribes.

MANCER – A Mancer is a warrior whose sole occupation is to defend the living against daemon kind and mages who have gone turned to the bad. They are often trained in magery in addition to combat. Part of an ancient order, Mancers exist outside most societies, do not claim citizenship, and give no loyalty to any ruler. They adhere to a code that incorporates most of the existing laws. They are few in number and seldom stay in one place for long. Frequently, authorities faced with a black or blood mage or other preternatural activity would send for a Mancer to aid them. In recent years, however, the Mancer Order had been faced with near extinction. Many Mancers were lost when the Dark Adept Ba'tvian Delthanurk destroyed their Guild House in Chalbrooke, and more were hunted down and slain by him afterwards. They have since reconvened at Destiny's Way and have been preparing for a final confrontation with the Dark Adepts. Under the leadership of Absol Omine, their numbers have grown, but not by much.

MASTERY TRIAL – A Mastery Trial is a test, or series of tests, whereby a student of magic proves his or her magical prowess. By passing this trial or trials, they are able to ascend to the next mage rank, whichever rank that may be. A mage's ability to pass the Mastery Trials is dependent on his/her skill, knowledge, and the amount of magic he/she can utilize at any one point.

MENIE – (pronounced *Meh-nay*) Menie is a minor port city on the western coast of Orthanor, to the east and slightly north of the Trinity. Though it has no king, it is a fully independent city-state ruled by a lord who holds the majority of the lands surrounding the city.

MERCHANTS GUILD – The Merchants Guild is the regulatory body of which Orthanor's mainland and maritime traders are members. Guild members trade primarily in high-end goods or wares garnered from other continents. They ply their trade for money, as opposed to bartering or services, and their guild fees are higher than those of the related Traders Guild. Their seal consists of an ewer, a small bundled sack, and closed wooden chest super-imposed over a coin. The guild's motto, "For Fair Value, In Goods, In Profits", is not featured in the seal. As proof of membership, every guildsman carries a medallion made from a real coin with the seal stamped on one side, and the motto engraved on the other. By tradition, the coin used to make the medallion is the first coin earned by the individual that carries it.

MONSTER OF MENIE, THE – (pronounced *Meh-nay*) The Monster of Menie is the label given to Ba'tvian Delthanurk after the events of *Descent Into Darkness: His Own*.

MOORLAND CATTLE – The moorland cattle breed is most favored by farmers for their durability, strength, and muscle mass. The bulls tend to be aggressive, especially if any cows are in heat. Both sexes of the species grow long, black horns that curve toward the front, then arch back. Bulls, however, will sometimes grow a second, smaller set just behind the first. The hides of the moorland cattle are brindled gray with varying splotches of white.

NAGUN – (pronounced *Nay-guhn*) A human servant of the half-daemon Labiyal Biyalban, Nagun looks after his master's personal abode, wherever that may be. He is a tall, muscular, bald man, and is Labiyal's most loyal servant, sharing a predilection for sadism.

NERISSE SE LI ASTORAE – (pronounced *Nehr-ees say lih Ahs-torh-ay*) An elven mage and Empath, Nerisse se li Astorae is the daughter of Nerthet si le Astorae and Elisse se li Astorae. She possesses the ability to hear, and speak to, the earth directly. For this reason, she was chosen to become a priestess of her people. Yet her mage talents prevented her from joining the priesthood immediately. Her people, the Elvanarae, are unable to teach a would-be adept and find her a teacher outside of their capital, Jevanel. She became a student of the Trinity College of Magery at age sixteen. She was apprenticed to the adept called Master Oknare in the aftermath of Ba'tvian Delthanurk's exile in 1304 AF. As a new student, she became fascinated with the story of the exiled blood mage, striving to understand what happened. By the time Ba'tvian returned to the Red Tower in his quest for vengeance, she was convinced that he'd saved the Trinity from destruction, and should have had mercy from the courts. Delthanurk took advantage of her naiveté, seducing her into being his ally. After he killed Master Oknare, Nerisse chose to flee with him. She traveled with Ba'tvian for two years before it is discovered that she is his helpmate. In 1306 AF, the Elvanarae severed all ties with Nerisse, including her earthbond, an act that would eventually kill her. Unwilling to lose her support, Ba'tvian ordered her to kill the race that birthed her. A young woman in love, she remains faithful to Ba'tvian, believing in him, helping him, even as he continues to mold her into his greatest tool.

NERTHET SI LE ASTORAE – (pronounced *Nehr-theht sih leh Ahs-torh-ay*) The father of Nerisse se li Astorae, Nerthet si le Astorae was married to Elisse se li Astorae. He was an Elvaneran cultivator, tending to small plots of crops grown on the surface ground above Jevanel. It is said that his eviscerated ghost can be seen by the ruined entry shed that once led down into his home in Jevanel.

NILBRE – (pronounced *Nihl-bray*) A city-state in the Gastaean Plains, Nilbre is located in the south-eastern part of the region. The area has an arid climate, bordering on the Arelle Desert. To grow crops so close to the Arelle, the city has instigated widespread irrigation and developed engineering to collect as much water as possible for use in the fields and the homes.

NORTHERN ICE FIELDS – A vast frozen sea in the northern polar region of Einlienn, the Northern Ice Fields are hemmed in by the Northern Ring and is largely featureless. At the very center of the Northern Ice Fields is an endless blizzard. The region is alternately called the Northern Snow Fields.

NORTHERN RING – The Northern Ring is an uneven ring of mountain ranges that enclose the northern polar region of Einlienn.

NORTHERN SNOW FIELDS – See Northern Ice Fields.

NORTHERN WILDERNESS – Located north of the Wood of Destiny and south of the Northern Ring, the Northern Wilderness of Orthanor is a largely wooded area with the Sradieen and Chal-Edon Trade Routes as the only maintained roads. Villages, lone trappers' cabins, and small towns are scattered far apart. Most villages and towns are stockaded as a defense against bandits and the occasional barbarian raid from the mountains. There is no central governing body in this area. Most of the economy is based on fur-trapping, logging, some mining, and alcohol distilliation from root vegetables and herbs.

OLEF ALTHESON – (pronounced *Oh-lef Ahl-theh-sahn*) A corporal in the Rathburn Watch, Olef Altheson was assigned to the investigation of a long string of murders thought to have gone on for several years. His sister, Claire, was recently murdered, the latest victim of his current investigation.

OKNARE, MASTER – (pronounced *Ahk-nayr*) Master Oknare was a human male serving as a teacher of advanced or prodigious students of magic at the Trinity College of Magery. Though commonly called 'master', he was in fact an adept level mage. He was mentor to Ba'tvian Delthanurk until the student's exile in 1304 AF, then subsequentially became the teacher of Nerisse se li Astorae. He was killed by Ba'tvian Delthanurk and his Shadowed Ones later that same year.

ONE, THE – The One is the supreme being who created the universe with the aid of His children, the Eldarae.

ORDER OF ON'DESAE – (pronounced *Ohn'Deh-say*) A monastic order devoted to worship of the One, the On'Desae Order is known for its generosity, open-minded acceptance of others, and efforts to preserve sites or monuments associated with the One or the Creation Myths. Their most renowned shrine is located at Destiny's Way, just outside the south-eastern edge of the Wood of Destiny. The order is less known for its other purpose: supporting the Mancer Guild as it fights against Daemons, blood magery, and black magic. They open their monasteries to traveling Mancers, supply them on their journeys, and offer sanctuary for Mancers who need healing, or survive their profession long enough to retire. The order also passes along news and maintains libraries of Mancer lore.

ORTHANOR – (pronounced *Ohr-thahn-ohr*) Orthanor is the largest of three major continents of Einlienn.

PALIN FERNICK – (pronounced *Pahl-ihn Fehr-nihk*) A Mancer killed by Ba'tvian Delthanurk near Edon Port in 1307 AF.

PIETE TOWN – (pronounced *Pi-eht*) A barricaded settlement, Piete Town situated north of the Wood of the Destiny and west of the Relds. It is one of the largest settlements in the northern wilderness. By tradition, the town's foremost healer, who is usually an Empath, lives just outside the town. An unspoken pact with local bandits grants the healer and his/her family immunity provided that they tend to anyone injured who arrives at their door.

PLAINS OF GASTAEIA – (pronounced *Gahs-tay-ya*) See the Gastaean Plains.

PORTAL – A portal is a rift in the time-space continuum that allows near-instantaneous travel between one point and another. The mage skill and power required to create a portal is such that only adept-caliber mages or higher are able to create and sustain them. Portals are also called gates or crossings.

PRIALLA FILOCHE – The illegitimate half-sister of Halvark Tretoan, Prialla Filoche is the product of a tryst between Lord Tretoan and a chambermaid of the household. Though her mother was let go by the Tretoan family due to her pregnancy, she was re-hired more than a decade later as their chatelaine after the death of Lord Tretoan's wife. Prialla, by this time in her early teens, returned with her mother. Though a servant, she forged a sexual relationship with both Halvark Tretoan and Raptu Carthier before Lord Tretoan revealed her true parentage. The revelation that Halvark was her half-brother did little dissuade either of them from their relationship. Together with Raptu, the trio became known for wild behavior and secretly delved into the study of blood magery. In 1306 AF, she participated in the ritual slaying of Halvark's father and her chatelaine mother, and took her mother's place as the head of the Tretoan household under-stairs. She has since prove to be an astute businesswoman, keeping the books and helping Halvark to manage the estate.

PROPHECY – Largely believed to be an iron-clad prediction of the future, the concept of prophecy first came about with the Eldarae. To aid the One during the Time of Creation, they were given the ability to speak things into existence, and eventually turned this power into dictating the course of events in certain parts of the universe. Hell was the first to use this power for his own selfish desires. To counter any prophecy Hell might speak into being, the One allowed free will and Hope into the universe.

PYRE CRYPTS – The Pyre Crypts are one of the three sacred grounds that were behind the Temple of Earth in Jevanel. When an Elvanarae died, he or she was taken to the Pyre Crypts, carried along a path lit by bowl of burning pyre rock, first through a largely barren "garden" of ash, rock, and *illiuss,* then through a forest of carved, totem-like familial memorials. At the other end of the path was a shallow bowl-shaped depression, large enough to accommodate several funerary pyres. Pyre rock was piled there, the body laid out on top, and the pile was lit. The mourners may stayed as long as they wished but the priesthood remained until the pyre was reduced to cold ash. Anything that did not burn in the pyre was cleaned with care and tucked into one of hundreds of wall niches or alcoves. The ashes were then collected and scattered in the "garden" at the front of the grounds. Along with the Temple, the Pyre Crypts were destroyed with Jevanel.

PYRE ROCK – A grayish-white rock, Pyre Rock has a chalk-like consistency. Its composition is such that it is flammable, burning slowly with blue-green flames. A fist-sized rock will burn for a day. The Elvanarae use pyre rock as fuel for their funeral pyres, hence its name.

RAPTU CARTHIER, LORD – (pronounced *Rahp-too Cahr-thee-ehr*) Raptu Carthier is the scion of a wealthy merchant family from the Rathburn area. The Carthier family grew rich from various business ventures, primarily the courier service that they run from their own estate. Though originally a middle-class bloodline, they eventually bought their way into the country nobility and began raising fast horses for their courier service as well as racing. The Carthier Estate's close proximity to the Tretoan family's holdings led to a close friendship between Raptu Carthier, Halvark Tretoan, & Prialla Filoche. Together the trio became known for wild behavior and secretly delved into the study of blood magery. In 1306 AF Raptu participated in the ritual murders of Halvark's father and Prialla's mother. He did the same with his own parents the following year. Now at the helm of the family business, he works hard to make it prosperous so that he aid in funding the long-term plans the trio have developed with their ally, Ba'tvian Delthanurk.

RAT ROOT – Rat Root is a medicinal herb used to prevent pregnancy. It grows wild throughout Orthanor's temperate zones, its leaves resembling the grasses of the moorlands. The differences lie in the reddish-brown tips of the leaves, how the leaves grow from the roots in smaller tufts, and the stalks covered with tiny orange flowers that spear up from the center of the leaf tuft. Its name derives from the shape of the roots as they resemble the bodies and tails of rats.

RATH WEED – (pronounced *Rahth*) Rath weed is a leafy plant, yellow -green in color, that grows naturally on the moors east of the Wood of Destiny. It propagates from parts of the root system, and often occurs in thick patches for this reason. Though it is used in tisanes and syrups to treat respiratory illness, the leaves are more often dried and smoked. The practice was once so prevalent among the farmers that originally settled the area that the region was given the name of Rathburn after weed they smoked. Once cultivated for trade all over the continent, rath weed is now considered the poor man's choice for smoke and is no longer farmed en masse. Instead, wild plants are harvested, or individuals grow their own at home.

RATHBURN – (pronounced *Rahth-buhrn*) The third largest city-state on the eastern side Orthanor, Rathburn's outlying regions along the Lathim River border those of Chalbrooke to the east. The city-state was founded by the Tretoan family in 1102 AF. As time went on, the family grew more distant from the day-to-day rule of the city, appointing others to do so and allowing them a great deal of autonomy. This eventually led to a somewhat democratic form of government, which was heavily influenced by the Tretoan family patriarchs. Rathburn's position at one end of the Chal-Edon Trade Route and its trade alliances with Chalbrooke and Edon assures that its commerce is prosperous. Initially founded to take advantage of the rath weed that grew in area, the main staples are now cattle and grain. As a relatively young city, it is still growing, attracting people looking for a different kind of life, as well more trades and crafts looking to set up shop. Because of its tendency to welcome new business, and also due to the practices of certain aristocratic offspring of the Tretoan family, it has become a center for black market tradesmen. Anything can be bought and sold in Rathburn.

RATHBURN WATCH – (pronounced *Rahth-burhn*) The secular law enforcement of the city of Rathburn, the Rathburn Watch is a small body of men that does its best to ensure the safety of the citizenry. Most of its officers came from the city militia when it was reduced due to government budget cuts.

REBIRTHING GROUNDS – One of three sacred grounds that were behind the Temple of Earth at Jevanel, the Rebirthing Grounds were filled with grotto, moss laden soil, subterranean glowing fungus and flowers. The soil here was rich loam. Here, petitioners who wished to leave behind some part of their old lives in order to continue into a new phase of living were symbolically "reborn of the earth". They were laid out in a shallow grave and buried, leaving only their faces exposed. By remaining thus for an entire night, it was believed that the earth would absorb the emotional baggage or negative influence of the spirit so that the petitioner would rise free of anything that weighed him or her down in their new life. Along with the Temple, the Rebirthing Grounds were destroyed with Jevanel.

RED – The name used by Ba'tvian Delthanurk to refer to the blood mage with whom he has an alliance. Once, the two had an agreement that Red would supply information to Ba'tvian in exchange for a victim to use in blood rites every full moon. This agreement gave way to a loose alliance in the aftermath of *Descent Into Darkness: His Command*. Both men now share information and services without expectation of payment, provided that doing so will further their own interests.

RED TOWER, THE – The Red Tower is the name for the Trinity College of Magery, as well as the natural stone column on which it perches. It is part of the Trinity and the nick-name is derived from the red tiled roofs featured on all school and town buildings.

REG MORRIN, CAPTAIN – Reg Morrin was the Captain of the Rathburn Watch. Reg Morrin once served in the city militia before they were incorporated into the Watch. He's fond of smoking his pipe, preferring rath weed. A contemporary of Veln Greenmeadow's father, he is sometimes referred to as the Old Man Morrin. A no-nonsense man of wiry build, silvered hair, and military bearing, he served in Rathburn's militia before joining the Watch. He has been captain for fifteen years as of 1311 AF and is old enough to remember what it was like when the Tretoan family took a greater interest in the welfare of the city – something that began to fall off around the time of Halvark's birth. He's a stickler for the law and rules, something that has garnered him respect from the citizens and derision from the criminal element. He was Veln Greenmeadow's senior officer prior to his leaving the Watch to become a Mancer, and had agreed to watch over Veln's mother in his absence until her death. In the summer of 1311 AF, he was confronted with a series of murders that could be traced back several years in the Rathburn area. Believing that they could be the result of blood mages operating in the area, he asked Veln to assist. Reg Morrin was killed and eaten by a possessed Olef Altheson within a week of the Mancer's arrival.

RELDS, THE – (pronounced *Rehlds*) A swamp in the northern wilderness of Orthanor, to the north and east of Menie, the Relds are located along the southern half of the Telmar River. In winter, the swamp is semi-frozen. As the ice tends to be thin and fragile in winter, and the area much too boggy for travel in summer, it is generally avoided. It is sometimes used as a haven by criminals or refugees as their pursuers are reluctant to follow them into it. However, the terrain is so hazardous that only one out of four men that venture into it survive.

SAGE – The fourth and highest class of magery, sages are extremely rare. They can be so powerful that a more primitive culture could mistake them for gods. They are masters at manipulating magic, dimensional space, and even time.

SAND WORMS – Sand worms reside in arid regions of sandy soil, hence the name, but have been known to bore through grout and hard sediment. Often found in colonies that range from a handful of worms to several hundred, they grow up to two feet long and three inches in diameter.   They possess firm, off-white bodies that are covered with tiny spines that they can independently of each other. The spines are used to help them maneuver through the ground. Their heads are all mouth, with a maw that flips the lips inside out to expose three rows of teeth and central boring tooth. The teeth rows twist back and forth as the central tooth strikes out repeatedly, allowing the creature can burrow through most materials. They feed by swallowing grit through slits around the boring tooth; it's the bacteria in the grit that provides them with nourishment.

SAERLAN SI LE THEIAN – (pronounced *Say-her-lahn sih leh Thehr-yee-ahn*) Saerlan si le Theian is the High Priest of the Elvanarae and resides in Jevanel. A gentle, compassionate man in his late fifties, he bears the slate blue skin and white hair of his race. As High Priest, he is also the theocratic ruler of his people. It was Saerlan who had noticed Nerisse se li Astorae's potential and claimed her for the priesthood, and it was he who had made the decision to send Nerisse to the Trinity to complete her mage-training before her induction.

SEA'S BURDEN – A small cargo vessel, the *Sea's Burden* was the ship Ba'tvian Delthanurk used to return to the Trinity in the winter of 1304 AF.

SHADOWED ONES – The cursed, first generation of daemons sired by Hell, the Shadowed Ones are condemned to be the lowliest of the low, and their once mighty origins have been forgotten by all but a select few. They exist as ethereal creatures that feed upon death. The more life force they consume, the stronger they become. Eventually, they are able take on a physical form for a time.   Once they are corporeal, they are able to hunt and feed upon anything, living or dead. Because of the danger they pose, they are routinely hunted by the Mancers.

SILMON OF WINEDE – (pronounced *Sihl-mohn* of *Wihn-eed*) Silmon is the proprietor and bartender of the only tavern in Winede.

SKELETON COAST – See Spirlan Coast.

SNOW BLOOM – A hardy bush whose flowers are a pale lavender color, snow bloom produces white berry clusters in the spring. The berries are edible. Their taste is described as being sweet with a hint of cinnamon. The plant can be found in the White Mountains of

Annia. A cousin by the same name, with bluish-white berries can be found in the Maltek Mountains of Orthanor. Both varieties are found in the Black Mountains and the Wilderlands of Annia. In Orthanor, the berries are eaten raw or are stewed, spiced, and served over fresh bread. In Annia, the berries are more often dried for inclusion in tea blends.

SOUTHERN ICE FIELDS – An area consisting of the outlying parts of the southern polar region of Einlienn, the Southern Ice Fields are dominated by frozen, rocky tundra and snow. Ice storms are frequent.

SPIR-GAS RIVER – (pronounced *Spihr-Gahs*) The largest river running through the Gastaean Plains, the Spir-Gas River is fed from several springs throughout the central and eastern portionsof the plains and flows west to spill into the Capil Ocean. Its name is a combination of the two major regions the rivers cuts through: the Spirlan Forest and the Gastaean Plains.

SPIRLAN COAST – (pronounced *Spihr-lahn*) The portion of the south-western coast of Orthanor, the Spirlan Coast makes up the seaside boundary of the Spirlan Forest. It becomes known as the Skeleton Coast once the Spirlan Forest died off in the aftermath of the Great Earthquake of 1304 AF.

SPIRLAN FOREST – A large forest, consisting mostly of the gigantic spire trees, the Spirlan Forest spanned a few hundred miles along the southwestern coast of Orthanor. That coast once bore the forest's name as its own, and was home to a human civilization that made built their towns in the trees. The Spirlan Forest was largely destroyed by the Great Earthquake of 1304 AF.

SPIRE TREE – A gigantic tree whose branches grow in a spiral pattern up its thick trunk, spire trees can grow up to a half-mile high on average. Because of the sturdiness of the tree, and the close proximity of the branches to one another, villages and towns were frequently built in them, with the spiraling branches acting as the only road.

SRADIEEN TRADING ROUTE – (pronounced *Srah-dih-een*) The main route for the northern fur trade, the Sradieen Trading Route winds through the northern wilderness of Orthanor and traditionally ends at

Glasten Port. Since the rise of Menie as a major shipping port, however, most of the traders stop there instead of heading on to Glasten. The trade route is one of the few roads that is paved with stone. The paving stones are ancient, having been laid down by a culture that existed before The Flood. Though that civilization was lost to history, some of their stonework remains with the names of roads and places carved deeply into the rock. The name Sradieen can be found etched into the stone pavers that have survived the onslaught of water and time, thus the trade route is known by this name.

SUNDOWN – A tiny fishing village, Sundown is situated on a desolate stretch of coastline between Menie and the Spirlan Forest. Its inhabitants were massacred by Ba'tvian Delthanurk in 1304 AF and the village was left to rot. In the years afterwards, the site became known as an eerie place. The villagers' spirits are said to reside there, still caught in the trauma of their deaths.

SUPPLICANT'S GARDEN – The Supplicant's Garden surrounded the entrance of the Temple of Earth in Jevanel. A variety of flowers, moss, vines, and glowing fungus were cultivated in beautiful beds around serene pools and stone benches. Tucked among the plants were small stone monoliths with ancient carvings that showed scenes from the creation myth the Elvanarae ascribed to. Atop each monolith grew a natural crystal. The Supplicant's Garden was a place for people to wait or meditate when visiting the Temple. It was destroyed with Jevanel in 1306 AF.

SURFACE FARMLANDS OF JEVANEL – (pronounced *Jeh-vahn-ehl*) Situated on the lands above the cavern where Jevanel resides, the surface farmlands were maintained by Elvanarae family lines, each accessing their plots via entry sheds that housed stairs leading down to their homes. The families worked the fields, sowed the crops, and harvested the bounty. Most of what was grown was food and textile crops. The land was fertilized regularly with a compost mixture that included decayed fish, rotted moss, vegetable leavings, and crushed oyster and clam shells. After the Fall of Jevanel, the fields collapsed into a bowl-like basin, the entry sheds went to ruin, and the area became the home of spirits. Elvanaraen ghosts wander the land now, weeping and screaming over their fate.

TAVOR JESTE – (pronounced *Tah-vohr Jehst*) A Dithume mage with an affinity for vermin hailing from the Isles of Narye, Tavor is the twin brother of Lakit Jeste. Of the twins, Tavor is more reserved and less emotional, often preferring to Lakit speak for them both. Unlike his twin, Tavor never developed the emotional attachments that most people, of any race, will as they mature. The two maintain a natural telepathic bond that allows them to know what the other thinking. This bond, coupled with Tavor's innate lack of emotional capability, is thought to have fostered the deterioration of Lakit's potential for emotional attachment. Since they have begun using blood magic, Tavor's emotionlessness has begun to eat away at parts of his personality. This has led to a dependency on Lakit for mental cues as to how to interact with others normally. In 1304 AF, Lakit, Tavor, and a cousin participated in a blood rite that saved the Isles of Narye from being decimated by a tsunami triggered by the Great Earthquake. Condemned for their crimes, there were scheduled to be executed but managed to escape mere hours after their sentencing. Lakit and Tavor split off from their cousin, heading for the Orthanor while their cousin set out to sea.

TELMAR BRIDGE – (pronounced *Tehl-mahr*) The bridge over which the Chal-Edon Trade Route crosses the Telmar River, the Telmar Bridge was built by the Traders and Merchants Guilds and is maintained by them. It is left unmanned in the winter, when traders are less apt to travel but is manned by guildsmen in the spring and summer when a toll is instituted to help fund the bridge's upkeep.

TELMAR RIVER – (pronounced *Tehl-mahr*) A freshwater river, the Telmar runs from the Maltek Bay, through the Northern Wilderness of Orthanor, through the Relds, and by the town of Goose-Bree. It is crossed by the Chal-Edon Trade Route. See also Telmar Bridge.

TEMPLE OF EARTH, THE – The religious center for the Elvanaeran faith, the Temple of Earthwas in Jevanel, and also served as the government building as the city was governed by the Temple's High Priest. The Temple was built in front of a large three-chambered natural alcove on one side of the large cavern holding the city. The alcove was part of the Temple grounds and held the Cleansing Pools, the Pyre Crypts, and the Rebirthing Grounds. The Temple was desecrated, then destroyed, by Nerisse se li Astorae and two other Dark Adepts in 1306 AF.

TERIK WAYFORD, CAPTAIN – Terik Wayford is the Captain of the small cargo vessel called *Fisher's Delight*.

THALENE – (pronounced *Thah-leen*) The Thalene were pre-Flood human civilization known for their advanced technology and sciences. When they became caught up in Hell's War, they began genetically engineering warriors to defend them, thus creating the shape-shifting race now called the Were-Clan. Unfortunately, their child race could not prevent their decline or protect them from the effects of prolonged global war. By the time of the Flood, there were no human Thalene left, only the Were-Clan they had created.

TIMBREL JODREK – (pronounced *Tihm-brehl Johd-rehk*) Timbrel Jodrek was a Mancer in his late twenties who patroled the Northern Wilderness of Orthanor. In 1306 AF, he tracked Ba'tvian Delthanurk and Nerisse se li Astorae after the death of Piete Town's healer. He was killed in an ambush the duo set up with the help of the barbarian Ibestor. As he died, he was able to relay a mage sending to Absol Omine, telling him of Ba'tvian's allies.

TIME OF CREATION, THE – The period in which the universe was created by the One, then populated with worlds and dimensions with the help of the Eldarae. Also see *Creation Myths*.

TRADERS GUILD – The Traders Guild is the regulatory body of which traveling mainland traders are members. Guild members trade primarily in low-end or raw goods. They are allowed to barter their wares for other goods or services. Their seal is a quartered circle ringed by the Guild's motto, "Provision of Goods to All, For Fair Trades or Barter". Each quadrant of the circle holds one of four symbols: scales for fairness, a book for accounting, a wool bundle for raw goods, and a candle for general goods. Every trader carries a chitty with their guild's seal on it as proof of their membership.

TRETOAN ESTATE – The largest land-holding in the Rathburn area, the Tretoan Estate lies to the east along the Chal-Edon Trade Route. It is reknowned as being the most prominent breeder and supplier of cattle and sheep, and owned by the aristocratic Tretoan family, who helped found the city of Rathburn 1102 AF.

TRINITY, THE – Three columns of natural stone rising out of the eastern Capil Ocean near the coast of Orthanor, the Trinity are about ten to twelve days sailing time out from the mainland. Atop each of the stone columns is a college of advanced learning and a small town. They, and the columns, are collectively referred to as the Trinity Schools, the Trinity Colleges, the Trinity, or the Trinity Towers.

UNBLOODED – A term used to describe someone unexperienced in true combat. It is also used to indicate that the person in question has never made a kill.

VELN GREENDMEADOW – (pronounced *Vehln Green-mehd-oh*) One of the older Mancers in the Order, Veln Greenmeadow was a contemporary of Absol Omine. He was formerly a member of the Rathburn Watch, as his father Farn Greenmeadow had been prior to his murder in a tavern brawl. After avenging his father's death, he left the Watch and Rathburn, eventually ending up in Chalbrooke where he became one of the few Mancers recruited as an adult in 1295 AF. He had the arcane affinity for death, which manifested as the ability to see ghosts. Though the affinity gave him little else, it did set some restrictions on the magic workings he was able to perform. Despite the limitations, he rose to the rank of a master mage within the Mancer Order. In 1311 AF, he journeyed to Rathburn as the behest of his old commander, Rathburn Watch Captain Reg Morrin, to consult on a long string of murders suspected to be the work of a blood mage. That investigation led to a confrontation between Veln and the Dark Adepts led by Ba'tvian Delthanurk. He was captured and underwent a series of mind alterations as well as a daemon possession, executed by Nerisse se li Astorae and Ba'tvian Delthanurk. Allowed to escape, Veln fled to Destiny's Way with the Dark Adepts coming in his wake. Given the orders to find I'k'Nole Kar'k'Eige and now completely in the control of the whyte that possessed his body, Veln managed to stop the whyte by using his own life force to destroy his heart.

VELTAN – (pronounced *Vehl-tahn*) Veltan is a small town west of Destiny's Way.

WANDERER'S TRAIL – The Wanderer's Trail is an unpaved path that cuts through the moorlands to the southwest of Rathburn and east of Destiny's Way. The path is marked by stone cairns that are placed within sight of each other. These markers shift from time to time as the vegetation grows to obscure the cairns. Its purpose was the lead wandering trading families of the Gastaean Plans to the Chal-Edon Trade Route which starts at Rathburn. Due to the influx of

Shadowed Ones on the moors, the route is rarely traveled.

WEATHER MAGES – A subset of mages, weather mages possess an affinity for air and weather so strong that it often renders them unable to perform generic magic workings. They are rare in most races, but are prolific among the maritime Dithume. They are highly valued by shipmasters all over the world, and most trading vessels contract at least one mage to travel with them on the high seas. Though their edicts prevent them from manipulating the weather outright in most cases, weather mages are still able to call up sailing winds, or direct ships around pockets of bad storms or hurricanes. Also called Weather Workers.

WEATHER SENSITIVES – A subset of weather mages, weather sensitives possess no ability to manipulate the weather but are able to identify or predict storms. They are more common than weather mages, and their services are cheaper for shipmasters and captains to contract.

WEATHER WORKERS – See Weather Mages.

WERE-CLAN – A shape-shifting race, the Were-Clan are descended from the ancient Thalene human civilization. Before the Flood that ended Hell's War, during a time when advanced technology had a place in the world, the Were-Clan had been genetically engineered as warriors to face the onslaught of Hell's daemonic forces. By the time of the Flood, the Thalene technology and civilization had been abandoned, or killed off. The Were-Clan went on to survive the Flood, eventually establishing themselves as clans of nomadic mercenaries on the continents of Genoria and Annia. Though individual Were-Clan have been known to venture into Orthanor, the race has never established there.

WHYTE – (pronounced *Whi-t*) One of the lowest castes of daemon-kind, a whyte is a being without physical form anywhere outside of its home plane, Hell. As weak daemons, they are unable traverse the dimensional barriers without aid. Sometimes, they accompany Daemon Lords as they breach the barrier. Other times, they are summoned through the barrier by blood mages. Once on Einlienn, the whytes are vulnerable to enslavement and can be weakened further by other forces outside of magic. When in Einlienn, a whyte finds its existence hard, as the world itself does what it can to suppress it, sapping its strength, memory, and will-power. This enables blood mages to trap a whyte for their own ends. Though their natural state in Einlienn is discorporate, the whytes have discovered that possessing the bodies of the newly dead can allow them to resist the world's suppression. They cannot possess living bodies by themselves as they lack the power required to displace a soul. In the instances where this has occurred, the magic required for the possession has been provided by a powerful blood mage, or the blood mage has displaced the soul for them. What happens to a whyte after the body is destroyed or slain depends on whether they inhabited a dead or living vessel. If the body is dead, then the whyte is merely freed into its incorporeal state and must be formally banished back to Hell. If it is a living body, the whyte is forced to follow the body's soul into the realm of the dead; from there, the whyte is able to return to Hell on its own as the barriers between death and Hell are thin.

WILTON LANNE – (pronounced *Wihl-tohn Layn*) The late seneschal of Raptu Carthier's holdings in 1311 AF, Wilton Lanne dared to inform the Rathburn Watch of the ritual murders his master performed with the other Dark Adepts. He mistakenly believed that they occurred on the Carthier Estate, when they actually took place on Tretoan's Estate. Fearful for his life, he stole a mule and attempted to run. His treachery was quickly discovered. He was pursued across the moors and apprehended. Ba'tvian Delthanurk and Rapty Carthier made him an example of the consquences of betrayal to the rest of the Carthier servants, feeding him to the Shadowed Ones while he was still alive.

WINEDE – (pronounced *Wihn-eed*) A village to the far northwest of the Wood of Destiny, Winede lies not far from the Sradieen Trade Route and is surrounded by a stockade.

WOOD OF DESTINY, THE – The world's most ancient wood, the Wood of Destiny was created by Xera before his death. The Wood has a collective consciousness that is aware of the myriad paths of the past, present, and future. The Wood sings, reaching out to touch its visitors through the endless song. Its mind has child-like, ageless qualities, and possesses a limited means of communication. Its main method of communication is through visions that it weaves around its visitors through song, drawing on the visitors' past, present, and possible futures to do so. This has often spooked people and, in some cases, driven them mad. The Wood is also believed to be the place where Xera died, and where Xera's father, the One, merged the pieces of his dismembered son with the world he loved so much. Because of this mythology, and the Wood's inherent uncanny nature, a monastery and shrine belonging to the Order of On'Desae was established on its southern border.

XERA – (pronounced *Zehr-ah*) Xera was one of the Eldarae and the creator of Einlienn. It is believed that, when Xera was torn to pieces by his brother, Hell, his remains were merged with Einlienn. It is for this reason that most of the races of Einlienn are referred to as Xera's Children.

ZERICK MANCERSON – (pronounced *Zehr-ihk Mahn-sehr-sohn*) The head of the Mancers' Guild, Zerick Mancerson resides in the Chalbrooke Guild House. As the Guild Leader, it is his responsibility to ensure that the Mancers numbers do not dip below a certain level, that all information concerning their training, techniques, and lore are recorded, and that rampant menaces are dealt with.

About the Author

DORIS Ross lives in Jacksonville, FL, where she drinks coffee by the gallon, writes, works, and occasionally plays video games. Her current favorites are *Halo, Minecraft, Diablo III, Destiny,* and the *Fable* series. Sometimes, when she's met enough of her writing goals, she gets to have LAN parties with family and friends.

A resident of the city since 1987, she began writing *Descent Into Darkness* in 2008 when she realized that the book she was working on was not the starting point for the story. Coinciding with this was the launch of TrinityGateways.net, where she posted samples of her writing. In June 2012, she co-founded the publishing house Trinity Gateways LLC with fellow authors and long-time friends LJ Gastineau and Tricia Sparks. Not long after, her father pushed to have *Blood & Rain* readied for publication. So after a final edit and revision, she did — much to her father's gratification.

Today, Doris is working to finish the *Descent Into Darkness* dark fantasy series and revise the completed draft of *Blood & Rain*'s sequel. You can follow her progress at DorisRoss.com, and find out what other publications she's been involved in at TrinityGateways.net.

Hidden Reaches
Book 1

Blood & Rain

by

Doris Ross

There is something dark in every city...

Jacksonville, FL, is a city with historic roots and character, much like many other cities in the United States. Yet the mundane façade hides a layer of reality not seen by the humans – except for a select few. Alex Rosselle is such a one. The IRS and her clientele know her as an artist, yet the city's paranormal underbelly see her for what she is: a Hunter, the latest in a long line of humans who ensure that the secretive supernatural side of life stays civil.

...that attracts peril like a moth to flame.

Like Alex's ex, the thieving bastard. But personal business takes a back seat when something monstrous begins stalking the streets of her beloved city. With every kill it makes, storms brew. In midst of the bloodshed she will discover an old nemesis, a new ally, and the interest of an ancient deity. Bearing down on them all is something only one of them can stop – provided Alex doesn't drown as the city becomes awash with blood and rain.

This hurricane season will be one she will never forget.

MANTLE OF THE GODS
BOOK 1

QUEST FOR TRUTH

BY
TRICIA SPARKS

A mysterious discovery leads one woman to stumble upon a startling secret of the ancient world...

Annalynn Gallagher is an archeologist working the find of the century with the last person she ever wanted to see again: Dr. Ian Broody, the man who'd ruined her life. Now trouble is brewing at the dig and Anna is determined to prevent the past from repeating itself.

Some secrets should stay in the dark...

As she delves for the answers about the rising turmoil she finds only more danger. From her dig site to her home back in the States, she encounters sabotage, ominous tails, and threats to her safety and sanity. Seeking help, she turns to a man with a history darker than her own.

...or they will drive you over the edge.

Sam Abrams left the blackness of his past behind a long time ago. With his career as a professional fighter on the rise, he has little interest in aiding a prim and proper archeologist with her issues –

especially when he has enough of his own. Then he catches sight of what's followed Anna and can't turn away.

Some things have to be fought...

At Anna's dig site, an ancient evil stirs awake. As it reaches back into the world, Ann and Sam land in the heart of a dark storm that could mean the end of them.

...others have to be survived.

The clock has started ticking and the world may never be the same.

ISBN-10: 0988195151

ISBN-13: 978-0988195158

www.ingramcontent.com/pod-product-compliance
Lightning Source LLC
Chambersburg PA
CBHW051513250626
47156CB00001B/79